SOLYN'S BODY

KLAUDEN'S RING SAGA

SOLYN'S BODY

AWARD-WINNING AUTHOR
JM PAQUETTE

DEDICATION

To the best superhero a sidekick could have.

TRIGGER WARNING

This book contains violence, gore, a lot of blood spatter, attempted rape, recollection of previous sexual trauma, and some steamy sexual content.

TABLE OF CONTENTS

ACKNOWLEDGMENTS

So many others stood along the path as I wrote this book; this page is for them. I stand in awe of the greats who came before, in whose words and worlds I have wandered through many a long night: J.R.R. Tolkien for the mythology, Stephen King for the audacity, Diana Gabaldon for the wittiness, Margaret Weiss and Tracy Hickman for the fantasy world, and all the others who have made me laugh and weep with their tales. I roll my d20 in honor of the roleplaying games that allowed me to create so very many characters (and to the DM who loved pool effects and gave my mage "Vampirism"). I raise my mug of tea (Thanks, Lisa!) to my fellow Ink Slingers, without whose steady encouragement I would never have gotten so far. I take my hat off to Nicole Dragonbeck, who not only creates amazing fantasy worlds, but translated my crazy crosshatches and chicken scratch marks into a delightful map. Thanking my family goes without saying—much appreciation to Remi (who gave Ev a bath while I was busy writing at night), to Ev (for making me put the laptop down and come play), to Nebi (for making me pause to give some much-required petting), and to Greyhame (who always keeps my feet warm when he isn't yowling). And finally, thanks to Phil, for helping me work out the logistics and catching not only my anachronisms, but any double spaces after periods. Any mistakes are mine alone.

I

Hannah Tallerin was standing over her forge, eyes squinting against the waves of heat baking off the blade she worked, when the stranger opened the door to the smithy. Though her senses were by no means what they had been, she still had the uncanny reflexes of someone who spent lots of time barely dodging lethal blows, and so she turned as the door began to swing inside, her long limbs ready to react if the visitor proved dangerous. The turn was a bad idea, as the hammer in her right hand continued its arc of movement and connected with the second finger of her left hand, mashing the tip and sending a shriek of agony up her hand and into her arm. She cursed, dropped the hammer to the anvil with a clatter, and cradled the wounded hand against her chest as she completed her turn.

A man had entered the smithy. He hovered in the shadowed front of the room, and Hannah's mortal eyes could only make out a sense of height marred by stooped shoulders, the lump of a traveling bag, and a slow measured step as he moved to one wall, examining the weapons hung there. When she saw that the newcomer wasn't intent on harming her, at least not outright, she relaxed a bit, but she couldn't ignore the little thrill that had been building in her chest as it was suddenly and distressingly dashed.

I've got to get out of here, she thought, remembering a time when she had been so thankful for slow time like this, for days and weeks of mindless simplicity, she working away with metal, Rory shaping the local farmers into serviceable soldiers, the two of them carefully sharing the small bed each night.

Safety. Comfort. The regularity of a common life. *And plenty of smashed fingers along the way,* she thought bitterly, taking a cloth from her apron pocket and carefully wrapping the injured digit, blotting at the blood seeping from beneath the broken nail, remembering a time when blood meant something so much more. Now it only meant pain.

The stranger hadn't approached the wooden counter that divided the customer area from the black bellied forge, squat anvil, and large water barrel that took up her work area, and so Hannah ignored him for a time, allowing him to take in the plethora of short swords, axes, picks, and shields that lined the walls near the ceiling. The lower portion of the front area was filled with pots and pans, and Hannah had a new display area for her knives right next to the counter. She surreptitiously watched as the potential customer scanned her wares, noting how he seemed to focus on the weapons, some dusty from lack of interest.

Maybe he would actually buy something. It had been a while since anyone in this village had needed the weapons Hannah excelled at producing, though she had a nice business in knives, pots, and metal clasps. The idea of someone able to talk shop with her was exciting. Still, she had learned that it never paid to seem too eager to sell, so she left him to his examination. Her finger throbbed, and she checked to see that the blood had stopped flowing. It hadn't. She sighed angrily and pressed down with more force.

This was what she had wanted. This had been what she was thinking of when she told Klauden almost a year ago that she wanted a simple life with Rory, a life without the complications that had plagued them both. Of course, that had been when she thought she was dead, or dying at best, and anything was a preferable alternative to what she had been expecting. She clearly hadn't thought this whole thing through.

Simplicity was nice, but it was boring. Unimportant in a way that made her wonder if all humans felt like this all the time, the days running together into a blur until the body grew old and withered and died. She would die now, too, just like them. Old and ugly like a mortal woman.

She shook the maudlin image away—thoughts like these came too often these past weeks—to check on her customer, another man doomed by time. He was standing idly before the counter, eyes scanning the walls still, but she could see he wasn't really looking at the weapons anymore.

"Help you?" she asked in the low voice that she sometimes still thought of as a stranger's.

The man looked at her, then seemed to realize something as he gave her a closer look. Hannah waited patiently for him to speak. The double-take was nothing new. She was accustomed to people giving her odd looks, though lately the reasons for them were a bit less clear than they had been. Before, they had looked at her because she made some blunder, some awkward revelation of her origins that marked her as a foreigner, as a freak, as something different. Now, they still gave her that look, but only because she was breaking their accepted notions of whom a black-smith should be and what he should look like. Rory had warned her, of course, and she had known it would be hard at first. She had been a smith in Talperin for a few months before meeting Rory and encountered some resistance there too. Still, it hadn't taken the people long to recognize skill, and that Hannah had. Of course, she didn't tell them where her knowledge had come from, and they hadn't asked, and then it hadn't mattered, but she and Rory had been in Severin almost eight months now, and some of the people here still gave her odd looks. She knew they were farther away from other towns, knew that the southern people were known for their particular expectations of what men and women should do, and she could understand that, having the background of her father's House in memory, but that didn't make it any less annoying when men stared at her for a few minutes before asking if she could get her man to come help them with something.

Some wouldn't even go that far. Some just walked out. Some gave her their esteemed opinions about female smithies. One had even gone so far as to grab her during one of these impassioned speeches, and he had learned the hard way that trying to strong-arm the new smithy was a bad idea, even when her man wasn't there to protect her. Rory had asked her if she wanted to leave after that, to go somewhere to the north, where people were less rigid.

She had declined, still lost in the fog of relief that was her life with him: the two of them sharing a home, eating breakfast together, doing all the little things that had seemed so impossible when she had first confessed to him in Kalford so long ago. *This is the life,* she kept telling herself. *This is what I wanted.*

And it was.

Sort of.

Except that when she told Klauden what she wanted, she hadn't imagined old men staring at her like this while she stood sweaty and disheveled, arms and back aching from a long day's work. She didn't mind the work. It was the waiting, the constant waiting, like she knew this fairy tale would end, and her real life would start up again. It just didn't feel right to be so secure, so settled, with no one chasing her, and no goblins, and no beast keeping her up nights.

Then again, Rory did his share of keeping her up at night, so that was a fair trade off. Better than that, even. She was fairly certain she had gotten the better deal on that exchange.

"You?" the old man whispered in front of her. Hannah focused on him again. He seemed ready to talk now, though she wondered what he was asking. She gave him a once over—traveling cloak, staff, pack—he definitely wasn't a local.

"Me," she replied, wondering if it was a language barrier. "What can I do for you?" She gave him a closer look when he paused. He had no visible weapons. *Maybe he really is looking to buy?*

She took in the state of his cloak, a bit tattered along the neckline, but well mended and obviously cared for. His feet were covered in old boots, worn as well, but in decent shape. The man did his share of walking, but he had chosen well in his footwear. Hannah's own shoes would never have lasted so long. He seemed a simple traveler, a man she had seen a thousand times over, an old man wandering from here to there, stopping in shops when fancy and finance took him. His eyes were low set in a deeply lined face, a face used to the elements. Hannah wondered if he had ever been north of the Vanya, then stopped herself. He would not have returned if he had been. Few mortals did.

"You don't remember me," he said, and this time Hannah tried to pick up his accent. She had been a keen student of language patterns once, back in her father's House, but it seemed the gift had left her over the months. Either that, or her new ears had never developed the ability to listen the way she once had. Whatever the cause, she couldn't place the man's history. *Remember him?* She ran through the list of towns that she and Rory had traveled through before settling here in Severin. *He doesn't seem familiar, but then again, why would I remember him? And who would recognize me now anyway?*

And then it hit her. He didn't recognize her. It was the body he knew: the slave girl who had been in the wrong place at the wrong time, the girl Solyn whose body Hannah had taken over during the ceremony that had been meant to purify her tainted soul. *Thanks again, Klauden,* she thought wryly, absurdly conflicted whenever she thought of her old friend. He had meant to help her. Surely that had been his intention. He just hadn't realized what putting her into a feeble mortal body would do to her. Nor had she. Then, it had just been a novelty, an exciting new toy to try out, a vehicle by which she could escape the castle with Rory and live out her childish ideas.

"Should I remember you?" she asked cautiously.

"What have they done to you, Hannah Hunter?" he asked, approaching the counter and placing large big-knuckled hands over hers. She pulled away, disgusted by the gesture, confused by the name, but then something in her surged, and she was allowing the old man to caress her hands. *What in the nine hells*—she began, Rory's phrase coming easily to mind, but then stopped as she realized more was happening. Someone was speaking, saying something rushed like, "Where have you been?" in a low voice that was familiar.

Something was moving her mouth.

Someone else was speaking through her.

"Oh, hell, Malfek, fehalon," she cursed in a rush of words, jerking back both control of her voice and her hands. She withdrew toward the forge, staring at the man.

What did he do to me?

He reached for her. "Oh, my dear," he whispered, his face filling with pity, his eyes a well of sadness. "What did they do to you?"

"Nothing," she spat at him. "No one did anything." She realized she was breathing hard, like there was something trapped inside her chest trying to break free. She ruthlessly shoved it back down. She calmed herself, regaining the emotional cool that had gotten her through so many difficult situations. "I don't know you, old man," she said stiffly. "I don't know why you're here or who you think I am, but you're wrong."

He paused, the emotions on his face loosening a bit as he considered her. She felt something snake out of him then, a low stirring across the room that prickled along her skin, and she recognized the feel of magic.

The old fool was using magic on her. She brought up her own defenses, ready to see what this spell would do, but when nothing beyond a small tickle of her face happened, she just stood there. She wanted to throttle him, to send a spear of ice into his chest that would make him regret coming in here, to use her magic to push him back against the walls and maybe even through the door to where he wouldn't bother her anymore, but there was something else in her now, too, a desperate need to keep him safe, to see him set free. She struggled with herself for a moment, then conceded the battle.

"Fine," she declared, "you can go free. Get out of my shop, and don't let me see you again."

"You are not yourself." It was not a question.

"I am not the person you are looking for," she said, as if that was obvious already.

"Not anymore," he observed, then his hands were raised in front of his chest, and Hannah knew that he was casting a spell again, and she wondered why she had been so stupid as to stand there and let this man into her shop and leave herself completely defenseless, when there was a sudden break in the room's air and a soft whooshing noise as the old man vanished.

Hannah stood from the semi-crouch she had assumed, ears popping, to stare at the space where the man had been.

Damn, she thought. *Vanishing magic. Serious spellcasting.* Even at her best, Hannah could manage a few offensive spells, but everything was memorization and stress for her. The power needed to simply disappear from the room was astounding. Or maybe he hadn't disappeared; maybe he had just gone invisible, as she could on occasion.

That was a hell of a lot of fuss just to go invisible, she thought, but she checked the room anyway, careful to cover every available space to make sure he wasn't still hiding in the building with her. When she was fairly certain she was alone, she barred the door and went to secure the forge for the night.

She had had enough of this for one day.

II

Rory was already inside the cozy one room house they shared when Hannah walked inside. He stood at the counter that ran along the back wall, a knife in one hand as he carefully sliced carrots and added them to the iron pot that held their dinner. As she shut the door and barred it behind her, he turned away from his work to smile at her.

"How was the forge today?" he asked, turning back to slide the carrots into the pot. He wiped the knife clean before setting it on the counter, then walked the stew pot over to the fireplace. He hung it on the hook and pushed the pot inside the fireplace where the stew could cook before he turned to her again, wiping his hands on his black pants. "Long day?"

Hannah sighed, grateful as ever that he had decided to take over the cooking side of their domestic life. It had taken almost a month of blackened chickens and charred stews before he had raised the question, trying not to insult her cooking but clearly starving for better fare. Hannah recalled one of the women in the village commenting that the sure way to claim a man was to cook such food that made him eager to come home for dinner, suggesting that a man who looked for dinner elsewhere would find more than just food. She had worried about that for a time, wondering if Rory would find other things along with his dinner, but she had come to see that the elf was nothing if not completely loyal to her. He was a good mate, kind and considerate of her, and now that she had examples to compare their relationship with, she was certain that Rory was one of the best men she'd ever met. He never struck her, as she knew that many men in the village did their women, and he rarely criticized her beyond a slight teasing that came from a good place. Not to say that they didn't have their share of arguments, mostly over how she was treating herself, but for the most part, Hannah's home life was fairly calm.

"Very long day," she said, plopping down onto the wooden bench before the table. There wasn't much furniture in the room, but the benches, table, chest, and bed always made for convenient places to rest when the floor wasn't appealing. The small area rug in the center of the room made the floor comfortable on occasion, though its function wasn't aesthetic as much as practical, since it hid the trapdoor that led to the basement and the tunnel into the woods beyond the fenced yard. Rory had learned to be careful over the years. So had Hannah.

Rory made his way over to her, squatting before her perch on the bench. He took in her smudged face, her sweaty hair, then her sloppily wrapped hand. She held up the wounded finger for his inspection. "I mashed it again," she explained, knowing what would come next. There had been a time when she had protested this, when it had made her furious to suffer his inspection, to listen to his long explanations of how she needed to be more careful, to take better care of herself, or, he was fond of reiterating, if she insisted on beating herself to a bloody pulp, to at least take the time to care for the wounds. It had been hard to accept not only his well-meant ministrations but just the idea that her body would not heal quickly on its own, would not bounce back from a wound with a fresh infusion of blood, or could even get worse if proper attention wasn't given to the area in question. That argument she had finally conceded to him when, after a particularly nasty cut on her hand from a slipped knife, she had gotten so sick from the resulting infection that Rory had to take her to nearby Salva for a real doctor and proper medicine. Now, she just let him check her over for wounds and took whatever advice he gave her.

As he delicately unwrapped her bleeding hand, Hannah wondered if she would ever be able to just look at a wound and know if it was serious or not. She had learned that pain wasn't a good judge at all. Everything hurt in this body; standing all day made her back ache, swinging the hammer made her shoulders scream, touching hot metal made her fingers shriek, even the mortal cramps she got every month curled her into a defensive ball of agony. She wondered if she would ever get used to the fragility of this form, the ease with which it was hurt and angry. Hannah winced as Rory first straightened her fingers, then he gently pulled her hand closer to him, into the slanting rays of sunlight that crossed the room from the window. He looked at it, then cocked a dark eyebrow at her.

"Not too bad," he observed, poking at the tip of her finger and sending a spike of pain down her arm, "though you'll probably lose the nail."

"Figures," she mumbled, pulling her hand back to rest on the tabletop. Her hands were filthy after the day's work, the grime and ash coating her up to the elbows, then spreading out across her shirt sleeves and onto her chest. She could see the line where her apron had been, the cleaner material beneath still in need of a good washing.

"Go wash," he said, turning back to his work. "We'll eat soon."

Hannah stood, keenly aware of how childish she felt, absurdly angry at how he treated her but knowing he only did it to keep her safe. Torn between frustration and appreciation, she headed out the door to the water barrel.

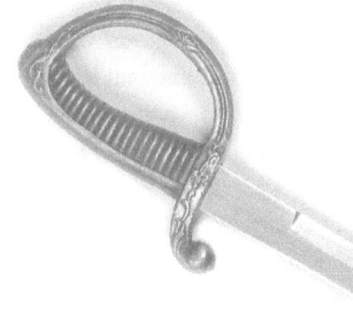

III

After dinner, Rory suggested they go for a swim. She knew he could tell something was bothering her, but as was his manner, he let her work up to it. They left the small house and followed the short path through the woods as the sun set behind them, making their way to the small spring that served as bathing facility and laundry site, not to mention sundry other events made more exciting with water.

She watched as Rory undressed, taking in the lines of his form, the hard muscles of his back, the scars that littered his chest, the long ears that marked his race. His hair had grown longer, shaggy around his ears, and Hannah loved knowing how it felt when she ran her hands through the dark mass. It was still a novelty to think of him as belonging to her. She had a brief flash of another man, another face framed with blonde hair and bright blue eyes that might have been hers, but that was in another life, another person.

The feeling in her chest returned, a yearning that seemed more than homesickness, and Hannah shoved it away. *What is wrong with me today?*

She disrobed, shoving her clothes into the water in a ball that could be dealt with after they soaked, and stepped carefully into the spring. Rory had taught her to swim, but the water still made her nervous, the feel of it pulling her down and under, the pressure against her skin tight as she grew extremely conscious of this body's need to breathe. She was still a paranoid swimmer, Rory told her, but she would adjust eventually. *When?* she wanted to ask him. *Ten years after I'm dead from old age?*

She ignored the thought, focusing on the feel as the water soothed her aching muscles. *I'm here now,* she thought. *Might as well enjoy it.*

Still, there was the old man to think of. He might come back, convinced that she was the person he was looking for. She walked out to where Rory was lazily sprawled on his back, chest rising and falling in the water as he breathed.

"A man came to the forge today looking for me," she said. Rory stopped bobbing, pushing wet hair behind his ear as he glanced at her.

"Who was it?"

She shrugged. "I don't know. He thought he knew me, but then changed his mind."

"Did you recognize him?"

She shook her head, wet hair swinging against her cheeks. "Not at all." Then, after a beat, she added, "Not really."

"Which is it, Hannah? Did you know him or not?"

She considered the strange feeling that had compelled her to let the man go free, that had stayed her hand when she wanted to blast him with a spell. Finally, she shook her head decisively. "I thought I knew him for a moment, but then I knew I didn't."

"Did he say anything else?"

"No, just vanished when he realized I wasn't her."

"Vanished?"

Hannah nodded. "Definitely a lot of power there. I couldn't have done it."

Rory considered this bit of information, then shrugged. "Just a traveler then. Severin's full of them."

"I know. He just..."

"Just what?"

"Just scared me a bit, that's all. He seemed so sure that he knew me."

Rory gave her a piercing stare. "Do you think he was looking for her?" he asked, and he didn't need to say anything else.

Hannah frowned, then shook her head. "I don't know. He called me Hannah." She gestured at herself. "This girl was called Solyn."

Rory nodded, then seemed to hesitate before continuing. After a moment, he asked, "She's not still..." He paused, gathering his thoughts. "I mean, you don't think she's still there at all, do you?"

Hannah reached inside herself, seeking that astonished girl she had met for an instant when Klauden placed her in this body. She remembered the shock, the outrage, but then she had taken charge, and after that, she hadn't been aware of anything. At least, not anything obvious. Though, what happened today could have been Solyn.

Is that possible? Could Solyn's spirit lay dormant for almost a year and then pop out and make me refrain from doing things or even speak using my mouth?

It was an unnerving thought. Hannah sometimes regretted stealing the body from the slave girl. *But really,* she thought, *what choice had there been? Should I have let the ceremony go as planned and allowed myself to be placed into Anna's body—the vampiric body of a sibling—or even worse, should I have refused a body and just gone wherever those without bodies went—hell or someplace worse—or even into nothingness?* No, she hadn't been willing to die, and Solyn hadn't been strong enough to keep hold of her own body; that in itself was justification enough. *If the girl wanted to stay herself, she should have fought harder.*

That was what Hannah told herself when she woke up at night anyway.

"I don't know," she answered Rory, awkwardly paddling over to him in the dimming light. Her finger ached with the motion, but the water was soothing. "I don't think so, but I don't know."

"He would know, wouldn't he?"

Hannah nodded her head, knowing that Klauden was a sore subject, even if they rarely spoke of him. Could she blame the elf for not being eager to talk about her once betrothed? It was enough that both she and Rory owed the vampire their lives; she tried not to remind the elf that she had once loved someone else, that she had once thought that her life would be quite different than it was. "He might," she admitted.

Rory nodded, changing the subject abruptly. "Let me know if this man returns," he demanded, then smirked at her. "I'd hate to have to fight for you again."

She returned the grin. "Liar. You'd love it."

He laughed, then caught her waist under the water. "Maybe," he admitted. "Though, I sometimes wonder if you were worth all that trouble."

"What trouble?" she asked breezily. "I happen to know that killing fledgling vampires in to-the-death tournaments is all in a day's work for you." He laughed again, then tugged her closer. "You earned this prize," she said, the water lapping against their shoulders as they rose and fell with Rory's breath.

"So I did," he said, then seemed to remember something else. "Speaking of prizes, I got you something today."

"Oh?" she inquired, allowing him to pull her to the water's edge. "To what do I owe this honor?"

He snorted at her. "Ungrateful wench. Here, I speak of prizes and you mock me. Some woman I've married."

Hannah giggled, squeezing the water out of her hair as she stood in the knee-high water. "Fine. Seriously, what did you get me?"

"A sword."

"Typical male present," she snapped. "Some women in the village get flowers or jewelry."

"Some women in the village can't even wield a sword. Flowers and shiny trinkets are all they can appreciate." He turned to her. "You, on the other hand, know how to appreciate a fine weapon."

"Point taken. What kind of sword?"

"Short sword," he said, illustrating the length with his hands. "It seemed a good weight for you, and you need something to balance Klauden's blade."

She nodded. For all that Rory disliked speaking of Klauden himself, he had no qualms about the sword Hannah carried, the blade that had been Klauden's by default that he had never learned to use. Hannah glanced at the delicately engraved scabbard laying on the rocks by the spring's edge near Rory's own discarded weapons, appreciative of both the sword's craftsmanship and its memories, then reached for her pile of wet clothes, spreading them out on top of the water and assessing the damage. "And to what do I owe this honor?" she repeated.

"I can't get my wife a sword?" he asked, spreading out his own clothes and beginning to scrub them.

She gave him a pointed look. "What am I doing for you now?"

He sighed, then grinned at her. "I thought that you might be so overwhelmed with gratitude that you would make Jaston a new sword. His father's is too long for him. He's ready for a blade of his own." Hannah nodded, picturing the lanky youth in her mind. He was one of the sixteen men Rory was training this month as part of his arrangement with Tarren, the village's mayor and head soldier. Severin wasn't known for its defenses, but even the simplest farmer could be taught to wield a blade in defense of his home, and Rory was an excellent teacher. The village paid well for his advice. "He's learning fast," she commented, then looked up at him with a scowl. "And what makes you think I'll be eager to do that just because you gave me a sword? You do realize I make pots all day long, right?"

"Yes, dear, I do realize what you do, but this sword is special."

"How so?"

"The man I bought it from said it had once been magical."

"Really? I could show you a ton of weapons that were once magical. Everyone that trades in a sword says that. You didn't pay a lot for it, did you?"

He tossed his shirt at her. "Thelash," he teased her. "And for your information, even I, the magic-deprived swordsman, know when something has magical capabilities. It's real."

She tossed the shirt back at him, grinning as it splashed his face. She was still skeptical. "What kind of magic?"

He shook his head. "I don't know. That's your thing. I just recognize runes when I see them."

Hannah stopped washing to stare at him. "There are runes on it? Are you sure?" She was getting excited now. Talk of a magical blade was all well and good but commonplace. Finding a blade with actual magical runes on it was something else entirely. "What kind? Where are they? What do they say?"

Rory squeezed out his shirt, then draped it over his shoulder as he shrugged. "Like I said, sweetheart, that's not my area of expertise. It was a good blade, so I bought it. The markings seemed like something you would appreciate."

Hannah squeezed out her own shirt, tugging it over her head, then tried to make sense of her skirt. After a failed attempt to find the center and step into it, she decided that the shirt was long enough to get her back home modestly enough. She twisted the skirt into a long line, getting rid of more water, then headed out of the pond, gesturing at Rory to hurry up with his pants.

"Come on! I want to see this thing."

He shook his head in surprise, eyes widening innocently. "But I thought you had a forge full of swords. What's the rush?"

She grabbed his arm to tug him along. "Don't play that way. I want to see what kind of runes it has."

He left the water but didn't move very quickly. "But it's just another sword. You would have preferred flowers or jewelry anyway. Maybe I'll just sell it..."

"You wouldn't dare!" she snapped, giving up on her tugging to face him at the spring's edge. She took a breath, then sighed. He was so particular about some things, especially gift giving. "Fine," she admitted. "You did well. Thanks for my gift."

He inclined his head, accepting her praise. "You are welcome."

"Good, now can we go see it?"

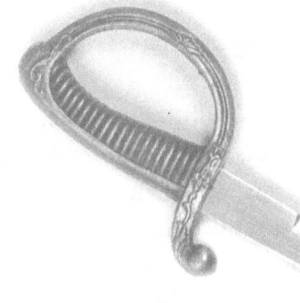

IV

Hannah was dreaming again. She didn't quite understand how she knew this, but everything about this room was wrong. First of all, it was built for colder weather than the house she shared with Rory, the windows covered by shutters and a rolled-up blanket pushed against the door to block the draft. She had never been in this place before, yet she felt at home here.

She sat on a wooden stool, her long hair pulled back in the standard braid, her hands working dexterously at a loom, long fingers leaping in and out of rows with thin colored threads. She seemed to be making some sort of design on the fabric, a scene of white and blue that might be the start of a mountain range. Hannah didn't recognize the picture, nor did she understand why she was using the loom with such familiarity since she had never used one in her life. Her fingers just knew where to go, the design a clear image in her head of numbers and blocks of color. It was strange to sit here, to know such things that she knew she shouldn't know. It had to be a dream, yet she couldn't recall ever knowing that she was dreaming while she was doing it before.

While she was pondering, the door to the small room opened, letting in a gust of cold air, and a tall man walked in. Hannah smiled at him, delighted at his appearance, suddenly wondering if her hair was in place, hoping he would notice how carefully she had applied her eye make-up.

Hannah knew that all of this was ridiculous. She would never worry about her hair, nor had she worn eye make-up in years, and she certainly didn't care what this newcomer thought of her. After all, he was too big for her—his shoulders alone had trouble getting through the narrow door frame—and his face was coated with a thick beard. In fact, he was far too hairy for her tastes. *What am I thinking?*

Yet she could feel herself responding to him, her heart picking up as her breath quickened, her formerly confident fingers now carefully aware of their placement, not wanting to look uncoordinated as he watched.

The newcomer strode across the room, and though Hannah wanted to move, to get into a defensive stance before the stranger got within range, she just sat there, hands skimming across the surface of the loom, placing another line of blues and whites that continued what Hannah knew was going to be a mountain scene—an image of the peaks that surrounded this village.

"It's lovely," the man said, standing behind her. Hannah was distinctly aware of his presence at her back, feeling exposed and nervous even as she was delighted with his praise.

There was something about the man's voice, something familiar, but it was gone before she could place it. She turned away from her weaving for a moment to glance at him, and she could feel her lips tilting up in a flirtatious smile.

"Thank you," she replied, feeling the warmth in her chest as he looked at her, their gazes locked in a smoldering connection. Hannah knew she should recognize something here, something about the man's eyes and his slow, careful appraisal of her that was tickling some memory, but she couldn't fathom what it was.

Then the door opened again, a blast of cold air breaking their locked eyes, and she turned quickly back to her loom, smiling perfunctorily at this new arrival. At first, Hannah thought it was the same man, but after a closer look, she noted subtle differences. This man was smaller in the chest, his hair a bit less shiny, and he had a tired, worn-down look on his face. His eyes had the same piercing gaze, but he looked defeated somehow, not strong and proud like the first man. Hannah thought they must be brothers, if not twins. She felt herself speaking to this new man.

"Greetings, husband. I didn't think you'd be home so soon." Even as she said the word "husband," Hannah felt herself losing touch with the scene. She was drifting away, losing the clarity of the man's face as he gave his brother a sharp look over her head. She heard his sharper voice ask,

"What are *you* doing here?" before the scene faded completely, and then she was awake in a familiar bed in a room thousands of leagues away.

Rory's arm tightened around her, and she snuggled into his warmth, his solid frame behind her a comfort in the darkness. She had been dreaming, that much was clear, but when had she had such a vivid dream before? It had been more like a memory, but not anything she had ever lived.

She held her hands up, the long fingers still a stranger's to her in the dim light from the banked fire. *Could I weave if I tried?* She twisted the fingers, picturing the smooth dance across the strings as she did so, and knew that the answer was yes. It was a familiar feeling, coming into knowledge like this, and she felt relieved at first. *Didn't I pick up my skill with metal in just this fashion, after taking the handsome smithy in Talperin?* He was filled with knowledge, and life, of course; there had always been the thrill of taking warm life.

Hannah shook her head. *That was a long time ago,* she reminded herself. She wiggled her fingers again, the shapes vague in the darkness. *Now you can barely see in the dark, never mind take down men twice your size.*

She sighed, the shock of this body hitting her again as it did often, too often of late. It was that damn old man. He had done something to her, woken her in a way that she was slowly beginning to understand. She knew how to weave because Solyn had known how to weave. Somehow, she was dreaming the slave's memories.

Hannah thought there was probably more to it than that since the nagging question of the man's voice and both of their faces still lingered, but as she tried to hold onto the images, they faded, ephemeral bits that her mind refused to recall. It was almost like her magic, she realized, when the memory of a spell faded each time she used it and she had to study her spellbook anew the next day. There were some things that her mind just refused to hold on to. It was annoying.

Of all the things she could forget—the warm rush of blood in her mouth, the sound of live blood pumping through stout veins—why could she not lose the memories of her old life that seemed determined to make her regret her decision? She pushed herself farther into Rory's embrace, feeling his steady breathing calming her fluttering heart. This was what she wanted: to lie here with him without anything between them. She no longer had to fight the desire to take him, no longer had to fear what she might do by mistake, no longer had to suffer when her body demanded fresh blood, no longer had to worry about divine magic, no longer had to wonder about what she was missing. Now it was just the two of them, and she was grateful for that. Grateful for this chance.

And, of course, she no longer had the nightmares. That had been a huge relief. She didn't have to relive her life at her father's castle every night in her dreams. In fact, she hardly dreamed at all now, except for tonight.

She readjusted herself, Rory's hand settling on her bare hip beneath the blanket. *Alright then,* she thought, *so now I know how to weave.* As she thought about it, she realized that she could probably paint and draw as well. The skill seemed to linger in her hands, the techniques crystallizing in her mind. It wasn't such a bad thing. It was the same thing she had always done, except now she learned in dreams and memories instead of through blood. It could even come in useful, especially since Rory's gift needed a careful hand to reform some of the runes that time and use had worn away from the blade.

Hannah didn't want to think about what else the dream meant; that is, that Solyn might have been awakened by the old man's visit and might soon want more than just to share her memories. That was something she couldn't believe, not only because it would mean that the girl had been alive somehow inside her for all this time, trapped deep within, but because it might mean that she could be trapped as well, taken away from herself, and Rory, never to return. Hannah pictured her body, but with a stranger's eyes, lying next to Rory in this bed at night.

Oh no, she decided. *That will not do.*

THE HUSBAND

Rory knew that something strange was happening to his wife, but he hoped it would pass before he had to do anything about it. He stood among the trees that covered their backyard, two swords poised in the ready stance, trying to imagine what he could do to help her. The routine of practice was comforting, his body carefully stepping into double thrusts, his feet landing precisely where they should be, his limbs executing the rhythm he had established through years of morning practices just like this one.

It's nothing, he told himself. He spun around, executing a twist and slice designed to catch opponents off guard, the twin blades whistling as they cut the predawn air. It was getting cooler again, the mornings hazy with fog and dew and a slight chill that reminded Rory of late spring back in Firene. It was still odd to realize that the seasons were backward this far south. He and Hannah had traveled a long way from her home in the far north beyond the Vanya mountain range and his own erstwhile origins in the Elven stronghold of Firene in the northeast; even Upsen, the port city that they had intended to reach when he had first met Hannah, was far to the north of this place. It would be spring up there by now, the deep chill of winter passed into another year.

Time had never mattered so much to Rory before. He swung the swords in an angry cross before his body, the dance degenerating into the pacing swipes that often calmed his temper. *It has only been a year,* he reminded himself. *One year, and what is that in comparison to the hundreds I will live still?* He was two hundred and twenty-nine years old already; even Hannah had been well into her eighties when they had met, a young age for a vampire, he had come to realize, but still almost more than a human life span.

The life span that Hannah would now live.

The thought of her mortality hit him as it always did, somewhere near his heart and chilling his spirit, and then his thoughts inevitably wondered if things would have been better had she stayed as she was. She had been a demon, that much was true, and he hated that her survival depended on the lives of others, but even so, that demon would have lived for hundreds of years, would never have gotten sick or nearly died from infections resulting from simple wounds.

And now she was even more vulnerable than ever. He paused in his pacing, hand braced on a tree trunk as he forced himself to face the issue.

Hannah always has moments, he told himself. She had days, even weeks, where she seemed like a stranger, but she came back to him before it caused a problem. He could always tell by her eyes. They were the only thing that remained the same from when he had first met her. Then she had been a short, frail thing, though he had soon learned how deceptive that frailty was, with springy red curls and a wiry body that knew how to move in a battle.

She had been full of secrets then, too, but he grinned at the memory of that girl and how he had found himself interested all the same, intrigued by the bright flicker in her green eyes. It wasn't common to find a human with such bold eyes, and he soon discovered the reasons why—she wasn't human—but even so, he could recognize the woman he loved in them. She had laughed during battles, too, her eyes flashing as she whipped this way and that, tossing her daggers with deadly aim before casting small but effective spells at their enemies. That was part of what he valued in her, the sheer love of life that overtook her when she was fighting for her own.

That and the fact that he had always been partial to redheads.

But things were different now. Hannah was blonde, as Galina had been—he had to scoff at the thought of his first wife, the image of her Elven face in his memory still enough to make him angry. He shook the thoughts away, seeing Hannah as she was now, her long hair often tied out of the way in a braid, her body taller and more curvaceous. She was still beautiful, but what he liked most was her eyes, that he could still recognize her in those brilliant green eyes.

Eyes that he had seen turn blue more than once in the last two weeks.

He turned away from the tree, hands a blur again as he began another dance, this one swift and marked with deadly thrusts to vital areas of invisible enemies. He closed his eyes, trying to concentrate without thought and failing miserably.

At first, he had dismissed it as a trick of the light, worrying on his part, a nagging uncertainty about the old man who had visited her forge looking for the slave girl.

Now, he was no longer able to deny the truth. For whatever reason, the other girl was back, showing herself in small slices, revealing snatches of a personality that Rory didn't quite appreciate.

The first time had been at the forge. He had gone to visit her at midday, the men taking a break from training for lunch, and had watched her work at carving a particular rune for almost a quarter of an hour. It shouldn't have been so odd, and it wasn't at first. She was trying to reform the faded runes on the blade's surface, it was a magical endeavor, and that required concentration.

Yes, he had told himself, *but wouldn't a magic user be concerned with proper shape? Shouldn't a magic-user have the book of runes nearby as a reference point?* Magic wasn't his specialty, but he had spent enough time with Hannah to have learned a few things about how particular spell casting could be. He knew she had the book with her at the forge. The night she first saw the sword, she had excitedly told him about the section in her spellbook on magical runes.

Klauden had made the book for her, she had told him proudly, detailing which ones she would use and where, and how they would make the sword even more powerful than it had been. She was so glad the vampire had thought to add that section. And then she had thanked Rory, her husband, again for his thoughtful gift.

Yes, Rory had smiled. *Good old Klauden.*

But when he had stopped to visit her for lunch, Hannah hadn't been concerned with magical runes. Her face had been a mask of concentration, but her hands, her big, long-fingered hands, were artfully carving another symbol into the blade, something that Rory became more and more certain were petals surrounding a broad stem with leaves.

A flower.

On a magical blade.

What the hell is she thinking? That had been his initial thought, but some instinct had forced him to stay put, to watch what he didn't want to see, to recognize every detail of the scene with his warrior's eyes. Hannah was working as an artist, a perfectionist at that, something Rory had never seen before. Hannah had always been the sort of person to do things on the fly, to take things as finished even if they were barely serviceable. She was definitely not someone who paid attention to details. As she turned the blade this way and that in the light of the forge, Rory had seen that her eyes were blue.

He didn't want to admit it, but he knew what that meant. Before he had met Hannah, he had spent some time hunting vampires, those he had thought of as demons possessing humans. Hannah had told him that these were actually humans bitten by vampires, not purebloods who were born with their gifts as she had been, and that some of them recovered, but Rory had not met one of those in his lifetime. The ones he had volunteered to hunt down had been mad creatures, wild with bloodthirst and violently strong. When they died, he had seen their eyes change colors, as the possessed always did when the true owner returned at the departure of the demon spirit. Some had even thanked him at the end.

If Hannah's eyes were changing colors, it meant that something was taking hold of her, and Rory knew better than to think it was a foreign demon. It was that damn slave girl, somehow waking up and influencing his wife.

Rory finished the dance with two sharp thrusts behind him, then stood still, panting a little. He knew he should talk to her about it, but since she hadn't told him about the dreams, he hadn't known how to approach the subject. Sometimes, Hannah was too guarded for her own good.

Rory had begun observing her dreams after the first night. He had felt her wake, stare at her hands for a time, then slip back into a calmer sleep. He had waited patiently for her to mention it. After all, she had told him when her nightmares had finally stopped; that had been a wonderful night, and an even better morning. They had moments like that still, though they were rarer now, and especially scarce this week. Hannah was changing right before his eyes.

Besides, he had always been able to dreamwalk; it was his Knack. He wasn't nearly as skilled as Caganasti, the elf who had helped him find Hannah's soul after her body had been destroyed by Malbrek, nor had he the abilities of the esteemed Klauden, but he knew his skill well enough to monitor his wife. She was somehow reliving the slave girl's memories in her sleep. Rory was detailing what he saw each night in Hannah's mind, trying to put the pieces together.

Clearly, the slave had been from Valrane, the human village that supplied Hannah's father's castle with human blood, but Rory couldn't tell how the girl had ended up at the castle in the first place. The fact that he didn't know a lot about the specifics of how the slaves got to the castle had a lot to do with it, but he still couldn't figure out why a girl who was clearly playing two men would choose death at the castle instead of life with one of them. Maybe she had been forced.

Damn, I just don't know enough about life north of the Vanya to make it out.

Rory sighed, sheathing his blades and wiping a hand across his face. He knew what had to be done. If he didn't act soon, Hannah might disappear entirely.

Still, he thought bitterly, *of all people, why does it have to be* him?

V

Over the next few weeks, Hannah realized that this problem with Solyn wasn't going away. She tried to focus on collecting herself more often, to consciously remind herself who she was and why she was here, but there were times when that story seemed so farfetched, and she found herself wondering why she hadn't left for home already. Surely her family would be worried about her.

What family? She shook her head to clear it. Surely her father wasn't missing her. The grand Magnus van Kreeosk hadn't paid much attention to his daughter when she had lived in his castle. *Why would he think of me after I've been gone for almost two years?* Though, she had to admit, for her father, two years was the space of a blink.

Hannah stood by the back door of the smithy, trying to use the mid-morning light to highlight the runes inscribed on the blade Rory had given her almost three months ago. She rubbed her forehead, wishing the muddled confusion that was a constant companion of late would relent and give her a moment of clarity.

My father, she thought bitterly, the old face swimming into her mind, his purple eyes, his thin lips, his permanent scowl whenever he looked at her, always bemoaning her flaws, her incapabilities at spellwork, at sword-play, even the appetite for blood that was shamefully absent in one of her status. *Oh, Father,* she thought, wondering about life in the castle now. *What is happening there? Has Livenna, my father's other daughter, replaced me by now? What has become of Klauden?*

She fingered the silver ring on the necklace she now wore. Rory had given her Klauden's ring again, silently asking her to accept the gift he customarily wore around his neck. "Maybe it will help," he had said. She had accepted the necklace, though it was a bit awkward for him to return what had been her unofficial wedding gift to him, knowing that she couldn't actually wear the ring anymore—it didn't fit this body's fingers. Touching the rune-carved surface of the metal now, she considered the item. *Does the magic of the ring still work?* Sometimes, it was hard to be so far away from everything.

As she stood there, the sun glinting off the runes on the blade, she felt the haze of uncertainty leave her. For a moment, she was wholly herself, despite Solyn, despite the body, despite everything that had been happening to her since the old man walked into her shop. She was Hannah van Kreeosk, now Hannah Tallerin, and her purpose was clear. Well, clearer than it had been for many weeks. She took a chance and searched for that other, the personality she felt hovering at the back of her mind, the sense of knowledge invading her hands and body.

Nothing.

She breathed then, a deep fulfilling sigh that still gave her a thrill. Breathing was such a wonderful thing. She had never appreciated it before; of course, her body hadn't really needed to breathe. It had gotten what it needed from the blood she took.

Hannah turned away from those memories, focusing again on the task at hand. The blade was a good weight for her arm; Rory had been right about that. Once she had all of the runes inscribed, it would be a weapon worthy of envy, a good helping hand in any fight. The past few weeks had been blurry with confusing memories, but when she worked on the sword, sometimes she felt that other presence leave her, not entirely, as it had for this moment, but stepped away, distant. She was almost finished with the sword now, and the thought scared her. *What will I focus on next? What can pull me together and remind me of who I am once this magical endeavor is completed?* Maybe she should start thinking about making a new sword and starting over. That would be challenging.

Challenges are something I was always good at, she thought idly, then winced as something clicked in her mind, *especially the challenge of becoming one of them.*

What? Hannah pushed the thought away, sighing now in earnest. The moment of solitude had passed. That damn girl was back in her head, making her think ridiculous things. If only she knew what the slave wanted! But that wasn't true because Hannah knew what the slave was after.

Her body, of course.

The dreams had been coming more frequently now, each new snippet a picture of a life that Hannah couldn't imagine on her own, even in her most outrageous moments. *Besides, when did I ever care about a slave before?* She scowled, moving the blade in the light, trying to decipher the problem with the last stubborn symbol. It was misshapen, that much was clear, but Hannah couldn't see where the problem began or how to fix it.

She glanced over at her spellbook, laying open on the cabinet against the back wall where she kept her more delicate tools. For a moment, her eyes blurred, and she couldn't read the writing.

Damn eyesight is awful, she thought bitterly. *I can't even shift from bright light to dim without taking forever to adjust.*

As she stared at the page, the words swirled into focus, Klauden's neat notes beneath the rune clear and concise. "Ice," the note read, "useful against flame, and cooling excessive heat." This description was followed by a brief addendum: "Essential to avoid confusion between Ice and Snow," and he had recopied the rune a bit larger and circled the swirl coming off the bottom right of the symbol. Hannah thought for a second that it looked a bit like a flower stem, then shook her head.

Of course, it wasn't anything like that—the curl was common in runes; it was just making it to the left or the right that differentiated. She could imagine how foolish she would appear if her new sword designed to inflict ice damage and searing cold suddenly caused the weather to change instead. The Snow rune was common for necklaces or staffs, but not blades. Ice was what she needed here. She turned back to the sunlight.

It just wasn't right.

The slave girl would appreciate the snow, she thought idly, shivering a little as she remembered last night's dream. Another day spent weaving, though this time the image was different, and she was sure that when the man stood behind her to watch—Matthew, her memory supplied his name now—that he would reach out and touch her, strong fingers gripping her shoulders as he turned her toward him for a deep kiss. She was ever aware of the door and hoping that it wouldn't open to reveal another face, even as she felt the soft caress of his fingers against her skin, his body warm and hard behind her. It was unnerving to want someone so much that she found a bit repulsive. Every time the man kissed her, Hannah felt sick inside, skin crawling with revulsion, and the feeling lingered even when she woke up.

This morning, she had looked at Rory when he gave her a familiar pat on the rump with that same feeling of disgust. The feeling was fleeting, but Hannah couldn't deny that it had been there.

If she was being honest, the feeling had made her ill. She had almost vomited, and then her morning had been filled with distracting thoughts of pregnancy, wondering if it could be true, alternating between giddiness at the thought of such an adventure and then sick at the thought of how the baby would have blonde hair instead of red, and big hands that could draw. For the first time, she was looking forward to bleeding again.

She was starting to hate the slave girl and the body she had lived in. Little things were beginning to seep into her everyday thoughts, her everyday life, and Hannah was powerless to stop it. She knew she should talk to Rory about it, should ask for his advice, his help, something, but she just couldn't find the right moment to do it. She hated Solyn a little more for driving a wedge between her and the elf like this.

But then again, she knew things now, things about Solyn that made her regret her harsh thoughts. She could understand how Solyn felt in her little life in that tiny village, how trapped she had been by a marriage to a man she couldn't love, and how agonized she had been to discover that the one she did want might have wanted her, too, if only she'd been less of a coward. The slave had vowed never to be afraid again, not like that. She would die first. The start of her little rebellion had been to take what she wanted, and Solyn wanted Matthew, the other brother. Hannah tried to remember Solyn's husband's name, but it kept leaping away from her.

Hannah tried to distance herself from this knowledge, to view it as just another tale that she had read with Klauden as a child. She tried to imagine how the story would end. *How did this slave get to my father's castle? Who owned her?* Hannah knew that she had never been valued by any of the vampires there. She had heard stories, though, about how some of the Kargin—those second sons—and on occasion even Vailen van Joosen, the lowest ranking son of the three elite families, had indulged in other sordid acts with slaves, but those had been dismissed as rumors, even for the brief moment she had considered them. *What exactly happened to this slave before I got her?*

She stepped away from the door, setting the blade on the anvil again, and stretched, her hands finally resting on the rough material of her dress over the smooth skin of her belly. *How many hands have touched this body there?*

She knew the body wasn't virgin; she got the impression that Solyn had known her share of men, both of the ones she dreamed of each night, and likely more again at the castle. Though Rory had been gentle with her, she knew that her body's experience disconcerted him, or maybe it was her own inability to fully express what she wanted that he thought about. She stepped over to the forge again, settling into her work, checking the right shape once more in the light from the open door before trying again to carve the stubborn rune into the right lines and curves. Rory would be so pleased when she could show him the completed weapon.

She had been working for a few minutes when she paused, staring vacantly into the white flames of the forge. *How could I not have noticed?*

Thoughts of Rory had sparked a realization. They had been sleeping together every night since this debacle began, but they hadn't been truly together for several days. She tilted her head, really thinking about it. *Malfek,* she thought, *it's been longer than days, hell, weeks even.* For a couple that happily jumped into bed practically every other day for almost a year, she was surprised that it had taken her so long to even realize that the sex had just about stopped. *Weeks,* she thought, *at least three weeks;* in fact, she had even had her last monthly course without really minding the interruption.

That was disturbing, but it was even more unsettling to realize that this abstinence wasn't at all on Rory's part. He still smiled welcomingly when she came to bed, still traced light fingers across her belly and over her shoulders, still kissed her when he saw her and held her hand when they walked together. It had been her. She just didn't want him.

What? That was insane. This was the elf she had lusted after enough to throw away her future; this was the elf that had occupied her every waking thought even when she knew that she was nothing but trouble for him. *How could I just turn off that kind of passion?*

Because it's not right for humans to mate with elves.

The thought was clear, concise, and not her own.

Malfek, fehalon, slave get out of my mind, Hannah thought immediately, the sentiment crowding out anything else she had been pondering. She stood, hands jerking away from the blade so suddenly that it tilted and fell to the floor. As it fell end over end to the straw-covered dirt, Hannah saw in the reflected firelight from the forge the dim outline of a flower, a picture mostly obscured by the Ice rune that had been giving her so much trouble.

Did I carve that? she wondered, big hands reaching for the blade to examine it more closely. She stopped halfway there, uncertain as she hadn't been in months. *What is the matter with you? A stupid thought about sex, and here you are, acting like a scared girl-child.*

Get a hold of yourself, Hannah. The voice was Klauden's, a comforting sound in her head that often appeared at odd moments, though it was a welcome change from the voices she used to hear—mainly her father stating the obvious or Kelvin Malbrek, her teacher and her father's second-in-command, barking orders. At least she always gave herself good advice in Klauden's voice now.

She took a deep breath, feeling the pull in her chest and the way her dress tightened around her breasts, then closed her eyes, keenly aware of the heat from the forge on her face, her hands balled into fists at her sides. It was alright, everything was alright, she was Hannah, and she was in charge of this body. She hadn't gone through all the trouble of facing Malbrek and fleeing her home just to lose control to a coward who couldn't marry the right man.

She opened her eyes again, feeling steadiness flow through her limbs. A break, that was what she needed, just a break from this heat and hard work.

VI

Hannah wiped her hands on her dress again as she walked, scowling at the two streaks of soot that smeared across the back of her hand instead of onto her simple blue clothing. She always looked a mess these days. It was amazing that Rory was willing to touch her at all.

She made her way down the main street of the village, moving slowly and trying to enjoy the cool afternoon air. It would be cold again soon, and though she preferred it to the baking heat they had passed through in Silva's summer, she hated how cold this body would get, the fingers numb and useless and her nose running like a sieve.

Wiping her nose, she wondered if she had just smeared the soot on her face. *Since when did you care so much about how you look? Idiot.*

She could feel the anxiety building in her again, the uncertainty that could overwhelm her if she would let it, and walked faster, rounding the inn and leaning against the boundary that marked the training grounds. She placed both hands flat against the post and rail fence, feeling the rough wooden slats press into her palms, grounding her in a sense of touch again. Looking up from the fence, she spotted Rory across the open space, both swords out as he worked three sweaty farmers through drills. Hannah leaned against the fence and took comfort in watching him.

His back was to her, his hair grown long around his shoulders now, and he was saying something in a low voice to one of the men. Hannah couldn't make it out, *damn these useless ears,* but she heard the man say "yes, sir" as he got into a ready stance before the elf. The farmer was exhausted, his chest sunken with the effort of his breath and his hair swirling in wet locks across his shoulders. Hannah thought his name was Bergin, but that might be his brother. There were two of them, both somewhat scrawny, but they worked the far field to the west of town. Hannah wondered if they got enough to eat. She turned, taking in the shape of the other two trainees.

One of them was Jaston, the boy for whom she had crafted the sword. Barely sixteen, he had the shadow of what would become a beard in a year or two and still hadn't lost the gangly awkwardness of mortal youth. *He is so young,* Hannah thought. When she had been sixteen, she had been in Essentials with Klauden, her mate to be; Vailen, a bore even as a child; and Anna, the half-sister whose vampire body she was supposed to have inhabited before Klauden changed the ceremony; she hadn't been able to cast even the simplest of spells but had been delighted by the rush of energy that fresh blood at the end of a lesson always brought.

Though she hadn't been quite so awkward, even then. Nor had Klauden or Vailen suffered from the pangs that haunted mortal adolescence; that seemed something the blood curse took care of, grooming them all to be powerful, untouchable, and indestructible beings.

But then, that had been a lie too. Her body hadn't been so hard to burn, after all. She realized that she was fingering the ring on the chain around her neck again, comforted by the cool metal band and its familiar markings. She wondered if Klauden could still see her with it, or if he would choose to if he could; it had been fairly clear when she and Rory left him that that part of her life was over. *Does he still think of me as often as I think of him?*

Rory crossed his swords before his body in the ready stance, then after a word, waited in place. Bergin stared at him, waiting for the movement that he could defend, but when Rory simply stood there, the man hesitantly took a swing at the elf. Rory stepped easily out of the way, taking the opportunity to slash at his opponent's wrist in the process, causing the man to yell and drop his sword. Rory yelled a sharp negative, then smacked the man on the top of his head with the flat of his blade before stepping back.

Hannah could hear him shouting. "Never attack unless you mean it, Fergus," he snapped, "and never let go of your blade!"

Fergus, huh? Hannah thought, squinting a bit to see the farmer's face. *Is he the older one, then?*

Rory bent and retrieved Bergin's brother's blade from the dirt and tossed it at the man, who squatted with his wrist in his hand. Hannah could see the blood trickling out from under his fingers. The blade landed at the man's feet, and he looked up at Rory with a bright hatred before turning back to his wrist. Rory must have seen the look, for he hit the man on the shoulder with the flat of the other blade, the force of the blow pushing the man to his knees.

"Get up," he snarled. "Do you think a goblin will wait for your wound to stop bleeding before he runs you through?" Fergus made his way carefully to his feet, but before he could stand upright, Rory smacked him again across the thigh with his blade. When Fergus growled something, Rory snapped, "Pick up your blade, idiot." The man picked it up awkwardly, still cradling his bleeding wrist.

Hannah had to smile. That was her man, whipping farmers into soldiers the same way she had been shaped into a lethal, dagger-throwing sorceress by Malbrek's constant scorn. It was funny how things turned out sometimes, how she could hate one almost as much as she loved the other. Rory's back was still to her, but she could picture his face, cold and impassive as it had been when she had watched him in the tournament her father had held for the prize of her soul. She thrilled at the knowledge that his face cracked and opened for her, sometimes only for her, revealing an inner sweetness and lingering playfulness that sparked a kindred response in her own soul.

But that's silly, she thought. Rory was always easygoing, ready with an eager smile for anyone, and always willing to lend a hand. But still, he could be so hard sometimes. The thought made her swell a bit with pride. That was her husband, that warrior, that confident teacher who once commanded the armies of Firene.

Klauden could never have been like that.

Or maybe he could have been if he'd had a different mate...

Hannah ignored the thought.

Rory turned his attention to the other two men, young Jaston and another farmer that Hannah recognized from the inn, but she couldn't recall his name. She really ought to work on that; she'd been in the village for many months now, and still, she only knew a few people by name. She should be more sociable; it was what a human did.

Rory was lecturing his unwounded students. "Now you two, think about what you're doing, but don't let it overwhelm you. Trust your instincts. They will never fail—"

Standing behind Rory, she caught the movement before she thought he did, Fergus's blade singing through the air at Rory's undefended left side. She wanted to shout a warning, but even as she started to make a sound, Rory spun about, one sword easily blocking Fergus's well-aimed thrust and knocking his sword to the ground again, while the other blade went to the man's throat. Fergus put both hands up in surrender, blood trickling down his wrist to drip on the dirt of the training yard.

"—you in a fight," Rory continued, as if nothing untoward had happened. He nodded at the two men, "Dismissed," before turning his attention back to Fergus. He cocked his head, then sheathed his swords.

"That was a good try, Fergus," he said, taking a deep breath, "but you lack conviction."

Fergus didn't look like he lacked conviction to Hannah. In fact, he looked like he would gladly spear the elf on the spot. When the man didn't say anything, Rory added, "If you really wanted to hit me, you would have succeeded." He picked up the sword that might have slain him and handed it to the man, hilt first. "Determination will often carry a man through a battle." As Fergus grasped the sword with a shaky hand, Rory shook his head in frustration. "Though, little good that will do you without a blade. Honestly, Fergus, you need to learn to hold onto your sword." He reached out to grab the man's wounded wrist. He poked it a bit, then released it. "Have your woman bind that for you. Not too tight, mind."

Fergus nodded, his face a mask of shock, disbelief, and growing awe. When Rory stepped away and said, "Dismissed," Fergus did not leave as the others had.

He waited a moment, then said, "You're not angry."

Rory glanced in Hannah's direction, grinned, and gave her a small wave. "Why would I be?" he asked his student.

"I tried to kill you," Fergus said, tucking his sword awkwardly into the sheath on his belt.

Rory laughed. "It will take more than you to kill me, Fergus."

Instead of growing angry as Hannah expected he might, the man broke into a sunny smile. "But, I..." He trailed off, nervous hilarity taking over.

Rory sighed, turned away from Hannah to face him completely. He placed a hand gently on the man's shoulder, watching as the would-be soldier winced. "You were angry. You lashed out. That's good. That's what this town needs you to do." He paused, considering. "You've got the instincts in the right place. Now you just need your body to catch up with you. Someday, if you keep practicing, a move like that will work for you."

Fergus seemed pleased by this little speech, nodded, and moved away to where his vest and jacket hung over the fence by the inn wall. Rory walked over to Hannah, running a hand through his hair and wiping his forehead in one motion. The gesture was familiar; Hannah wondered if he even realized that he did it. It was something he always did after fighting, whether in practice or in reality. The movement comforted her, reminded her how well she knew him and his little quirks.

"What brings you out here?" he asked, and Hannah could tell he was pleased to see her.

"I thought I'd take a break and watch you torture the locals a bit."

"A woman after my own heart," he observed, then leapt over the fence in a smooth bound, offering his hand to her as he headed away from the training field. "Have you eaten?"

"No," she answered, thinking again of how long it had been since he'd had his hands under her dress, his bare chest glinting with scars in the firelight, and felt her face grow warm.

Rory quirked an eye at her but said nothing about it. She took his hand and began leading him down the street at a brisk walk, heading back to their house. "What's this?" he asked, hurrying along behind her. When she didn't respond, he didn't ask again.

When he shut the door of their house behind them, she turned to face him, desire hopefully plain on her face, and waited for him to kiss her.

He gave her another curious glance, then leaned down to give her a brief kiss. When he would pull away, Hannah stopped him, her hands winding in his hair and pulling him across the room toward the banked fireplace.

"Hannah," he said against her mouth in that voice that made her shiver.

She waited for the voice in her head to speak and was relieved when it didn't. Sinking to the carpet on the floor, she tugged the elf down with her.

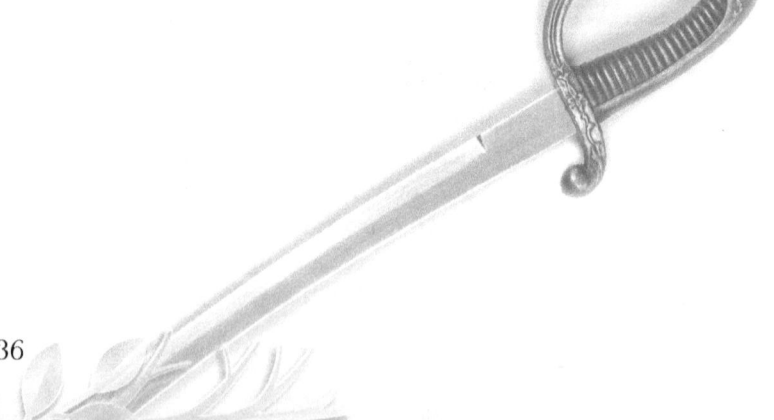

VII

"Talk to me, Hannah," Rory whispered against her hair.

Hannah tightened her grip around his waist, squirming even closer to his warmth. They were on the rug before the fireplace, slats of late afternoon sunlight illuminating the ridges of scars on Rory's shoulder and making the locks of her blonde hair glisten against his skin. She stared at the strands of her unbound hair, recognizing them as her own, and for once not minding that they weren't red.

"About what?" she whispered back, though she knew perfectly well what he was talking about.

He moved away from her a bit, readjusting so he could watch her face. She settled for resting her head on his upper arm instead of in the crook of his armpit. "I'm serious," he said. "What is it?"

"Nothing," she said automatically, needing the security of keeping everything a secret, while hating herself for not facing the truth. *If I tell him,* she thought, *if I talk about it, then it's not just something I'm imagining. It's real, and what the hell am I going to do about it?*

That was cowardice, though, and she knew herself well enough to realize that it had only been a matter of time before she faced facts. Hannah was thoroughly pragmatic, and though she might try to delude herself at times, it always came back to this moment, the unveiling of the mystery, the barefaced truth staring back at her.

Rory sighed beneath her. "Nothing," he repeated, frustration bordering on defeat in his voice. "Right." He watched her face closely, staring into her eyes until she thought he might bully the answers out of her. Then he shook his head. "You never did like to talk about things."

"That's not true," she snapped, rising to an elbow to look at him. "I just prefer to leave unpleasant things for later."

"Unpleasant things like what? That you were a bloodsucking demon? That you had a crazed vampire wizard following you?" He paused, smirking. "I thought we learned how well that doesn't work out for us the last time you didn't tell me everything."

"I don't want to talk about it," she said. "It's different."

"What's different?"

"Everything!" she snapped, pushing away from him to sit up. She stared at her hands in her lap, her golden skin chilled in the absence of his heat.

Rory sat up, too, put an arm around her shoulder, and turned her face to his. "I know—" he began, but she cut him off.

"You don't know!"

He jerked his arm away, face reddening a bit. "Well, you don't talk to me!" He glared at her. "Hell, Hannah, you can't even tell me what's happening to you. Why?"

She looked away. "I don't know," she mumbled. But that wasn't true either. She knew. *Stop this,* she heard Klauden say. *This is not like you at all.*

That voice was forever reminding her of how she had been, how she was supposed to be, who she really was.

"Fine," she said, to no one in particular. "You want to know what's going on?" She faced Rory again, face warming as frustration overwhelmed her. "I'm becoming her—that's what's going on. She's taking over. This stupid mortal body is not always under my control anymore. I can't focus on things. I am starting to think like her. I am starting to behave like her. I can't even look at you without knowing what she thinks about it!"

"It's that bad, then," he said, watching her face carefully again. *Why does he keep staring at me like that?* It was disconcerting.

"Not all the time," she admitted. "Like this afternoon. I was wholly myself again when I was with you. It was nice."

He grinned. "So that's why you jumped all over me. Trying to force out that girl's spirit by having lots of sex with me."

"I'm sorry," she said. "I didn't mean to use you like that."

He shrugged, taking in the disarray of strewn clothing and weapons that littered the floor around them. "I don't mind. Anytime you need a reminder of who you are, just throw yourself at me. I'll be here." He paused, thinking. "So, the physical act brings you back, then?"

It was Hannah's turn to shrug. "I don't know what it is. I think it's being with you, but there are times when this body isn't all mine, and it's hard to get it back. I can't hear her clearly yet, but I know that I will, and I don't know what will happen then."

"But this works," Rory repeated. "Touching me, being with me helps."

Hannah nodded. She couldn't tell him that sometimes his touch made her want to vomit. That had probably been a fluke anyway.

No, it wasn't. Honesty, Hannah. Stop deluding yourself—and him.

She stopped her agreement, shaking her head. "Well, not exactly."

"What do you mean?"

"Sometimes it helps, like today, but there are other times when she doesn't want to be touched at all."

Rory looked at her for a long time, and Hannah wished she could see what was going through his mind. "By me," he added finally.

Hannah couldn't look at him. "I don't know. No. I don't think so." *Gods, I am rambling again. Get a hold of yourself!* She let the weight of her fear fall on her then, allowing the possibilities that she refused to consider flood her mind, thoughts of Solyn pushing her into a dark corner, or even worse, thoughts of Solyn letting her watch while she lived with Rory. But that was foolishness. Clearly, Solyn wanted to go back home. She would never stay with Rory.

Would she?

Hannah didn't like to think of it. She put her face in her hands, tears jerking out of her in little sobs. "What's going to happen to me?" she asked, hating how broken and weak she sounded, how pathetic and small.

Rory took her hands in his. "It's alright," he said, though she knew it wasn't true. Hannah stopped her watery deluge and looked at him, grateful for his support.

"I don't want to leave you," she said, wishing he would tug her closer to him again, instead of this tenuous connection through linked hands and fingers.

"I won't let you," he promised, reading her mind and yanking her over to his lap.

He kissed her, then pushed her hair behind her shoulders. "I got you something today," he added, hands brushing her neck and the necklace she still wore.

"Another sword?" she asked.

He shook his head, pushed her gently to the floor in front of him, and reached behind him to the ball of his pants on the floor. Locating his belt pouch, he dragged it over to them and loosed the strings. Hannah watched him curiously. *What is this all about?*

Carefully, he withdrew a small gold band from the bag. It was caught up in some string, and it took him a moment to free it. While he fussed with it, Hannah tried to keep a grip on her emotions. A ring. He had gotten her a ring.

It doesn't really matter, she told herself. They were married as any mortals got married—a verbal agreement, taking his name, the decision to share a home—but even still, there were times when she regretted the lack of formality, the lack of a symbolic link between them. Until recently, he had worn Klauden's ring on his neck, the only thing she had to symbolize her part of the bargain, but now that he had given the ring back to her, it was a bit odd.

Rory managed to free the ring, and Hannah saw that it was not engraved but molded with thin braided coils. It was an Elven ring. She looked from it to him.

"Where did you get that?" she asked. There were no other elves in Severin. In fact, there were few elves in nearby Salva.

"I ordered it when we were in Salva last spring. It came today." He pulled her hand out to him. "I know it's been some time since we made this official," he said, holding out her fingers, "but I was wondering if you would do me the honor of wearing my ring." When she nodded, he slipped the ring over her finger. It fit perfectly.

"Thank you," she whispered, feeling the odd weight on her hand, knowing it would take some time to get used to it. She hugged him then, crawling closer into his lap and resting her head on his shoulder. "I didn't get you anything," she commented.

"There's no need." He shook his head, then pushed her away so that he could look at her face. "Just stay with me, Hannah." Hannah could feel the palpable presence of Solyn between them again, even with the new ring to keep them connected.

"I'm so afraid," she admitted, and it seemed that the confession soothed her, as if acknowledging the fear somehow made it less powerful.

Rory placed both hands on her shoulders, his solidarity and strength a comfort. "You have to fight her, Hannah."

She nodded, hoping that would actually work in the end. "I will," she promised, then added, "I am."

Even as she spoke, she wondered how long she would remain willing to fight, how much more time she had left.

VIII

Hannah stood before her forge, twisting the magical blade this way and that, trying to distinguish between the Ice rune she was trying to carve and the stupid flower that Solyn had managed to sneak instead. She squinted in the half light from the glowing coals, willing her eyes to see as they once had, to see what was right there in front of them.

It didn't help. The markings blurred and ran together anyway.

After shoving the thin rod she was using to carve the lines into the blade into her apron pocket, she tossed the sword down in disgust. It clanked loudly against the stone anvil, rocking back and forth for a moment before settling into place.

Nothing helps anymore, she thought bitterly. Her eyes were no longer reliably her own. There were times when she thought that nothing in this body was reliably hers anymore. Inhabiting the mortal body had always been awkward, a strange adjustment that she still hadn't outgrown these many months, but even in those first moments of recognition, when she finally understood what Klauden had done to her, even then, she had not felt such a stranger in her own skin.

It was one thing to understand that she had stolen the body, however unintentionally, from someone else. It was entirely different to realize that the person was still there, growing stronger every day, not exactly meshing with Hannah's own personality, but slowly infecting bits and pieces of her, taking over in a slow, methodical way that would leave Hannah with nothing to cling to by the end.

She closed her eyes. Even if they didn't see the right way, she could at least still control them. She could feel that other, that slave girl rising to the surface, the foreign emotions bubbling along her skin, could hear her thoughts getting ever closer. Hannah wiped at her eyes, Rory's new ring a comforting weight on her finger, rubbing dirty palms against her cheeks and forehead, wishing she could wipe away her problems along with the sweat. She shouldn't be so sweaty anyway; it was early winter now, the ground crisp with frost in the morning. She felt at her waist, her armpits to test the extent of the damage. She was damp through her dress. That would be a problem when she had to walk home later in the cold dark. It seemed the forge was extra hot today.

She stretched then, contemplating. Maybe she should just go home now, call it quits for the day and walk home in the light. Rory would still be working with the farmers—*soldiers,* she thought hastily, *they are soldiers now, Rory's soldiers*—by the inn. She would be alone at home as well. The idea was not comforting.

Yes, but maybe I could take a bath. The thought was strange—they didn't have a tub inside the house. For the past few months, they had made due with the spring out back. Last winter, they had been up in the Vanya Mountains near Hannah's father's castle. By the time they made it this far south, it had been spring already, almost summer. The people here said it got cold in the winter, but Hannah hadn't really thought about how she would wash. *What about Rory? Will he still swim every morning now that it's getting colder?*

For a moment, Hannah felt the sharp pang of homesickness. At her father's castle, there would have been a metal tub filled with hot water, perfumed water at that, and all of the trouble of heating it and getting it ready out of Hannah's reach, done by the slaves of her family. She tried to shake the feeling off. It wasn't as if she wanted to return to that place, to those people. Still, a hot bath would be nice right now.

She frowned, wondering where they might find a tub in this town. *Do I have enough spare metal to make a small one? It couldn't be all that hard to heat water and fill it.*

<*Obviously, you never drew a bath in your life.*>

The voice was sharp, bitter, and not her own.

Hannah turned around, searching for the speaker, but the area before the counter was empty, the wooden door shut tight, even the one window was latched and shuttered. She was alone.

That is, physically, she was alone. Her head was another story.

Hannah took a deep breath, trying to keep the little whimper she felt building in her throat from emerging. When she felt it creep back down inside, she steeled herself, readying her mind and body as she had done before other battles. *Fine, then.*

< *You finally speak to me, and that's all you have to say?* > She retorted, hoping to incite the voice to continue. *Solyn,* she reminded herself, *not the voice, not some random haunting or unexplained event. Solyn, the slave girl.*

Do not make this more than it is, she heard Klauden say. *It is only what you expected.*

And she had been expecting this. It was only a matter of time. From the moment Solyn had woken up, or had been woken up by that old man's spell, Hannah had known there would be a confrontation.

Hannah could deal with confrontations; in fact, she was almost looking forward to it. Any sort of direct action was better than the uncertainty of wondering when Solyn would appear again, in what area of Hannah's life she would emerge.

Get them out in the open, she heard Malbrek, her old teacher, instructing her. *That's the only way to truly crush your enemy for someone like you.*

< *Honestly, with all the people you hear in your head, girl, I'm astonished that you even noticed I was here.* >

< *Shut up.* > It wasn't the best thing to say or what she wanted to convey, but Hannah didn't know how to explain her thought process or why she always heard different voices in her mind, and she certainly didn't want to discuss her method of advice-giving with this slave girl. She settled for asking, < *What do you want, anyway?* >

< *Isn't it obvious? You've stolen my body. Pardon me for taking offense at that.* >

< *I didn't exactly steal it,* > Hannah objected. < *It wasn't even my idea.* >

< *I don't care whose idea it was,* > Solyn snapped. < *I want it back.* >

< *Well, you have it now, don't you? Why not just reach out and grab it?* >

Hannah thought it might be dangerous to prod the girl like that, but she couldn't help it. She had to reach some sort of solution here, or she might very well go mad from the strain of it all.

She could feel Solyn's resentment, and underneath that, she could feel the girl's impotent rage. *She hasn't done it yet,* Hannah realized, *because she can't. Maybe she doesn't know how, or maybe she just can't do it at all, but either way, she's not strong enough. Yet.*

<*I could do it,*> the voice insisted. <*I just don't want to right now.*>

<*You don't want to?*>

This was getting ridiculous. She was finally talking to the stranger, conversing with the woman who shared her body, and they were bickering like children barely out of Essentials. Thoughts of her childhood made her think of Klauden again, then she was remembering how Klauden had let her inside his body so that she could watch Rory fight in the tournament. That had been sort of like this; maybe that was why she didn't find it so unnerving. Not that it wasn't disconcerting—it was—but it was something she could relate to, something familiar, and that was helping her maintain calm.

<*Ah, now that one had promise.*>

Hannah's mind was shifted from her own memory of Klauden's actions that day to another image of her one-time mate. He was younger than the Klauden she remembered from her last trip to her father's castle. Perhaps Hannah's flight, return, and subsequent flight had aged him somehow. It wasn't that he looked old, not by any means. He was barely into his adulthood at all, even at a hundred years old. What Hannah had noticed was the weight around his shoulders, the knowledge in his eyes that was not yet present in Solyn's memory of him. Seeing this image of him from another time, Hannah had a dark moment to ponder what she had done to her old friend, what great price he had paid for her.

Solyn ignored the thought, the image pressing forward. In the memory, Hannah's new memory, Klauden was standing in a doorway, face impassive, long fingered hands reaching out to pick her up off the floor.

<*What were you doing on the floor?*> Hannah asked, curious despite herself. She could feel Solyn's aching body in the memory, the way her bones sang, her lips swollen and one eye unable to open.

<*That was how they left me,*> Solyn replied, and there was no emotion in her voice. Hannah had a sense of where this was leading and revolted. She didn't want to hear Solyn's story. She didn't want to know what kind of pain lay behind that flat voice. She didn't want to know anything else about this girl's life, and she certainly didn't want to know what Klauden had to do with it.

<No. I don't want to see this.> The young Klauden was helping her stand up, and when her legs buckled, he picked her up, carrying her out of the room that she had thought would be her death chamber.

<Stop,> Hannah said. *<I said stop it.>*

But Klauden was laying her down someplace soft. Hannah recognized his room and the tapestry on the wall next to his bed, the picture she recalled from a distance; she had not been so far into his rooms since they were very young. Most of her time with him had been spent in the front room, where his desk sat amid all of the books he had carted up from the library in the basement, and the rest of her memories were of them romping through the caverns below the castle.

Well, she had romped. Klauden would never do something so undignified. Even in this memory, he was so cordial, so formally concerned for her welfare. Hannah wondered what would ever break that shell. And then she was feeling the soft sheets beneath her battered body, and it was warm, and he was looking at her with those big blue eyes, and she thought he was going to—

Hannah let her legs buckle, allowing her body to crash to the floor of the forge in an awkward seat, then slapped herself across the face as hard as she could. The jolting of her fall and the sting of the slap shocked Solyn into silence and banished the memory of Klauden's face from Hannah's mind.

<I don't want to know that,> she repeated, hands holding her face, covering her eyes like a child. *<I don't want to know what he was doing with you. I don't want to know what happened. Please just leave me alone; just go back to sleep, and leave me alone.>*

When there was no response, Hannah risked opening her eyes. She was sprawled awkwardly on the floor, her cheek aching where she had slapped herself, but she was alone.

For now.

IX

A week later found Hannah sitting on the stool in her forge, her spell-book laid open on the counter that ran beneath the window, pale slats of afternoon daylight spilling across the spiky handwriting. She sighed, ran a shaky hand over her forehead, and tried to steady her breathing.

This isn't happening. It can't be.

The slave's eyesight had never been spectacular, that much was clear to her, but even so, Hannah had always been able to see well enough to survive in her new world. In fact, there had been days when she thought her sight rivaled even Rory's.

Not today, though.

She sniffed, willing the heaviness in her chest to loosen, the dark dread in the bottom of her throat threatening to rise in a wave of panic. No matter how hard she squinted, the words in her spellbook would not come clear. For a time that morning, she had thought there was something wrong with the book, that somehow the magic of the pages had been tainted, causing the letters to blur and fade into one another. Klauden's gift was not so easily tainted, though, and Hannah knew that whatever problem she was having reading her spells rested in her own eyes, not the book's magic.

It's not fair, she insisted, shoving the book toward the windows in a burst of anger. Not only was she the only one who couldn't seem to remember her spells, the only one who required a damn spellbook at all, but now she couldn't read the words in order to memorize them. Her morning ritual, though often procrastinated and detested, was something that she never neglected; without the hour spent memorizing the words that allowed her to focus her magic toward specific purposes, Hannah was helpless. Yes, she could use a sword, but her true power lay in her magic, and each morning, she committed at least a dozen of the multisyllabic incantations to memory.

Except this morning. And this afternoon. And, she feared, watching the slats of light slowly fade as the sun sank lower, this evening.

No, she told herself. *It's nothing. It's the light. It's the book. It's my eyes. It's the spells. That's it,* she decided. *It's just the spells.*

Dragging the book back toward her, she flipped through until she reached the page that she knew held the words to her spell for invisibility. She recognized the page by the stylized figure at the top right-hand corner, a tall woman veiled in a shimmering outline of wavy lines. Klauden always did have a nice hand for artwork. Her eyes lingered on the picture for a time, unwilling to drift farther down the page to where the words lay, fear freezing her gaze as she anticipated what would come next. When she could delay no longer, she let her eyes slip down the page and couldn't contain a small sob from escaping her throat. The words would not come clear. The letters swirled for a moment, but after she focused, directed all of her will toward seeing what was on the page, they solidified into a definite shape.

To her dismay, the shapes of the letters were foreign to Hannah's mind. She knew that logically the shapes hadn't changed. What had changed was her mind's ability to understand what they meant.

Though it galled her to admit it, not only because of what it meant for her magic, but for what it signified about her odd relationship with the previous owner of this body, Hannah knew what was happening: she could no longer read because Solyn didn't know how to read. The slave's inability to decipher letters was somehow overwhelming Hannah's knowledge, rendering her helpless.

If she's in me enough to stop me from reading, Hannah thought, *where else is she invading? What other things that I can do or think today will I be unable to do tomorrow? How long until she takes over completely?*

And even worse, what if I don't even notice when it happens?

With a shaky breath, Hannah slammed the book closed.

X

When the first refugees came trickling into town, Hannah didn't know anything about it. She was shut up in her smithy mending pots for Annie Whithers and sharpening knives for Ivan Grawse—she had given up on the sword for the time being—but when young Scotty Pailin burst through her door, he began excitedly to tell her all about it.

Hannah didn't tell him how close he had come to getting a chest full of ice for his troubles—she was still a bit nervous when it came to people bursting through doors at her, and instinct was a hard creature to tame. Still, she would have to cast the spell at him first, and she couldn't do that anymore, not with her inability to read and memorize the spells each morning. She tried not to mourn the loss of her magic this day, as it had likely saved Scotty Pailin's scrawny hide.

"Slow down," she ordered the boy. "Who is here?"

"People!" he shouted. "Lots of people!" Hannah wondered how he defined "lots." Severin was a decent sized village of nearly six hundred people, nothing compared to the thousands of nearby Salva or even the hundreds of thousands that made up Upsen, the port city at the end of the Marin River, or Rasa, the trading city on the edge of the Rasan Mountains. This far to the south, she wondered how many more people there could be in one place. Before leaving home, the most she had ever seen at one time had been nearly one hundred, the number of occupants of her father's castle, and that included all three families, the slew of second sons and daughters that made up the Kargin, a host of fledglings, and a number of servants and slaves. Such numbers still boggled her mind.

"Where?" she asked Scotty, trying to get some sense of what was happening.

"They came from Salva," he explained, "so said the first few. They said it was attacked! Goblins and giants and lizardmen burned it down, they said!" Hannah gave him a quizzical eye.

Does this kid honestly believe that Salva, that great city, could be sacked by a few goblins? It seemed impossible to the point of ridiculousness. Now, she had seen goblins sack Talperin, the small village where she had first met Rory, where he had saved her from those creatures, in fact, but the thought of such unorganized creatures destroying a city was unfathomable.

"Who told you such stories?" she asked Scotty, a sad smile crossing her face as she wondered just how many other tall tales would fool him before he learned to discern truth from fiction.

"They're outside," he declared, sensing her disbelief. "Rory and Tarren are talking with one of them." Hannah sighed, still thinking this part of Scotty's imagination but thankful for the break it offered, and began untying her apron. She laid it across the counter, checked that the forge would stay for a time, then followed him out into the street.

There were people everywhere. Hannah had an odd moment of recollection where, instead of seeing the buildings that lined the main street and dozens of Severin's villagers milling about in nervous knots and clusters, she saw a series of burned-out buildings with smashed windows and a main street littered with bodies. It was Talperin she was remembering, the village destroyed by the goblins last year. *Is it possible that force held together, that it became an army?*

Hannah didn't want to think about that. Such things seemed so far away from this place at the edge of the world.

She spotted Rory through the crowd and made her way through the people toward him. He was deep in conversation with Tarren, the portly mayor who had hired Rory as a trainer for what he called his city guard, and another figure. As she approached, Hannah could see the tattered state of the stranger's clothing, the dried blood on his face that matched the black singes that scored the bottom of his cloak. He had no traveling bag, and his eyes were bleary with exhaustion.

"We had some warning," he was explaining in a strained voice. "The guard got the call out before the gates were overrun, but still, there were so many of them, and we only barely escaped."

Rory gave Hannah a concerned glance over the man's shoulder. No doubt he was recalling what Hannah had just thought of—the strange series of attacks that had caused their first meeting. Goblins sacking a village was out of the ordinary, but not unheard of, and once they had realized that other villages had been attacked as well, there seemed a pattern, but then, everything had gone crazy with Jamison and Malbrek, and she and Rory had had other things to worry about. She hadn't even thought about that raid for months.

But what if it wasn't a raid at all? What if it was the start of something much more complex?

From what this man claimed, there was now an army of goblins, among other creatures, to the north, and they would eventually head this way.

"But why?" Tarren was asking the stranger. "What did they want? Plunder? There has to be a motive." The mayor looked at Rory. "Maybe we could pay them off."

The refugee was shaking his head. "That wasn't the worst of it," he said. "I only heard tell of it, mind, but even so..." He trailed off, eyes closing as exhaustion bore down on him. He swayed a bit, and Hannah caught his arm.

"Easy," she told him. "You need rest." She looked over at the other refugees. It seemed like a large group was heading over to the inn, but even that building could only hold so many people. She looked at Rory. "Where can he sleep?" The elf shrugged, glancing around at the mass of people and seeing what she had just seen. Hannah could see the question on his face, and she sighed, then nodded.

It was the right thing to do, taking the man into their house, but she didn't have to like it. The thought of the stranger sleeping in the bed she shared with Rory made her uneasy. "I'll take him," she said, trying to keep her face from revealing her true feelings.

"I'll be there soon." She watched him move away with Tarren, the two heads close together in consultation.

As soon as Hannah assured the man, who introduced himself as Martin, that he was perfectly welcome to lie down in the room's only bed, the refugee had fallen fast asleep. After she determined that he was not feigning exhaustion, Hannah tried to calm herself.

It's too much, she thought again, too much and all at once. Strangers in her body, strangers in her bed, strange armies marching nearby. *What happened to my quiet life with Rory?* Even as she pictured the lazy mornings they shared at the spring, the afternoons spent training in the back yard, the images seemed distant, less real than the last three months.

It was Solyn. She had been slowly creeping into Hannah's life since then.

If it wasn't so cold outside, Hannah would have gone into the woods to sit and think. As it was, she had only the sleeping man for company, and he made her a bit uncomfortable. She told herself it was nothing, that she was doing the right thing in allowing him to rest and recover, but even so, his presence unnerved her, another item on a long list of problems.

Finally, she settled for sitting in front of the fireplace, quickly replacing her sweaty dress with a thinner housedress and wrapping herself in Rory's old cloak. She laid her swords on the floor by her knees—the scabbard bearing Klauden's family crest glimmered in the firelight while the magical sword seemed to absorb the light. She knew it was the magic, but she couldn't see such things with any reliability anymore. Staring at the subtle planes and valleys in the metal, she saw that the sword needed a scabbard, and soon, or the runes she was working so hard on would just get rubbed away again.

She ran a finger along the blade, feeling the thrum of unspent and stirring magic in her arm. It was comforting to know that she could still feel it, the memory of magic reminding her of what she had once been capable of. That was one thing she couldn't blame on the body; Solyn too had been a spellcaster, at least with Hannah inside her. Hannah didn't know if the slave had been able to cast on her own before that; probably not though, since she would not have been trained for it as a slave and the villages around the castle were not known for their tolerance of magic among their own.

She sighed, wrapping her arm back inside the cloak, pushing her hair out of the way as she readjusted. Her hair hung in disarray past her shoulder, the braid of this morning coming unraveled in the day's work. Her mind lost in thought, Hannah's fingers began untangling the braid slowly, carefully spreading the long tresses until her hair hung free on both sides of her neck to puddle in her lap. Her hair was so long now. She stood up, awkwardly using the cloak blanket as a makeshift toga and carefully holding one sword at her waist—one could never be too cautious, especially with strangers about—and walked to the table beside the bed to retrieve her hairbrush.

The silver brush was part of a set that included a matching mirror, the only things Hannah had that had belonged to her mother. She had managed to keep hold of them through many miles and even more mishaps, and they were always a comfort to her. She shuffled back over to the fire, settling the brush by her side next to the two swords as she rewrapped the cloak to cover her exposed shoulders.

The necklace hung heavy around her neck, Klauden's ring resting between her breasts, and Hannah pulled it off, staring at the arcane markings that circled the band as they reflected the firelight. She knew that if she still had her old eyes, she would have been able to see the tinge of magic that surrounded the band of metal, the careful spell woven by Klauden before she had left home the first time. *If he knew what was happening, could he help me?*

Would he?

Solyn's memory of Klauden had been more disturbing than Hannah wanted to admit. She told herself that she had been gone for a long time, that she was no longer promised to Klauden, that what he did wasn't any of her concern, but nothing helped. She kept returning to the hungry look on his face when he watched her on his bed, a look that Hannah had never seen directed at her, not even when he had confessed his love to her inside the Star of Elgiva, not even when he had sent her away with Rory. It was just so unlike the Klauden she knew and remembered.

And loved.

There was that, of course. Sure, she loved Klauden. She had been raised for more than seventy years to believe she would one day become his mate. He had been her best friend, her confidante, her teacher and companion. She couldn't just forget all of that.

But didn't I? Didn't I forget all about that when I chose to be with Rory, when I chose my elf over any chance of returning home to my old life? She was being ridiculous, of course. She couldn't possibly be jealous of a memory that wasn't even hers.

Still, the feeling wouldn't go away. She heard a low snicker in her mind, Solyn enjoying her frustration.

Hannah picked up the brush and began pulling it through her hair. She had an impulse to slow down and do it right, to take care of her gorgeous hair as it ought to be done, and in response, she brushed more furiously, tearing at the few tangles and quickly rebraiding it when she was finished.

It's just hair, she told Solyn. *It's nothing.*

XI

Hannah woke to someone's hand on her shoulder. She opened her eyes, a bit disoriented. She was lying in bed, her bed, and Rory was looking down at her.

"Where did Martin go?" she asked blearily, rubbing her sleep-filled eyes. "When did I fall asleep?"

"He went to the inn to help with the others," Rory said. "He just needed some rest." He smiled at her. "So did you, apparently."

"I didn't mean to fall asleep," she said, rolling onto her side and readjusting the cloak she still had wrapped around her. "Is it night already?"

He nodded. "You were on the floor in front of the fire. Martin came to get me. He didn't want to disturb you. I put you in the bed. You were very out of it."

"Oh," she yawned, then stretched, feeling life steal back into her limbs. Her stomach growled. "Have you eaten?"

"No," he said. "I'll make us something."

As he busied himself with the cabinets beneath the counter that ran the length of the opposite wall, Hannah sat up, shivering a bit when the cloak slipped off her shoulder.

"What do we have?" she asked, drowsily pleasant as she watched Rory bend down to take something out of a cubby, then pop to his feet as he placed it on the counter. He moved so quickly, so easily, so confident in their house. She sighed, the sight familiar and warming. Yes, this was how things had been between them.

Cozy. Safe.

"Just some vegetables," he answered, dagger flashing in the firelight as he diced and sliced the few stalks before using the blade to push them into the cook pot. "Stew alright?"

"Sure," she said, scooting to the edge of the bed. "I'll get the water."

"No need," he told her. "Stay there. I got it before I came home."

"Thanks," she laughed a bit. "You're always so prepared."

Rory walked the pot over to the fireplace, then used the poker to draw the metal arm toward him. He hung the pot on the arm, then kicked it lazily back over the flames with a booted foot. Hannah loved to watch Rory cook. He was so skilled at it. Her own attempts to make anything edible had always been accompanied by frantic shuffling and spilled pots as she tried not to burn everything. Rory made it look so damn easy.

Then again, even when they had been on the road, he had been competent, often hunting for their meal if they wanted meat, pointing out edible herbs and vegetables for Hannah to collect along the way. He could make a fire in the pouring rain and make a stringy rabbit taste like heaven. She was so glad he was capable. Hannah had never been one for survival skills; it hadn't much mattered before.

"So what's going to happen now?" she asked when he walked back to the bed and sat beside her. "Will there be a war?"

He shrugged, tugging off his boots and then his shirt. "I don't know. Could be. From what they told us, they were at least five thousand strong when Salva fell. An army that size will take its time with the city—plunder, food, and such."

"Then they will come here?"

He nodded. "Maybe. No one seems to know if they have a higher purpose beyond slaughter. We did learn that they are led by a red demon and an Elven warrior, though."

Hannah smirked. "Red demon, huh? That sounds like fun. Right in your line of work."

He shrugged, smirking a bit at her reference to his occupation when they had met. "Who knows what to believe? Some of the people claimed they heard the story from someone else about the demon, but at least the elf is a certainty. Several saw him ordering the goblins about."

"Why would an elf lead an army of goblins?" she wondered, shaking her head.

"Who would want an army of goblins?" Rory retorted. "Useless creatures, really, unless you've got them in great numbers, that is. Still, they never work well together. Might as well organize a group of snakes."

Hannah nodded, trying to decide between the growing anticipation in her chest—*a battle, a real battle again!*—and the fear that followed. Fear for him, that he might get hurt in a fight with so many, and fear for herself, that she might get this frail mortal body killed.

"What will we do here?" she whispered. "What are the people going to do?"

Rory shook his head. "Tarren wanted to pay them off, but I doubt that will work. Why take some payment when they could have the whole village? The others though..." He trailed off, then gave Hannah a direct look. "They're fairly keen on fighting."

"Your men, you mean," she said.

"The city guard," he corrected, but Hannah knew better. Rory had been training the men in small groups for half a year now. They were decent enough, but still farmers, deep down.

"They want to stand and fight," she said, making sure she was hearing him correctly, "against five thousand goblins."

He nodded. "They said it was their town, they had carved it out of the wilderness, and damned if some foul creatures were going to take it from them."

"Rory," she began, scorn creeping into her voice, "it took barely three hundred goblins to sack Talperin. They will not survive."

"Perhaps not." He paused, then added, "They have the tunnels."

Hannah considered the system of tunnels that ran beneath Severin, the old mine shafts abandoned now; they could be useful for the fighting, and there was the cave to make a stand in, but still, it was hardly the ideal place to defend against such numbers. "What's 'perhaps' about it? Even with the tunnels, it's impossible. That's what it is." She stared at him, a growing fear doubling with a queer excitement in her stomach. "You're not planning on staying with them, are you?"

"As you said, they are my men."

She grabbed his shoulders, letting the cloak fall in a puddle around her waist. "Rory," she began again in a softer voice, but then paused. *Of course, he will stay. Why did I ever think he would run? This was what I admire in him, this damn honor, this unyielding need to defend those who need his help. Didn't he help me in Talperin out of that same need?*

Even so, she knew when to toss honor aside and save her own neck. She had learned that lesson on her first few nights away from home so long ago. Sometimes, survival was more important. Looking at him, though, the set of his shoulder, the grim look in his eyes, she wondered about the cost.

What would it do to him if we left, knowing that we abandoned these people? They were nothing to her; no matter how much she tried to fit in, she couldn't lie about that. She would kill them all if it meant her and Rory's survival.

But he would not. Could not.

She thought of what she had cost Klauden, of what her happiness had meant to so many others, and couldn't let that happen all over again. Rory would have to stay; she couldn't spoil him by making him leave. It was an intrinsic part of who he was. A hero. *My foolhardy, impossible, insane hero,* she thought.

And she, stupid idiot that she was, loved him even more for that. Klauden would never stand up to such odds. He was utterly practical, like she was. But still, there was something amazing about the idea, the very thought of staging a defense here, in this tiny village at the end of the world. She felt that strange excitement run through her at the thought, at the hope of such a fight, extinguishing the fear she had felt moments before.

I may not be as strong as I was, but damn, I can still be useful in a fight. And they do need us.

Hannah had decided, but still, she had to try, to be certain she hadn't thrown her hard-won life away on a suicidal stand without at least examining every option.

"They are just mortals," she whispered. "They will die anyway."

He gave her a hard look, and she was sorry that she had said it, but the feeling passed, and she returned his gaze, every inch the vampire she had been when they first met. She knew something about her coldness appealed to him. He liked her ability to get right to the bottom of the situation.

"But they shouldn't die. Not yet."

"It's true, though. They'll all die with or without you."

"I know it's true. Believe me," he said, staring at her intently, "I know that humans die very quickly." Hannah wondered what else he was saying to her with that comment. *Has he thought of my death, then?* "We could help them, though," he said, changing the subject. "We should help them."

She sighed, then smiled at him. "And so we will."

Now it was his turn to grab her shoulders. "You're sure?"

She shrugged, nodding. "Why not? Things haven't been exciting enough around here lately anyway."

"I knew there was a reason I married you." Rory laughed, then kissed her. "You'll need to finish that sword," he said, mouth close to hers, excitement making him talk faster. "And you've got to work on your balance. We'll start again tomorrow."

She nodded, lips against his again. "Definitely," she agreed. "There's lots to be done."

"I know," he answered, hands tightening behind her back, slipping the straps of her dress off her shoulders.

"In fact," she breathed, smiling at him, hands lingering on the waistband of his pants, "we should get started right away."

He grinned back at her, hands wandering lower amidst the cloak and blankets on the bed. "I thought we were."

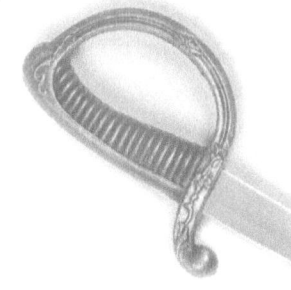

XII

"There's the next three," Hannah said, handing the blades over to Scotty, who promptly dashed out the door with them held against his chest, the straps meant to attach them to belts flapping over his shoulders. The boy had become quite the little assistant over the past few days, running here or there with her weapons as she directed. It made him feel useful, something everyone was trying to be now. It helped to avoid thinking about what was to come. She sighed, wiping her sweaty brow with the back of a filthy hand.

It had been a long week, making enough swords and axes for the townspeople and newly arrived refugees of Salva. She glanced at her ever-dwindling stock of hilts and leather grips, then at the last bit of ore the mines had brought in last week. There should be enough left to arm most of them, and those who lacked skill with blades could make do with the bows and arrows that Morris Cameron and his lot were frantically crafting. Hannah thought of the feather-coated Mrs. Cameron, the way her red-rimmed eyes squinted each time the woman sneezed, and was thankful that she dealt in cold steel instead. *If feathers gave the woman so much trouble,* Hannah wondered, *why then had she married a bowyer and fletcher?* She pictured Rory then, and their problems, and thought she could understand Mrs. Cameron's decision.

Will things ever be the same between us again? Despite their closeness of a few days ago, she could still sense the distance in him, the careful way he looked at her, the thoughtful glances her way, and the nervous tension he worked through each morning when he practiced behind their house.

She knew he was thinking about training the men, but he still worked with her in the mornings too, offering tips and criticism as she went through the motions, but by the time she rose and went outside, she could see he had been at it for some time already. He was practicing more seriously than she had ever seen before, and she could see the mastery in his movement. Even as she watched him, though, she kept reminding herself that he was just one man, and one man alone, even one like Rory, could not defeat an entire army.

Something else had to happen if they were going to live, but Hannah couldn't think of what. Besides, she was focusing enough energy on her own training.

Solyn could wield a sword, could hold her own fairly well with two blades, in fact, but Hannah's true specialty had always been in throwing daggers. She had been a magic user, and distance had been her ally. Now, she had to get used to fighting in close quarters, and though she had some skill, it was still something she needed to work on.

She thought of her spellbook, abandoned in her old traveling pack at the house. She couldn't read it anymore now, and as a result, she had no spells at all at her disposal. If it came to close fighting, she would have to stick close to Rory. The thought galled her, to think how dependent she was on him, and yet, part of her was comforted by the knowledge that he would protect her, would keep her safe.

Hannah wondered if the thought was her own or something echoing from Solyn. She hadn't spoken directly to the girl since that day in her forge, but she could feel the slave's presence all the time now, a creeping sensation under her skin that Hannah feared more than she could admit.

Do not make this more than it is, she reminded herself. She didn't advise herself in Klauden's voice this time, though it was something he would have said. Since the disturbing memory Solyn had shared, Hannah had tried not to think of her old friend, tried not to wonder what other secrets he was hiding beneath that inscrutable face. It didn't matter now anyway.

She stretched, feeling the muscles in her back pop and crackle, then reached out for another unfinished blade. She could pound out at least two more swords today before her arms gave in to the strain of the work. She pulled another blade from the forge, careful with the white-hot metal as she went back to work.

Hannah was settling the blade on the anvil, drawing back the hammer and placing her hand over the thick cloth that braced the other end of the blade, when the door opened again.

"Scotty," she said irritably, without turning around, "I know you didn't bring those all the way down to Rory already. I don't care how far they've gotten with the fence already, or what Harry Squinton told you about red demons. Quit your lollygagging." She swung the hammer down, pinging the first dents into the blade that would eventually smooth the metal into a serviceable weapon.

"Lollygagging?" asked a familiar, accented voice she had not expected to hear again outside of her own mind. "I had never thought to hear you utter such a word, Hannah."

She let the hammer fall, shock paralyzing her limbs for an instant, but when the ball smashed into her other hand, the same error in judgment she had always made, the pain jerked her into motion. She whirled, facing the man standing just inside her forge.

He was still tall, but not as much as he used to be. She knew it was because her new body was taller than she had been, but it was still odd to think of him shrinking as she grew up to meet him. His blonde hair was down to his shoulders now, some of the wisps working their way free from the tie at his neck to frame his face. He was flushed, as if he had been running in the cold weather, but Hannah recognized that rosy glow of health in his cheeks—Klauden had been feeding quite well on his journey south of the mountains. She couldn't deny how strangely beautiful he was to her, how he seemed to sparkle with some unearthly glow; it was how all mortals saw her kind—well, the kind she had been. No wonder Rory had found her irresistible.

She drew her wounded finger to her mouth by reflex, sucking the blood that welled from beneath the mashed nail, and when she spoke, the words were muffled around it. "Klauden," she breathed. "How did you find me?"

Hannah sensed that the question was not entirely her own. She felt Solyn surging in her, something in the slave beating savagely against her insides, and suddenly Hannah was seeing another new memory. This time Klauden was speaking to her, offering small soothing words against her pain, smoothing away her aches with his long thin hands. She wanted those hands to do more than just touch her shoulders, to feel more than just the sense of magic rushing into her, the healing power of Klauden's spell a welcome thrill, but not the only one she wanted.

If only he would...

Hannah dragged herself back to the present. Klauden was watching her curiously. He nodded, as if to confirm something, then took the few steps toward her. Hannah stood frozen behind the counter, staring at him with wide eyes. He reached out slowly, taking first her arm, then with a gentle tug, her hand. He murmured a few words, and Hannah felt the healing power go through her with a jolt. Her finger was no longer bleeding. In fact, the nail wasn't even broken anymore. She knew Klauden practiced the art of healing humans—one of the only ones at her father's castle to bother with such a hobby—but she had never been on the receiving end of that kind of magic.

Solyn was whispering something that disagreed with her, but Hannah ignored it.

"It's almost like getting blood," she whispered, unaware at first that she was speaking out loud, "healing like that." She wiped the remaining blood across her apron, wondering at the power of such magic.

Klauden nodded, then looked her over with a critical eye. "You are not well, chaivin," he declared. Hannah tried to ignore the shiver that went through her when he called her that, his old pet name, "Fire soul"; a reference to her red hair or her temperament, she had never been sure. "I had thought your elf could do better for you."

His mention of Rory brought her back to herself, all speculation and Solyn forgotten for the moment. "Why are you here?" she asked, arms crossing over her chest defensively.

"I thought you might need some assistance," he responded, taking in the rest of the smithy—the worn forge, the scarred counter—and then Hannah again—her old dress, her slumped shoulders, her sweaty brow and thinning cheeks. The stress of the last few months was beginning to show around her eyes.

"How did you even find me?" she snapped. "This is practically the other end of the world."

He reached out again, and Hannah caught herself before she flinched away. His fingers closed around the chain on her neck, tugging it up and out of her dress until the silver ring spun at the end. "You're still wearing my ring."

Her first impulse was to tear the ring off and throw it at him, to toss the magical item at his feet, and damn him for always watching her. But then the impulse passed. She was the one who had chosen to wear the stupid thing, even after she knew what it could do. "So, it still works, then," she said when nothing else came to mind.

"I enchanted it myself," he snapped. "Of course, it still works."

"But Klauden," she began, struggling for the right words, "what are you doing here? Why did you leave home in the first place?"

The door to the forge swung open again, and another voice spoke. "Because I asked him to."

Hannah stared at Rory, noting the heavy rhythm of his chest, as if he had run there. The elf stood perfectly still for a moment, taking in the scene, Klauden standing across the counter from Hannah, the necklace in his hand, her body leaning toward him. She took the necklace and the ring back from Klauden and stepped away from him.

"Rory, why—" Hannah started, but the elf cut her off.

"Later," he growled, and Hannah quieted, the harsh tone of his voice allowing for no opposition. He had never spoken to her like that, not in the year she had known him.

What is going on?

Before her human eyes could catch that he had started to move, the elf flung himself at Klauden, shoving the vampire against the wall, a drawn sword to Klauden's neck. "Start talking," the elf growled at Klauden. "Now."

"Rory..." Hannah began but could think of nothing to add. This was a side of Rory she had seen before in bits and pieces but never quite so ferocious and up close. Staring at him now, she could understand the rage that had caused him to kill his cousin and earn a banishment from his home city of Firene. Oddly enough, this side of him didn't repel her; in fact, she felt more drawn to him than she had in weeks.

Klauden hadn't made any move to extricate himself from beneath Rory's blade. He scoffed instead. "You cannot kill me with that, elf."

Rory pushed the blade closer. "It worked well enough on Matthew Hunter," he snarled, and Hannah had a sudden vision of the fledgling's last moments in the tournament, when Rory had spun about and cut off his opponent's head with one swift strike. Something inside her rejoiced at the sight, and Hannah knew it wasn't entirely her thought, though why Solyn would be glad at a death in the tournament, she didn't know.

The vampire smiled, still unmoving. "I cannot be killed as easily as a fledgling like that," he commented. "Besides," he added with a glance in Hannah's direction, "you asked me to come here in the first place."

Rory sighed, withdrawing his blade and sheathing it in one smooth move. "So I did." He glanced at Hannah, and she could feel a slow burn working its way up her neck.

What exactly has my husband been doing behind my back?

He looked guiltily away from her, back to the vampire. "So speak."

Klauden stepped away from the wall, fastidiously wiping his hands against his robes as if Rory had somehow disheveled him. "What do you want to hear, elf?" he asked. "Solyn is back—that's plain to see. What more do you need?"

There was a new look on Rory's face now, and it took Hannah a moment to recognize it. She had last seen it when he sat with her in Kalford, when she had been burning with bloodfever and he couldn't help her.

It was desperation.

"Help her," he said simply. "Get Solyn out of there. Do whatever you have to do to keep Hannah safe."

"It's not that simple," Klauden answered.

"I know that," Rory snapped, "but you're the one who put her in that body in the first place. You must be able to do something."

Klauden nodded. "I did do something. When I first directed Hannah into the body, I put Solyn into a deep sleep. She wasn't supposed to ever wake up. Something must have gone wrong."

"Well, make it right," Rory said.

"That is hard to do when I don't know what exactly went wrong. I need some time to study the situation."

"You don't have time," Rory said. "Goblins are coming. Hannah is losing herself. You have to act now."

"I can't."

"Can't or won't?"

Klauden rolled his eyes, voice still calm. "If I act now, as you so boldly put it, I may cause more harm than good. Patience, my dear elf, patience."

Hannah could see Rory restraining himself, could see how desperately he wanted to strike Klauden, and she spoke to break the tension.

"I know why she woke up," she blurted.

"You do?" Rory asked. "Why?"

"The old man. He cast a spell on me. He did it."

Klauden stared at her. "What old man?" he asked.

Hannah shrugged. "I don't know. He came in a few months ago, asked what had happened to me, then cast some magic at me. When nothing happened, he vanished."

Klauden's eyes widened. "Vanished?"

Rory nodded. "I searched for him afterward but found nothing. It was like he was never here at all. Hannah was the only one who saw him."

Now it was her turn to stare. "I was?" Then she rallied, focusing on the real point. "You checked up on it?"

Rory didn't even look at her. "Of course, I did. I scoured this place from one end to the other to find him." He glanced at her meaningfully. "No one admitted to telling him your name."

"But he called me Hannah," she insisted, then her memory clicked into place and she remembered more of it. "Hannah Hunter," she said. The name registered something further back in her memory, and she tried to cling to the thread. It wasn't Solyn that was blocking her; in fact, Solyn seemed to have stepped aside to let Hannah think about it.

"Wait a minute," Rory said. "You didn't tell me that before. He called you Hannah Hunter?"

"I didn't?" she asked, not really paying attention to him. *Why is that name so damned familiar?*

<*Honestly, you are ridiculous,*> Solyn snapped. Suddenly Hannah was seeing another memory, but one she had witnessed before. She was weaving the tapestry in the house in the mountains, Matthew standing behind her—*wait, Matthew?* But the memory flooded past her questions—and the door was opening to reveal another face, a familiar face, once she saw past the beard.

Jamison Hunter, Solyn's husband. The man who had betrayed her to Malbrek and gotten her killed in the first place. The man whose brother Rory had killed in the tournament for her soul.

"How could I not have realized?" Hannah asked.

<Because you are terribly stupid,> Solyn replied.

"Oh, shut up," Hannah said, then realized both men were staring openly at her. Rory with that damning concern that had grown so familiar and Klauden with something between academic curiosity and dawning hope. As she watched, the vampire's face rearranged itself, and he was closed to her again. "Solyn was married to Jamison Hunter," she announced.

Rory flung Klauden against the wall again. "Why? Why of all people would you pick this body for Hannah? The wife of the man who betrayed her? The brother of the fledgling I killed? What sick game is this?"

Klauden frowned at this newest assault. It seemed like Rory's blunt force was distasteful to him, a show of emotion that revealed the elf's lack of breeding. Hannah knew that thought wasn't hers. She wondered how long she would be able to tell the difference.

"Stop it. Both of you," she said, taking a deep breath to calm herself. She looked at Klauden. "Did you know who she was?"

"I did." He nodded. *I bet you did,* she thought but refused to allow the anger to grow. *Not yet.*

Rory started to object, to speak again, but Hannah cut him off. "You put me into the body of the woman whose husband turned me over to Malbrek."

Klauden shrugged. "I did not know that he had turned you in." His face was clear, hiding nothing. "If you recall, I never asked how Malbrek managed to capture you."

"Fine," Rory snapped, "but you knew she was sleeping with Matthew Hunter, right?"

Klauden's face clouded over for a moment, then cleared. Hannah felt Solyn bursting forth, charging forward, then she was speaking in Hannah's new voice. "I wouldn't have had that man in my bed for anything. You know that, Klauden."

Rory stared, then scoffed. He cleared his throat, then said, "But you were having an affair. I saw it."

Hannah had been paralyzed by the speaking demon in her throat. Now she was paralyzed by Rory's words. She pushed her way forward, shoving Solyn out of the way. "What do you mean you saw it? When did you see it? How did you know?"

There was that guilt again, overshadowing his face, but he faced her this time, unwilling to flinch away. "I can dreamwalk, Hannah. You knew that."

She took a few deep breaths through her nose. *Is he saying what I think he is saying?* "You... you've been spying on me?"

"Not spying," he said quickly. "I was worried about you." He looked to Klauden, then back at her. "That's how I knew to contact Klauden, to ask him to come help you."

"You asked him to come? How long ago? How long have you been watching my dreams?"

"They're not your dreams, Hannah. They're her memories."

"I know! How long?"

The elf shrugged, his face worn and tired. "Since the start," he admitted in a low voice, "since she woke."

Hannah knew that he had been trying to help, to save her in his own way, but the idea was still too upsetting. It was too close to the betrayal she had felt when Klauden told her that he had been watching her.

Everyone is always watching me! Worrying about me, telling me what to do!

"I see," she said, looking each of them over. "I see. Some saviors I have. One of them spies on my dreams and the other puts me in the body of a... of a..." She trailed off, unable to continue. "The hell with both of you!" she shouted, then stalked out the back door. She heard Rory call after her, but she ignored him, slamming the back door behind her, walking briskly through the layer of snow that coated the small yard behind the forge.

She didn't know where she was going, but she just had to get away, to be alone for once. She dared Solyn to show herself, but the slave remained silent, and Hannah gave her a silent, unwilling thanks.

XIII

The next time Hannah looked around, she saw that her angry stalking had taken her to the spring in the woods behind their house. She found a space that was mostly dry and plopped down, shivering a bit as the cold seeped through her dress.

I should have grabbed my cloak. I should have taken my sword.
I should have killed both of them.

She scowled, wishing that she had someone she could confide in, someone more experienced with men who could advise her. At least then she would know if she was the only woman who had to deal with such foolishness. She took a deep breath, loving that in this body, such a small movement really did offer some comfort, and tried to work everything out.

So, this girl had been something to Klauden; that was why he had chosen her. She couldn't have meant so much, though, since he effectively killed her when he took her body for Hannah's use. That didn't necessarily mean anything, though. The important thing was that this girl was human, and Klauden was a vampire. He wouldn't hesitate to do what had to be done. He might feel some guilt later on, but even so, she was only a slave— one of hundreds he had seen and known and fed from over the years. If the girl had meant something to him, no doubt he would have turned her.

No. Maybe he took her blood in other ways, shared something with her, but he never bit her, never crossed that crucial line that converts a meal into a fledgling. Maybe he remembered the vow we made as children not to make another. Maybe he just didn't think her worthy.

<*Maybe it's none of your business,*> Solyn quipped.

Hannah couldn't hide a smile. She had wanted someone's advice, right? Maybe this duality wasn't all bad. *<Hey,>* she thought at Solyn. *<What brings you to the surface?>*

<Where else would I go?>

Hannah recoiled. *<I was trying to be nice,>* she thought sharply. *<This doesn't have to be a battle.>*

<It doesn't?>

She closed her eyes, shaking her head in disgust. *<Fine, then.>*

She went back to her thoughts. Matthew Hunter had become a fledgling, either before or after leaving Valrane, and Solyn had followed him. Wasn't that the story Jamison had told about his wife?

Wait. He said his wife was called Hannah, named for the princess in the castle. Named after me.

A soft step in the snow caught her attention, and she jerked up, hand reaching for the empty space on her hip where her sword should be. Rory was standing across the clearing, near the ice that rimmed the spring. The elf held an extra cloak, and when she looked at him, he walked slowly over to where she sat. When she didn't make any inviting gestures for him to sit down, he held the cloak out to her.

"I thought you might be cold."

She took the material without a word, wrapping it around her shoulders and enjoying the warmth it offered. After an awkward moment of silence, Rory sank to his knees in the snow before her.

"I am sorry," he whispered. "I should have told you."

Hannah sniffed. She knew she should be apologizing to him. It was what she should do when her inability to communicate caused trouble between them. *Why can I never just come out with everything? Why do I always choose what information to share? Don't I trust him?*

She didn't realize she was crying until he wiped a tear from her cheek. *What a sobbing fool I've become lately,* she thought. *Klauden would never approve.* Thoughts of the vampire passed, and she was alone with Rory again. She pushed his hand away, wiping at her cheeks.

"Don't cry, Hannah. You'll freeze your cheeks solid," he commented.

"I'm fine," she said, using the cloak to mop up the rest of the mess. "I just..." She paused, trailed off into silence. *I just what?* She didn't know. She was still angry with him, so angry, but then, she knew it was right.

What he had done was right. What other choice had she left him but to dreamwalk her? She hadn't said anything at all about Solyn, nothing beyond a general hint of what was happening. She looked at him, head cocking. "So what else do you know?"

He rearranged his legs so that he sat instead of knelt in the snow. "Well, I know that she uses your mouth to speak now. How long has that been happening?"

Hannah shrugged. "Today was the first time, but I've able to speak to her for a while now."

He nodded. "I thought so."

"How did you know?"

"I know you. I know when she's very close."

Shaking her head, she asked, "How often does it happen?"

"More often than you realize, I think." He shook his head, scraping some snow off the edge of his boot. "I'm glad that he's here, you know. He can help."

"But will he?" When Rory looked sharply at her, she added, "He knew her, this girl, this body. I mean, I think he really knew her." When his eyes widened in understanding, she continued, raising her hands in exasperation, "Or maybe he just healed her. I don't know. I don't want to know."

She didn't say her deepest fear—that Klauden had chosen this girl so that he could have the body he wanted with the mind he knew and respected, that perhaps his months of journeying to this remote place had been motivated by more than pure altruism, that maybe, just maybe, her old friend had come to collect at last on the debt she owed him.

"What are you thinking, Hannah?" Rory asked, eyes narrowing. "What do you think it means?"

Before she could answer, another voice spoke from the trees behind them. Rory jumped to his feet, sword in hand, then re-sheathed the weapon as Klauden appeared. Soft flakes of ice were caught in his hair, and Hannah realized that it had started snowing.

"There is something you should know before you condemn me."

She rolled her eyes, waiting for him to speak. When the vampire said nothing else, she snapped, "Have you ever heard of privacy?" She glanced at Rory. "We were having a private conversation between husband and wife," she added, watching the words sting Klauden's face. He deserved it.

Instead of the reaction she expected, for him to seize up and walk away, Klauden gave her an incredulous look.

"Oh, and what ceremony was it that bound you together? I fear I never received an invitation."

She stared at him, at words she had never thought to hear from his refined mouth. *What is he suggesting? That we aren't married, that Rory and I are lying?* Instead of responding with what she wanted to say, that humans didn't always have big ceremonies, that an agreement between partners was enough, that no one need hear the vows exchanged, she snapped, "I wouldn't have thought you would come anyway, Master van Sherinak, the situation being what it was." *Ah, there's the look I wanted.* He had enough sense to look ashamed at least. She hadn't addressed him by his formal name since they were children, and he was being a bastard.

He shook his head, exasperated as always with her. Hannah had the brief thought that it was probably best that they hadn't become mates; she would have made him crazy.

What am I thinking? I already make him crazy, always have.

That was Solyn again, though why she should have insight into Hannah's relationship with Klauden raised even more questions about the girl's relationship with the vampire.

"Well, you are here now. What have you to say?" Hannah asked, unconsciously reverting to the formality of her childhood.

Klauden glanced around at the clearing, the snow, and then her cheeks, which must be pale with cold. "Is there no better place for such discussion?" He didn't say it, but Hannah knew what he was implying—yet another jab at Rory's ability to care for her.

"You came out here; you interrupted us. Obviously, you've got something to share. Spill it," she ordered. "Or leave," she added when he didn't speak.

Inside, something in Hannah wept at the thought of these words between them; they had been such friends once, so close, and here they were, bickering like enemies.

What has happened to me? To him?

"Please," she added as an afterthought, softening her voice. Rory gave her a sharp glance, scowled, and looked expectantly to Klauden. Hannah saw that the elf had not taken his hand from his sword hilt.

"As you will," Klauden said. "I thought you should know that when I gave her body to you, Solyn was ready to step off the closest cliff into the nearest gorge. She had no will to live."

Something tried to force its way into Hannah's mind as he spoke, something that Solyn wanted her to know, something important that would justify her despair. "No," Hannah told her, closing her eyes. "No." She looked at Klauden, adding, "Let him tell me, then."

Klauden swallowed, clearly trying to find the right words. "Solyn had some difficulties with some of the men in the castle."

"Matthew? He didn't want her?" she asked.

Klauden shook his head. "Matthew did not want to turn her, but he was not averse to other pastimes. He had some influence among the Kargin. He was a close friend to Vailen van Joosen."

At the mention of the name, Hannah's mind pictured the first son of the lowest ranking family in the House; Vailen had never meant much to her. He'd been salvageable with a weapon, nothing with magic, and beyond negligent at anything requiring serious thought. Hannah hadn't thought of him since she saw how Livenna, her father's other daughter—a member of the Kargin as a result of her birth order—had flirted with him, trying to improve her status by mating high.

As she remembered the idiot boy she had quickly bested in both steel and spells, the image faded, twisted, and she had a different view of that same face, except now it was smeared with blood, as if he had just fed. Hannah was vaguely embarrassed, as if she had wandered in on an acquaintance in the midst of a personal act, but then she took in other details of the scene—the way he was looking right at her with a satisfied smirk on his face, the dagger in his hand dripping with fresh blood, and Hannah felt the shriek of her body, the ache of her limbs, and the fear tighten her chest as he brought the blade close again, this time running the tip across the sensitive ridge of her collarbone, and she felt the wet ripple of more blood. She realized that she was naked from the waist up, her dress a tangled mess around her hips; she felt the restraining hands of the male Kargin holding her down, knew that this was only the start, that there would be more pain, more blood, and then even worse invasions, and she remembered wishing they would hurry up and get it over with so that she could be with the kind one again, the one whose touch did not involve pain, whose quiet need didn't require more blood...

Hannah was lying on the ground when she opened her eyes, her head cushioned in someone's lap, and she vaguely recalled slumping over with the force of the memory. Still overwhelmed by the pain, the swirling emotions, the hatred and fear intolerable in her head, Hannah rolled onto all fours, then vomited into the snow with the force of her revulsion.

<*I didn't know,*> she told the silent Solyn. <*I didn't.*>

<*Please,*> the slave replied sarcastically. <*Don't lie. You knew. You didn't care.*>

Hannah couldn't reply. The girl was right. Maybe she had always known about the perversions enacted on the slaves by some of the Kargin. It hadn't been her concern. Nothing that involved the slaves had been her concern.

<*I...*> she tried, then tried again. <*I am sorry?*> It ended up sounding more like a question, like she was asking herself if it was true more so than commiserating with the slave who had every right to wish for death.

<*I don't need your pity,*> Solyn stated, and Hannah could feel the emptiness of Solyn's pain, the blankness that only recently had begun to fill again with desire, with longing and wishing for small things again—the first of which was the wish for her own skin again, for control of her body and her future. Hannah felt the slave's anger flare up again, not only for what she had endured time and again, but for Hannah's attitude. <*Stop trying to care,*> she snapped. <*You didn't even know my name, though I laid out enough of your dresses to know much more about you.*>

Her name.

Hannah sat up, ignoring the rest of the thought, pushing Solyn and her terrible memories away for a moment. The puddle of vomit was steaming in the snow. Someone was rubbing her back, someone else was holding her braid out of the way. She put out a hand for support, grateful for the warm hand that held her steady—Rory's, then. Klauden's skin would be cool to the touch by now, so long after he had fed, and standing in the cold wouldn't help.

"My name," she whispered, opening her eyes to stare at two concerned faces. Klauden had knelt to her right, while Rory still partially held her on his lap. He must have caught her when she fell.

"Hannah," Rory answered, his face constricted in a knot of worry. "You are Hannah." It was not a question, but she could sense that very soon it might be.

"But her, the girl, her name is Solyn, not Hannah. Why does everyone call her Hannah Hunter?"

Rory looked to Klauden, and the vampire sighed, taking his hands away from Hannah's back and rubbing his face. "Her name was Hannah when she arrived," he muttered.

"What do you mean?" Hannah asked.

"They rename the slaves," Rory mused. "That's it, right? To keep them under control."

Klauden nodded, but added, "Only if they share names with the elite."

"Is that common? Why would the humans name their children after the vampires who would kill them?" Rory helped Hannah to her feet, holding her very close to him when they stood. He pulled the hood of the cloak up to cover her head.

"It is more common than you think, a form of hero worship I have yet to fully grasp. It is an ancient custom, though. Almost as old as the castle itself." Klauden rose gracefully to his own feet.

"Solyn is her slave name," Hannah repeated, trying to grasp that. "Why that name?" She was rambling a bit, allowing her rampaging thoughts to rage as they would. She wasn't making a whole lot of sense. Rory's hands rested on her shoulders, a solid reminder of his presence.

"It means 'Fair One,'" Klauden commented, "in the old tongue." He was wiping snow out of his hair.

Hannah shook her head, feeling the last of the nausea fading away as the cold seeped into her bones instead. "You would know that."

"Of course, I would," Klauden snapped, all authority again. "I named her."

XIV

By the time the trio arrived at Hannah and Rory's home, Hannah had realized two things—there was going to be a terrible snow storm that night, and Klauden had nowhere else to sleep. She glanced at Rory as they walked through the packed snow of the back yard, willing him to do something about the situation. The elf blinked wet snow out of his eyes, brushing his dark hair behind his ears as he frowned, looking from the small thatched-roof home, to the vampire, and back again.

She could see the debate going on in his mind. He thought of Klauden as his responsibility since he had summoned the vampire here, but he was worried about the villagers' safety with the blood drinker among them, knowing that to send Klauden somewhere else for the night could result in a fresh body in the morning. She wondered if he would have felt the same way about her eventually, treating her with careful wariness every time they came to a new town and he had to leave her alone.

Then again, she knew enough about Elven culture to know that hospitality was of grave importance to them. Casting out a guest was a serious offense, and abusing the host's hospitality was even worse. That was partly why Rory had only been banished from Firene after killing Marten—if he had discovered his wife with the prince in the palace and not his own home, his fate would probably have been much worse. Since the insult had taken place in his home, though, those who remained were inclined to be lenient. Maybe Rory was just considering his obligations.

Klauden paused a few feet from the door, his face impassive as he took in their home, the wet wooden walls, the stone blocks of the chimney a dark hump near the back door. Finally, he shook his head, then looked expectantly at her. He was waiting too.

He seemed so odd to her there—his red robes still clean and his blonde hair falling back into perfect waves around his face even with the wind beginning to whip around them—she had never thought to see such a sight in her backyard. Klauden van Sherinak out of his element and let loose in the wild, and yet he never lost that sense of aristocracy. It was hard to think of him without his books and papers, the massive desk in his study piled high with history and his fingers wet with ink. She thought of her own filthy hands, the grit from the forge never really coming out from under her fingernails.

How did he manage to stay so clean? There were times when Hannah noticed how far she had come from her upbringing, from the fastidiousness that was expected of Magnus van Kreeosk's daughter, yet living here with Rory among the simple villagers, it had seemed a paltry loss. *It's not like I'm filthy; so my hands are still dirty, so what?*

She had the absurd urge to fix her hair under the hood of the cloak, to look presentable to please the vampire. Hannah forced her hands to keep still against her side, willing Solyn and her ridiculous obsession with her looks to stop doing things like this to her. Rory had reached the back door now, and he paused before opening it, turning to face them.

"You are welcome here," he said in a low voice. He wasn't being rude or reluctant, she noted. In fact, his voice had lost all sense of emotion, falling back on some customary Elven tradition that didn't require thought. He reached for the doorknob, tugging the door open with sudden violence as he peered inside, hand on the hilt of his sword. Hannah knew this was something he did every time he opened the door to a room. Whether out of paranoia or long practice, Rory never walked into a new room without a hand on his blade. In fact, the elf never seemed comfortable inside until he had locked and barred the door.

When his quick scan of the interior revealed no intruders, he stepped out of the way to admit them. "Please," he said, gesturing toward the door. Hannah waited, watching Klauden.

The vampire seemed to consider something, then sighed. "No," he said. "I shall find my own lodgings tonight."

Rory swallowed before speaking, and Hannah could practically read the thoughts on his face—relief, excitement, annoyance, regret, then grudging acceptance. "I insist," he said, gesturing again at the door.

The vampire stood where he was for another moment that drew out into awkwardness. Hannah had the odd thought that his cheeks should be red, as Rory's were, from the cold. That was silly, though, since Klauden's face wouldn't grow red or even really warm without fresh blood. She wondered how long it had been since he had fed and what he would do when he needed to do so again.

He's lasted this long, she thought. *He'll be fine.* But she couldn't keep the image of young Scotty squirming in those arms, or the youngest daughter of Tarren, a girl of wide smiles and flyaway blonde hair—certainly irresistible to any child of the mountains. Hannah wondered if her own mortality called out to the vampire, if he could hear the blood in these mortal veins, and if that was the case, how Rory must be an even bigger beacon, the temptation of Elven blood nearly too much to bear. *Didn't I only barely resist his blood?*

The wind gusted, blowing her hood off her head, and a cold draft of icy air drifted down her back. She shivered, then decided it was too cold to stand out here debating.

"Look, the inns are filled with refugees," Hannah said, "and it's going to snow tonight."

"The weather will not bother me," he said, "as you well know." The vampire's eyes glinted in the dim light, the red tinge marking the start of his nightvision, and Hannah wondered how he had managed to stay hidden among the mortals with such obvious differences. She looked away, knowing that he spoke the truth, that his body would be fine outside all night long. He would be cold, but he wouldn't die or anything. The body of a vampire was notorious for its endurance. *But even so,* she thought, *such endurance has its limits, as I discovered.*

The snow began to fall more heavily, and Hannah shivered again, stepping closer to the doorway and the promise of heat inside. Rory stayed where he was, snow melting on his long eyelashes as he blinked in the wind. He gestured at the door again. "Please. I invited you here. You must stay with me."

Hannah knew what it cost the elf to say those words. Of everyone in the village, strange refugees included, Klauden was the last person Rory would want in his home. If he invited him to stay tonight, that would mean that Klauden was staying there for good until the attack came or he went home.

If he goes home.

But that was silly. Of course, he would go home. Klauden didn't belong anywhere except her father's castle. The fact that he left at all was shocking.

Klauden peered through the doorway, taking in the single room, the sparse furniture, and the lack of a private room for him to sleep in. He seemed on the verge of refusing again, but Hannah spoke quickly.

"You have to stay here, Klauden. There's nowhere else. Come inside before we freeze to death." Without watching to see if he obeyed, she walked into the house, stamping her booted feet on the mat by the back door to get most of the snow off. When she turned around, bracing an arm on the wall as she tugged off her wet boots, she saw that Klauden had followed her and Rory was shutting and barring the door. She set her boots down, then hurried to the fireplace, using the poker to shove the old embers in a better position under the bigger logs. The small orange glow grew brighter, but not fast enough. She stood up, retrieving the tinderbox from the shelf across the top of the fireplace, but before she could strike a new flame, Klauden was beside her. He mumbled a phrase, and a bright streak of fire leaped from his open palm into the fireplace, igniting a cheerful flame. Hannah backed away from the sudden light and heat, remembering a time when she could have done that. It was strange to think that she no longer had her magic.

"Thanks," she said.

The vampire gave her a curious look, nodded, then began shrugging off his traveling cloak, the fine material only slightly stained along the bottom despite his months of journeying, and looking around for a place to put it. Hannah took the soft material from him and walked to the front door, hanging first Klauden's and then her own cloak on the pegs next to the main entrance. Rory was unlacing his boots, a look of grim determination on his face.

"So," Hannah said, to break the silence. Both men looked at her, Klauden out of place in front of the fireplace in his long flowing red robes with their intricate designs along the edges. Hannah knew how much effort went into such details now, seeing the clothes through Solyn's eyes.

He looks like some prince in an old story, she thought, *with his finery and his manners.* She looked at Rory sitting on the edge of the bed, unbelting his weapons and laying one blade on the floor next to his side as always, sheathing the other and sliding it under the pillow but always within easy reach.

"Are you hungry?" he asked her. "There's some soup left from this morning."

When she nodded, he stood, walking past a frozen Klauden toward the cupboards that held their dishes, and began spooning dinner into two bowls for them. After he finished the second, he glanced at Klauden. "You want some?"

Klauden considered, staring at the food with cautious inquiry, then shook his head. "No, thank you."

"Your loss," Rory said, then slid both bowls onto the table, taking his customary seat on the bench along one side.

Hannah sat down across from him in her typical spot, aware of Klauden's eyes on her back. Finally, after she couldn't stand the silence anymore, she snapped, "Oh, just come sit down already."

Klauden moved awkwardly, sinking onto the bench on her side of the table, but at a decent distance from her.

"So," she began again, trying to fill the silence, "how was training today?"

Rory shrugged. "Fine. The guard is ready, but the newcomers leave something to be desired. Most of them have some experience with weapons, but nothing serious. It's going to take some time to get them prepared."

"How much time?" she asked, taking another sip of her soup. "Will they be ready, you think?"

Rory sighed. "That depends on how much time we have before they get here."

He glanced sharply at Klauden, his face alight with realization. "You came from the north. Did you see the enemy lines?"

The vampire shrugged. "I saw a number of goblins around the settlement to the north, but I do not know about any lines."

"How many did you see?"

Klauden glanced at Hannah, then at the elf. "A lot of them," he said, and Hannah realized that Klauden wouldn't know. He probably had never seen so many people in one place. She thought of how much he was like her in her first few months south of the Vanya and felt sudden sympathy. *He must be so lost down here, so out of his element and confused. And he did all of this, risked everything, for me.* A cold lump settled in her stomach, and she pushed the soup away. *Will he ever stop paying for my mistakes?*

"How many is a lot? Hundreds? Thousands? Are they ready to move yet? Was it just goblins?"

Klauden wilted under the barrage of questions, glancing again at Hannah before speaking. "I do not..." he began, then tried again, "I am not sure."

"How could you not be sure? You did see them, didn't you?"

"He doesn't know anything about armies, Rory," Hannah explained, sensing her old friend's discomfort. "He's only read about them in books. I wouldn't know much about it either, except that I've lived with you and learned what you know."

Rory sighed, taking a last spoonful of soup and pushing away his own empty bowl. "Well, what can you tell us?"

Klauden frowned, his face a mask of recollection. "I passed at least a dozen of more than I had ever seen in one place." He looked to Hannah. "Like everyone in the castle standing in a line. Slaves too."

Hannah considered. "Groups of a hundred, likely. What else?"

"They were setting up camps in a circle around that city. I thought it might be a siege."

Rory shook his head. "No, everyone who could have left did. According to the refugees, there's no one alive to resist them." He gave Klauden a thoughtful look, then pushed his empty soup bowl to the center of the table. "So, if this is Salva—the walled part of the city, mind—then where were the camps you saw?"

The vampire squinted, peering at the bowl, then asked, "Where is this village?"

Rory slid his spoon to the edge of the table nearest the fireplace. "That's Severin down there." He grabbed Hannah's spoon from her bowl, sliding it up and to the right of the spoon representing Severin, "and that's the mountain range to the east of here."

"Alright," Klauden said, glancing around for something to use as a marker. Hannah pulled the gold ring off her finger and set it on the table, then tugged her necklace off and set that down too. She could feel both of their eyes on her, so she didn't look up at first, settling for pushing her bowl into the mess as well.

When she looked up, Klauden was eyeing the gold ring—the ring Rory had given her—with distaste, but he used the tip of one finger to push it very close to the bowl that stood for Salva. "The biggest one was here," he said, then pushed the necklace a few inches toward the fireplace, so that it sat about a third of the way toward the Severin spoon, "but there were two more over here." He pushed her bowl next to the necklace. "And there were several in a cluster over here."

Rory looked over the mini map, eyes creasing in consideration. "They've spread out a little, that's good." He saw that Hannah's bowl had some soup left in it, and grabbing the spoon that stood for the mountains to the east, scooped up two mouthfuls as he nodded.

"Why is that good?" Klauden asked.

"It means they're settling in some. If they meant to press on immediately, they would just camp in tight to the city." He gestured to the spaces between the two rings and the bowl. "They're giving each other space to avoid infighting, likely they're different tribes." He looked up at Klauden. "What else did you see?"

"Well, it seemed like there were a lot of men around."

"Fighting with the goblins?" Hannah asked.

Klauden shook his head. "Not exactly. They were clustered in smaller groups within the camps."

"Prisoners?" Rory asked.

"I do not know. I did not get that close."

"You didn't want to feed?" Hannah asked, the words tumbling out before she realized what she was saying. Klauden stared at her. She had never asked about his feeding habits before, except to say that he was getting pale again and should probably eat soon. It was rude. "I'm sorry," she apologized, then spoke quickly to Rory to hide her blunder. "So there were roughly a dozen groups of a hundred, with some men in the middle."

The elf dropped her spoon into the now empty bowl and continued. "That's a lot better than the thousands first reported," he said, "though I'm sure there are more inside." He leaned back, hand rubbing his chin in thought. "I wonder why they were keeping the men alive. What would they need prisoners for?"

"Slaves?" she suggested, pushing both bowls together.

He shook his head. "Goblins don't use slaves. They're cannibals, Hannah. They eat men."

"So maybe they ran out of food."

He stretched, hands rubbing his face as he considered. "Maybe."

Hannah took the lull in conversation as her cue to rise. She collected the bowls and spoons, unbarring the back door to dip them in the water barrel outside. After breaking the ice on the surface to get at the cold water, she rinsed the dishes, tossing the dirty water in an arc to the right of the door. The first few times she had done this, she had made the mistake of dumping the water right in front of the door and had slipped on the resulting ice the next morning as payment for her stupidity. Now she was careful of where the water went. She scooped fresh water into both bowls, holding the clean spoons in an awkward grip as she used her bare foot to tug the door shut behind her. Rory had risen as well, and now he set a metal pitcher on the tabletop, taking first one bowl and then the next from her as he poured the water inside. Hannah stepped back to the door and barred it for the night.

"What is that for?" Klauden asked, peering at the pitcher.

Hannah smiled. "It's water for the night," she said, then continued when his face only grew more confused. "So we don't have to go outside anymore."

She walked over to the small table by the bed, picking up her brush and walking back to the table. She began unbraiding her hair as she spoke. "We drink most of it during the night, but sometimes I need it to calm my hair or wash my face and hands." Rory had retrieved a bigger wooden bowl from beneath the counter, and he set this on the counter next to the pitcher before pouring a small amount into it. He splashed some water on his face and hands, wiping himself dry on his shirt before settling in to watch Hannah begin to finger comb her hair, a half-smile on his face.

"Here," he murmured, moving to stand behind her as he picked up the brush. Despite her complaints about her hair, Hannah loved this part of their nightly ritual. He moved the brush in long even strokes, the feel of his hands working through her hair reminding her of their first morning they spent together after they escaped her father's castle. It had been a mostly wonderful night, but their first dawn had been awkward, and then he had brushed her hair, careful hands working through the length, and things had settled.

They had settled.

Hannah let out a contented sigh, the feel of the brush in her hair as relaxing as always, and then she remembered that they were not alone, that this stage of the night's routine would not lead to a lingering kiss or a longer embrace. She opened her eyes, not remembering when she had closed them, and saw Klauden watching her, a slow patch of red working up from beneath his collar. When he saw her looking at him, he quickly looked away at the fireplace.

"Rory," she murmured, turning around to catch his hands. "That's good." She took the brush from him, turning to pick up her ring and necklace from the table. She slid the gold band on her finger, then grabbed the necklace and slipped it over her head, Klauden's ring landing heavily against her chest. "It's late."

The elf nodded, hands pulling her hair out from beneath the necklace, not looking at Klauden as he spoke. "Shall I get you a blanket, or do you have one?"

At this question, Hannah turned around to study the vampire. He wasn't carrying a bag. In fact, he had nothing at all except his clothes. "Where are your things?" she asked curiously.

Klauden stood up, spreading his hands before his chest. "I found everything I needed along the way."

Hannah raised her eyebrows at him. "You mean to say that you left home without anything?" The idea was preposterous. If there was ever a man attached to his belongings, especially his books, it was Klauden.

He nodded. "What did I need? I am here, aren't I?"

"But—" she began to protest, but he cut her off.

"As you said, it is late." He looked at Rory. "I will take that blanket."

As Rory headed toward the chest at the foot of their bed, Hannah couldn't help but ask, "Where's your spellbook?"

Klauden smiled at her. "I do not need a spellbook, Hannah. I remember all of my spells. You were the only one who still had to study them." As he said it, he gave her a curious glance before looking around the room.

"Where is your spellbook?" he asked.

Hannah looked away, remembering how the words blurred and smeared in her vision. "I put it away."

"Why?"

Rory came back and handed him the blanket, then gestured at the rug in the middle of the floor. "It's the next best thing to the bed," he said.

Klauden nodded, then knelt to spread out the blanket. He looked expectantly at Hannah when she didn't answer him. "Why did you put the book away?" he repeated.

"Because she can't read it anymore," Rory answered for her, and she looked away, a wash of sorrow filling her chest as the loss of her magic hit her again. It was the only thing she still had that made her Hannah, and now that too was gone. *How soon before everything that I once was disappears?*

"Solyn can't read," Klauden said, a note of understanding in his voice.

Hannah whirled on him, suddenly angry again. "No, she can't. At the very least you could have taught her that."

He scoffed. "She was a slave. Why would I teach her to read?"

"So she wasn't good enough, then?"

Rory was watching the conversation but seemed unwilling to get involved. He moved back to the bed and sat down, watching Klauden rearrange the blanket on the floor. "It was not a matter of worth. It wasn't even something I considered."

"Not even when you planned on putting me in her body? You didn't consider it then?"

He shrugged. "She was going to sleep. What did it matter what she knew or did not know?" He started to remove his boots.

"It matters now," she said. "It matters to me."

"Well, if it matters so much to you, I'll teach you," he said, setting the boots down at the edge of the blanket. "Or rather, I will remind you."

"What do you mean?"

He sighed, settling in the midst of the blanket and giving her one of his oh-will-you-please-focus looks. "She's not going to take over. You are still the one in command of that body. You just have to be more assertive."

"I am assertive. I try," Hannah said, stepping away from him and walking to the chest at the foot of the bed. She wondered if she should take off her dress and sleep in her slip as she normally did. She glanced at Rory. The elf looked at her, then smirked and pulled his shirt off.

Klauden glanced at the elf's bare skin, the muscles clearly defined across his arms and shoulders, the scars crisscrossing his chest, then quickly down at the blanket. Hannah knew he was thinking of blood, of strong Elven blood coursing through those veins, the smell of live human skin, and the promise of strength and satiation. She paused, hands at the neck of her dress. Maybe she should keep it on.

"What do you try?" Klauden asked, bringing her back to the conversation. His voice was thicker somehow.

"I fight her," she said.

He turned around on the blanket, his own hands loosening the belt at his waist and setting it aside with slightly more violence than was necessary. "You do what?" His voice was mostly back to normal, the bloodlust contained again.

"I fight her," she repeated. "I need to beat her to stay in control."

Klauden glanced at Rory sitting on the bed, then her standing there. "And where did you get that idea?"

"What should I be doing, then? She can speak through my mouth now. How long before she can take over completely?"

The vampire shook his head at her, then tugged his own robe over his head. Hannah stared, hypnotized by the suddenly bare chest he revealed, then curious about the shorts he wore beneath that. She had always wondered what Klauden wore beneath his robe. The vampire was lean, not quite as scrawny as some of the men Hannah had seen in the village, but not as muscular as Rory. His skin was so pale, she could see thin tracings of veins beneath it. She knew if she touched him he would be cool, his body still retaining the cold air from outside, though the side that faced the fire would soon warm up. She caught herself staring, felt the blush beginning to creep up her chest, and looked quickly away.

"Well, you certainly cannot win in a fight."

"Why not?" Rory asked. Hannah looked at him, then back at Klauden on the floor. *Was my stare obvious? It was a bad idea to have the vampire stay here,* she thought suddenly. She shifted her focus, thinking of Rory lying shirtless in bed next to her. *What's to keep Klauden from draining him dry during the night? He wouldn't,* she told herself, *not Klauden.*

Not tonight, at least. Not yet.

"Because Solyn is always going to be in that body with her," Klauden explained. "She's awake now, and she is not going anywhere." He turned to Hannah. "The only way to stop this split is to blend with her."

"Blend with her? What do you mean?" Rory asked, voice carefully neutral.

"Hannah has to accept Solyn as part of herself. If she doesn't, the two will drive each other to madness."

"Or she'll take over," Hannah whispered. "She'll win."

Klauden scoffed. "You would let her win? You would willingly give over your body to another?"

"No."

"Well, then. The only thing to do is to work together. Find out what she wants. Give it to her. Come to a compromise."

"You're not serious," Rory said, and Hannah sensed something else in his voice, an odd note that she couldn't explain.

"It is the only way," Klauden said. "Fighting will only delay the inevitable."

"So, you're saying that Hannah should let herself become more like Solyn, is that it?" When Klauden nodded, the elf continued, "That's ridiculous. Hannah is herself. She can't suddenly blend with someone else. It doesn't make sense."

"It would not to someone like you."

Hannah heard what he was saying, heard what they both were saying, but she couldn't quite focus on it. She was stuck on that tone, the way Rory's voice had sounded, and she suddenly began to wonder how he felt about Solyn, how he would react to a person that was half-Hannah, half-slave-girl, and she felt a lead weight settle in her chest. He wouldn't want her then, not as some amalgamation. She was lucky he still wanted her now in this body.

No, there had to be another way.

She shook her head at both of them. "It's late," she repeated, rubbing her hands over her face, "and neither of you is making any sense to me." She sighed, then tugged her dress over her head. She could feel them watching her as she crossed to the wall, could sense both pairs of eyes tracing her movements through the thin slip as she hung the thick winter dress on the hook by the door. She didn't care, she told herself as she turned around to take the few steps to the bed. Rory was still watching her, but Klauden was busying himself with the blanket on the floor, tucking the edge around his waist as he lay on the floor.

Her eyes caught again on the pale smoothness of his chest, the sharp angle of his collarbone, and the way his hair brushed against his shoulders.

<Now there's a body worth dying for.>

<Shut up,> she told Solyn, feeling the slave's desire echoing in her own skin. <He is not for you.>

<For you, then?>

She took a deep breath, willing the slave into silence, then tore her gaze away from Klauden to stare at Rory. Her husband's face was red, or seemed flushed somehow, but he was otherwise expressionless. She wanted to talk to him, to have him hold her, but knew it wasn't possible, not with Klauden there. As she took the few steps to the bed and slipped in beside the elf, she wondered how long it would be before they were alone together again. She settled herself in the blankets, Rory pressing himself against her as he always did, but there seemed something automatic, almost obligatory in the way he held her.

She had a horrible thought then, one that kept combining with that tone she had heard him use before and refused to leave her be. *Did he invite Klauden to stay with us because he doesn't want to be alone with me?* Maybe the thought of Solyn in her skin was too disturbing for him, but he didn't want to say anything. She struggled to contain the growing knot of panic, settling farther into him, slightly comforted when his arm came around her more protectively than before, his lips close to her ear as he bade her goodnight.

Hannah fixed the pillow under head, trying to calm her whirling thoughts. She remembered life in her father's castle, how everyone had always been able to read her thoughts, and she wondered if Klauden could hear her now. If he could, she would likely keep him awake all night with her yammering. She took a deep breath, very aware of the elf behind her, one arm around her waist, the other tucked under the pillow and close to his blade.

<Rest easy, chaivin.>

The voice was familiar in her mind, the thought both reassuring and horrifying. *Was that real or just more of my imagination?* Hannah shivered, very aware of the hump that was Klauden on the floor, the vampire lying on his back, his eyes glowing red in the dimming firelight as he stared at her, his patient expression both a comfort and a warning.

XV

Hannah woke to the sound of a distant scream. She sat bolt upright in the bed, unaware for a moment of who or where she was. A nervous glance around the room jogged her memory some—the glow of the fireplace, the wooden table and benches, the hooks by the door with cloaks, and her dress hanging on them—it was all familiar. The only thing missing was her loom. The image of the room shifted suddenly, and she was staring at a similar place, but there was a large vertical loom against one wall with a small bench before it, a half-finished image on the screen and bits of colored string hanging down from all sides.

Hannah closed her eyes to the image, knowing that it was only Solyn again, the slave girl pressing her memories into Hannah's waking mind now. When she opened her eyes again, the room was hers. The only thing out of the ordinary was the blanket piled up on the rug in the center of the room.

Wait, she thought, her sleep-sluggish mind trying to put pieces together. *Why is there a blanket on the floor?* She had another image flash into her mind—this one of Klauden laying half covered by that blanket, his bare chest pale in the dim light. *Where did he go?*

She glanced to her right. Rory was lying on his back, arms cast up and underneath the pillow, no doubt clutching his sword, chest rising in the rhythm of deep sleep. As she stared at him, he mumbled something, took a deeper breath, then settled into a steady rhythm of almost snores. Hannah knew he was in no danger of waking. Once the elf started snoring, nothing short of the roof caving in could wake him. Hannah always wondered how much of that was due to his dreamwalking, if the concentration he needed to walk the other planes was what kept him in such deep sleep. Well, if he was dreamwalking now, it wasn't her dreams.

Who is he watching, then?

She frowned, then remembered what had woken her. Someone had screamed.

Or did they? Did I dream it? Hannah tried to recall her dream, but the images slid from her grasp, elusive bits and pieces of fragmented sensations. She had a brief glimpse of Klauden standing over her, watching her as she pretended to sleep, but it melted away into the kaleidoscope of dream pictures and disappeared.

She considered the empty blanket on the floor. Obviously, Klauden had gone out, but where had he gone? *Is he hunting? Did he hurt someone? Is that the scream I heard?* That was ridiculous, though. If Klauden had found a victim, she wouldn't scream like that. Klauden was far too careful for such dramatics.

Maybe it had been a wildcat or something.

Either way, she was awake now, and aware of a growing pressure in her bladder. She considered the chamber pot but decided that she wanted the fresh air instead.

Tossing the blanket aside, she stood up, wincing as her bare feet hit the cold floor. She hurried to the cloak on the peg by the front door, then stepped into her boots, not bothering with the ties for now. She grabbed one of Rory's knives from the countertop as she left; one could never be too careful when going outside at night. Hannah had once been surprised by a foraging wolverine in the backyard between her and the house and had woken Rory up with her loud attempts to get the beast to flee. Hannah had been lucky it was a harmless beast that time. Since then, she never left without some weapon.

Still, it wasn't like a wildebeest was going to jump on her when she left. She lifted the bar from the door to go outside and paused. The door had been locked. *How did Klauden leave?*

She gave the room another quick glance but couldn't see the vampire hiding anywhere, not that there was anywhere to hide. *Unless...*

She pulled the door shut but leaned the bar against the wall as she crossed to the center of the room. She pushed the blanket and the rug out of the way, revealing the trapdoor beneath. The escape tunnel that lay beneath had been the main reason Rory had chosen this house for them to live in. Others had been closer to the center of the village or more elaborate, but he had felt, and she had agreed, that the extra exit was worth the distance. They didn't know who had built it; even Tarren, when he had shown them this home, hadn't known. The previous owners, Haley and George Lathscomb, had both succumbed to the winter fever two years before, and Tarren had never asked George about it. She slid the locking mechanism aside, then lifted the door slowly, peering down into the darkness. Did Klauden go that way? If so, he had managed to rearrange the blankets overhead after leaving. The fact that it was still locked was no clue; the door locked automatically when it was shut. Having a trapdoor for their use was one thing; having strange people able to climb into their house was another. She gave Rory another look before making up her mind. The elf was sound asleep still, hands wrapped around the pillow. He had let go of his blade. He must be in a very deep sleep.

She retrieved a candle from the counter, managed to light it from the fireplace, then settled on the edge of the trapdoor, feet dangling into darkness. She tightened her grip on both the knife and the candle, then slid forward, dropping the few feet to the wooden bench they had placed just under the opening. She set the candle down, the flame making weird shapes and shadows on the earthen walls of the small room, and she stepped off the bench to the dirt floor, the cold damp walls glimmering in the candlelight. She took the two steps to the wooden panel in the wall of what had once been a simple cellar, pressed the latch that allowed it to open, stepped into the tunnel that lay beyond, and slid it shut behind her.

It didn't take her long to reach the end of the tunnel and step through the bare branched bush that hid the exit, and it took her even less time to find a convenient spot to relieve herself. As she squatted, mind focused on the cold snow blowing in her face and the fact that she had neglected to put her winter dress on before venturing into the night, a sudden noise made her pause.

It sounded like someone trying to cry out was being muffled, and nearby at that. She snuffed the candle, crouching low against the tree as she righted the slip and cloak she wore, then peered into the night, trying to locate the source of the sound. As she concentrated, it came to her. Footsteps in the snow, heavy sounding, as though several men were stomping in boots through the woods. She concentrated again, automatically reaching out with her senses as she had once been able to do, seeking the presence of other minds.

She hadn't really expected it to work—she had thought her magic gone for good—so when she was suddenly enveloped by five foreign minds, she pulled back for a moment to orient herself. Solyn was moaning something in the back of her mind about magic and privacy, but Hannah ignored her, focusing on the sudden reappearance of some of her magic.

She knew it was the magic in her that allowed this ability. It had never really been a spell after all. Relieved to know it still worked, Hannah sharpened her will and eased out with her senses again, brushing lightly against the other minds in the darkness. One was frightened, a young girl, Hannah guessed, from the panicky run of her fear. She waited, trying to see if she could catch a name in the madness, and eventually it came to her.

Elsbeth. Tarren's youngest daughter. *What in the nine hells is the girl doing out in the woods in the first place?* Hannah tried to get more of an impression but couldn't. She shifted her focus to the other minds and received a wash of anger and hatred, savage intentions driven to a violent purpose. Definitely men, likely more refugees, but of the sort less likely to find a welcome in Severin. Maybe they had been criminals in Salva, maybe they were a wandering band of rogues. Neither was unlikely in this part of the world. Bands of thieves were common enough south of the mountains, though Hannah wondered how long they would survive in the winter without steady shelter.

She caught a flicker of something else then, her mind brushing up against some foreign presence in the woods with them, but it was gone before she could pinpoint it. Some sort of wild creature? She opened her eyes, waiting for them to adjust to the sliver of moonlight that lit the small clearing ahead. Tightening her grip on her knife, Hannah slipped out from behind the bush, taking careful steps as Rory had taught her, not quite sure what she would do when she got to the men but determined that Elsbeth would not come to any harm if she could help her.

The group came into sight after she had maneuvered around a few trees, her boots landing softly in the new snow, her breath slow and steady to avoid notice. The wind was still whipping about, the snow limiting her vision, but she could see them well enough. They were moving at a steady pace, Elsbeth held by two of them, her whimpering cut off by a strip of cloth in her mouth that wound about her head. Hannah could see that she had been crying, was still crying, but her struggles seemed to have dampened a bit from what they could have been. Perhaps she was growing tired from the ordeal. Her feet were twisting and tripping against the long nightgown she wore, and Hannah caught sight of her bare feet, blue tinged and bleeding in the snow.

How did this mob get a hold of her? Tarren's house was near the inn, toward the center of the village. *Did Elsbeth go outside to the privy and get captured there?* The wind gusted, sending a shower of snowflakes into her face and down the neck of her slip, and Hannah shivered in the night.

Damn mortal body, she cursed, willing herself under control. She held her ground, waiting for the men to move beyond her before darting quickly to the next tree. She could easily pace them, but what happened when they stopped? Perhaps she could have taken on four men with her magic intact and her vampiric strength at full tilt, but with this body, she was little more of a challenge than poor Elsbeth. Still, she was the only one around who could help. If she went back to get Rory, she might not be able to find them again, and even if Rory could track them at night and in this weather, Hannah didn't know if the girl had that kind of time.

She had a good idea of what they were after; it hadn't taken Solyn's memories of Vailen for her to know that. But it wasn't like Elsbeth was a friend or anything. Hell, she barely knew the girl, except to note how she occasionally mooned after Rory when he trained the men. She had worried about it for a time, before she realized that Rory had eyes for no one but her, and Elsbeth mooned after every boy she saw. Still, a flirtatious nature didn't justify this.

Hannah moved again, outdistancing them as she kept carefully ahead of their trail, trading a scrawny pine for a thicker oak, then paused as she caught the dim glow of a campfire through the trees ahead. *Well, that must be their goal, then,* she thought, peeking out from behind the tree to see how close they had gotten to her. If she was going to do something, it should be before they reached their companions. As soon as she decided to act, she heard Solyn in her mind again.

<You are crazy! What are you doing? You're going to get us killed!>

Hannah ignored her, pulling the hood of her cloak tighter over her head and stepping out into the path before the quartet and their prisoner.

"What?" the one holding Elsbeth asked, coming to a halt before Hannah. He was scrawny and clad in old clothes, his pants worn through at the knees and his eyes rimmed with the gray tinge that followed a lack of sleep. He was surprised by her appearance and stood staring at her. She hoped she looked frightening there, a sudden figure materializing out of the darkness. Maybe she could play on their fear.

She heard Solyn's horrified yell: < *You don't even have a plan!?* >

"Release the girl," she ordered, not allowing them time to regroup. "Now."

The one who hadn't spoken reacted instantly, hands coming away from Elsbeth's shoulder and jerking to his forehead. Hannah recognized the gesture of prayer to Valerian. The fool was praying to his god. She smirked as he backed away from her, lips mouthing another prayer to the night.

The other three were less inclined to obey, she saw, as the one still holding the girl shoved her back into his comrade's arms and drew a rusty short sword from his belt. From the way he held it, Hannah thought he probably wasn't so familiar with its use. She tightened her grip on the knife but didn't move. Instead, she focused her energy at the armed man, willing him to see her, to see only her, remembering how the spell she had once used to charm her victims into complacency had felt, if not recalling the actual words. She could feel Solyn helping her, the slave's desperation fueling Hannah's will, and she could feel the magic growing in her, not striking out as it had when she said the words but pulsing in concentric waves toward the man. He paused, blinking suddenly and shaking his head as if something had confused him, and Hannah knew she had him.

Two down, two to go, she thought giddily, adrenaline racing through her. "You," she said, pointing at the one to the right who held Elsbeth, a younger man with a scraggly beard and a smudged face, "untie her hands, and send her this way."

The bearded man looked to his remaining comrade, a tall willowy man with a scar across one eyebrow, then back to Hannah. He seemed to draw strength from his companion's presence, though she could see that the way the leader was just standing there, frozen with his sword out, was unnerving him. She had to play off of that fear. "If you free her, I shall let you live. Your leader will not be so lucky."

He didn't have a weapon, none of them aside from the leader did, and Hannah knew that was part of the reason why she had been so successful thus far.

"Why should we?" the scarred one asked. "Who are you?"

The wind gusted then, and Hannah thanked the gods for dramatic flair. Her hood blew off, her hair twirling wildly about her head. Hannah hoped she looked like some fey creature come to light out of one of the stories she had heard as a child—a wild fairy or a nymph—and then hoped these men had heard the same stories she had. "I demand payment for passage through my woods," she declared. She pointed to the girl. "Young girls are particularly fine for my tastes."

<*What are you doing?*> Solyn asked.

Hannah shushed her. <*Help me,*> she thought to the slave. <*We have to scare them away.*>

Then her voice was speaking, Solyn using her mouth again. "If you do not give us what we want, we shall exact payment from each of you in turn," the slave added, and Hannah had to work to keep her face impassive and serious. They seemed unnerved by her sudden use of the word "we," and the scarred one began scanning the surrounding woods for her companions.

"We?" he asked. "How many are you?"

"We are many, and you are none," Solyn said. "Give over the girl, or die where you stand."

<*That's good,*> Hannah thought to the slave. <*Where did you get that from?*>

<*I loved the stories as a child. A great many wonderful quotes. Darnier says that to the woodsmen when he reclaims Thea from them at the end of their story.*>

<*Oh,*> Hannah thought, deciding to ask Solyn who Darnier and Thea were at some later point.

The faithful man backed away even farther, and Hannah narrowed her attention to the two remaining threats. The older man was squinting at her, probably contemplating the odds of her story being true, and the one holding Elsbeth glanced nervously from Hannah to his companion.

"Decide your fate," Hannah said, trying to push the men into fleeing. They seemed so close.

She thought the man was about to shove Elsbeth in her direction, to give in and leave, when a strange expression crossed his face, and instead of the wary concern he had been giving her, he smiled, something catching his eye that he liked.

Oh no, Hannah thought, *someone is right—*

And then something hit her on the head, and everything was warm, wet darkness.

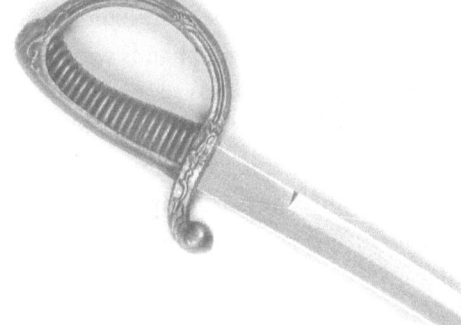

XVI

When Hannah came to, she was lying partially on her side with her face in the snow, hands bound before her, palms pressed hard against one another as her hands dug into her stomach, head aching. She tried to sit up using her elbows as leverage, but the world was spinning too quickly, and she stopped moving.

<Brilliant idea,> Solyn commented. *<What did you have in mind next?>*

<It was working well enough,> Hannah quipped. *<Where are we?>*

<Captured.>

Hannah moved her hands a bit, feeling the ropes bite into her wrists. *<Obviously. What else?>*

<See for yourself, brave heroine.>

Hannah opened her eyes a bit more, taking in her surroundings. Her lower back was pressed up against something hard, probably a tree. She could feel the cold wet wood behind her as she took stock of her body, her legs tucked up, knees a few inches away from where her hands pushed into her belly. Looking down, she saw that her bound hands were tied to a rope that trailed away for a few feet in the snow in front of her before coiling back behind her to wrap around the tree. She could move a little bit if she could get to her feet, but she wasn't going to get away while still tethered like that. She was near the campfire she had glimpsed earlier, and there were a lot more than four men. When she got her vision to stop whirling and blurring at the edges, she could make out seven people, and a covered bump that must be Elsbeth, similarly bound to a different tree to Hannah's right. *Nearly twice as many men,* she thought. *This is not good.*

One of the men, a boy, really, with his smooth cheeks and scrawny legs, noticed she was awake and nudged his comrade—an older man who lounged near the fire, tossing a knife end over end with careless ease. The new man approached her as she finally managed to get part of her body upright, using the tree for leverage as she leaned away from him, glad that her legs were still free, even as she realized it would do little good. She didn't think she could stand up yet anyway.

Hannah took in the small details of his clothes in the firelight; the red shirt was worn, but clearly the best piece of clothing among the group, and his pants did not have any holes in them. The easy way he held Rory's knife in one hand spoke of practice, and there was an air of command in his presence.

He's the leader, then.

She studied his long black hair, the bright eyes a slash of color in a face that had seen its share of sun and wind. Her first thought was that he had never lived inside, had never been tamed or owed allegiance to anyone.

<Tame?> Solyn thought angrily. *<Look at him. He's dangerous.>*

<We are dangerous,> Hannah thought back at her. *<He's just free.>*

"Well, well," the man said, revealing a missing tooth along his upper lip as he spoke. "Look who has decided to grace us with her presence."

Hannah tried to sit up straighter, to address the leader with what grace she could command, sitting there tied up and weaponless. When she had secured a more sturdy position, back to the tree, knees drawn up to her chest, and bound hands resting casually on top of her bare knees, cloak falling to either side in the snow, she gave him her best aristocratic stare. "State your purpose here, sir," she ordered.

He chuckled a bit, gesturing from her to his men with her knife. "Listen to her," he commented. He glanced at one of them—the scarred man from the woods who had held his ground against her. "You were right, Garin. This one will fetch a fine price." Garin smiled broadly at the compliment, inclining his head in deference to the leader.

"I thought you would like her, Len."

Hannah shook her head at Len the leader. "I am not for sale."

The man cocked his head, knife moving a few inches closer to her face. "No?" he asked, the blade a menacing reminder of just how fragile this body was. She should watch what she said if she planned on buying time.

<Time for what?> Solyn asked. *<Who is going to save you now?>*

<Time to think of something better,> Hannah snapped. She didn't want to admit that she had been thinking of Rory, who would surely notice she was gone, or Klauden, who had gone hunting in these very woods. *Surely one of the men who are so determined to have me could show up and rescue me, right?*

"No," she insisted, staring at the leader's face instead of the blade. *Stay strong,* she ordered herself. *Don't submit. This one will respond to strength.*

He gestured with the knife at Elsbeth, who lay in a heap nearby. "What about her, then? Surely one of you must be worth something."

Hannah glared at him, at the man who would mock her weakness like this. "We are all well beyond your price, sir." If only he would keep looking at her like that, she thought she might be able to charm him as she had the man in the woods. *<Yes,>* she thought at him, focusing on the magic again, *<stare at me, only me, think of me, and be my fool...>*

The man blinked hard, once, twice, and Hannah was sure she had him, but then he shook his head violently back and forth and slashed the tip of Rory's knife down her cheek.

Maybe he is dangerous, too, she thought stupidly. The pain was immediate, a sharp line of heat across her face, and though Hannah managed not to cry out, she felt Solyn start to seize up, the slave girl reacting instantly to a wound she had no doubt experienced dozens of times. Hannah wanted to be angry, to lash out at the man for hurting her, but she could feel the slave rising inside her, taking over, her frantic fear threatening to drown Hannah completely.

Without her consent, Hannah's limbs began to thrash, her bound hands jerking forward to strike out at the man, fingernails catching at his cheeks, and even though she knew the move was all wrong if she actually wanted to cause any real damage, Hannah couldn't get Solyn to realize that, never mind listen to her.

<Solyn!> She shouted inside her head, trying to get the slave to stop her thrashing. Len reacted instantly, knife hand slipping deftly to her neck and his body tumbling down on top of her. Her lower back scraped against the tree as they slid to the side, her shoulder hitting the ground hard. Even when he had her pinned on her back, hands pressed awkwardly into his stomach as she struggled vainly, Hannah couldn't get the body to stop

trying. It was useless, of course; he had the advantage of weight and size, and he wasn't tied up. The only thing this jerking around was doing was tiring her out and annoying him. He seemed flustered by her continued resistance, taking the opportunity to smack her hard across the face as he used the rope to pull her hands over her head, pinning her even more closely with his weight. Hannah got a whiff of stale sweat when she gasped in response to the pain, her face aching with the blow, tears running down her cheeks. She tried to calm Solyn down—<*Stop moving! You're making it worse!*>

Solyn finally obeyed, more as a result of the leader's body pinning her to the wet snow than Hannah's command, but at least she wasn't struggling anymore. Hannah could hear the other men laughing at them, at her, but she focused instead on the man's face. He was giving her an appraising look, and Hannah knew he would not misjudge her, not after this little explosion. He had seen something during her fight with Solyn, something that made him very wary. She felt a surge of hatred run through her, black rage at the man who would do this to her.

"Are you through, princess? I can keep this up all night," he commented, knife precariously close to her skin. He paused a moment, pushing himself up onto one elbow over her, and the knife drifted down to the neckline of the slip she wore beneath Rory's cloak. "You know, they're not too particular about what the women look like when we bring them in. You'd be worth just as much to me bruised and bloody as you are whole."

Hannah took the warning seriously, swallowing her anger as her stinging cheek reminded her of how suddenly this man could turn deadly again. Her mouth felt swollen, awkward and hot as she spoke. "Fine," she said, hating to submit, but unable to do anything else. "I won't fight you again." *Not until I have something to gain from it*, she added silently.

He smiled at her, the movement revealing unexpected dimples that made him look like an eager young man instead of the jaded criminal he was. Hannah tried not to associate that look with Scotty, her young assistant this past week. The boy deserved his dimples; this man was a fraud. "No more resisting?" His smile broadened, and she felt that heat rise in her again, fury that could destroy cities if only she could harness the power. "However will I entertain myself, not to mention my men, until morning?"

"You won't stay here until morning," Hannah snapped. "Only a fool would stay so close to the village with captives."

"For a woman who weeps at the slightest pain, you talk too much, dear," he observed.

"I get that a lot," she retorted. Len grabbed her earlobe with his free hand, strong fingers pinching the sensitive skin hard. Hannah cried out, unable to stop it, though the noise shamed her. She was furious, but she forced herself to stay perfectly still. *Wait*, she ordered. *Not yet.*

He glanced at one of his men; Hannah saw it was the one who had been frantically praying to his god when she arrived. "For a woodland sprite who demands tribute in her forest, she seems quite mortal to me, Benson," he said, a finger tracing down the mix of blood and tears on her cheek. When she didn't respond quickly enough, he pressed down with the thumb, the pressure igniting a new series of explosions in her face, and Hannah had a terrible moment of doubt. How long could she stand this kind of pain?

<Don't worry,> Solyn advised. *<This is nothing.>*

Hannah swallowed, suddenly very nauseated, her gorge rising against the pain. She saw the world shiver, dark spots of night overwhelming her vision, and wondered if that meant she was close to passing out. She had seen victims do that before, mortals who couldn't stand the pain of the bite and just drifted away. *Oh, yes,* she thought fiercely, *let me go.*

A fresh surge of agony swept through her then as the man shoved his thumb into the sensitive hollow beneath her jaw, bringing her back to this mortal body with a horrible jerk. She moaned, unable to stop the sound from escaping.

"That's right," the man whispered, lips close to her aching ear. "You will not avoid me, princess."

Okay, she wanted to tell him then, *alright. Anything, I'll do anything if you just stop hurting me.*

The thought was so outrageous that Hannah jerked back to herself, the words that must have been Solyn's echoing in her mind.

The hell with that, she thought.

Steeling herself, Hannah tried to think around the pain as she once had been able to do, distancing her mind from her body and focusing on exterior details, the stink of the man's breath, the glint of her blood on

Rory's knife, the way the firelight cast shadows on the leader's face, the vague shapes of the other men across the fireplace, the carefully blank look on Benson the believer's pale face, the way Garin licked his lips in anticipation, the cold snow beneath her body, melting against her cold skin, freezing her through the cloak and slip she wore. The technique worked some, and Hannah could breathe again, working through the pain as best she could.

He removed his finger then, and the relief was overwhelming. She felt fresh tears squeezing out of her eyes, unable to stop them. "Oh, beauty," he whispered, wiping a tear away with a calloused finger, "don't cry. Not yet anyway."

Hannah had the sudden image of Vailen, the young man whispering soft words into her ears in a language she didn't understand as he moved in her.

Don't cry, he had whispered near the end, deigning to speak in her tongue when he wanted to be sure she understood, not yet. Hannah heard Solyn start to scream, both in memory and inside her mind, the slave girl beyond consolation, beyond reach, and pushing Hannah beyond the bounds of patience.

<*SHUT UP!*> She ordered the girl, wishing her hands were free so she could slap herself into silence. <*I don't care about your problems. I don't care what terrible things happened to you. I don't care how hard it was, or how much pain you've suffered. I care about getting out of this alive and mostly unscathed, and I can't do that if you insist on shrieking like that! If you can't help me, at least shut up!*>

<*You don't understand,*> the girl began muttering, <*you can't understand. It's going to get worse, and I can't take this again. I'll die,*> she insisted. <*I'll die, I'll die, I'll die.*>

<*I will not die,*> Hannah told her sternly. <*I may get hurt here, but I will not die.*>

She glared at the leader, took a deep breath to calm herself, then spoke to assure both herself and Solyn, "He will not win."

Len gave her a curious look, then slid the knife inside her slip, using the tip to cut a small hole in the material between her breasts. Hannah heard the small pop of the fabric giving way, and it seemed very loud in her ears, her entire being focused on the small movement of Rory's knife. She lay motionless under the onslaught, knowing that such slow movement was meant to wear her down, to break her will. It was what she might have done, once upon a time.

"I think I shall win, princess," he commented, tracing a small line across her skin with the knife tip. The blade was sharp, as all of Rory's weapons were, and it took a moment for the pain to come singing up from her chest, the bright sting of a new wound hammering at Hannah's control. "In fact," he said, rolling himself on top of her again, "I think I have already won."

Hannah waited until he was very close to her, his hips worming underneath her slip, the cold air rushing underneath her clothes, the wet snow crunching under her back, waiting for the moment when he was most unprepared, knife hand awkwardly supporting his weight on the snow beside her, blade useless against the ground for a second, other hand busy with his pants, eyes glancing down to watch what he was doing.

"Not quite," she whispered, then lurched forward, knocking her forehead into his face, the pain exploding in her own head as she collided with his nose, feeling the wet spurt of blood, his blood, cover her eyes and cheeks. She simultaneously shoved her knee up between his legs, the sudden jackknife of her body a double weapon. When he cried out and jerked away from her, she used the rest of her momentum to roll to the right as far as the rope would let her, ignoring the slash of the blade as it cut her arm, getting her knees beneath her and using the rope as leverage to keep her hands out in front of her body.

As the leader stumbled to his feet, bellowing as the blood ran down his face, Hannah leaped to her own feet, trying to get into a defensible position while still bound. She saw Garin dart forward to catch Len's pinwheeling arm and caught the look of confusion breaking through the mask on Benson's face.

This may actually work, she thought. She would get to her feet, she would use the tree to make sure none could get behind her, and she would make her stand right here. There were only a few feet between this tree and the fire, and Elsbeth was lying right next to her, so the only ways for them to attack would be from her open left, which she could defend now, through the fire, which was unlikely, or over Elsbeth's prone form to her right, which was even more unlikely. Rory would be proud of her, she thought, raising her bound hands to wipe the blood from her eyes so she could see clearly. Her head ached with the memory of impact, but her heart was pounding, her entire body shaking with the excitement.

I can do this.

XVII

E xcept then she stepped on the untied laces of her boots, the snow-slick string catching on the rough bottom of the shoe, and when she tried to catch her balance, she stepped back, as Rory had always taught her to do—*Always step away from your enemy, Hannah, never into him, not until you're sure you've got him*—except that she wasn't standing up all the way yet, and her foot caught on Rory's cloak, then she was falling backward, tripping over her own feet, and colliding with the tree she meant to use as her defense. The tree pushed her sideways, and she fell in a heap on top of Elsbeth, her other barrier, bound hands tangled up in the cloak as she struggled to right herself.

She saw the movement out of the corner of her eye, a sudden pull back and thrust, and then her chest was on fire as the force pushed her away from Elsbeth into a curled up ball on the frozen ground, the boot that kicked her winding back for another go, and Hannah couldn't do anything except lay there in a heap and take it, the second kick knocking the rest of the wind from her lungs and paralyzing her.

She lay in gasping agony for a minute, looking up at the bearded man from the woods as he began to grin, boot drawing slowly back for another bout, this time aiming for her face, and she wondered if this was the end.

<*Not quite,*> she heard Solyn comment acidly, the girl's calm restored. <*They're just getting started.*>

When the bearded man set his boot back on the snow instead of kicking her again, Hannah wanted to breathe a sigh of relief, but when she tried to inhale, her chest hitched painfully.

<I can't breathe,> she thought desperately. *<I'm choking to death.>* Hannah realized she was perilously close to panicking and struggled to maintain control.

<You'll be fine. Just relax and breathe through your nose. It hurts, but it goes away.>

Hannah could feel the slave's sense of superiority, as though she had vast experience in this area and Hannah was a foolish child.

<Great,> she thought at Solyn, a slip of air burning down her throat with a horrible sound, *<you know all there is to know about getting beat up. Congratulations.>*

<I certainly have enough experience,> Solyn commented. *<Hopefully, Klauden will show up in time to heal us. He's good that way.>*

As she lay there, breath coming back in burning hitches, Hannah took a chance, asking what had been on her mind all along. She thought of Klauden standing aside, waiting for Vailen and the others to finish with Solyn before showing up to collect the pieces. *<Why didn't he just stop them altogether?>*

She could feel Solyn's embarrassment, her inability to give a truthful answer. *<I don't know.>*

<He could have,> Hannah thought. *<If he'd wanted to, he could have saved you with a word.>*

<I know that, alright? It's nothing, really. It's just what they do.>

From Solyn's tone, Hannah realized that she had been terribly rude, pointing out Klauden's complete lack of concern for the slave while her intention had only been curiosity. *<I'm sorry,>* she thought at her, a sudden wave of pity washing over her, pity for the girl who had been so brutalized that she expected this kind of treatment from men.

<Look, I was just grateful that he helped me at all.>

Hannah's breath was back, but the blow had made her start to cry again, and the tears were now making her nose run, and it was harder to get air than it had been before. Rough hands grabbed her shoulders, someone tearing the cloak from her back and nearly breaking her neck before the tie gave way. She gagged, gasping again for air as she was pushed forcefully to her knees on the ground, more hands gripping her shoulders like iron. She tried to remember a time when air had been so precious to her and failed. *Ridiculous mortal body*, she swore. *No wonder they always died so often.* One of her boots had come off, the bare top of her foot cold against the snow.

<How could you deal with this?> she wondered idly at Solyn, trying to focus on the blood-smeared face that swam into view before her. Her body was an agony of pain, a firestorm of aches from her face sinking down to meet the dull roar of waves from her chest. She wondered if the kicks had broken any ribs, remembering the black bruise across Rory's chest after Malbrek had nearly suffocated the elf with his magic. It had taken the elf weeks to truly heal up from that, even with her magic. She managed to separate herself from her body, divorce her mind from the pain, and focus on her surroundings again. Someone was kneeling before her, someone with mad fury in his eyes and a maelstrom of power in his mind. It was Len, and she had likely broken his nose. Hannah hoped it hurt like the nine hells.

"That was very foolish," he said to her, his voice nasally and wet, a hand trying to stop the blood from flowing.

"Right," she muttered, giggling madly at the strain of it all. "I should have tied my shoes."

The hand came away from his face, a lightning strike that rocked her head back on her neck. *He's so fast,* she thought, *even without a weapon, he's too strong and too fast.*

<They are always too strong and too fast,> Solyn commented. *<That's why they always win.>*

<Not this time.> Hannah pulled her head forward, barely registering this newest attack. She tried to brace herself with her hands, reaching for the snowy ground to the side of her knees, noting the spray of blood that covered the area, but one of the men holding her reached out and snatched the rope that tied her wrists to the tree, tugging her arms up and over her head, pulling her upright so that her knees barely touched the ground.

The leader shuffled forward on his knees, face dark with intent. "You will learn to respect your betters, princess," Len insisted, "or I swear I will cut every inch of your body until you beg for the end."

He punctuated this promise with another slash of Rory's knife, and Hannah felt the warm flood trickle down her shoulder, puddling against the ruined material of her slip. "You'd better be careful," she whispered, the pain making her a bit delirious. "So much blood is bound to draw all manner of creatures this way. Don't you know they can smell it?" She glanced around at the men she could see, eyes lingering on Benson. "You know it, don't you, believer? Can't you feel them all around you?"

The man drew himself upright, hands going back to his forehead, and the scarred man—Garin—pushed him violently on the shoulder. "Sit down," he growled at the faithful man, and Benson obeyed, sinking to his knees and closing his eyes. *He may want to help me,* she thought, *but he won't.*

Len had given the woods behind them a casual glance. "There's no one out there to save you, princess," he said. "There's nothing there at all."

"Shows what you know." She reached for her magic then, the power somewhere within, a desperate gamble to save herself, and for a second, it was there, a glimmer in the horizon of pain, but then Len rewarded her words with a sharp punch to the stomach, and she gagged again, this time retching up the remains of the soup she had eaten for dinner so many long hours ago.

Len leaned away from her, but the vomit mixed with the blood running into her mouth, and Hannah managed to spit at him, her blood smearing with his on his face. She wondered why she wouldn't just quit now, just stop resisting and give in. It wasn't as if she could get free, not now, not with so many of them holding her and her body a mess. She was too tired to reach for her magic, even if she could figure out how to unleash it without the words.

Len wiped at his face with disgust, stuck the knife into the snow at his side with a sharp movement, and reached for her neck, strong fingers wrapping around her throat and cutting off all breath. "I've had enough out of you," he growled.

Hannah tried to move her legs, to get some sort of solid ground beneath her so she could fight him, but they didn't respond. She knew that the tops of her feet were resting in the snow, tucked behind her knees, but one was numb now, numb like her hands and part of her face. Hannah wondered if she would freeze to death before or after they finished beating her. She could feel his fingers digging into her skin, her body bucking involuntarily against his grip, against the rope, against the hands that held her tight, and then suddenly, she wasn't really there at all anymore.

She felt something snap; was that her neck? Her will? Whatever it was, she was no longer tied to the clawing, biting, fighting thing that was her body. She could still see everything, could focus on the way the leader's face didn't change much as he throttled her, but she couldn't bring herself to care.

< *There you go,* > Solyn commented softly, and Hannah could feel the slave at her side, just two girls having a chat while a maniac choked their body to death. Was this where she lived most of the time, just below the surface? It wasn't so bad in here.

< *I was wondering how long you'd take to figure this out.* >

< *What is this?* >

< *A place to go, to get away when it gets too much,* > the slave explained. < *I wait here for Klauden. He'll bring me back.* >

Hannah thought of the vampire, of the empty space on her floor, of the locked door and the dark night, and was suddenly sure that if he could find her, it wouldn't be soon enough. He couldn't save her. Besides, who was she to constantly demand Klauden rescue her? *I'm not entirely helpless, am I?*

Maybe, she thought, *but if I'm halfway there, Elsbeth is even more helpless. I won't leave her alone.*

Fine, she decided, then pushed forward again, ignoring Solyn's sigh behind her, propelling herself back into the screaming skin that was her body.

The leader's hands were gone from her throat, but there was a sudden silence between breaths that seemed to last a bit too long. *Am I too late?* Rough hands smacked her chest, and then she was hacking, burning air screaming into her lungs and making her choke with effort. Hannah focused entirely on breathing, knowing that something else was happening to her, someone was moving her, but unable to care. Caring had gotten her into this mess in the first place.

And what had all of this accomplished? She had set out to find Klauden, then to rescue Elsbeth, and all that she had succeeded in doing was getting captured and serving as a punching bag for this monster. Thoughts of her initial purpose made Hannah think of Elsbeth again, and Hannah wondered what would become of her. Hannah opened her eyes, aware that she was sitting up on her butt now, legs akimbo, strong hands still holding her shoulders and something hard that might be a leg supporting her back. She could make out the small hump of the girl's body to her right, hopefully unconscious during this fiasco, safe in her mind. For now.

The leader was reaching for her again, and Hannah tried to pull away but couldn't, the tensing of her muscles only serving to hold herself in place when he latched both hands onto her slip, tugging at the small slit he had made with his knife and baring her skin. Hannah had the desperate thought that if she could get him to talk, maybe he would slow down, maybe she could buy time, maybe she could do something besides sit here and allow this to happen.

She got a lungful of air, expelling it in a question. "Why are you doing this?" she whispered, glad when her voice sounded desperate, a frantic plea for understanding. He would like that.

He cocked his head at her, hands settling on her thighs as he scooted closer to her before glancing around at his men, and Hannah got a sense of huddled bodies beyond the fire, eager minds waiting their turn, though her vision was a bit hazy at the edges now. "Why?" he repeated, busy fingers pushing the remains of her slip to her waist. "Why do you all ask that?"

Hannah swallowed stiffly, eyes closing, trying to keep the fuzziness in her vision from taking over. He would only hurt her awake again. She forced herself to look at him. "There have been others?"

He smiled at her, hands pausing in their pursuit of her bare skin, dimples showing again through the blood on his cheeks and chin. "Many others, princess, though none quite so entertaining as I think you will be."

Hannah heard him, knew that what he said was important, but she lost the feeble hold she had on her willpower. "You know," she commented dreamily, watching the blood continue to drip from his nose, "if you lie down, that should stop bleeding."

"Funny you should say that, princess," he said, and then she was on her back again, limbs heavy and useless all around her, and there was something she should be doing, something she was supposed to focus on, some reason she had come back from the haven within, but she couldn't remember. It was nice to lay here and just stare up into the sky, the snow still falling in little whorls to land on her eyelashes.

< *You promised.* > The voice was cold, accusing, and it took Hannah a moment to recognize it.

< *What?* > she asked Solyn, trying to rouse herself.

111

<You promised he wouldn't win, and here you are, just lying down for him. I knew it. I knew this would happen.>

<What's happening?> Hannah wondered. She couldn't feel much of anything, just the snow on her face, soothing her aches, and something cold and wet beneath her, likely more snow, and something hard and warm against her legs—

Hannah jerked back, suddenly more aware than ever of her surroundings. She slid up and away, flailing with her arms to push the man off of her, amazed that she had been so stunned, so delirious that she had practically laid there and let him rape her.

"No!" she shouted, amazed at the ferocity of her voice, at the sudden strength that flooded her limbs. Then she was struggling away from him, rocking her body back and forth in an effort to break free of the hands on her shoulders.

With a desperation she had never felt before, Hannah lunged at the hand closest to her, a calloused thing with hairy knuckles, and bit it. She didn't have the teeth for it, not anymore, but the attack was unexpected, and the hand leapt from her skin. She turned her head to the other side, an instinct older than she could recall guiding her movements as she dug into the soft flesh between thumb and forefinger. The second man cried out, trying to loose himself from her grip, and suddenly she was free from their hold. She scooted back, her numb hands useless as she struggled to get out from under him. Someone was shouting, and the leader was lunging after her, his hands trying to get a solid grip on her arms, but she didn't stop.

She kicked out with her legs, feet crashing into something solid and pushing her back another few feet, and then she bumped into something warm and heavy. Looking behind her, she saw the huddled hump of Elsbeth, and then the body moved, and she was looking at the very wide awake, very aware eyes of Tarren's youngest girl. Hannah wondered if he would recognize his daughter now. Though the girl was bound and gagged, there was something new on her face, something dangerous that warned Hannah to get out of the way. She kicked out again, still trying to fend off the leader who was trying to crawl his way back up her body, and managed to roll to one side, a well-aimed foot managing to lift the would-be rapist up and off of her. She scrambled again, knowing that even if she could gain her feet, it was all pointless.

There were too many of them. She didn't have any weapons. She couldn't cast any magic. It was only a matter of time before they cornered her again. They only had to grab the end of the rope to tug her back to them. The next time, she wouldn't get away.

Still, she had to try. She sat up, rolling onto her knees as she tried to stand, but her legs were numb and useless beneath her, refusing to support her weight. She saw Len getting up again, ready once more to tackle her, saw the excitement in his eyes, could tell how eager he was, how pleased he was that she had decided to fight back at the last, and then she felt something entirely unexpected.

An explosion of magic surrounded her, encasing the entire campsite.

Hannah watched as blood began to pour from the leader's eyes, leaking from his broken nose and the corners of his mouth. He stared at her in sudden surprise, as if he couldn't believe what was happening to him, and then dropped to the ground in a heap. He didn't move again. Before Hannah could understand what was happening, another blast flew past her, and a man to her left screamed, Garin clamping both hands over his ears and closing his eyes, and Hannah watched as he too began to bleed from the eyes, nose, and mouth. He crumpled slowly, eyes fading even as he sank first to his knees and fell onto his face.

Did I do that?

When she looked to her right, Hannah saw that Elsbeth was sitting up, eyes narrowed, the girl's entire being focused on the man lying on the ground, and then she understood. It was Elsbeth. The girl must have some latent magical ability, and the stress of the situation had brought it out. Hannah didn't waste any more time being amazed; she lurched uncertainly to her feet, squaring off between the girl and the other five men, who were still trying to figure out what was happening. A few scanned the surrounding trees, no doubt looking for the attackers who had killed their comrades. Everything had happened so suddenly; even the men she had bitten were only now regaining their feet. Hannah's first impulse was to grab Elsbeth and run, but her legs weren't steady enough to get far, and even so, they were both still tied to the trees. Head reeling, she tried to think of a plan.

Weapon, she thought frantically. *I need a weapon.* Glancing around, she spotted the hilt of Rory's knife sticking out of the snow a few feet away where Len had abandoned it and lunged. Her numb hands were no help, but she hooked the pommel between the two dead appendages and used the rope wrapped around her wrists to tug it free from the ground. She lurched backward, regaining a semi-steady stance before the tree, already deciding that to twist the knife around for a proper grip would take too much time, even if she could make her fingers obey. Instead, she drew her arms up, bending her elbows, the blade pointing out at her enemies. It wasn't any way to hold a knife to do damage, but anyone who rushed her would probably get cut a little bit in the approach.

"Don't come any closer," she said to the men, then added in a rush, "or you'll suffer the same fate." Hannah didn't know if Elsbeth could repeat the magic or if the girl was tapped out, but the men didn't know that either. She saw that the leader of the party in the woods was considering an attack, fingering the rusty blade at his belt. She addressed him.

"You," she said, gesturing with her bound hands, knife bobbing in his direction. "You will be the first to die." Hannah tried to reach out then, to call on any magical ability she had left, focusing on making him stop, making him fall down, making him do anything except continue to stand there of his own free will. She didn't know what spell it was, but she felt the magic rise in her, the power emanating out in a small wave, a weak attempt at best, but still, he felt it, and something changed in the way he stood. Instead of aggressive, he was wary and took a few steps back. Hannah staggered but caught her balance, the effort of that last spell nearly overcoming her.

She glanced at Elsbeth, saw the girl concentrating on the same man, eyes narrowing to slits as she tried to conjure the magic again, but Hannah thought it was too late. Without training, she wouldn't be able to do it again. Hell, Hannah had training, and even she had trouble getting magic to work right under the best of circumstances.

There was a long moment when no one said anything, five men considering the two women before them, one wavering and tied to a tree, the other sitting and glaring for all she was worth. Hannah had a moment where she thought they might make it, that she and Elsbeth had a chance of getting out of this, but then a man across the fire, one whom Hannah hadn't gotten a good look at before, spoke. "They're only women."

It seemed that was all the others needed to hear, and Hannah watched as they split up, three men heading her way and two rounding the fire toward Elsbeth.

<I tried, Solyn,> she thought desperately. *<I'm sorry, but I tried.>*

Before the first one could reach her, however, something leapt into the clearing between them, something red and tall and angry. The men began to stumble about, some crying out, but not before the creature struck, a savage bite to the man's neck, and Hannah saw the blood spray, and she knew that she was safe.

Her vision grayed out as the blur that was the vampire made short work of his first victim, leaping to tackle another as he tried to run away, but another sound caused her to open her eyes again.

It was a sword being drawn, the tell-tale sing of metal released from a scabbard, and when she looked across the fire, Hannah saw the tip of a sword appear from the middle of Benson's chest. The blade withdrew, and she saw another shape dance into the mob of dying men, slicing across the chest of another man as he turned to flee. The elf didn't pause to be sure his blow was mortal, instead stepping carefully over the body of the man Elsbeth had killed with her spell and knocking aside the feeble defense of the man who would be leader. Though he was the only one with a sword, he didn't stand much chance against the enraged elf who sent the rusty sword flying before shoving both of his blades deep into the man's chest. Hannah smiled. It was such a pleasure to watch Rory move.

Then the world tilted, and she was looking up at the elf's concerned face from the cold ground. He had a smear of blood on one cheek, no doubt spray from one of his victims.

"You found me," she whispered, eyes closing as her body tried to give in and pass out, but Rory shook her.

"Hannah," he said, voice heavy with concern, "stay with me."

She forced her eyes open. "I'm here," she said, but for a moment, she couldn't see his face. She blinked, the whiteness receding to the edge of her vision. "You're here."

"I'm here," the elf said, and she could feel him moving her arms, likely taking the knife out from between her hands, could hear the soft sound of a blade cutting the ropes that bound her wrists, felt the thin fabric of her slip as he pulled it up to cover her, and the gentle touch of his warm skin made her realize just how cold she was. And if she was cold, Elsbeth must be frozen by now.

"Elsbeth," she muttered, "is she…?"

"I'm alright," the girl answered, and Hannah caught a glimpse of her sitting up, Klauden crouched in front of her, the gag pushed down around her neck. Klauden said something to her, but Hannah couldn't hear it.

There was another long gray moment, and when Hannah could feel again, she was aware of someone's hands on hers, a stream of warmth running into her limbs, giving her energy and willpower again. She opened her eyes, saw the vampire kneeling at her side, a soft glow encasing his hand as it held hers.

<*See?*> Solyn said. <*I told you he was good like that.*>

Hannah ignored her, turning to face Rory, who knelt on her other side. He was holding her other hand, gentle fingers pushing strands of hair out of her aching face. "How did you find me?" she asked him.

He took a deep breath, anxious gaze flicking between her face and Klauden. "I woke up, and you were gone," he said. "I met him outside, and when we found them, we followed the tracks in the snow."

"I'm glad," she said, the warmth sinking into her, making her want to close her eyes again and disappear. She sighed, thoughts of the men trying to work their way into her mind again. "The others?" she asked. She had to be sure.

"Dead," Rory said. "We killed them all." He gestured to the clearing around them, then eased Hannah off the snow and into his arms so she had a better view. Klauden released her hand, turning to Elsbeth behind him. "See for yourself."

"I saw it," she murmured, settling into the elf's warmth. "Thanks," she added after a moment.

"Hannah, what happened?" he demanded, lips next to her ear. She could hear the worry blending with the start of anger in his voice.

"I heard a scream," she said, swallowing painfully. "I went to investigate."

"Why didn't you wake me?"

"I don't know. You were sleeping so soundly. It seemed wrong to disturb you. Besides," she added, "I didn't think there would be any trouble." She paused. "Actually, I thought I could handle whatever trouble came my way."

"Hannah..." He sat her up gently against his chest, his body heat echoing into her, running fingers along the knife cuts on her face and chest, checking their depth and seriousness. The only one he focused on was across her shoulder, and he tugged the remains of her slip up to staunch the bleeding.

"I know. I know. I'm mortal now. I have to be careful." She winced as he applied pressure to the cut.

"Sorry," Rory said, but his fingers did not ease up. He sighed. "You're not helpless." Hannah knew he was trying to be supportive, but his face creased in concern that contradicted his words. "You just have to learn some limits."

"What limit? To never go outside because someone might hurt me?"

He frowned at her, hand covering her numb fingers, lifting the hand so he could examine the color of her skin. "That's not what I meant." He began rubbing her hand briskly between his own, then paused to check her skin again.

"I know." She paused, trying to make some sense of things. "I just thought I could take them." She drifted then, mind trying to grasp the lesson here.

Rory shook the hand he held, bringing her back to him. "Don't do that," he ordered. "Don't you ever do that again." Hannah wondered if he was talking about her attempts to pass out or what had happened to her in the woods.

"I won't," she promised on both charges, closing her eyes again. "Trust me. I'll never leave your side again." There was a long moment of silence again, then Hannah heard a different voice speak up.

"She saved me," Elsbeth was saying, and Hannah tried to focus on the girl's eager face above hers. "She rescued me."

Hannah snorted, the movement making her chest hitch and her ribs ache. Rory pressed a hand against her chest, sensitive fingers feeling for damage. "Some rescue. More like a punching bag."

"You didn't have to follow," the girl was gushing now, fresh tears running down her white cheeks. She turned to Klauden, what she had seen him do finally registering on her shocked face. The vampire stared impassively back at her. "And you," she whispered, undeterred by his expression, "you attacked them like a monster."

Her eyes narrowed, taking in the smear of blood on the vampire's chin before glancing at Rory and then Hannah in turn. "What are you people?" she asked, complete candor in her still young voice. Hannah was glad to see that she hadn't been permanently hurt by this ordeal.

<*Not that you can see,* > Solyn observed quietly.

"None of your concern," the vampire snapped, and Hannah watched his lips move, the simple spell to ensnare the girl quick and efficient. Within seconds, Elsbeth was staring blankly at the vampire, face expressionless.

"What did you do now?" Rory asked, fingers checking the wound on Hannah's shoulder and frowning. She saw Klauden reach for something behind her and was surprised to see him retrieve her lost boot.

"She will be fine," Klauden said, settling her foot into the shoe. "It's just a glamour, but you need to take her home."

"After I get Hannah safe," the elf said, but Klauden stopped him with an arm to the shoulder.

"She will be safe with me," Klauden assured him.

Rory glanced from the blood on Klauden's chin to the blood that coated Hannah's face. "Somehow I doubt that."

"Think, man," the vampire snapped, giving Rory an impatient look that Hannah knew quite well. He looked at Elsbeth, still sitting there quietly impassive. "This girl needs to be brought home. They will not be pleased to find a complete stranger returning her, will they?"

Rory sighed, shaking his head, but not relinquishing his hold on Hannah.

"They know you, yes?" Klauden prompted.

The elf nodded. Hannah could see his sense of obligation warring with his need to care for her. "I'm alright," she whispered, head sinking back into his embrace, managing to thump his arm with the lump that was her hand. "Go. Just come back to me."

"I can't leave you here," Rory said, torn between Elsbeth and Hannah, "not with them."

"I will take her back to the house," Klauden assured him. "She will be fine."

"Don't let her out of your sight."

"I will not." Klauden reached for Hannah, strong, thin arms sliding beneath her and lifting her off the ground. She shivered in his embrace, newly thawed skin starting to feel again in little snatches of fire. Rory didn't quite let go of her until she was secure in the vampire's grasp, and even then, he seemed reluctant.

"Keep pressure on it," he said, moving Klauden's hand so that it pressed hard against the cut on her shoulder. "She's so cold," he said, hands trailing along her exposed arms. He glanced around the clearing, taking in the strewn bodies, the blood streaking the snow, then saw what he wanted. He took three steps to the cloak, the material a puddle on the ground, wet with snow and blood, but still better than nothing. He went to drape the cloth around Hannah, but Klauden stopped him.

"Elsbeth is in need of it more. It is a long walk to her home, yes?" In his frustration, Klauden's voice had reverted to more of an accent than Hannah had heard in a long time, old habits raising in him as he tried to take charge of the situation.

The elf paused, glancing from Hannah's battered form to the girl sitting in the snow, teeth chattering in the night. "Fine," he agreed, settling the material around the girl's shoulders and helping her to her feet. She obeyed, movements sluggish and pliable. "What will I tell her father?" he contemplated, more to himself than to anyone else, but Klauden chose to answer.

"Do you think that concerns me?"

Rory scowled at him. "I wasn't asking you." He glanced from the dull look on Elsbeth's face to the vampire. "How long will she be like this?"

"Until she sleeps," Klauden said.

"Will she remember?"

"Everything until we showed up," the vampire declared. "You may want to claim responsibility for this little rescue on your own."

Rory shook his head. "Take care of Hannah until I get back."

Klauden nodded, clutching Hannah a bit closer to his chest. "I will," he assured the elf, starting off into the woods.

"And Klauden?" Rory's voice echoed from the clearing.

"Yes?"

"If you do anything to my wife, I mean anything, I will kill you."

Hannah felt the chuckle bubble in Klauden's chest. "I would expect nothing less of you, elf. I will not harm her, I assure you."

XVIII

The journey home passed in a blur for Hannah. She was cold, shivering and aching in someone's arms, and she nestled closer, trying to burrow into the warmth of that chest. She heard a voice curse in a familiar accent, then she realized it was Klauden who was holding her, the vampire fighting to keep her steady while opening the back door.

"Kick it," Hannah suggested. "Use your foot."

Klauden took her advice, tugging the door open with the toe of his leather shoe and stepping inside. Hannah thought he would lay her on the bed, but he rested her on the floor instead, settling her carefully on the blanket he had abandoned earlier that night. She watched the vampire walk back to the door and bar it, unwilling to move at all. She was so cold.

Klauden crossed to the fireplace, gesturing casually, and approached her as the flames roared to life behind him. He folded himself into a sitting position behind her, then lifted her up so that she rested against his chest. It was the same thing Rory had done out in the snow. He pulled her slip away from the cut on her shoulder, running a finger over it to check the bleeding. Hannah felt him stiffen, finger tracing the line of the cut delicately, a small amount of blood collecting against his skin, and when he raised the finger to his mouth, out of sight behind her head, she didn't move to stop him. It wasn't like she needed that blood anymore anyway.

"You certainly are a lot of trouble," Klauden commented.

"You're one to talk. Where did you go?"

"Out." Something in the way the vampire spoke didn't sit right with Hannah, and she struggled to sit up, feeling the aches and pains of her body waking up as heat stole through her. When he saw she would not be deterred, Klauden helped her sit up, hands resting gently on her shoulders, avoiding the depressions that Hannah knew would be purple with bruises tomorrow—the men who had held her had not been gentle. He held her steady as he crawled deftly around her, long limbs rearranging themselves as he sat before her. She took in the blood smear on his cheek, the wet leather of his shoes, the few bits of snow clinging to his hair. Her own hair was wet and tangled with snow and blood. Wherever the vampire had been, it was not out in the weather.

"You weren't outside," she said.

"I was," he said.

"Your hair is barely wet."

"Yours is soaking, chaivin." He reached for her, pushing wet strands behind her ears. "Let me see to you."

His hands were warm on her skin. Hannah knew it was from the fresh blood he had taken, but they grew warmer as he began to speak in a low voice, the magic seeping into her and easing the worst of her pains. His touch stirred a memory, and Hannah was sitting on the edge of a bed in a vaguely familiar room, Klauden kneeling before her, blue robes a swirl around him, whispering foreign words as he held her hands.

"You did this for her," Hannah murmured, opening her eyes to her immediate surroundings. "Often."

"I did."

She fixed him with a glare, sudden anger washing through her. "Why didn't you stop it?"

He shrugged, hands settling on her face, a finger resting gently on her chin. "It was not my place to stop anything," he said, using the finger to turn her head slowly back and forth. "She belonged to my family, but you know how things are."

Hannah felt herself start to sink forward into his grasp, anger dissipating, the energy that kept her upright seeping away, and Klauden moved again, this time shuffling beside her, a strong arm around her back to keep her steady, long thigh pressed hard against hers where they sat on the floor before the fire. "She meant nothing to you, then?"

Klauden used his other hand to steady her drooping head, making sure she could see his face when he spoke. "I wouldn't say that," he whispered, gentle fingers tracing the curve of her jaw, the swollen outline of her cheek, the blood trickling from a cut on her lip.

"Did you love her?" Hannah didn't know why she was asking this, but it seemed like the right thing to do. She felt Solyn inside, the slave girl motionless and silent.

He licked his lips, and Hannah could see how big his fangs had grown in his mouth. "You know I appreciated you, Solyn," he said.

"I'm not her," Hannah insisted. "Don't call me that."

"No," he agreed, mouth moving in a familiar motion, and Hannah knew he was tormenting himself, running his tongue against his teeth, teasing the hunger while resisting it. It was a game she had played when she debated taking Rory, a way to both rouse and contain the hunger. "You are not the same."

"Stop it," she said, unable to look away from his mouth, the way his lips kept moving, his eyes glazing over with the start of his nightvision, the red glow that also signaled the start of an even stronger hunger.

"I'm not doing anything," he whispered.

"But you will," she whispered back, wanting to pull away from him, wanting to stop sitting here with blood on her face in the arms of a vampire who wanted her. She was so foolish, always so foolish.

"Perhaps," he agreed, then he was leaning toward her, thin tongue slipping out to flick the blood from her lip, hungry eyes promising comfort, solace, warmth, everything Solyn had ever wanted from him. He paused, his breath against her lips as he spoke. "Perhaps I should have done this years ago." Then he kissed her, soft lips warm against hers, his teeth and tongue running against her sensitive skin.

<Yes,> Solyn whispered. *<Finally.>*

Hannah fell into the moment before she could think about it, her own mouth responding to the touch, knowing he wanted both her mouth and her blood and willingly offering both, and then she remembered who she was and who she was kissing, and jerked away.

<No, Solyn,> she thought bitterly, staring at Klauden, the wet smear of her blood across his lips.

"No." Her voice was thick but determined.

He pulled away from her, hands withdrawing to a carefully neutral spot on her shoulders.

"No," she repeated, pushing away from him to fall slowly to her back on the blanket. He caught her before she hit, of course, soft hands resting her on the floor before he withdrew.

"You are a mess, chaivin," he observed, peering down at her. "Let me help you."

As he reached for her, Hannah slapped at his hands. It was a feeble gesture, but he got the idea, hands pausing in mid-air before withdrawing to his lap. "Don't touch me," she told him. "You've helped me enough."

She shuffled onto her elbows, pushing farther away from him to the edge of the blanket, then using the side of the mattress to ease herself to a sitting position against the bed, as far away from Klauden as she could manage on her own.

He had the decency to look ashamed, at least. "I shouldn't have done that," he whispered. "I am sorry."

"You say that," she retorted, "but for some reason, I just don't believe you."

"Have I ever lied to you?"

"Before or after you forgot to mention that Anna wasn't really dead?" she quipped, knowing that his omission of her half-sister's survival was a sore spot. She had only found out that the girl lived when Klauden told her that Anna's was the body they intended her to inhabit during the ceremony. What had become of Anna's soul was still a mystery.

"We already covered this," the vampire snapped, and Hannah saw his teeth receding in his mouth, the moment passing, and relief swept through her. If Klauden reached for her again, she didn't know if she had the strength to resist him. "You did not want to know."

"You make a lot of judgments about what I would or wouldn't want to know," she observed, flexing her hands as the returning feeling brought a wash of pins and needles with it. "You hardly know me anymore."

"I know you still," he insisted, eyes creasing as he took in the way she clenched her fists, her shallow breathing. "You are in pain. I can ease that."

"No, thank you. I don't want your kind of easing," she said, though she couldn't contain a wince as the rope burns on her wrists came back to life with a fiery sting.

"You are impossible," he snapped, reaching out to grab her hand with both of his.

"Don't," she said again, but when he only began to massage her palm with gentle fingers, she let him. When he reached for the other hand, she didn't resist, the smooth motion of his fingers pushing life back into her, easing the ache. Her face had started to throb again as well, her chest joining the general agony as she took a few deep breaths.

Maybe it wasn't so bad, then, having him touch her. Hannah closed her eyes, falling into the peace he offered.

< Yes, > Solyn whispered. *< This is what I want. >*

Hannah tried to ignore her, but she couldn't deny the memory of Klauden's words from a few hours before. *Find out what she wants and give it to her,* he had said.

She wondered what would happen to them if she refused, if they really would go mad as Klauden suggested, but when she finally drifted into a dreamless sleep a few moments later, she couldn't help wondering what would happen if she didn't.

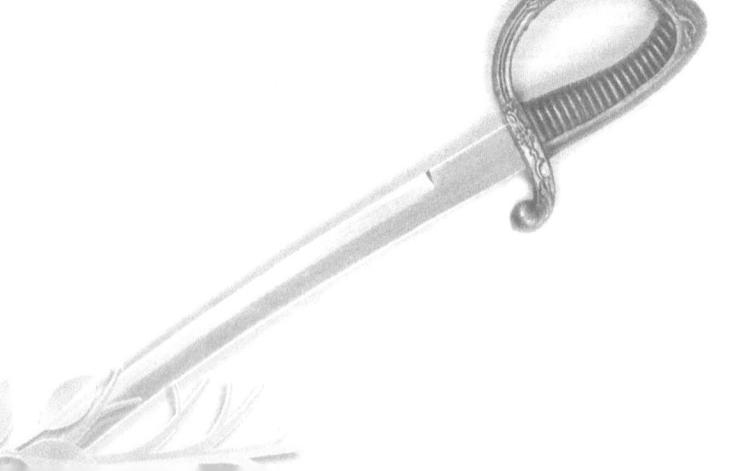

XIX

S he had only closed her eyes for a second, letting the moment stretch out, but when she opened them again, she was lying in bed, Rory's gentle hands wiping her face clean with a damp rag. "Easy," he said, dipping the cloth into a bowl of water next to her, and running the clean sponge across her chin, the warm water thawing her skin and soothing her aching muscles. She glanced down, saw that she was no longer wearing her slip, and wondered how Rory had managed to get her out of it without Klauden seeing. She had on a pair of Rory's shorts and one of his vests, the buttons covering most of her chest but leaving the knife cuts open to the air. The cut on her shoulder was an angry red line but no longer weeping. Klauden's magic had done its work. She glanced around the room, spotted the vampire sitting at the table, hands steepled before him as he watched the elf wipe her face. He saw her looking at him and nodded graciously.

"You're back," she whispered, turning back to her husband. "Is Elsbeth alright?"

He nodded. "A bit shaken up, but otherwise unharmed. Her father put her to bed." He shook his head, taking in the damage to Hannah's face and chest. "How do you feel?"

"Honestly? Like hell." She shifted in the bed, trying to find a comfortable spot. "But I'll be fine in a few days."

He frowned at her. "Do you know what they wanted, aside from the obvious?"

"I think they meant to sell us, but I don't know to whom," she said, readjusting her head on the pillow as she saw his face struggling with something.

"We did..." he began, hands pausing in his cleaning, fingers resting lightly against her cheek. "We did get there in time, right?"

Hannah knew what he was asking and nodded quickly. "I gave them some trouble."

"I see that." He smiled at her, the darkness around his eyes fading some. "You did very well."

"I shouldn't have gone," she answered. "It was stupid."

"It was," he agreed, resuming his dip and wipe process, "but you did manage to save that girl's life."

Hannah started to smile, but the movement made her face hurt, and she stopped. "More the other way around," she said.

He ran a finger across her lips. "What do you mean?"

"She's got magic," Hannah explained. "She killed two of them and gave me the chance to get to my feet again. Were it not for that, you would not have been in time."

"I see." He nodded, face clouding over with guilt.

"Don't," she ordered, reaching a sore hand out to land on his.

"What?" he whispered.

"Don't blame yourself. I'm fine." She smiled, ignoring the pain. "We're both alive and well. This is not your fault."

"I should have known there would be bands of men in the woods. Not all of the refugees came into town. I knew that, and I should have warned everyone."

"You couldn't have known that," she said. "Don't be stupid."

"You could have died."

"But I didn't."

"You could have been—" He couldn't bring himself to say it.

"But I wasn't. I'm alright now."

Hannah saw the anger in him, the need for vengeance not entirely quenched by killing the men in the clearing, and hoped he wouldn't turn it on himself. The tendency to be hard on himself was something Rory took a bit too seriously for her taste at times.

"Listen to me," she said seriously. "There are other things to think on right now. That might not have been the only band of them. You should send word."

"It's already done," the elf said, sitting up. "Tarren was seeing to it when I left him."

"Did he know Elsbeth was gone?"

Rory shook his head. "No. No one had even heard her leave. He said she never went outdoors in the cold, though. He thought something must have drawn her outside." He gave Klauden a meaningful look, his anger finding a suitable target nearby.

"Do not look at me," the vampire said. "I was nowhere near that girl's house. Besides, she is far too young for my taste."

"What else could it have been?" he asked.

"Maybe she had a mortal urge," Klauden suggested.

"They have a chamber pot inside," Rory countered.

"Maybe she arranged to meet a lover outside," the vampire guessed.

"Who would have a tryst in this kind of weather?"

Klauden threw up his hands. "Maybe she wanted a breath of fresh air. I do not know what the silly girl was thinking of when she went outside, but it is hardly my fault every time a maiden leaves her house!"

Rory glanced down at Hannah, lying bruised and beaten in the bed. "What about Hannah, then? She went outside to find you."

"I did not see her leave."

"Where did you go, then? What were you doing outside in the first place? Looking for a meal?"

Klauden stood up, hands clenched at his sides. "I do not feel the need to explain myself to you, elf, nor do I need to subject myself to such treatment. If you would prefer, I can find other lodgings."

"Stop it, both of you," Hannah ordered. "You're making my head hurt." She glanced at Klauden, the tall vampire so foreign in her house. "You. Let us know if you're going to leave so we don't look for you." She glanced back at her husband. "You. Stop trying to accuse him of everything. It's too late, and I'm too tired."

The elf gave her a silent perusal, then glanced at the vampire. "I didn't mean to accuse you," he said mockingly.

"Yes, you did," Klauden responded.

"You're not helping," Hannah quipped. "Look, there are bigger things here than us. Can't we focus on that?"

"Fine," Rory said, "but only if he stays where someone can keep an eye on him."

"I'll watch him," she promised. "He's not going to hurt anyone."

Klauden was shaking his head. "And to think you invited me here, elf. I travel three months and thousands of wheels to help, and this is how I am received. No wonder you were ostracized from your people. You are a disgrace."

Hannah felt the elf's muscles tense as he jumped off the bed, hands reaching for his blade as he gained his feet, the sing of metal still ringing when he held the blade out toward Klauden. "Keep it up," the elf promised, "and I will kill you, Hannah's will or no."

"Do try," Klauden goaded. "Please, continue breaking your promises to her. Soon she will realize that staying with you was a mistake from the start."

Hannah wanted to get up, to throttle both of them, to shout at them for being fools, but her body was too weak to obey. "Enough," she said, her voice quiet but audible. Both men paused to stare at her. "This is ridiculous. Rory, you asked him here to help me. Kindly let him live long enough to try." She continued, this time reverting to her natural tongue, the language of her father's castle, when speaking to Klauden. "<I see what you are doing,>" she told him, "<and I ask that you take heed. If you hurt my mate in any way, I will seek my vengeance.>"

He smiled at her use of the word "mate," shaking his head slowly back and forth. "<What would you do to me, betrothed? What could you do now?>"

"<I am still my father's daughter,>" she reminded him. "<You would be amazed.>"

He stared at her, and Hannah thought he might really be looking at her for the first time. Up until now, he had seen Solyn's face, Solyn's body, heard Solyn's voice, and habit had made him careless. Hannah could see the understanding glowing in his face, the idea that she really was Hannah, the Hannah he had known since childhood, finally sinking in.

"You are different," he said in the common tongue.

"I am."

Klauden bowed his head, though not very far since Rory's blade was still lingering near his neck. "Forgive me," the vampire said.

"I do," Hannah said, then looked at Rory.

The elf struggled for a minute, clearly wanting to have things out with Klauden once and for all, but eventually he gave in and sheathed his weapon. He started back toward Hannah on the bed, but Klauden's voice made him pause.

"I have offended you, host," the vampire said, eyes lifting from the floor to stare at the elf. "My apologies."

Rory seemed taken off guard by this, hand flicking to his blade in anticipation of a trick, but when the vampire did not move to strike him, he nodded curtly. "Yeah, sure. Your apology. Whatever." He turned his back on Klauden, sitting again on the bed with Hannah.

Still, when he came to bed a few moments later, Hannah noted that he kept both weapons very close at hand. Klauden sat at the table, and when Hannah finally closed her eyes, the vampire was staring off into the flames of the fireplace, brows heavy with thought.

XX

"You are not concentrating hard enough," Klauden said, and Hannah hid a smile in her hand. The vampire sat cross-legged on the wooden floor of the inn's back room, Elsbeth a mass of frustration as she lounged across from him, and Hannah watched the entire lesson from her comfortable perch with a glee she could hardly contain. Finally, someone else could annoy her friend, show him that his expectations of students were inflated impressions of greatness that none could achieve.

"I'm doing the best I can," Elsbeth complained, covering her face with both hands as she tried to focus. The lessons had been the girl's idea. After the debacle in the woods, an episode that Hannah's still purple face and shoulders recalled quite vividly, Elsbeth had told her father what she had done, how the men died after she just thought about it. Though Tarren had been reluctant to believe at first—he told Rory there had never been magic in his family—he had agreed with his daughter that having such a power without practical training was not only neglect, it was dangerous.

Rory told Hannah that the deciding moment had come when Elsbeth had asked her father what she was to do when she got mad at someone and they dropped dead. Originally, Tarren spoke to Rory about Hannah teaching his daughter, but after a lengthy discussion that had Rory leaping around in a verbal sparring match that left Hannah's problem a private matter, he agreed to let Hannah and Rory's new guest teach his daughter together.

Klauden had made an impression on the villagers, both men and women, with his foreign clothes and odd accent. Half the girls were smiling madly whenever he passed, and the rest were glaring at Elsbeth with undisguised jealousy. Hannah hadn't heard the specifics of their whispered conversations, but she knew Klauden was the topic of much discussion among the villagers.

Everyone wanted to know who the new guest was, where he had come from, and why he was staying with them. Though Rory had assured as many as he could that Klauden was a friend that Hannah had known from her childhood in the north, a magic user like she was, people were still skeptical of the stranger—half intrigued and half afraid of him.

Hannah saw how Klauden handled all of this with the ease of one accustomed to such a reaction, but she knew his lack of response was due more to his complete unawareness of the effect he had on people more so than any natural modesty. Among her people, Klauden had been one of the elite, but he'd never been noteworthy beyond his name and his position as promised to the First Daughter of Magnus van Kreeosk. Even Hannah had never noticed his appeal.

That had been before she was mortal, of course. Now, it took most of her considerable willpower to not think of his handsome face, his quiet calm, the soft press of his lips on hers, the comfort he represented—everything familiar and home. Watching him now as he worked with Elsbeth, this time having the girl focus on a small ball of clay—"Now squeeze, Elsbeth, focus your mind and picture the ball denting in where you press"—Hannah couldn't help but remember hours, days even, spent with him talking to her like that. *"Now, Hannah, focus—you can do better than that. Honestly, you're not even trying! Don't give me that face—do it again."* It was funny to see him in such a position again. He really was an excellent teacher, even with a terrible student like her.

Elsbeth was proving to be a similar challenge, and Hannah found herself liking the girl more because of it. It wasn't that she enjoyed watching Elsbeth struggle to get control of her power; it was that Hannah loved watching Klauden work. He was so intense, so totally focused on the prize that he never faltered.

If only I had half the intensity, Hannah mused, *I would not have had nearly so many problems in my life.*

Sitting propped up in the most comfortable chair the inn offered, Hannah was still acutely aware of her injuries, the aches and pains of numbing cold giving way to more specific ailments. Her face still hurt, her ribs were only just starting to heal, and her face was a kaleidoscope of color that even Solyn had not imagined in her most elaborate painting. Hannah had seen injuries before, had watched men and women heal from grave wounds, but she had never exactly been on the receiving end of such agony. *My mortal body is so weak,* she thought over and over again. *No wonder there is an entire school of magic devoted to keeping mortals healthy. It is amazing I am alive at all.*

Still, from what Rory had told her, these injuries were fairly minor in nature. He had seen men disemboweled on the battlefield, had watched what happens to limbs and skin when steel clashed and armies charged. Not that Hannah hadn't seen her own share of death and dismemberment—she had killed many people during her years as a vampire—but the suffering was something she had not witnessed. Her victims died, and usually died quickly and painlessly, well, most of the time. Even in the tournaments her father was famous for holding, there wasn't that much suffering to be seen. The victors lived; the others died. There had never been hours or days of lingering agony. Hannah couldn't understand why a body that was so very fragile could hold on to life with such desperation.

As she readjusted in the chair, pulling the new cloak tight around her elbows, Hannah suppressed a groan. She should probably get up and move around; her muscles would appreciate the change. Elsbeth glanced at her from her spot on the floor.

"Are you alright, Hannah?"

"Fine," Hannah assured her, squinting at the clay ball that lay on the floor between the girl and Klauden. It bore no marks yet, still as smooth as when Klauden had rolled it into shape an hour ago.

"Concentrate," the vampire instructed. "See the ball crushing," he repeated.

"I am," Elsbeth whined. "It's just not working." She flopped back on her elbows, blonde hair tossing as she shook her head, the tan line of her throat exposed. Hannah noted the way Klauden's lower jaw nibbled for a second at his upper lip, teeth a bit bigger than they ought to be. He saw Hannah watching him and looked quickly at the fireplace, mouth working silently.

"Maybe I don't have any magic, after all," Elsbeth was saying. "Maybe it was a fluke."

"It wasn't a fluke," Hannah told her. "I felt it, and trust me, power like that is not a mistake." She sat up some, trying to think of how Elsbeth could master her ability. "Look, you were angry the last time, right?"

Elsbeth nodded. "Furious."

"Exactly. Use that." She lowered her voice, reaching a soothing hypnotic sound. "Remember how you felt when those men were coming after me, recall precisely what you were thinking, feel the anger running through you as you picture their faces..." Hannah let her voice trail off, watching Elsbeth's face darken as she allowed herself to remember.

"They just kept hurting you," the girl whispered fiercely, "and they wouldn't stop. They just kept coming, and I just wanted them to leave you alone."

"And you made them stop, didn't you?" Hannah asked, her voice a low whisper.

"I made them stop," Elsbeth agreed.

"So make that ball stop now," Hannah suggested, redirecting Elsbeth's gaze to the floor before the fireplace. "Crush the life out of it. Destroy it."

Elsbeth focused, and Hannah felt the power leap out of the girl, the magic so nearby leaving a tingle in Hannah's fingertips, blood rushing to the surface of her skin. The clay ball seemed to expand for a second, then it crumpled, mashed flat to the floor with surprising force. Elsbeth took a second to realize what had happened, to acknowledge her success, but Hannah earned a pleased smile from Klauden for her own efforts, and she couldn't ignore the small fire that lit in her chest, how happy she was to have made him happy. The feeling passed quickly, Hannah managing to throw Solyn and her damn obsession into the back of her mind again, but it was getting harder and harder to distinguish between her own desires and Solyn's wishes.

"I did it!" Elsbeth shrieked, a broad grin lighting her face as she looked at Hannah. "You knew I could do it!"

Hannah nodded. "Just get mad. That's all."

Elsbeth scoffed, rubbing her hands along the rough wool of her green skirt as she sat up. "That's no trouble. I always get mad easy."

"Take care over the next few weeks, Elsbeth," Klauden suggested. "Until you master this power, you cannot get angry at anyone. You might hurt them unintentionally."

Elsbeth nodded, all serious now. Hannah could see that her words to her father had not been those of a daughter trying to wheedle her dad into giving her a coveted prize, but those of a concerned young woman who was more worried than she let on about this newfound ability. "I will mind my temper," she promised.

"Good," Klauden nodded at her, the deep bow of his head a sign that the lesson was ended for the day. "You did well."

Elsbeth smiled at him, the vampire's charm working on her as it always did, combining with her own flirtatious nature to make Hannah uncomfortably aware of a new emotion each time she watched them—jealousy. It was ridiculous, of course, the entire idea was preposterous. It wasn't like Klauden belonged to her. She was married! Sometimes, Hannah wondered how much of Solyn's personality had bled over into her own. After all, the slave girl had a penchant for wanting other men besides her husband.

<I hear you.>

Hannah closed her eyes, not watching as Elsbeth got to her feet, curtseying to Klauden as was the custom in the south. *<Not now,>* she told Solyn. *<Not ever again.>*

She opened her eyes in time to see Elsbeth nod deferentially to her before the girl turned and left the room. Hannah remained where she was, not willing to vacate this back room and fend off questions from the crowd that always seemed to occupy the inn these days.

Even her forge was no longer her own, the small area before the counter thronged with curious visitors who stopped by to wish her good health but really wanted to hear the story from her—an eyewitness account of the men who had tried to steal Elsbeth and how Hannah had bravely defended the girl. From the way some of them talked, Hannah sometimes thought they saw Elsbeth as some sort of princess, and she the brave heroine who had rescued her—or actually held off the men until the real rescuers could arrive—Rory and Klauden. As far as Hannah could tell, the elf had dealt with the victory slaps on the back and congratulatory winks with charm and grace, his usual ebullience making the people respect him even more.

Though, she thought with a wince, she hadn't seen much of her husband over the past few days. Since her attack, he had been occupied with the refugees, training the men daily, as well as setting up a patrolling guard in the surrounding woods. People were nervous, he told her, but they were growing more confident by the day as the village's defenses grew. The wall might even be completed in time, they said, though Hannah wondered how a mere eight foot wall of wood would keep out a determined army. Walls were more for the mental defense of the people, Rory had told her. They never actually kept the army out, but they let the defenders feel safe until the end, giving them the edge they needed to fight as best they could.

Hannah had even heard some people speculate that the army wouldn't come this way at all, that they were content with Salva and whatever spoils that city could offer them. *What can they possibly want with Severin?* Though she wanted to believe this, Rory had told her that it was only a matter of time, was always a matter of time. It may take a week, a month, maybe even a year, but the army would come this way eventually, and they had be as ready as they could be.

"You are concentrating very hard, chaivin."

Klauden's voice broke her reverie, and Hannah realized that the vampire had gained his feet, standing a few feet from her, hands clasped before him in the typical Klauden stance she recalled. He was taller than most of the people in Severin, she noted, and his head was quite close to the ceiling of this room, the low beams that supported the upper levels of the inn making this back room a bit cozier than the common room that lay beyond. Though it had a fireplace, this room was probably where the original owner had lived, since it had several doors—one to the kitchen next door with its multiple fireplaces and cooking utensils, one that led to the courtyard outside where Hannah had watched Rory train with the men, one that led directly into the common room itself, and one that led to a stairwell. Hannah knew that Tarren and his family lived in two rooms upstairs, rooms that were carefully sectioned off from the rest of the inn.

The mayor was friendly enough with his patrons downstairs, but he would not hazard any guests wandering into his family's rooms while they slept. Hannah knew the wall he had built across the second floor hallway was something different than other inns, but Tarren made up for it by devoting the entire third floor to rooms. There was even an attic that he rented in extremity, though Hannah had heard that it was unbearably hot in the summer and freezing cold in the winter. There was no fireplace up there, though it was surrounded by the stone blocks of the chimneys that ringed the building.

Hannah shook her head, thoughts of Tarren's inn drifting away when she looked at Klauden again. She couldn't get over how clean he was, how strong and imperial he looked standing there.

"Come," he said, gesturing with his hand. "We can go back out."

She shook her head. "I don't want to go back out there with them."

"Very well. Where then?"

Hannah thought. She really wanted to be outside, but it was too cold to stand out there for any length of time, especially wearing the thin shirt and Rory's vest that she had on, her wounds still too fresh for her old dress to be comfortable. Actually, Hannah found she liked the new style, the white shirt and black vest complimenting her bustline, and the new black skirt Rory had gotten from Mrs. Edgeton—her eldest had outgrown the garment, swelled as she was in pregnancy—was a welcome return to what Hannah had worn when she first met Rory. She liked skirts, she had decided. Maybe when she finally healed up, she might not revert to the dresses she had been wearing. Maybe a new wardrobe was in order.

Hannah had always had an eye for clothing; she had grown up putting on the latest designs her slaves laid out. Still, there was something freeing in changing her style of mortal dress. The dresses had been convenient, the style Solyn had worn when Klauden had first put her in this body. A return to skirts and sweaters would remind Hannah of who she had been when Rory had first seen her, and that would be a good thing.

"Hannah?"

"I'm sorry," she apologized, remembering Klauden standing there again. "I'm off in my own head today."

"That's nothing new," he observed. "Come." He held out his hand, and she decided that she could brave the cold after all.

Hannah struggled to her feet, stepping carefully on to the wooden floor with her securely tied boots. "Where are we going?"

The vampire shrugged. "Let us walk."

"Alright." She let him lead her out the side door, slipping past the line of men running drills in the courtyard and making his way toward the small street that ran behind the inn. Hannah looked for Rory but didn't see him. There were so many men in Severin now; the elf could be anywhere. The inn's yard was no longer big enough to house them all. Some had moved to the field behind John Sebring's house—it was level and without rocks—and others had moved to the town square between the general store and Joseph's inn—the only other inn in town. Though he owned the building, Joseph rented a small house next door to the inn, choosing to live alone instead of taking a room with his patrons. He was cordial to Hannah and Rory but had never quite warmed to them, probably resenting their connection to his only business rival, the man who had beaten him in the mayor's race of two years previous.

No doubt he's reveling in travelers now, Hannah thought, though she knew Joseph had taken in a number of refugees without payment. Everyone in town seemed to be doing their best to help out.

They made their way down the icy back street, their feet not leaving any marks in the slick snow. The movement made Hannah's sore muscles ache at first, but once they had walked in silence for a time, her body warmed to the exercise. Hannah felt Klauden watching her and turned to glance at him.

"What?"

"How are you today?" he asked, and she knew he wasn't referring to her injuries. Hannah had refused to let the vampire use his magic to heal her after that first night, afraid what might happen if she let him touch her again. It had been a long week, but she was feeling much better now; even walking was no longer such a trial. It was nice to be outside and alone, away from prying eyes and eager words. Even so, Klauden wasn't concerned with that—he wanted to know about Solyn.

"I'm fine." The answer was automatic, not really true, but something to say to fill the space.

"Hannah," he said, pausing to look at her.

"What?" she snapped, pausing to peer back at him.

"You still hear her in your head, yes?"

She nodded. "So?"

"So, that means she is still a separate entity in your body. This cannot continue."

"I don't know what you want me to do about it," she said, shaking her head and moving faster down the street. "I can't make her leave, and you can't make her sleep."

Klauden hurried to keep up with her. "She can't leave, Hannah. This is her body."

"I know, alright? What am I supposed to do: leave and let her have it?"

He shook his head. "You aren't even trying," he said. "You spend all of your energy in fighting her. You'll never win that way."

"You know that for a fact, then?"

"You know I don't. There aren't any records of anything like this that I've been able to find."

"And you looked?"

"Of course I looked. I've spent the greater part of the year researching you."

She stopped walking and stared at him for a long moment. He looked away.

"Have you." It was not a question. She sighed, shaking her head. She didn't know if the idea surprised her. Of course, Klauden would research her. It was his way. "So, what have you discovered?"

"In the history of our people, of all the records I can find, you are entirely unique."

"Gee, thanks," she muttered, toe kicking out at a chunk of ice nearby. It skittered into the back of a water barrel that stood next to the general store's back door.

Klauden touched her shoulder, tentative hands careful to avoid her bruises. It was the first time he had touched her since the night he carried her home, and Hannah tried not to flinch away. "You are," he repeated. "Two souls in one body—it has never happened before."

"Wonderful," she said. "I'm an object worthy of study, then, yes?" Klauden nodded at her, eyes curious. "I know that probably thrills you, Klauden, but all that it does for me is make my life more difficult."

"It doesn't have to be so difficult."

"Well, it is. I wish like hell things were different."

"So do I." Something about the way he said it made her stop her run of pity and consider his feelings. He seemed to be pondering something, and she had the dark thought that he was debating whether or not to tell her something or to continue with his secrets.

"Look," she began, distracting him, "I know you think that somehow blending with her is the answer—"

138

"It is the only answer."

"But I can't see how I can do that. Even if I thought it might work, how do I go about becoming one with a complete stranger?"

"Stop your fighting," he suggested. "Let go and allow Solyn to have some control."

"And what if she takes over, huh? What if your precious slave decides not to let me back in control?"

"Solyn is not like that," he said. "She would be willing to share."

"How do you know?"

"I know her."

"Do you? Do you really? What, you think after a few healing sessions in your bedroom you know everything there is to know about a person?" He seemed taken aback by that, understanding dawning as he realized just how much Hannah knew about him. "Oh, I've seen it," she said to his apprehensive face. "I've seen your bedroom. I've seen you lay her on your sheets. I've seen you feed from her." The last wasn't true; Solyn hadn't allowed Hannah to see quite so far into her memories, but Hannah had a sense that it was true, and the look on Klauden's face confirmed it.

"I never bit her."

"Congratulations," Hannah quipped. "You refrained from turning a battered slave. To be honest, I think turning her would have been a favor." She thought a moment, Solyn's emotions close to the surface of her own. Hannah knew the girl wanted to speak, but she was holding back for some reason. She liked to watch. She was always watching. "In fact, that was why she went to the castle in the first place. Right?" She paused, listening to the silence inside that confirmed her idea. "You wanted to find Matthew, to join him in his new life, but when you found him, he didn't want you."

Hannah stopped, eyes staring into a memory of Matthew laughing at her, his face lighting up in that new inhuman beauty as he actually laughed at her, at the very notion that he would want someone like her, his brother's leavings, when he had the chance at a new life. Hannah could feel Solyn's anguish, her black impotent rage, and then she was being taken away, everyone shoving and prodding her along, until the tall one came and showed her kindness. He had given her a new name, and he had always looked after her. So, when she had started to have trouble with the Kargin, with Vailen and his men, it was only natural to turn to

Klauden for help. And when she could see how starved he was, how much his betrothed ignored his needs, it was only natural to offer the only thing she had left—her blood. She knew he wouldn't turn her, some dim vestige of loyalty to that woman, Solyn thought, prevented him from doing that, but it was nice to just be with him, to bask in his presence, to revel in his soft touch as he swiped the blood from her wounds onto a finger and sucked it off, careful not to infect her with his bite.

"I would not turn her," Klauden said, and Hannah returned to the present with a jolt. *How odd,* she thought, *to think as Solyn when she was thinking of me.*

"Why not?" she asked, a bit breathless. "Tell me the truth, Klauden."

He shrugged. "It wouldn't be right," he said after a moment. "She was always hurt, and I didn't want to take advantage of her."

"But it was what she wanted."

"Was it? I didn't know."

"If you had known?"

He shrugged. "I don't know."

"Yes, you do. Tell me."

"No, I would not have turned her," he admitted. "Is that what you want to hear?"

"I want to hear the truth."

He nodded. "That is the truth."

"Why not?" she pressed.

He scowled, hands moving to tighten her cloak around her neck, long fingers tucking loose strands of her hair into place. Hannah tried to ignore the trail of his fingertips. "I do not intend to ever turn anyone," he said finally. "Didn't we make a promise to that effect?"

Hannah nodded. "We did."

He smiled softly at her. "We made a lot of promises that didn't stay true," he commented.

"I didn't mean to turn anyone," Hannah defended, thinking of the Elven healer in Kalford, how he had attacked her, had forced her into biting him in self-defense, then managed to escape before she could finish him off. "It was a mistake." She remembered how close the bond between them had been for the brief moments she had spent near him; she had felt his pain when she hurt him, had, in effect, hurt herself as she tried to knock him down and escape. She wondered if he had lived when her body had died. Probably not.

"The healer?" he asked. "I know that."

"He's probably dead anyway," she muttered.

Klauden nodded, seemed to consider something again, then cocked his head to one side. "Hannah, what do you think would have happened if things hadn't turned out this way?"

"What do you mean?"

"If you hadn't been captured that day, if you hadn't been turned into a mortal, if you hadn't come home, what would have become of you?"

"You mean of me and Rory," she said.

He shrugged. "Either way."

She sighed. "I don't know. Maybe we would have made it to Upsen. Rory would have gotten a job there same as he has here, and I probably would have stuck to blacksmithing. Seems mortals always have a great need for new weapons. Upsen's a big place, I hear. Maybe I would have been able to feed on travelers and the like."

"You would have been happy in such a life?"

She shrugged again. "I don't know."

"Are you happy here?"

She gave him a look. "I was until Solyn showed up again. I was perfectly fine."

"You like being mortal, then?"

"It's alright. It has its moments, I'll tell you that." Hannah paused, realizing that she was thinking of sex with Rory, knowing that she could never explain to Klauden what that meant to her. For her people, she had the feeling that sex was tied to the hunger, to blood, to feeding and mating. Her physical relationship with Rory was one of the best things about them, she thought sometimes, though they had good conversation as well. Since Solyn had returned, that relationship had been badly damaged, and Hannah tried not to wonder if it could ever be repaired. Certainly not if Solyn remained a factor, as Klauden kept insisting she would.

"Like what?" Klauden asked.

"Well, it's nice to breathe all the time," she said, saying the first thing she thought of.

"We breathe," he said.

"Yes, but you don't have to. You don't know what it's like to be out of breath, or breathless, or feel like you're never going to breathe again. It's a curse sometimes," she admitted, thinking of how she had felt when the man had kicked the wind out of her, "but there's something about taking a deep breath that makes the body feel so," she paused, stumbling for the word, "so ... alive."

"The bloodthirst makes one breathless."

"Yes, but it's not the same."

Klauden considered for a moment, then put both hands to his sides, closed his eyes, and inhaled deeply. He held his breath for far too long, and Hannah had to tap him to bring him back. "You went too long," she said. "Watch me. Like this." She took a deep breath, wincing as the pain in her ribs spiked, but let the air fill her lungs, relishing in the rush of life and vitality that filled her as she let the air out in a slow whoosh. She smiled, loving the feeling of needing the air, the cold air making her cheeks flush and her eyes glisten.

The vampire watched her breathe, face creasing in wonder as he tried to appreciate something Hannah knew he could never understand. He took a few deep breaths, but nothing had the same impact. After a while, he asked her what else made being mortal so wonderful. Hannah wondered if he was trying to make her defend her decision.

"Alright," she said, thinking. "Try stretching, then." She illustrated, moving from her toes up through her torso and ending with her arms over her head. "I can feel every muscle in this body," she explained. "It's almost like getting a small taste of blood, a tease that wakes the senses but doesn't satisfy them."

"I would not make a very good mortal," Klauden said suddenly, and Hannah peered at him. The vampire started walking again, a hand on her arm to keep her steady if she should slip. They passed a few more buildings before they reached the edge of the village proper, and Hannah didn't object when he led her into the woods. She thought she would be frightened to enter these trees again, but with Klauden at her side, she wasn't afraid at all. The sword belted at her waist made her feel even safer, too; Rory had insisted she never go anywhere without a decent weapon again.

"What makes you say that?" she asked after a time. "Why wouldn't you be a good mortal?"

He shrugged, shaking his head as the wind gusted, pushing fine blonde waves away from his cheeks, defining the angular features of nose and chin. *He is so different looking from the rest of the men down here,* Hannah thought. *He almost looks like an elf but without the ears.* That was what she had thought the first moment she laid eyes on Rory, that the elf rivaled Klauden in handsomeness. Now, of course, she would say that Rory was better looking, more suited to her tastes, but she couldn't deny that the vampire had a certain amount of charm for her eyes, charm that seemed to increase every time she looked on him.

"I think I would resent it," he said finally.

"Resent what?

"Time."

"Time?" she repeated. "What about time?"

He steered them toward a small stone outcropping that was mostly free of snow, easing her into a sitting position on the edge and standing before her. "I have been alive for one hundred and six years, chaivin," he began. "I have learned a great deal in that time, and I am still young by our standards. I will live several hundred years in the future. Had I been born mortal, I would have been dead many years ago. There just isn't enough time to learn all there is to know."

"There's more to life than learning," she said.

"I know that," he agreed. "But what kind of person could I be if I died before I was even halfway complete?"

"Mortals are entirely different from us, Klauden. They don't spend so many years studying as children. Everything is rushed. They marry young, they build families, and they live their lives because they know their time is limited." She sniffed, nose beginning to run in the cold. She wiped it with a hand. "Think of Solyn," she suggested. "She's only twenty-four, and yet she's lived a great deal in her life. When I was twenty-four, I was barely out of Essentials."

"Nor I," he agreed, eyes creasing in consternation. "I suppose it just seems like a waste."

"Solyn is a waste?"

"No, not her." He paused, trying to gather his thoughts. Hannah remembered dozens of other times when they had spoken like this, theorizing and philosophizing, he always trying to break down her views with his flowery words, she always sticking to her position with dogged single-mindedness, certain about things as she always had been. Hannah rarely changed her mind. Once she had an idea of something, she tended to keep it that way. Klauden was always improving on his theories, though, each new text he read making him redefine and re-evaluate his views. "It just seems foolish to let such wonderful creatures die so soon."

"Mortals are wonderful creatures?"

"Of course, they are. Everything about them is intoxicating," he said, stepping forward to take a deep breath of her. "They smell so good, and their blood is so strong. A walking temptation of power and delight. It is a wonder that they live as long as they do, I suppose."

Hannah could see the effect her mortal body was having on the vampire, knew that her closeness was calling to him, that her blood was running very close under her skin, and she pushed herself off the rock, landing on unsteady feet in the snow. One foot slipped a bit, and Klauden was there, an arm around her to keep her steady, lifting her off the ground, his teeth long and frightening, his face alien and distant, the bloodlust taking him over.

"Klauden," she said loudly, hoping to bring him back to the moment. "Klauden." When she saw his face begin to clear, humanity coming back into those eyes, she asked, "How long has it been since you fed?"

The vampire let her go, setting her on the ground and moving a few feet away from her. "I am fine."

"You're not fine," she said. "You're starving."

"It is fine," he repeated.

She sighed, shaking her head at him. "You need to feed," she insisted.

"I will manage."

"No," she ordered. "You should go feed now."

"You show such concern for my well-being, chaivin. It warms my spirit." He gave her a very un-Klaudenlike grin, and she felt something in her respond to the charm. Hannah knew that this was Klauden, her old friend, but she suddenly realized that he was also a vampire, a blood-drinking creature that could kill her without any effort at all. It was so easy to fall into old habits with him that she forgot just how dangerous a vampire could be. She took a few steps away from him.

"I just want to see you well," she whispered, trying to ignore the growing emotion inside her chest. She knew it was fear, and it was wrong, unnatural to fear Klauden.

"I will not harm you," he whispered, head cocking as he stared at her. "You need not fear me."

"I know," Hannah said. "I know that, believe me, I do, but this body knows a little something about hungry vampires, and it wants nothing more than to be very far away from you."

"Really?" he asked, licking his lips a bit as he stared long and hard at her. "You forget, chaivin, that I know how to read the body of a mortal."

Hannah frowned, knowing that he spoke the truth. She hadn't been entirely honest with him, though. The truth was that the sight of him, face cold and hungry and somehow desperate, made her ache with the need to touch him, to sate him, to somehow ease the pain she could feel radiating out from him in waves.

<*Dammit, Solyn! Stop doing that! He's not some lost waif who needs tending!*>

<*I could help him,*> the slave girl said. <*Let me help him.*>

<*No way,*> Hannah thought.

<*But it would be so nice,*> Solyn insisted. <*It feels so good.*> The slave tried to submerge Hannah in a memory then, an image that started with the touch of Klauden's finger running along her shoulder blades. Hannah slapped herself hard across the face, and suddenly she was alone, standing in the snow a few feet from the vampire.

"No," she whispered.

He stood a bit straighter. "I see."

"You don't see," she said. "I don't know why you're really here, but if you've somehow come for me, you're wrong."

"Why do you say such things to me? I came to help you."

"Did you? Then why do you keep trying to," she stumbled a bit, then forged on, "to seduce me somehow? You know I'm with Rory. We're married!"

"Stop saying that," he retorted. "You aren't properly married, and you know it."

"I love him."

"So you say, but I can sense what that body wants, Hannah, and it is not entirely certain of that."

She narrowed her eyes at his use of her name for once. "Well, I am."

He nodded. "As you say." He gave her an appraising look. "You cannot conquer her. It will not work."

"You don't know that. Not for sure."

He shrugged. "True, but all of my research suggests that the only solution is a compromise."

"There will be no compromise," Hannah declared.

"As you wish," he repeated, hands clasping before his chest in the customary pose for departure among equals.

"Go," she ordered him. "Go feed on someone deserving. Don't come back until you've fed."

"Someone deserving? What a conscience you've developed, chaivin."

"I mean it."

"I know. Don't worry. I will not feed on anyone you know."

"Good."

He paused, on the verge of leaving, but something made him try. "Allow me to walk you back to safety."

"I will be fine," Hannah assured him, patting the sword on her hip. "Besides, it's the middle of the day."

"Still, I promised the elf—"

"Don't use Rory as an excuse to stay by me," Hannah warned. "Go."

The vampire turned away, disappearing into the trees abruptly. Hannah sat back down, letting the air fill her lungs and chest a few times before she felt steady enough to walk back to town.

It was strange to think of Klauden as a threat. It felt all wrong, but she knew him well enough to see the signs. He was hungry, and hungry vampires did foolish things sometimes. Hadn't she killed three men in one night once out of desperate hunger? She could not give Klauden the chance to do something he would regret. That she would regret.

Hannah stood, tugging her cloak tighter and gripping her sword hilt. The magic wasn't complete, not yet, but it was a good blade, and it would serve her well in a fight. She hadn't trained with it in a while, though. Maybe now was the time to train more with Rory. She set off into the woods to find him.

XXI

Hannah found Rory in the field behind John Sebring's farm. The elf was taking a break, face red and sweaty as she approached, swords belted across his hips as he took a swig of water, dumping some over his face and flipping his wet hair back over his shoulders, his body steaming slightly in the cool air. Hannah stared at him for a moment, a small glow in her belly as she appreciated the fine lines of cheek and shoulder. And he was hers, her husband.

Something of her thoughts must have shown on her face, for he gave her a crooked grin as she approached, an eyebrow quirking in interest. "Hannah," he greeted. "What brings you this way?"

She shrugged, hands reaching for the sword at her hip. "I thought I might get some practice with this."

He gave her a critical once over, taking in the shape of her face, then her shoulders. "Are you ready for that?"

"I am."

He nodded. "Sounds good." He took another sip, pushing his hair behind his ears. Hannah had the odd thought that he looked a bit like a drowned rat with his hair all slicked back like that, his long ears poking out through the mess. He was so different from the men he trained. Hannah glanced at them.

There were two groups of ten milling about, one getting in line to run drills as the man on the end—Hannah recognized Fergus, the man who had tried to stab Rory a few weeks ago—barking orders, the other spread out along the edge of the field, resting and stretching as they took a break. Hannah walked to the tree stump that held the men's cloaks and laid hers on top. It was cold without the extra protection, but the cloak would impede her progress. Besides, the exercise would keep her warm soon enough. She made her way back to Rory and took a sip of the water he offered, then followed him as he began getting his ten men back in line. Hannah took up a position near the end, boots taking a moment to stamp out a new line in the snow so she wouldn't slip and fall.

When everyone was back in the line, Rory took his place before them, bowing as was his custom. Hannah saw that some of the men had already unsheathed their swords; these were the ones who were still new to the weapon, she observed. They couldn't draw them fast enough, and so were now training with them always out.

"Huh!" Rory's guttural noise signaled the start, and the elf drew both swords in a flash, blades swinging around in a double arc before halting in a crossed position before his chest. Hannah drew her own sword, the simply carved hilt glowing in the sunlight, swinging the one blade across her chest in an arc and bringing it up in a salute, eyes staring beyond the craftsmanship of the would-be magical weapon. She heard the clang of metal as some of the less skilled swordsmen banged their weapons together when they reached the point across their chests. She smirked, knowing that even if she had brought Klauden's sword with her, she had enough skill to keep her blades from smacking each other.

Rory continued with another shout, this time stepping forward and to the right, swords slashing both before and behind him in a smooth figure eight. Hannah mimicked the right side, feeling the tightness in her arm as she swung the blade forward and backward, ending with it held taut before her. *It's so good to train again,* she thought. The men were now in a line behind her, and she was very aware of the blade hovering a foot away from her back. *Just how green are these recruits?*

With another signal, Rory turned again to the right, this time circling the blades up and over his head, stepping in a twist that had him facing the opposite direction. The men were a bit less organized for this move, and it took them some time to reorient the line. The elf frowned, then motioned for Hannah to take position on the opposite side of the line so the men had examples in both directions. She saw the expression of some of the men as she took up her new position, the way they rolled their eyes or scowled at the thought of a woman leading their training sessions. This group was mostly refugees; they hadn't heard much of Rory's wife, the magic user who could wield blades as well as she made them.

Hannah straightened her shoulders, then with a sudden thought, stepped quickly to the tree which served as a makeshift weapons rack to collect another short sword. Since the tournament, they had both trained with two weapons when possible. She found one of a decent weight, then hopped back into line. Rory had waited for her to begin. When she had the new sword belted around her waist and had cleared a decent space on the snowy ground, she nodded to the elf.

"Hah!" he shouted, then she was stepping to the right again, arms drawing the blades in a smooth motion and whipping them back and front in sharp jabs before settling into the second position, blades crossed before her chest, right foot slightly in front in preparation for the next step. The training exercise was ingrained in her now. After a year of living with Rory, it was hard not to know this most basic of his exercises, the first one he ran through each morning in the yard behind their house. Even during their months on the road, the elf had always maintained his morning ritual, and Hannah had always enjoyed sharing in the practice. She could do most of these movements in her sleep.

That was the idea, of course. All of this training was about muscle memory, about getting the body to react in a certain way without thinking. Hannah had thought a lot about muscle memory over the last year, wondering if all of this training would stay with her if she ever returned to her body. It was a silly thought, she knew, since her body was destroyed, but she still wondered. She could still remember the moves she had done when she had thrown her daggers, though the slave's arms hadn't been built for that activity then. Hannah had worked on it, but it seemed that Solyn's talent lay with short swords, and so Hannah had obliged the body.

Stepping through the moves over the next hour, aware of the flawless execution that would earn the respect of the new recruits, Hannah also appreciated the chance to not think. It wasn't that she had to focus all of her will on remembering the moves; it was more like her body moved on its own and she didn't have to think.

The emptiness was a relief.

Emptiness.

Hannah finished the last step, swords slipping back into the sheaths with practiced ease, feet solidly planted beneath her, knees bent and ready to react to anything. She paused, breath whistling a bit through her chest as her heart pumped madly, waiting for something, anything to remind her of the constant presence within.

Nothing. Silence.

She could have screamed with relief.

Rory was congratulating the men, voice warm with praise as he sent them on their way. Hannah had seen him do this before too. After a long practice, the elf was careful to have the men leave on a high note. He would beat them into submission again the next morning. Hannah waited for the last of the men to leave, working through a few more practice routines as Rory spoke with Fergus for a moment, the two heads close together as they compared observations on the progress of the men.

It was late afternoon before she and Rory headed out of the field, and the sun was low on the horizon. Hannah had put on her cloak again, but she was soaked with sweat, and the extra material wasn't doing much to keep her warm. Rory saw the shiver run through her and put an arm around her shoulders, careful of her bruises as he pulled her close. They walked slowly, taking comfort in one another's company as they hadn't done in many months. Neither spoke, each enjoying the silence as they walked.

When they reached the house, Rory opened the door, glanced inside warily, then let Hannah walk in first, a rare gesture of chivalry that was not lost on Hannah. He always took such care for her safety; it was a relief to know that he believed in her ability to take care of herself should some stranger lurk in the house.

As she heard the door shut behind them, Hannah wondered if other couples behaved as they did, if having faith each other's abilities was a rare thing or the thing that made relationships work. She wished suddenly that she had a friend with whom she could talk about such things, someone who would know if she and Rory were so very different from other people. She leaned against the wall to untie her boots as Rory made his way to the fireplace to restore the flames. She watched him pile the tinder into a feasible stack, then took a chance and reached out with her magic. No words this time, just a small fierce desire for fire in the fireplace, and she felt the energy echo out of her in a small wave, Rory jerking his fingers back as the pile lit, then tossing a grin over his shoulder at her as he reached for the poker to shove the flame underneath the bigger logs.

"I see you've got some of your magic back."

She nodded, plopping the second boot onto the floor and walking over the fireplace to warm her hands. "I suppose near death experiences will do that to a person. It's different now, but it still works."

"I'm glad."

They stood in silence for a moment before the flames, each relishing the heat and light from the flames. Hannah ran a hand through her sweat-tangled hair, and Rory reached out to unbraid it.

"We could wash," he breathed, stepping closer to her, "at the inn."

"We could," she agreed, her hands reaching out to touch him, fingers pressing hard against his chest as they hadn't in many long weeks. His shirt was still damp, the material cold. "You must be freezing," she murmured, reaching to pull the shirt over his head. He let her, then reached for the vest she wore.

"This is soaked," he said, beginning to unfasten the buttons. Hannah was very aware of the small shifts in the material as he unhooked the vest. She smiled shyly at him, a slow hand tracing the curve of his shoulder in the firelight.

He finished with the vest and pushed it slowly off her shoulders, careful of the bruises there. When he reached for her shirt, he paused, glancing around the room.

"Where is he?" he whispered, eyes lingering on the door.

Hannah had to think a moment before she realized who he was referring to. "Oh," she breathed. "He's out. Feeding, I think."

The elf nodded, then backed away from her. For a moment, Hannah thought he might be rejecting her, but he only stepped to the door and barred it before taking confident strides in her direction.

She smiled again at him, this time in invitation, and he didn't pretend to misunderstand.

XXII

Solyn waited until Hannah was involved in a particularly private moment to intrude, the slave speaking quite clearly in her mind.

<You do realize that Klauden would be much better at this.>

Hannah jerked upright, the mouth that had been lingering on the sensitive area of her husband's collarbone curling into a frustrated snarl, hands fisting at her sides. Rory's hands on her hips grew tighter as he stared up at her, wariness crossing his features.

<He would not!> Hannah thought angrily at her. Then, after realizing exactly what the slave had suggested, couldn't resist a laugh. *<In fact,>* she added, *<he would have no idea what he was doing.>*

Hannah moved her hips, feeling Rory's response as she tried to recapture the excitement of the previous moment. The elf moaned, a low sound that always pleased her, and she redoubled her efforts.

<Now Rory,> she added, just in case Solyn hadn't gotten her point, *<knows exactly what I like.>*

<You don't even know what you like.>

Hannah closed her eyes, trying to ignore the girl, focusing instead on the small twinges of fire that ran through her limbs. The hands on her hips slipped upward, tugging her down to him, then she was kissing him, warm mouths together, and she was happy.

This moment, this closeness, this was hers. Completely and utterly hers.

<Yes,> she thought, *<this is what I want.>*

<It's not what I want.>

The voice made Hannah pause again, and this time, Rory did not dismiss the sudden change in her. She watched his eyes open wider as her hands tightened on his shoulders, lips a few inches apart, and then she was falling inside herself, somehow shoved to the side. Rory's face faded from immediate view, and Hannah disappeared into deep darkness. She tried to scream, to warn Rory that something was happening, that she was being controlled, but the elf's face in her memory remained impassive, curious at her movement but not alarmed, not concerned as he would be if he understood what was happening to her.

<*Until I get what I want,*> Solyn whispered as Hannah retreated, <*I will sate myself with this.*>

Hannah's silent scream echoed off the walls in her mind, but no one heard.

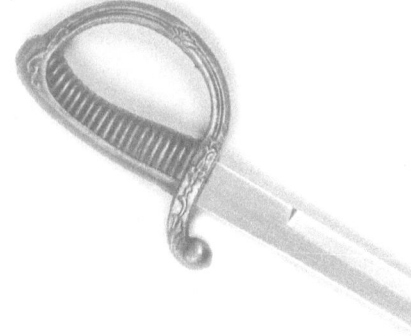

XXIII

When Hannah opened her eyes, she was sitting on the floor, bare bottom cold against the wooden floorboards and aching in a way that suggested her movement there had not been gentle. Rory was standing over her, hands fisted and held shaking at his sides, his face red and betrayed.

<Have your elf, then,> Solyn snapped, and Hannah wondered what the hell she had missed. Glancing around, she determined that not much time had passed.

"Rory," she said, shaking her head and getting to her feet.

He stared at her, breathing hard, part of him still hard for her as he stood naked before her. "It's you again." He nodded. "Good."

"She pushed me back," Hannah said, blinking to clear the aftereffects from her mind. She flexed her hands, wiping her face as she readjusted to control.

"Is this the first time?"

She nodded, overcome by a sudden wave of nausea. "I hear her a lot, but she's never done that." She gulped hard, regaining her composure.

"Good." He sighed then, an angry tic in his jaw as he looked past her to the fireplace.

"Rory," she tried again. "I'm sorry."

"There's nothing to be sorry about," he replied, but the cold look on his face didn't fade when he looked down at her.

"Yes, there is," she snapped, but instead of focusing on him, she turned to the table. *If Solyn wants to fight back,* Hannah thought bitterly, *I am willing.* But if the girl thought she could sneak in and steal Hannah's body whenever she wanted, or if she could just burst in on private moments like that, that was a step too far.

If it hadn't been her own body she was fighting, Hannah would have followed her impulse to destroy the creature who would dare to defile her in this way, to steal precious moments with Rory and pervert them like this.

But it wasn't as if she could hit herself or beat herself up.

No, that wasn't the answer. Scanning the table for what she sought, Hannah had already decided on another route to victory. Her eye caught on one of Rory's knives, and she grabbed it.

She heard the elf's choked cry as she raised the dagger to her neck, but he was silent when she dragged the long rope of Solyn's hair across the blade, severing the long strands to land in a silent hump on the floor.

Solyn's shrieks were deafening, but Hannah ignored them, knife sawing back and forth as she cut her hair just above the nape of her neck. By the time Rory approached and wordlessly helped even out the chunks in the back of her head with a steady hand, Solyn's yells had subsided to a defeated sob. Hannah waited until the pile of hair on the floor contained most of what Solyn had considered her most important asset before speaking.

<If you ever take over again,> she promised, *<I will do more than just cut some of your pretty hair.>*

<Alright! I give in!>

<Promise me,> Hannah prompted. *<Swear to it.>*

The slave girl consented, fading away from Hannah's consciousness with another jab of fierce resentment, then Hannah stood before Rory, hair shorn and body goose bumped in the chill air. He looked at her closely, eyes studying her own, then pushed a lock of stray hair behind her ear. It slid forward into her eyes again.

"Is that it?"

"It won't happen again," Hannah swore. "I made her promise."

"Will she keep it?"

Hannah shrugged. "I hope so." She glanced nervously at him. He wasn't angry anymore, she saw with relief. She knew he had never been angry with her, not really, but it was still frustrating to see how badly timed Solyn's little appearance was. "I'm sorry," she whispered again.

"It's alright," he said, hands reaching out to wrap around her back. "Come here."

Hannah buried her face on his shoulder, loving the feel of his body near hers, the never-ending warmth of his skin even in the coldest days. She had teased him about that during their journey south, claiming he had some sort of magical heat spell at work on him all the time. Hannah was always cold.

The elf rubbed her upper arms briskly, then moved to rub the newly bare space between her shoulder blades. His hands moved upward, skittering across the sensitive skin of her bare neck, then buried themselves in her hair, fingers wiggling against her scalp and working through the few remaining snarls. Hannah lifted her head, allowing him to push the front part of her hair behind her ears again. It stayed this time, but Hannah had the idea that hair in her face might be a problem for a time.

"You know," Rory mused, hands drifting from her hair to her hips again, "I always cut my hair before a big battle."

"You did?" Hannah's own hands lingered in the neutral zone of Rory's hips, uncertain if the moment was still salvageable.

He nodded. "Most soldiers did."

"Why?"

"Long hair is a liability in a battle. It gets in the face and blocks sight. I was toying with the idea of cutting it soon, before the army gets here, but," he paused, fingering the hairline that now matched her jaw, "maybe now I won't. People might think we're trying to match or something."

Hannah moved her hands to touch Rory's hair, the dark strands longer now than when they had met, brushing up against his collarbone and curling behind his ears. "I like your hair," she said. "Don't cut it."

He turned her chin this way and that in the firelight, looking at her new profile. "I like your hair," he repeated. "It suits you this way."

"It does suit me this way," Hannah agreed, then peered at him. She was wondering something and didn't know how to ask.

"What?"

"How did you know?"

"Know what?"

"That it wasn't me."

"Oh," he paused, considering. After a moment, he tapped her cheek, whispering, "Your eyes."

"What about my eyes?"

"They change color, Hannah. When she's near, they turn blue-green. When she's very near, they turn blue."

Hannah raised a hand to her face. *Is that true? Am I so transparent?* "Really?"

The elf nodded. "I knew she was talking to you at first, but that happens all the time now, so I didn't think it mattered, but when they turned blue completely, I knew you were gone altogether."

"How often does it happen?" she whispered.

"More often than you think," he admitted. "In fact, this afternoon was the first time I've seen you entirely yourself in a very long time."

"Is she there now?" she asked. "Is she in my eyes?" Hannah widened her eyes at him, staring intently.

The elf chuckled a bit. "Easy, Hannah. Yes, she's there, but on the edges only. You've pushed her far away, but she's still there."

"She's always there," Hannah muttered, hands falling away from his body to her own.

"Not always," he whispered, reaching to pull her close again. He kissed her softly, warm hands soothing. When they parted, he whispered, "She will not always be between us."

"What if she is?" Hannah whispered back, voicing her deepest fear.

"She won't be," the elf insisted. "I know it."

"But how can you be so sure?"

Before Rory could answer, there was a soft knock on the door, and Rory headed for his discarded clothes strewn about the room. "Just a moment," he said loudly, handing Hannah her shirt as he stepped into his pants. He helped her with the buttons on the vest as she adjusted her skirt. Before he turned to answer the door, however, he kissed her again, taking his time with it, and Hannah wished violently that they were alone again. She was still fixing the angle of her skirt when the elf tugged his shirt over his head and removed the door bar.

When Klauden stepped into the room, he took in the elf's untucked shirt, the bedclothes in disarray, and then stopped at Hannah's hair.

"What have you done to yourself now?" he asked, head shaking in disbelief.

XXIV

Hannah was in her forge the next day, hands carefully carving the last details of the final rune into the magical sword Rory had gotten her months before. Klauden sat on an upside down water barrel beside her, careful eyes measuring each fraction of the line she pounded into the blade. His presence was unexpected, but not unnerving; since their encounter in the woods the day before, Klauden had not questioned her intentions, and she had not mentioned his feeding habits.

Rory had left earlier than usual, leaving her alone with the vampire, so she had allowed him to come to the forge, knowing that she had to finish the damn sword soon, or it would never get done. Besides, she reminded herself, as long as he stayed out of her light and didn't give her any of those new hungry looks, she didn't mind his company so much. He helped her focus, his presence reminding her of childhood lessons learned through dedication and perseverance.

She was about to strike the small chisel to make yet another mark in the blade when the vampire's hand darted out to catch hers.

"Not there, chaivin," he said. "Look." Hannah wondered why he had suddenly gotten so accustomed to calling her that. Back home, he had only used the endearment on special occasions; lately it seemed he never called her anything else. It was strange, a reminder of home and their history together that she didn't always appreciate.

Hannah sniffed, moving the chisel away from the metal, and looked. She brushed at the blade with the bundle of leather cloths to smooth away the residue of her last few taps, then replaced the chisel tip, hammer in her other hand. "It goes here."

He shook his head. "You're not looking."

Hannah scowled at him, pulling away from her work, and his hand, to stand up straighter. She rubbed her face with the back of a dirty hand, glancing over at the open spellbook lying in the light of the back door. A lock of hair fell into her eyes, and she brushed it behind an ear. Short hair could definitely be annoying. She looked from the image of the ice rune to the almost completed carving in the blade and back again. *The line should curve down another two notches,* she thought, *then loop back up and around. What is he talking about?*

"I am looking," she snapped at him. "It goes here and then around." She illustrated her intentions with a slow arc of the chisel, showing him where the lines ought to be.

He shook his head, then squinted at her. "Solyn," he said abruptly, "let her see."

"Don't talk to her," Hannah snapped, her anger at the slave girl still very close under her skin. "She's not even here now."

"She is," he contradicted gently. "She's so near you can't even sense her." Hannah cocked her head, reluctantly reaching out for the slave as she had done in the past. Solyn had been distant since the haircutting incident of the previous evening. Hannah almost hoped that she might be quelled into silence for good. *Maybe Klauden is wrong about his blending theory,* she thought, *and a good threat is all the slave needed to disappear.*

Hannah waited, but nothing happened. "She's gone," she repeated. "I'm telling you, she's not here."

Klauden's long finger reached out to touch her sweaty face, the tip running from her chin, down the line of her neck and pausing over the delicate shape of her collarbone. Slow fire blossomed in her skin, and Hannah suddenly wanted more, wanted that finger to keep moving more than anything.

"What?" she whispered, eyes closing in a half swoon of delight.

"Solyn," Klauden said again, "I said to let her see."

Then Hannah's mouth was speaking, but the words weren't hers. "Come, come, Klauden. You don't have to be so serious all the time."

The finger that had raised such desire in her seconds before was joined by the rest of his hand, but instead of continuing with his teasing—*Wait,* Hannah thought frantically, *Klauden is teasing?*—Klauden wrapped his hand around her throat. The gesture was slow, deliberate, and thoroughly clear in its meaning. "I said," he repeated again, "to let her see."

The slave girl sighed angrily, a small huff of breath sneaking out beyond his hand. He had not tightened his grip yet, but Solyn knew he would. "Fine," she conceded, "but I'll be back."

"I shall count the days."

Hannah felt the girl recede, and her mouth was hers again. "What?" she repeated, though this time, anger fueled her voice instead of desire. "Malfek, Klauden. How could you?"

The vampire removed his hand from her neck, nodding instead to the blade. "Come, chaivin," he said, as though nothing had happened. "She will not trouble you again."

"No," she said. "What was that all about?"

He frowned at her, then shrugged. "She likes to play games sometimes."

"Play games?" Hannah repeated. "You call taking over my body playing games?"

"It's not important," the vampire snapped. He gestured to the blade. "Can you see it now?"

Sighing angrily, Hannah stared at the blade lying on her anvil. She wanted to ask him what he meant, to continue this conversation, but she knew he wouldn't let her, not until the task was finished. Klauden had always been single-minded. She looked at the image in the book, then back at the blade again, trying to see where the rest of the line belonged. The shapes were distorted in her eyes, each covering and recovering the other. Hannah blinked hard, trying to get the two images to quit blurring in her mind. She put the backs of her hands to her eyes, pushing slightly against her eyelids and causing an explosion of colors. When her vision returned, she finally saw the rune clearly.

With a look at Klauden that promised a respite, but not an end to this discussion, she grabbed the chisel and hammer again, eager to work while she could. She wiped her sweaty brow with the back of her hand, tucking an errant strand of hair behind her ear, where it promptly slipped out and fell in front of her face again. Hannah decided she could see past it and rested the chisel against the blade again, picturing how the rest of the rune would look.

The only sound for the next few minutes was the high-pitched ding of the hammer as it forced the chisel into the blade, her hands steady and certain as she engraved the last loop. When it was done, she let out a breath she hadn't been aware of holding, then wiped the blade with the bundle of rags to check the design. She picked up the sword, the pommel comfortable in her hand, flipping it upright in the sunlight streaming through the window. The runes flickered in the light, the line of them suddenly illuminating with a blue glow and a hiss. Hannah watched as they flared brightly, then faded to a light blue. She felt the magic of the blade thrum up her hand and into her wrist. The weapon was suddenly much lighter. She swung it a few times, getting used to the ease with which she could wield it.

"Excellent," she whispered. She decided a small test was in order despite the evidence of the glow and gently tapped the tip of the sword against the doorframe. There was a small hiss, the runes lit up, and the area surrounding the tip began to frost over, a smooth sheen of ice coating a small circle that quickly engulfed the frame and spilled over onto the wall. Hannah pulled the sword away, noting the fade of the runes as she did. The ice patch on the wall did not fade but remained a white smear.

She reached out with her other hand to touch the ice, watched as it melted beneath the heat of her fingertip, and smiled when the edges began to disappear slowly, small drips of cold water running down the wall.

"Perfect," she said, turning to Klauden. It galled her to admit it, but without his intervention, she likely would have been fighting with the rune for much longer. She bowed formally, sword held upright before her face as Rory had taught her. "I thank you."

"No need," he said, nodding at her. "May I see it?"

"Sure." She handed him the sword. He took it awkwardly, not knowing what to do with the sharp edges as he studied the runes she had carved.

"Decent work," he observed. He looked up at her. "You only had trouble with the last one?"

Hannah nodded. "I couldn't see it," she said.

"Solyn wouldn't let you finish it," he corrected.

"No," Hannah argued. "I just had some trouble with the bottom."

He peered closely at the rune again, then gave her a pointed look. "She was trying to carve a flower," he said.

He leaned back on the barrel, hands clasping before his chest. "What did she do?"

"She took over!" Hannah explained angrily, hands waving in the air as her frustration grew. "She pushed me away completely, and during a very—" She broke off, realizing what she was about to say and to whom. Her arms fell to her sides, hands grasping the twin pommels she now carried. "It was a bad time."

"So you cut her hair to get back at her," he mused.

"I had to do something."

He reached out to touch her hair, but she pulled away from him, afraid of what that touch might do to her. "She had beautiful hair," he whispered.

"Well, it's not her hair, now, is it? It's mine." Hannah moved farther away from him abruptly, pacing in the small space between the forge and the counter.

"It belongs to both of you," he commented.

"I don't want to share it," she snapped, aware that this queer sense of double intentions was going to drive her mad. She wanted nothing more than to take the few steps to where the vampire sat and throw herself into his arms, and yet she knew, she knew that she wanted nothing of the sort. In fact, the only thing Hannah wanted was to be free of this lustful slave girl that inhabited her body. She put a hand to her head, willing the confusion to end. "In fact, I don't want to share anything with her!" She was angry then, suddenly, violently angry at the events of the last few months, and even more so at the one who had done this to her. She whirled on Klauden. "How could you do this to me?"

Klauden frowned at her, eyebrows arching in confusion. "Do what?"

"You put me in this stupid mortal body! You knew she was still in here!"

He shrugged. "I didn't know she would wake up."

Something about his tone, the offhand way he replied, as if the presence of the slave girl now awake in her body was nothing worth mentioning, or at the very least, was no fault of his, made her want to strike him. Before she had made a conscious decision, both blades were in her hands as she faced him. "I don't believe you!" she shouted, wondering what she intended to do with the weapons.

Klauden leaped to his feet, hands before his chest in a gesture of peace. "Hannah!"

"No! You're way too happy about this whole situation," she accused him, advancing on him with both swords. "This suits you just fine, doesn't it?"

"Now, Hannah, think about what you are doing," Klauden said, standing still before the counter.

Hannah took another step toward him, ranting, "Me in this body that you find so intriguing, with the slave that you found irresistible, driving a wedge between me and Rory, pushing me right toward you!" She paused, hands shaking a bit as she contemplated the future.

Klauden stood perfectly still, but she knew how fast that body could move, how easily he could outmaneuver her.

She took a deep breath, willing her hands to steady. *What am I going to do? Try to kill Klauden?* Even if the idea wasn't ridiculous, it was pointless. She could no more defeat the vampire in this body than she could hold off the entire army. She sheathed her swords violently, the weakness of this mortal frame more degrading than ever before. She sighed heavily, the adrenaline leaving her limbs heavy with unspent nerves. She stepped back from him, leaning against the wall as she closed her eyes.

When she opened them, the vampire was staring at her, face impassive as he waited for her to speak, but she could still feel that undeniable tug that was Solyn, the slave girl pushing her inexorably toward him. "Let me tell you something, Klauden," she whispered, shaking her head. "Even if you succeed, even if this little plot of yours works out the way you want, I hope you realize that it won't be me." She glared at him. "I would not be with you."

"That's a lie," he whispered, and there was something new in his voice now. Hannah wondered if he finally getting angry with her.

"Is it?" she asked, chuckling a bit. "The only reason I want you now is because of her. It's all because of her. Do you understand?"

He was in front of her instantly, moving so quickly that she couldn't get out of his way, then he was staring at her, face inches away from her own, eyes darkening as he breathed deep of her scent. Hannah knew he was thinking of blood, of soft mortal skin and delicate mortal veins, and how she could sate him, could fill him, could soothe the burning inside him. What bothered her was that not only could she imagine what he felt, but she was also aware of this body's reaction to him. He was inhuman in his beauty, his eyes arresting and strange, and she wanted to fall into him, to surrender to his strength, to give in to that magnetism that she knew belonged to all vampires.

He could do this to anyone, she thought absently. *This is how he gets his victims to come willingly.*

"Deny it all you like, chaivin," he whispered, words soft as he moved closer, lips nearly brushing hers, "but I know you. It doesn't matter what body you are in. Your soul knows me and knows where it belongs."

"I belong with Rory," she answered levelly, refusing to look away from him. "At least he doesn't use charms to get my attention."

"This isn't a charm, chaivin."

"No, but it's something. You're doing something to me, to her, to get me to give in to you. Do you think I can't tell? I used to hunt victims, too, you know. This is just another version of that, no matter what you call it."

He pulled away from her. "You think I hunt you?"

"Don't you?"

He sighed, hands fisting at his sides. "You are the most frustrating person I've ever met."

"You haven't met that many people," she retorted.

"I've met enough," he said. He looked around her shop, quickly jumping up and over the counter in a flurry of red robes and blonde hair to stand in the customer area out front. He moved to the wall, fingering an axe in contemplation. Hannah took the moment to calm her pounding heart. "What is it that you want here?" he asked suddenly. "What is it about this place, these people, that makes you want to be here?"

"What are you talking about?" Hannah turned to face him. This was comforting, her on her side of the counter, him on the other. *Like a regular customer,* she thought. This was safe. "I live here," she said, thinking of the small house she shared with Rory, of the spring in the woods beyond that was so beautiful in the summer.

"But why?" He moved away from the axe to touch an old shield in the corner. It was not one of Hannah's best, but it would serve in extremity. He shook his head. "I know you always loved your weapons, but is this really necessary?"

"I don't carry a shield," she said stupidly, knowing where he was going and not quite willing to follow.

He gave her a look, and she sighed, giving in. "What do you want to hear, Klauden? I like it here. This is my forge. I have a home. I have a life." She paused, thinking of Solyn. "Well, I had a life."

"You don't belong here."

"Where should I be?"

"You belong at home, chaivin. You belong in your father's castle." He paused, staring at her with those eyes again as he added. "You belong at my side."

"I do?" she scoffed. "Why? So that I can stand there and look pretty at parties?"

"You are not meant for this life," he repeated.

"You gave me this life."

"Had I known what I was consigning you to, I would not have done so."

"What is so bad about this place?" She looked around. "This is a nice forge," she said. She picked up the poker and shoved the wooden pile inside the forge, using her magic to lessen the flames. It pleased her to know that her control of the power was growing every day. "It stays hot longer than any other I've worked on. I think the builder put something special in the metal." She picked up the hammer and chisel. "And these are excellent tools. They work quite well," she frowned, walking to place them in their respective places on the rack against the far wall, "well, when my hands can guide them to the right spot, of course, they work better, but still." She stepped back to the counter, hands resting against the worn edge. "This is a great place, Klauden. It's where I want to be."

"This is the middle of nowhere," he said, walking over to her. He grabbed one of her hands, pulling it close to him and flipping it over to reveal her palm. "Look at your hands," he ordered. "Calluses. What kind of lady has hands like these?"

"Your precious Solyn had calluses," she said. "You didn't mind them."

"Solyn was a slave. Her hands should be rough."

Hannah jerked her hand away. "You just don't get it, do you?" She turned around, refusing to look at him. "This is my life," she said slowly. "This is the life I want."

"But why?"

"You wouldn't understand."

"Help me."

Hannah was about to try when she was interrupted by a shout from outside. Klauden had opened the door and was peering out before she had even turned around.

"What is it?" she asked him, hopping up on the counter and swinging her legs over to the customer area. The vampire shook his head, then came back inside, a hand out to help her down. She took the offering without thought, landing lightly on her feet and moving to the door.

"More refugees," Klauden said, following her as she went to stand outside. Hannah looked at the ragtag band of men making their way up the street. "No doubt your elf will relish the chance to train them."

"Hush," she said, watching as a few villagers closed the gate that blocked the street, a part of the wall that now circled the entire village. There were only about a dozen men, she saw, tattered and bloodied by their trials as they stood before Angelina's clothing shop. Several villagers, including the ones who had closed the gates, were approaching the newcomers, and Hannah saw Tarren holding out a hand in welcome to the one in front, a tall man with black hair and a red shirt.

She was about to step into the street to head that way when something prickled the back of her neck, her brain trying to tell her something about the way the newcomer was standing there, waiting for Tarren to approach. At the same moment, Klauden's hand landed on her shoulder, holding her in place. "Wait," he whispered.

Hannah paused, trying to understand the cold feeling in her gut. She was still standing there when Tarren shook hands with the stranger, and when the man used the handshake to pull the mayor close and bury his face against Tarren's neck, she didn't realize what had happened. When Tarren began to scream, however, something in her broke the paralysis, and she was running, blades singing as she drew them both, booted feet taking her unerringly into the fray. Someone was yelling behind her, but she ignored it.

"Don't!" she screamed at the people who were still unaware of what was happening. "They're fledglings!" When the people's gaping attention moved from the spectacle of Tarren struggling in the man's arms to her flying full tilt toward them, Hannah realized they didn't understand the word she had used.

"They're vampires!" she shrieked. "Get away!"

That worked, she thought, as the frozen villagers began to flee. The fledglings took off after them, a dozen bodies leaping in random directions after easy prey. Hannah barreled into the closest one, knocking him aside as he focused on a small boy. Hannah saw that it was Scotty Pailin, her would-be assistant before Klauden had arrived and claimed all of her attention, and she stood defensively in front of him, swords drawn as she gauged what the fledgling would do next.

He recovered from her shove, spinning on his heels as he whirled to face her, mad eyes ignoring the swords she held and focusing on the exposed skin of her neck. He lunged, and Hannah ducked, one blade swinging up to catch him in the midsection, but he anticipated her move and dodged deftly aside, body twisting impossibly fast. Hannah had a hard time following his movements with her mortal eyes, and she knew that she was probably outmatched.

Someone was still shouting behind her, and it took her a second to recognize her name. She didn't look in the direction of the call, focusing instead on the fledgling's next move, but when Klauden barreled into the man, knocking him aside and securing himself between her and her attacker, she figured it had probably been him. Seeing that she was safe for the time being, Hannah darted a look behind her.

"Scotty!" she shouted. The boy, who had been crouching in fear against the wheel of a wagon, looked tearfully at her. "Get Rory!" she ordered. "Run! Now!" He kept staring at her for a second, and Hannah thought he might be frozen in place with terror, but then his eyes narrowed, he nodded once, and then he was off, a small shape running swiftly down the street.

Hannah watched him go, saw a blonde fledgling notice him, and then she was moving again, placing herself in the way to give Scotty some time. The fledgling looked over her shoulder at the retreating shape of the boy, then grinned at her, huge teeth rubbing against his lips as he took in her mortality.

"Come," she told him, gesturing with the blades. He leaped at her, but this time Hannah was ready for such speed. She spun her blades around in the move Rory had taught her, one blade out front to catch his leg and make him stumble, and the other shooting out over his back and driving down for the kill. Her first blade succeeded in tripping him up, but he recovered smoothly, back arching so that her blade skittered off bone instead of sticking deep in flesh.

Still, the blade flashed blue, and a streak of ice covered the fledgling's back. She turned to keep him in front of her, feet determined to keep solid ground, but the fledgling had also spun, one foot hooking around her knee and pulling her to the ground. She went down awkwardly, but used one blade to keep herself from a complete tangle, the other crossing quickly before her exposed body to protect her. The fledgling shrieked as he nearly impaled his hand on the sword in his eagerness to grab her, and he backed up, seeking a less painful way to approach his prey.

Hannah scuttled back on her knees, gaining ground and time as she increased the distance between them. The fledgling cradled his wounded hand, eyes carefully gauging the swords she held, and Hannah used the break to jump deftly to her feet, swords carefully out before her. There was a loud explosion from her right, and when the fledgling turned to see what it was, Hannah lunged, both swords streaking out and around in a smooth circle to catch him across the shoulders. He gave a cry of dismay as both blades found purchase in flesh, and he sank to his knees. Hannah did not relent, tugging up on both blades once to free them, ignoring the small circle of ice that surrounded the wound from the magical blade, then whipped them quickly before her body, the double motion cleanly lopping off the fledgling's head.

She took a deep breath, turning to the sound she had heard. Part of Angelina's shop was in flames, the porch of the wooden building a charred mess of broken wood and shattered glass. The twisted body of what Hannah assumed had been a fledgling lay smoking in the wreckage. Hannah turned to stare at Klauden, the only one who could have cast such magic, and the vampire shrugged, a small grin on his face, before turning to face another fledgling who dared approach.

Hannah did a small circle, unable to repress the smile that crossed her lips. It was so much fun to fight like this! She had just selected her newest target, a fledgling with red hair and a stained shirt watching her from twenty yards away, when something hit her from behind. She went sprawling into the street face first, too unprepared for the blow to even catch herself, and in the seconds it took to get her hands underneath her to push to her feet, she felt the sharp pain of teeth biting the back of her neck.

She screamed more in outrage than in pain, and shoved violently to dislodge the attacker. Her motion lifted them both off the ground, and she used the momentum to roll to the right, an elbow digging into the man's ribs as she landed on top of him.

When her second blow to his side with her other elbow did not knock him off, Hannah reacted instinctively, banging her head back as hard as she could and knocking her skull into the man's face. She felt the pain dull in her head as wet warmth squished into her hair. The teeth holding her neck released, and she scrambled away, crawling on hands and knees to grab her forgotten swords. She grabbed the magical one and got to her knees, the blade glowing as she slashed out at the one who had attacked her.

I've been bitten, she thought dully. *I'm infected.*

She felt Solyn surge in her then, the slave girl enraged as she took over Hannah's arm, wielding the blade with more skill than Hannah thought she possessed, twisting it deftly over the prone fledgling's chest, and when the man—Hannah saw it was the black-haired one who had bitten Tarren—slipped out of reach, Solyn lowered the blade level with the ground and jabbed it into his exposed side. He cried out, but Hannah had managed to grab her other sword with her remaining arm, and she brought this one down full onto the fledgling's chest, the point driving through his body to lodge in the dirt beneath. The man wriggled against the blade, trying to free himself desperately, but Hannah was on her feet then, the magical sword held in both hands as she brought it down in a smooth arc, chopping off his head before he could break free. The body went limp, and Hannah sagged over it for a second, aware that she had been hearing more shouts for some time now.

She withdrew the sword from the chest, grabbed the other sword, then got to her feet and scanned her surroundings for another threat.

I've been bitten, she thought again, looking around in a daze. *Bitten.*

A few yards in front of her, Klauden was dodging around the red-haired one Hannah had been considering, the vampire easily avoiding blows as he chanted, and then the fledgling was paralyzed, limbs frozen in place under the power of Klauden's spell. The vampire hesitated a moment as he looked at her, then a quick look around had him darting to the right again, where he faced another fledgling, this time with streaks of flame shooting out from his hands.

Hannah heard Rory's voice in her mind, a question from long ago: *Is that all it takes then? Just one bite?*

Hannah let both swords fall to the ground beside her, hands clutching the back of her neck as she felt the telltale wound there. She kept her eyes on Klauden, watching as the vampire reached out with both hands to engulf the fledgling in flames. The man shrieked and fell writhing to the street. Klauden turned to stare down the street, and Hannah heard what he had already seen. More men were pouring noisily down the lane, blades and boots clanking as they ran.

Reinforcements, Hannah thought, hands busily pushing her hair down to cover the wound, wishing she could cover what it meant as easily. Her knees buckled as a tremor went through her, and she sank heavily to the ground.

Rory's men, she thought, hands pushing the collar of her shirt up and over the wound, desperate to hide it.

It's not fair. Hannah didn't know if it was her own thought or Solyn's.

She watched the new arrivals pile into the seven remaining fledglings, the recruits holding their own admirably as they ganged up on the attackers. She saw Rory roll easily out of the way of one fledgling, gaining his feet as he slammed both blades into the soft skin of the man's back in the move she had tried to use. The fledgling fell, Rory's attack having been more successful than hers, then the elf was moving again, blades out to counter the lunge of another attacker, and Hannah's vision went blurry. Rory wouldn't get bitten, she knew, closing her eyes. He wouldn't be so stupid.

She was still kneeling when she opened her eyes to watch Klauden's red robes come into view. The vampire knelt before her, his body blocking out the chaos of the street behind him. Both hands held her face for a second to get her attention, then one hand reached around to push her hands out of the way, his fingers feeling the wound on the back of her neck. She winced, letting her hands fall into her lap, and he pulled away, sinking back on his haunches with wide eyes.

"Oh, chaivin," he whispered.

XXV

By the time Rory made his way to her side, Hannah had regained much of her composure. She got quickly to her feet and reclaimed the blades that had fallen by her sides. After she wiped the offending blood from the weapons, she sheathed them with more violence than was necessary. She was still breathing heavily from the fight, her body beginning to tremble with aftershocks of battle. Her hands twitched, and she steadied them on the pommels on both swords.

The elf was winded as well, though he bore it with more grace, cheeks flushed and eyes sparkling, his hair in disarray around his face. He seemed wild to her then, like a feral and strange creature out of myth, and her first impulse was to launch herself at him, into his arms, melt into the strength and solidarity of the magic that somehow belonged to her.

"Hannah," he breathed, quick steps leading him to her side, busily cleaning his own blades on his pants before sheathing them. He had a spray of blood on one cheek, the spatter of one of his victims, and she took the few steps to meet him halfway. He caught her easily, arms wrapping around her waist as he pulled her close for a kiss.

Normally shy in public, Hannah realized that she no longer cared about the people scrambling around her, the early shouts for aid and more reinforcements, the bodies of slain fledglings lying all around them. She didn't even mind Klauden still on his knees before where she had been sitting, eyes carefully averted from their embrace. She kissed Rory back, reveling in the feel of warm flesh after the heat and excitement of the fight, knowing that this impulse, this mad desire was the inevitable result of such action, knowing that it was their way of reacting to the brush with death by affirming life. Rory was as excited as she was, but he still managed to break the kiss to mumble against her lips.

"Scotty told us you were under attack," he said, kissing her again. "He said that you were in desperate trouble."

"I was," she replied, mouth hungrily finding his through the conversation. "I couldn't hold them off."

"You should have waited for help before engaging them," he remonstrated.

"I know, but there wasn't time. I only realized what they were when they attacked Tarren."

"You are so brave," he whispered, pausing long enough to look down at her. "When I rounded the corner and saw you fighting on the ground, I thought you were done for, but before I could even reach you, you had regained your feet and killed him." He paused, kissed her again, then pushed her hair out of her face and cradled her cheeks with both hands. "You were magnificent."

"I had a great teacher," she told him, but then his hand brushed the back of her neck, and she winced, the pain reminding her how unmagnificent her performance had actually been.

It might be alright, she told herself. *Sometimes people survive. Sometimes nothing happens to them.*

Yes, and sometimes they turn into monsters, she answered herself, this time not needing Solyn or any of her other demons to supply the voice of reason. But usually, she had to admit, those who were bitten became fledglings. From what she could recall, Hannah thought that entire transformation would take only a day or so, depending on the constitution of the body. She remembered the hunger in the fledgling's eyes, the raw bloodlust still unsated or calmed, and she wondered just how newly turned he had been. Older, stronger fledglings could turn others into their kind, but the new ones were usually too frantic in their need or too uncoordinated in their attack to actually succeed in turning anyone. Usually, those bitten by a newly turned fledgling just died. Hannah tried not to think about that.

"Are you alright?" Rory asked her, their frantic kisses slowing as their hearts regained a normal pace.

"I'm fine," Hannah lied, astonished at the words as she spoke them, but before she could correct herself, Rory was kissing her cheek, her forehead, her nose.

"I'm glad."

"Are you?" she asked distractedly, hoping against hope that she was right, that she might be one of those who recovered from the bite.

<*What in your history makes you think that you would escape so easily?*> Solyn asked quietly. It was the first time the slave had spoken in some time, and Hannah forced her face to stay impassive.

<*If anyone deserves to escape,*> Hannah thought at her, <*it's me. I didn't go through so much trouble to get this mortal body only to be forced back to the beginning.*>

<*You forget yourself,*> Solyn commented, though without any heat. <*It is my body that will be turned fledgling. Or worse.*>

Hannah ignored her words and the small stab of guilt that accompanied them. Rory had pulled away from her to survey the carnage around them. He shook his head, then began to lead her toward a small contingent of his men who stood nearby, huddled over a body. Hannah saw that the fledglings had been defeated, but near them were many bodies of villagers as well.

She spotted Tarren, the former mayor slumped on his side, open eyes vacant and staring at nothing. Blood spattered his chin and cheek, dyeing his white shirt and shoulder red and pooling in the icy mud of the road. He was surrounded by three other bodies, two women and a man. Hannah recognized the startled expression of Angelina, the former shopkeeper who made clothes in the store three buildings down from Hannah's shop.

Something moved in her chest, but before it could materialize, it disappeared. Hannah wondered if it was some mortal emotion like grief or pain, but then thought it was probably just pity. It was an awful way to die, caught in the embrace of a newly turned fledgling. They were still half-mad creatures, unable to control their thirst or their teeth, mauling the victim severely before even hitting any decent veins.

Some of the new soldiers were seeing to the bodies, straightening twisted limbs and laying them out for their kin to claim and bury. So many, she realized, as Rory helped her over the flung out arm of a young man, a soldier who had dropped his sword and paid for his error with his life. Though there had only been a dozen fledglings, nearly fifty villagers lay dead or dying in the street.

I was so lucky, she thought. *Even bitten, I am lucky to be alive at all.* She looked at the fledglings then, took in their tattered clothing, their gaunt cheeks, their empty hands. *These were untrained and newly turned. What will happen if there are more of them?* Likely there were, she knew, and the next time, they would be well fed and armed. A small group of decent fledglings could destroy this village in an afternoon, she realized, a chill working its way up her spine. The move turned her neck a little, reminding her again of the wound, and she wondered if, when the attack came, which side she would be fighting on.

Fledglings newly turned were dangerous, unpredictable things.

She bit her lip, maintaining her expression as she allowed Rory to lead her to the cluster of men. When they neared, the others moved aside for them, and she saw a young man lying on the ground, a comrade kneeling beside him and holding his hand. The young man was crying. Hannah was glad for a moment that she did not recognize him. He was a new recruit.

From the angle of his body, she could see that he had taken a wound in the belly somehow, though without a sword, she wondered how the fledgling had managed it. As Rory knelt on his other side, leaving her standing near the man's feet, Hannah caught a glimpse of ragged flesh beneath the remains of his shirt. Not a sword wound, she realized, glancing quickly down at her own hands and nails. Soon, she too might have the ability to tear through flesh with her bare hands, her staggering strength allowing her limbs to destroy anything in their path.

Hannah closed her eyes, willing this to be a dream, for the last few moments to somehow turn back and allow her to catch that bastard before he bit her.

The man on the ground was more than just doomed by his gaping guts, though, she saw when she opened them again. He too had been bitten, a bloody, pulpy spot on his right forearm evidence of the crushing force of a fledgling's jaws. Even if he could recover from his torn belly, the bite was damning. He would turn, or go mad, or just die.

Hannah's hand stole to her neck, adjusting her shirt and tugging on her hair. When her hand came away bloody, she wiped it on her skirt, the evidence blending with the marks from her swords. Though several men stood around her, none seemed to pay attention to her shuffling. They were watching the man on the ground, listening to his gasps and choking sobs as his mortal body tried to understand what had happened.

"Easy, Thomas," Rory was saying, a hand on the man's shoulder. "Rest easy now."

"He's been bit," one of the men behind Rory said. Hannah saw that it was Fergus, the man who had once tried to stab Rory from behind. Apparently, that sentiment had passed, since Fergus was looking at the elf with a loyalty that surprised Hannah. She knew Rory's men were devoted, but she had never realized just how much the elf commanded their respect and attention.

"I know," Rory replied in a low voice. He looked at the young man kneeling across from him, their eyes meeting in silent assent.

Tears ran from the young man's eyes as he nodded, but he removed one hand from his dying companion's to draw the blade from his belt. Thomas, lying on the ground, glanced from Rory to his friend and back again.

"Tell my mother," Thomas wheezed, blood bubbling on his lips and running down his chin. "Tell her..."

"I will," his friend said, "I'm sorry, Tom." Then he brought the blade swiftly across Thomas's throat. The boy's eyes bulged a bit as he bled out, but when the light faded from his eyes, Hannah thought he looked peaceful. As she continued to stare at him, however, Hannah thought of her own neck and what she would soon have to do, and then she couldn't stop staring at the way the blood splashed around his lips, lips too inexperienced to have kissed their share of girls, and the way the red puddled around his collarbone, the color seeping darkly through his shirt and soaking into the dirt and ice of the road. She felt her stomach rise then and knew she was going to be sick.

"Others have been bitten," Fergus said in a low voice.

Rory nodded, glanced at Hannah, then frowned. "You know what you have to do," the elf said. "Some may recover. The others..." Rory left the words unspoken.

Hannah didn't hear Fergus's reply. Instead, she managed to stumble away through the crowd of men to the other side of the street before letting go, the puddle of vomit steaming in the chilly air. When she had regained herself, she sat back, and saw that Klauden was standing beside her.

"<You did not tell him,>" the vampire commented quietly in their native tongue.

Hannah wiped her mouth, feeling an ache building under her skin. "<Some people recover.>"

"<And you are one of those people?>"

"<Perhaps.>"

He sighed, hunkering on one knee beside her. His hand rested lightly on the back of her neck, and she was about to pull away, but then he mumbled something and she felt the low thrum of magic pass from his hand into her body, and the stinging faded immediately. "<Very soon,>" he said, "<I will not be able to help you like this.>"

"<I may not turn,>" she insisted.

"<You may turn mad,>" he snapped. "<The number of those who recover is almost as few as those who lose their minds. Mostly, though, those who are bitten turn. You should prepare yourself for that.>" He removed his hand, standing up. "<And him.>"

"<I—>" she began, but then another wave of nausea caught up to her, and she vomited again, this time remaining on hands and knees for a longer moment. She could feel the icy ground seeping into her palms and knees, her breath showing in hot puffs beneath her.

Is it starting already? Is my body reacting to the infection, even now my blood changing, my body transforming?

She was about to speak again, but then someone else was by her side. Rory, she realized, recognizing the scabbard as it swung into view beside her. She turned her head slowly, aware of a slight pounding in her temples. "I'm alright," she managed, wiping her mouth again with the back of her hand.

The elf squatted beside her, a hand on her back to steady her as she sat back again. "Are you?" he asked, concern in his voice now. "Were you injured?"

Hannah shook her head. "No, no." She glanced to her right, and the vampire stared blandly back at her. She looked back at Rory. "I just... All that blood," she settled for saying. "It's been a while since I saw so much blood."

Rory chuckled, wrapping an arm around her back and helping her to feet. "Really? I wouldn't think that blood would ever bother you, Hannah."

"Hah," she said without cheer. Her head felt light then, and she struggled to breathe. Rory's arms came more tightly around her, and he gave her a serious look. "Hannah." There was real worry in his voice now. His hands began a quick exploration of her body, no doubt checking for wounds. When his hands skittered over the wet patch around the back of her neck, they paused, and he turned to check the area. "You're bleeding," he said, and Hannah was grateful that Klauden had managed to heal the bite wound.

"It's not mine," she explained, tugging his hands away from her neck. "I bashed my head into his nose, and he bled all over me."

The elf grinned at her. "That's my girl."

Hannah managed a weak smile in return. *Gods, I feel awful. Some people recover,* she told herself. *They do!* She wouldn't acknowledge the deeper fear beneath her conscious mind—*the fledgling was so young, too young...*

"Still," the elf said, "you must have bashed your head too hard. That will make you throw up when it's really bad. You need to rest but don't sleep." He turned to the vampire at Hannah's side. "Can—" He broke off then, realizing what he was about to say.

"I will watch her," the vampire offered, saving Rory the trouble of trying to ask for help.

"Thanks," Rory said, then gave the vampire a long look. "And many thanks for being with her today," he added. "You defended her very well."

"Not well enough," Klauden replied, and before Rory could ask what he meant, Hannah said, "You fought well, Klauden. I didn't know you could make such a huge fireball."

"I can do many things," the vampire replied but gave her a cordial nod.

Rory gave the street a look and shook his head. "Where did they come from?"

"The army?" Hannah asked.

"But fledglings in the army, along with the goblins..." His voice trailed off as he stared at Klauden again. "You," he said quietly. "You said there were men among them. You never mentioned anything about vampires."

Klauden shrugged. "I didn't know they were fledglings."

Rory looked at Hannah. "Can't you tell?" Hannah ignored the fact that he was asking her as a vampire, which she wasn't, well, which she wasn't right now, and considered.

"Sometimes," she admitted, "but only in close quarters. He didn't get very close to them."

"You can't sense them?"

"Only if it's someone of his own blood or someone he knows," she explained. "At least, that's all I could ever do, and only when I wanted to find others like me. It doesn't work by itself."

Hannah could have expanded on her explanation, could have told him that vampires can sense other vampires, but that fledglings were entirely different. Unless bound by the blood bond, most fledglings could go unnoticed by other vampires if they were careful. Though they might resemble vampires in their lust for blood, fledglings were quite different creatures—they didn't age, and though they were much stronger than the average mortal, they could not rival a true vampire in strength and magic. The only one to ever defy that convention was Kelvin Malbrek, Hannah's father's second-in-command.

"So if he wasn't looking, he wouldn't have seen," the elf concluded. When Hannah nodded, he gave the vampire a solemn look. "Apologies," he said. "I shouldn't have assumed."

"You seem to have a habit of apologizing for assuming things about me," the vampire replied, and Hannah was quick to interrupt them before sparks began to fly.

"Look," she said, "we have to find out how many are left."

Rory nodded, his face grim. "We'll send out scouts."

"No need," Klauden said, then stepped lightly away from them, making his way to a fledgling who sprawled in the middle of the street. Hannah had thought him dead, but now she realized he was just paralyzed, Klauden's spell holding him fast. "Just ask this one."

Rory took Hannah's arm and stepped carefully across the bodies. He nodded to Fergus, who had stood a good distance away during their exchange, and said, "Start gathering the wounded. You know what has to be done."

Fergus nodded and bowed briefly, an officer before a superior, and marched away, shouting orders at the men who milled about in small groups. She had heard their confusion about vampires attacking during the day and had to repress a surprising swell of pride—her people's myths had spread far and wide.

Now, though, she wondered about how the stories would change in this place, with fledglings running amok. It was a Klauden thought, she realized. He would care about such things.

She watched Fergus's back as he walked away, no doubt to issue orders. The ones who were seriously wounded would die, but she didn't think they would outright kill the bitten. They would guard them though, ready and waiting for any sign of the change. Hannah thought about saying something, anything—that maybe not all would turn, or that those who turned may not lose themselves—but then she was being tugged forward, and the thought faded. She had other problems at the moment.

Klauden's work had not passed unnoticed. Several soldiers were standing before the fledgling with weapons drawn, waiting for orders. Rory motioned them back, but not before one asked. "What is it, sir? Magic?"

Klauden nodded at Rory, then at his handiwork. "He is frozen for the moment, but I can release him at will. What would you know from him?"

"Everything," Rory said, stepping forward in front of Hannah, careful to guide her hand to his shoulder so she could lean on him from behind if need be. "I want him to tell me everything."

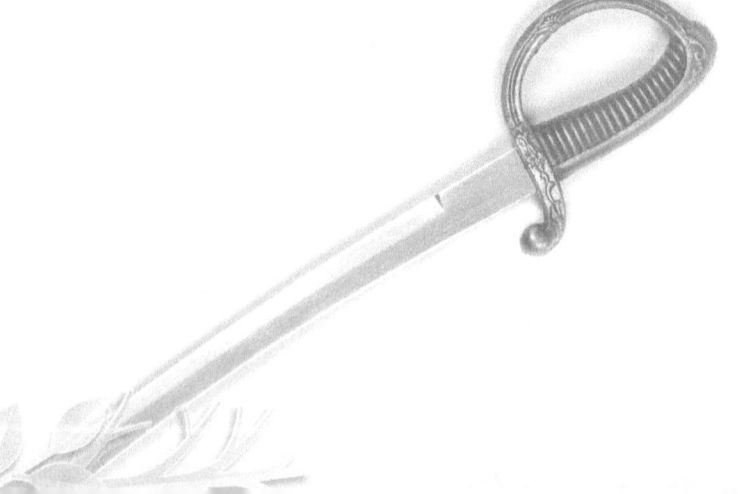

XXVI

They brought the fledgling away from the street, behind Hannah's forge, where most of the villagers couldn't see them.

"Who is your leader?" Rory asked again, and when the bloodied fledgling refused to answer, the elf punched him. Klauden caught him neatly, standing the man back on his feet.

"You will speak," the vampire said. "You must know that."

The fledgling stared silently past them at the wooden wall of Hannah's forge. Hannah could see the way he struggled to keep his balance, to keep his will, and she knew that the only thing powerful enough to keep the creature from breaking was the strength of his master's will. Klauden had to know that fledglings were bound by the wishes of their makers; a promise made or an order given had to be obeyed.

"Klauden," she whispered, amazed at how dry her throat had become. She was worsening at an alarming rate. "He can't tell you."

"What do you mean?" Rory asked, turning to face her, blood on his knuckles smearing on his chin as he wiped at his face.

"He's bound," Hannah said. "Whoever made him must have made him swear not to tell." When both men stared at her, she added, "It's what I would do."

"Can you overcome the bond?" Rory asked, glancing at the battered fledgling again. The creature swayed a bit, then spread his feet a bit and settled into a sturdy stance. He looked up then, at her, eyes very much alive, and there was a strange hunger there, a savagery not quite tamed. Whoever had made him, it had not been very long ago. He was still a half-crazed thing, desperate for blood. Though he was overpowered by the magic that held him in check and the blows that had cowed him into submission, he was still a fledgling, and soon enough the lust for more blood would overcome any control they had over him.

"I can try," Klauden was saying, and he gestured to Hannah. "Come here, chaivin," he ordered. Hannah saw Rory's face darken at the pet name, but that was soon overshadowed as he watched her lurch away from the wall and take the few steps to Klauden's side.

"Hannah," he said, concern heavy in his voice. "You don't look well."

"I'm fine," she said, steadying herself at the vampire's side. The fledgling was still looking at her, face resigned to his fate. "What can I do?" she asked Klauden.

"Concentrate," the vampire ordered, then grabbed her hand and placed it gently on the fledgling's cheek.

"I don't—" Hannah began, but Klauden cut her off.

"He is a fledgling made of the same master that made the others. You can reach him." She knew what Klauden was saying. Because she had been bitten, she too was connected to that master, though the link would be tenuous at best since she had not only slain her maker but never come into contact with the other vampire. Still, it was worth a try.

She closed her eyes, concentrating on breaking through the fledgling's defenses, reaching out with her magic and her blood to connect with him. At first, nothing happened, and she was about to quit, but then she was no longer seeing him in the bloody snow before her, but shivering in a cold tent. She was bare-chested, her skin frigid in the cold air that leaked through the thin walls, and she was starving, though this hunger was the mortal need for food. Hannah realized she had somehow jumped inside his memory, just as Solyn often fed her memories. As she watched, someone entered the tent. She put up her hands in a feeble defense, the memory of screams from those who had been dragged outside still quite vivid in her mind, but instead of dragging her through the flap to the waiting monsters outside, the newcomer approached and gave her a quizzical once over.

"You will need to be shaven," he said, and as he spoke, Hannah felt her mind crack a little. She knew that voice. The Elven healer from Kalford, the only one she had ever made, the one she had fully intended to kill, was standing before her. She wanted to shout something, to react in some way, but she was trapped in the fledgling's memory, unable to do anything except what he had done during her fledgling's visit.

"I don't understand," she was saying in a male voice.

"She wants you," the elf explained in a bored voice. "You must be made presentable."

Despite her continued protestations, the elf didn't answer any more of her questions. Instead, he sent for a razor and some soap, watching carefully as she ran the blade over the scruffy beard on her face. It was odd to be on this end of shaving, feeling the scrape of the blade against her skin, the tug of the short hairs as they parted with her skin. She had watched Rory shave on the odd occasion when he grew enough facial hair to warrant it, but elves were mostly smooth skinned, much like vampires, she thought, remembering the smoothness of Klauden's cheek against her hand.

Soon enough, she was shaved, and the elf took a moment to examine her hands, rough blunt-fingered things with stubby nails, before moving on to her hair. After a bit more trimming, she was deemed acceptable, and the healer called out in a voice that the man didn't understand. Hannah understood it perfectly, however.

"He is ready for you, mistress," the elf had said, and in Hannah's mother tongue, the language spoken by the vampires who ruled north of the Vanya.

As she turned to face the tent flap, Hannah had a horrible moment of anticipation.

It is not possible, she thought frantically. *There is no way this is happening.*

But when the woman entered the tent, and Hannah stared into her own face, she knew exactly what had been happening in the town to the north.

It's me, she thought stupidly. *It's my body. Someone is using my body to make an army of fledglings.*

<*I thought you said your body had been destroyed,*> Solyn quipped, the voice drawing Hannah back from the edge of a screaming abyss.

<*I thought it was,*> Hannah told her, calming herself.

<*But there it is.*> A pause, then <*You know what this means?*>

<*I can get back,*> Hannah thought desperately, clinging to the only hope she had left. <*I can be what I was.*>

<*You can leave me alone.*>

<*But your body,*> Hannah began, rallying again, <*it's been bitten.*>

<And?> The question hung in the air between them. Hannah's body approached slowly, narrow hips slinky in black leather pants and her pale skin shining in contrast to the black vest she wore. Hannah ignored the revealing outfit, trying to focus on the important issues.

<You're not upset about that?> She asked, aware of how much damage she had done to Solyn's life.

<Why would I be? It's what I wanted all along, don't you see?>

Hannah paused to absorb this, feeling Solyn subside a bit, and she refocused on the memory before her. Even in the skimpy clothes, her body was looking well, her skin pale and clear, her hair bright and shiny in curls around her face.

As the woman occupying her body approached, the man found himself unable to move to defend himself, clearly a victim of magical paralysis. Hannah watched until she sank her teeth into his neck, and that was when she noticed her eyes.

They were purple, blazing bright purple. There was only man Hannah had ever known who had eyes that color. Magnus van Kreeosk. And if her father was safely tucked away in his castle, that meant that the eyes must belong to the only child who had inherited his eyes, Anna, the half-sister Hannah had lost to a childhood accident, the body she had been supposed to occupy in Malfek's machinations.

They said her mind went elsewhere, Hannah thought in a panic. *He took it. That bastard took her soul, held it all this time, and then he put it in my body! Malfek,* she cursed. *Goblin armies, fledgling fighters, the Elven healer, and Anna in my body! What is Malbrek planning next?*

She felt the man jerking in his memory, body fighting death as the vampire released him. He tried to move but couldn't, and Hannah faded away then, not only from his memories, but from any conscious thought at all.

XXVII

When Hannah woke, she was lying face down in a bed, her body alternately shaking with chills and burning with fever, and for a moment, she was convinced that everything had been a dream, and she was back in the inn at Kalford, Rory nervously leaning over her as she slowly went mad with bloodfever. Then her vision cleared, and she was staring at Klauden through a veil of blonde hair, the vampire sitting on the edge of the bed, a wet cloth in hand that he used to wipe her neck and shoulders.

"What?" she croaked, her throat aching with dryness.

"Hush," Klauden told her, brushing her hair out of her face. "You must rest."

"The fledgling," she blurted. "It was me. I made him. Don't you see?"

Klauden shushed her, hands twisting the cloth in a bowl and ringing it out over her face, the drops cooling her burning skin.

She was desperately thirsty, but she knew that water wasn't what she needed. She looked around the room, recognizing her house, and looked up at Klauden.

"My body," she whispered. "It's still alive."

Klauden nodded. "You aren't dying," he insisted. "You're just changing." There was something about the way he said it that made Hannah pause. She twisted to turn onto her back, but settled for lying on her side, Klauden's wet cloth resting on her neck. The vampire seemed very agitated about something.

Hannah shook her head. "No, that's not it," she tried to explain, but then she realized what he had said, and her stomach sank. "Changing?" she repeated, hands working their way up from her sides to feel the inside of her mouth, to the teeth that were huge against her lips. "No," she moaned. "Not everyone changes," she insisted.

"But you are," Klauden said. "You will," he declared in a fierce whisper that made her give him a closer look. He put the cloth on her forehead, then reached for her hands, holding them tightly in his own.

"What is it?" she asked him. "What?"

"Rest," he told her. "You need all of your strength."

"Does Rory know?" she asked.

Klauden shook his head. "He will, but he doesn't yet."

"What happened?"

"You fainted," he said. "I brought you home." At her expectant look, he said, "The elf is on his way. He had to deal with the fledgling, then confer with the men before he could come back." He shook his head. "You picked a dedicated man, Hannah, but he certainly knows how to be loyal to his community before himself."

"The men need him," she whispered.

"More than you do?" he asked, and Hannah was struck by the concern in the vampire's voice. *Does he think Rory is neglecting me right now?*

She changed the subject. "Did the fledgling crack?"

Klauden nodded. "Once you touched him, he started talking. I don't know exactly what you did, but once he began to speak, he couldn't stop." He gave her a level look. "There are at least a hundred fledglings in Salva, training day by day with weapons. They follow the orders of an elf, but they are loyal to—"

"A woman," Hannah finished. "Me."

Klauden nodded. "It appears so."

"Did you know?"

He shook his head, hands caressing hers on top of the blanket. "I wondered that your body had been destroyed so easily. If Malbrek truly wanted to purify you, he wouldn't have given it up so quickly. But when I saw that Rory had your ring, I assumed he must be telling the truth when he said he saw your body."

"So, what then? Malbrek burned another body to throw him off, even putting my ring on the corpse so Rory wouldn't suspect anything?"

"That seems likely," Klauden said. "I was with you for a time inside the Star, so I didn't see what happened after you were taken, and I don't know what he did with the body between then and the ceremony. I watched him most of the way and saw nothing suspicious."

"So my body is still out there, but with someone else in it. You know what that means, right?" He looked at her. She grinned, the idea loosening the ball in her stomach. "I can get it back," she whispered. "I can be myself again."

"You're turning into a fledgling," Klauden said. "You cannot be yourself anymore."

"No," Hannah said. "Solyn is turning into a fledgling."

"Hannah," Klauden said, his tone making her pause, "you are very ill," he said.

She gave him a suspicious look, a chill working through her limbs. "Doesn't everyone get sick during the change?"

"They do, but..."

"But what?"

"You were bitten by a very new fledgling," he began. "He was only a few weeks old."

She wanted him to continue, knew that she could believe it when she heard him say it, but he was interrupted as the door swung open, Rory entering through the back door and practically leaping to the edge of the bed. Klauden quickly released Hannah's hands and grabbed the cloth from her neck. Hannah could see it was pink with blood. Klauden must have cleaned the remains of her wound. The vampire collected the bowl and stood up, walking over to the table to leave her and the elf alone.

"Hannah, what is it?" Rory asked. "What's wrong?"

"I..." She was going to say that she was fine, that nothing was wrong, but she thought it was beyond cruel to lie at this point. "I will be alright," she settled for saying.

Rory touched her face, his hands cold on her flushed skin, and stared at her. One of his hands touched the swollen skin of her mouth, feeling the fangs beneath her lips. Before Hannah could stop him, his hands slipped down her face, working under her hair and to her neck. She tried to move, to protest this investigation, but she was weak, and he was determined. When he didn't feel what he sought, he reached down and gently pulled her up to a sitting position.

"Don't," she whispered, but he ignored her, eyes now seeking what his hands could not feel. She was no longer wearing the bloody shirt she had been bitten in, and Klauden had closed the wound, but he could still see the white marks on her neck. She heard the sharp intake of his breath as he saw the mark, and when he laid her carefully back down, she avoided his gaze.

"Oh, Hannah," he whispered. "Why didn't you tell me?"

"I didn't want you to worry."

He sighed, taking both her hands into his much as Klauden had done, though there was little comfort in the gesture. "I remember what you said," he said quietly. "Just one bite. That's all."

She nodded. "I'm so sorry."

He shook his head. "What will happen to you?"

Hannah glanced beyond him to Klauden, standing before the kitchen table. "I will change, I think," she said quietly. "I will become a fledgling."

"I see."

"There's more, though," she said, sudden hope fueling her voice.

"What?"

"My body," she began. "It's not dead. I saw it."

"What are you talking about?"

"My vampiric body," she tried to explain. "When I touched the fledgling, I saw his memories. My body turned him. My body has been turning all of them."

"Are you sure?"

She nodded. "There's someone else in it right now, but it's there. You know what that means, right?" She wanted to tell him more, to explain everything, but he cut her off.

"Can you reclaim it?" He looked to Klauden. "Can she reclaim it? Can she leave Solyn to this body and get her own back?" Hannah couldn't ignore the hope in her husband's voice.

"I don't know," the vampire said. "I would assume so, but I'm not positive."

Hannah winced as another shiver went through her, and this time, her body did not stop. She felt her gorge rising again, and she lurched out of bed, barely reaching the bowl Klauden had left on the kitchen table before vomiting again. Rory caught her when her knees gave out, and Klauden gave her a serious look from across the table.

"Malfek," she cursed, wiping her mouth with a weak hand. "Is this normal?"

Rory looked from her to the vampire. "Can't you help her?" the elf asked. "Can't you make it easier?"

Klauden shook his head. "Look at her," he said. "Mortal magic cannot help her now."

"Surely you've seen fledglings turn before, right?" When Klauden nodded, the elf continued, "How long will this last?"

"Typically, it takes a full day for one to turn completely, but..."

"But what?"

"When fledglings turn," Klauden explained, "they are often bitten by a pureblood vampire. Fledglings do not bite mortals to make more fledglings, not until they are much older. There is a certain kind of blood magic required. These were newly turned, still half mad with the change." He looked away from them, eyes focusing on the fireplace.

"What are you saying?" Rory asked. Hannah knew what was coming, and she rested back in the warmth of Rory's embrace. The elf did not help her back to bed, instead supporting her in the middle of the floor as he stared at Klauden.

"She cannot change," the vampire stated. "The one who bit her was too young, and there wasn't nearly enough blood. I've seen it before."

"What happens?" Rory asked.

"Usually death, following madness." He stared at Hannah. "You know the fehalon, yes?" Hannah nodded, remembering vividly the few fledglings who had been driven mad by the change, half-crazed beasts that her father had delighted in watching fight in the tournaments. "You haven't had enough blood to turn, and you've been infected enough that your mortal body cannot live."

"Are you telling me that I will die?" When he said nothing, she asked, "Or go mad?" *Well, at least the villagers don't have to worry about fledglings from the attack.*

"Do something," Rory said. "You're a vampire. Can't you help it?"

"I swore never to make a fledgling," Klauden said, and Rory stood up, dragging Hannah with him.

"You'd let her die, then?"

"You don't understand," Klauden said. "The bond between master and fledgling is forever," he continued.

"She would live," Rory said.

"She would be bound to me," Klauden said, trying to get the elf to see reason.

"She's already bound to you," Rory snapped, and Hannah winced.

"Not like this," Klauden replied. "You can't understand." He turned to Hannah. "Tell him," the vampire said. "Tell him about the bond between master and fledgling."

Hannah remembered the healer, remembered sharing his pain, and wondered if she could stand such a connection to Klauden. "It's very intense," she said finally. Rory picked up her sagging body and set her down on the edge of the table, an arm resting on her shoulder to keep her upright.

"How intense?"

"She would always know where I was," Klauden said. "She would know what I thought and felt. She would have to obey my every whim, come whenever I called. She would be utterly mine."

There was a long time when no one said anything. Hannah fought another wave of dizziness, squeezing her eyes shut to regain her senses.

When she opened her eyes, Rory was still contemplating, his face smooth as he considered the possibility. His mouth worked, his teeth biting his lower jaw, and Hannah had a strange rushing moment where she could sense the blood in him, the life pulsing beneath his skin. Then it was gone, and she struggled to take a breath. Her body refused at first, chest seizing in a painful tightness, but then it relaxed, and Hannah took a slow deep breath. Rory watched her struggle with a blank face, then turned to Klauden.

"But she would live," he said finally. "Otherwise, there's no hope at all."

Klauden shrugged. "I don't know," he admitted. "From what I've seen before, though, I don't think she will recover from this. Her body is already trying to change and can't."

"But if you bite her," the elf said, "she would change. She would be your fledgling, but she would be alive."

The vampire nodded. Rory looked at Hannah, still shuddering a bit as she tried to breathe. "What do you want, Hannah?" he asked.

Hannah shrugged, head pounding and mouth dry. "I don't know," she answered honestly. After a moment she added, "I don't want to die."

"Even if I were to bite her, she would need more blood," Klauden said quietly. "She would have to feed right away."

Rory looked at them evenly. "I understand."

"No," Hannah said, her will strengthening as she understood what the elf meant. "Not you."

"Elven blood is powerful, right? What would kill a mortal will only weaken me. Use my blood."

Klauden frowned, then shrugged. "It would work."

Hannah shook her head. "No."

"Why?"

"I will not use you like that," she said. "I will not taint what we have with more blood." She stifled a cough then, noting the blood on her hand as she rested it on her lap. Things were very bad if she was coughing up blood.

"You are steeped in blood, Hannah," Rory said, wiping the blood from her hand. "You always have been." He winked at her then, the motion oddly out of place in the serious discussion. "And in case you didn't notice, I went for you anyway." He paused, taking her hands in his. Hannah felt herself start to slide forward on the table, but Klauden's hand grabbed her back and held her upright. "I know what you gave up to be with me," the elf said levelly, ignoring the vampire completely. "I know what it cost you to do it, and it has been a wonderful year with you." He paused again, seeming to find the words within himself. "But it's time now. You're no longer mortal. Your body is still alive. We have the chance to set things right, but we can't do that if you die tonight out of stubbornness."

"It's not stubbornness," she insisted. "I just want you to understand what it is you are asking for."

"You don't have to bite me," Rory said. "You can just take my blood, and that will be the end of it."

"You would do that for me?"

"Of course," he said. "I love you." Hannah smiled at him, unable to stop herself. Though they lived together as husband and wife, though they shared their lives with each other, she couldn't remember the last time he had actually said the words. Neither of them were very open with their emotions, especially when it came to words of love. Mostly, she knew that he loved her through his behavior and the way he worried about her, but it was still nice to hear it spoken aloud.

"I love you," she answered, feeling the words burn in her chest. "But I don't think you realize what this means."

"Hannah, you will die without this. What else do I need to know?"

Hannah risked a small glance at Klauden, but the vampire's expression gave nothing away. Her mind was whirling, plans forming and being discarded as she considered the possibilities. She could wait and see if her body could withstand the change; she could let Klauden change her and accept all that would come with such a change; or, she realized suddenly, she could use the powers of a fledgling to reclaim her own body, and then Solyn would be Klauden's fledgling. *The bond wouldn't follow me into another body, would it? But...*

Hannah looked past both men into the fireplace, trying to understand the new feeling in her chest. *Could I,* she wondered, *could I do that to her?*

<*Believe me,*> Solyn answered her unspoken thought, <*I would love any plan that gave me back control of my body. Hells,*> she added, <*as a fledgling, I would be strong. No one could ever hurt me again.*>

<*You want this?*>

<*It's all I ever wanted.*> The girl paused, then Hannah caught a small sense of laughter. <*You know,*> Solyn said, <*all this time I thought Matthew refused me out of arrogance, but it turns out that he couldn't do it. How that must have galled him, to know that for all of his newfound power as a fledgling, he couldn't make more like himself.*>

<*Fledglings can eventually turn people,*> Hannah said. <*Kelvin Malbrek is a fledgling, and yet he managed to finish turning that healer I bit in Kalford.*>

<*I thought you said you turned him.*>

<*I bit him, and he fled before I could kill him. Even so, he couldn't have lived without help.*>

<*Much like us right now.*>

Hannah nodded, glancing back to look at Klauden. <*I think this is a bad idea,*> she told Solyn. <*I think I'm going to regret this.*>

<You might, but it's not like you'll have long to fuss over it,> Solyn answered. *<When you get your body back, I'll be his fledgling.>*

There was something in her tone that let Hannah know that such an idea was not at all displeasing to Solyn; in fact, the girl seemed excited by the prospect. Hannah ruthlessly shoved down the burn of jealousy that threatened to fill her chest. This was not the time to be foolish.

Still, it was a big step to take, and Hannah feared what even a short time as Klauden's fledgling might do to her.

"He might not even want to do it," she said suddenly, and both men looked at her. "You swore," she addressed Klauden. "We both swore never to make another of our kind." She looked away. "I was unable to keep that promise," she added, "but you still can. I would not begrudge you."

Klauden gave her a long look but said nothing.

<It's me,> Hannah heard Solyn say after a moment. *<He doesn't want to do it because it will bind him to me.>*

<Hush,> Hannah told her. *<Don't be ridiculous. He chose your body for me to occupy. Clearly, he has some feeling for you.>*

<He does,> Solyn quipped. *<Disdain.>*

<He's not always like that,> Hannah said, then wondered why she was defending him. When she looked at Klauden again, he had taken on that eerie otherness that she associated with the way Solyn saw him. *He is so handsome,* she thought, with his high cheekbones and blonde hair always perfectly arranged. His manner was impeccable, his powers daunting, his self-control an iron cage around his heart.

<Except for you,> Solyn said sadly. *<He only cares about you. There isn't room in him for anything else.>*

<I'm sorry,> Hannah said, not knowing what else to say. After a moment, she added, *<Look, if we do this, then you'll be close to him forever. Will that be enough?>*

<I have lived with far less,> Solyn agreed.

Rory broke the silence then. "Let's have it out, then. Will you do this thing for Hannah?"

Klauden shook his head at the elf. "You know I would do anything for Hannah. I just want it clear what you are asking me to do."

"You will be close to her. I understand."

"You can't understand," Klauden snapped. "But you aren't meant to, I suppose." He took a deep breath that went on for far too long, then licked his lips. "Are you certain this is what you want this time?" he asked Hannah.

She shrugged weakly, another bout of nausea weaving its way through her guts. "I have no idea," she replied, "but as per usual, I appear to have no other choice." Without looking at either of them, she turned aside to vomit into the bowl on the table beside her, noting that, this time, there was blood in her bile, a sure sign that her body was not doing so well. When she was finished, she sat up again, this time leaning heavily on Klauden's arm around her back. "So, let's get this over with."

"Have you ever watched a fledgling being made?" Klauden asked her.

She shook her head. "I've seen them bitten, but I never watched the change before." When it seemed as though the vampire would say something, she cut him off. "Look, I know how it works, alright? You bite me, I bleed out." When he raised an eyebrow at her casual manner, she added, "Fine, I bleed out a lot. Then you give me some of your blood. I drink. When I've had enough from you, I'll need more fresh blood. That's what Rory's here for." She paused long enough to give the table a quick glance. "Grab a knife, Rory, and be ready with it. I don't want to bite you." The elf reached over to the counter and grabbed a knife, holding it carefully in one hand.

"Where is best?" he asked. "My arms, wrists, neck? What?"

"Not the neck," she said. "I might hurt you." She gave Klauden a look. "What do you think? The wrist?"

"That should suffice." The vampire helped her to her feet then, propelling her over to the bed. Hannah sat down nervously. She hadn't lied when she said she had seen others bitten before, but her understanding of the process was far different than actually experiencing it. She had a brief flash of the fledgling's memories she had shared behind the forge. When he had been bitten, he had been so aroused that he couldn't stop himself.

Is there any way to keep the sexual tension out of this? She looked at both men as they seated themselves on either side of her. She had heard stories of what one woman could do with two men, but she hadn't ever pictured herself in that position, and certainly not with these two men. *How will they keep from killing each other if things get out of hand?*

"Listen," Klauden was saying, "when she changes, it will be sudden. She will not be herself for a time." He seemed about to say something else, then shook his head, and said instead, "Just remember that when you offer her your wrist. There is a chance she will lash out and harm you."

"I understand," Rory said.

"No," Klauden said, "you do not, but very soon, you will."

XXVIII

"Get to it," Hannah breathed.

The vampire looked at her, nodded, then reached out a hand to touch her cheek. He stared at her for a long time, and she knew he was doing something, preparing himself somehow. His other hand slid around her back, and he moved closer to her, the length of his body resting against hers as they sat on the bed. She could feel Rory's gaze on her, on both of them, and felt a wash of guilt as she realized just what letting Klauden turn her might entail.

Klauden ignored Rory completely, looking at Hannah as though she were the only one in the room, and she had a sudden memory flash. She was a child again, and she and Klauden were standing at the edge of a cliff, the Vanya Mountains stretching up and around them both. She had managed to get him out of the castle again, dragging him from his books and rooms to explore yet another tunnel she had discovered in the canyons beyond the castle proper. They had been exploring most of the day, and it was getting late. Hannah had stepped to the edge of the cliff at the end of this newest cave, looking out over the valley below, feeling the wind tugging at her hair, whipping her skirt around her ankles.

"Come on," she coaxed. "Come and see."

Klauden was somewhat afraid of heights, she had realized later. He had been reluctant to get so near the edge, but after her incessant nagging, he finally gave in. When he reached the edge, she had grabbed his hand, taking comfort in the closeness of her friend, her promised mate, her confidante. He had taken in the view slowly, eyes savoring each detail in that careful manner before turning to look at her. They had been so close then, beyond the need for words. *What happened to that feeling?*

Hannah sat on the edge of the bed again, back in the present, except that instead of that girl she had been offering Klauden her hand at the edge of the cliff, it was Klauden who was offering his hand, and it was her turn to take a chance for him.

His arm was still around her back, and she knew Rory was still on her other side, but at that moment, it was just her and Klauden, the sense of his closeness, his hand on her cheek.

<<*Come to me.*>>

The voice was a whisper, and Hannah recognized the language it was in. When she had agreed to this, she hadn't realized just what she was getting into, apparently.

<<*I will,*>> she replied, to no one in particular. Even Solyn was silent now.

Klauden was leaning toward her, and for a second, she was sure he was going to kiss her again. She didn't move, willing to let him do what he would for the moment. At the last second, he dipped down, warm lips sliding along her chin and moving slowly down her neck. Hannah shivered, and she hoped it was the result of the sickness.

She had closed her eyes at some point, but she was very aware of Klauden's every movement, the way his touch seemed to start little fires in her skin. She leaned her head back, knowing that he would eventually bite her, and when he did, he would need access to her neck. Still, as she did it, his mouth continued its journey along her skin, moving up to her ear and then back again and she forgot why she was doing this at all. Time stopped for a moment, and everything in her receded to Klauden's mouth on her skin, his hand around her back, his body touching hers. She had completely forgotten Rory's presence until she let out a little moan and heard the elf's sharp intake of breath. She was about to open her eyes and push Klauden away, but then she heard the vampire's voice in her head again, sharp and commanding.

<<*No!*>>

Hannah paused, staying where she was, caught in the moment between fantasy and reality.

"Do not interrupt me again," she heard Klauden say in a soft voice from very far away.

"You said you had to bite her. You didn't mention this," the elf replied in a steely voice that was dangerously quiet.

"There is more to converting a fledgling than just biology," Klauden replied softly, hands moving again on Hannah's back, lips very close to her skin. "It requires magic as well."

"What you're doing isn't magic," she heard Rory observe coldly.

"I have never made a fledgling," Klauden said, and this time his voice held a hint of anger, "and I shall never do so again." He slid a hand up under her hair, tilting her head to the side so he could kiss her neck. "I will not ruin the moment because you are having second thoughts," he whispered against her skin. Hannah knew she should be paying attention to this conversation, that it was important, but at the moment, she couldn't really focus on anything more pressing than the feel of Klauden's breath against her neck, the temptation of his body so close to her own.

"But…"

"I told you it was intense," the vampire admonished and began kissing Hannah's neck again. "I can't just bite her and run," he added, his other hand sliding up from her back to caress the bare skin of her neck, slowly moving his head to the other side so he could kiss that skin as well. "That is what fledglings in the midst of their passions do." He took a deep breath, then blew on Hannah's neck. She shivered, her body intensely aware of his every movement. "I am no fledgling, and this will be done right."

He tilted Hannah's head into his shoulder, long fingers running along her jawline, up to her cheek, and tangling in her hair. Hannah could smell his skin, that odd mixture of old books and ink and indoors she recalled from childhood, yet now there was something else in it, something wild and exotic.

"Making fledglings is more than biting," he was saying, speaking against her skin. "She has to want me." He paused, then she could hear the smile in his voice. "She will want me," his voice changed then, turning from silk to darkness, "but it is you that she will have, your blood that she will demand, your soul that she will drink in." His hand slid down the outside of her arm, her skin prickling in response to his touch, and as he ran his hand back up again, he began pushing down the neck of her shirt, revealing her shoulder. He pushed her hair to the side, sliding cool fingers across the sensitive skin of her neck, then leaned down.

<<*Look at me,*>> she heard him say in her mind, and Hannah obeyed. He was so close to her, face hovering before hers, fangs huge against his lips. She blinked, feeling the roiling sickness in her body trying to surge forward again. Both of his hands were on her skin now, long fingers moving in slow circles that she had never expected in one as inexperienced as he was. For all that he was still a virgin, Klauden had done a lot more research in this area than she had before her first night with Rory.

Thoughts of the elf nearly knocked her off course then, as she remembered that he was still sitting on her other side, still watching as Klauden caressed her. She started to pull away, to say that this wasn't worth it, that she would rather suffer any pain than to put Rory through this, but then one of Klauden's hands found bare skin under her shirt, and his mouth found hers.

This isn't right, she thought, but it was distracted, her mind commenting on events while her body raged with desire.

<*This is wonderful,*> Solyn whispered. <*I told you he would be good.*>

Hannah did pull away then, but Klauden refused to release her, hands tugging her over onto his lap, her legs wrapping around his waist. It felt so good to sit there, bodies close and her heart pounding, not only in her chest but the sound echoing in her head, and no doubt in his skin. When she couldn't stand it anymore, Klauden finally released her mouth, sliding down to her neck in measured kisses.

She was gasping for air, her body aching for something she couldn't name. Though it was close to sex with Rory, she knew that this desire went far beyond a need for physical completion, and she suddenly understood that for Klauden, this was sex, or at least the start. He could never be satisfied with a simple joining of bodies; he needed blood in order to enjoy himself. Hannah wondered if she would have made the same connections if her first experience had been with a vampire and not the elf. *Have I been somehow shaped by Rory so much that I don't relate to sex as my own people do?*

<<*Chaivin,*>> she heard Klauden say, and she realized that he had paused in his movement.

"Huh?" she mumbled. It was the first time she had spoken in a long time, and it was loud in the silence. She opened her eyes and stared at the vampire.

Klauden shook his head at her, grinning broadly. "<You never did know when to be quiet,>" he said in their language.

"<It's not in me to be silent,>" she replied in the same tongue. "<You know that.>"

"<So I did,>" he whispered, and then he sank his head to her neck and bit her.

The pain was instant and intense, then faded away into a slow burning that threatened to devour her. She closed her eyes again, drifting away into the sensation. The world faded away, and there was nothing except Klauden's body beneath her, his hands on her skin, his mouth working against her neck, then she was fading away from that as well.

Her own sense of self dissipating as he drew her blood, Hannah became slowly aware of several things. First, there was the lazy thought that if this was what her victims had felt for all of those years, she didn't really have much to be guilty about. It was wonderful, this floating, drifting state, and she could sense Klauden's deep satisfaction as he drank her blood. He was contented, the burning in his own body easing as she fed him. Hannah hadn't realized just how powerfully the bloodthirst burned in him. She was astounded that he had refrained from leaping on people and drinking. If her own need had ever been so great, she couldn't recall.

<<It was,>> Klauden whispered in her mind. <<You've just forgotten.>>

<<How do you stand it?>>

<<How did you?>>

Hannah paused, words drifting away as she drew closer to Klauden's emotions. The vampire didn't seem to be thinking the way she did. Instead of a series of words, the way that Hannah often felt inside her head, and the way Solyn felt in her head at times, Klauden was a wash of colors and images, sensations and fragmented memories.

She caught a glimpse of herself standing at the end of a tunnel, face nervous and hair blowing in a slight breeze, looking out of place in her new mortal clothes and belongings. *That's the morning I left,* she recognized, *when I left home the first time.* The image vanished, disappearing into another memory of her, this time in Solyn's body, standing at the end of a similar hallway, now accompanied by an elf and more weapons.

<<*You are always letting me go,*>> she thought faintly. <<*How do you do it?*>>

<<*You are always making me,*>> Klauden responded, but his voice was distant. Hannah tried to get closer but found that she was trapped somehow in the limbo of his mind, unable to follow his voice.

<<*Klauden?*>> Her word echoed, rebounded, and she focused all of her energy on finding him. <<*Klauden!*>>

Then someone was shouting at her, and she had a body again, a body that should have been racked with sickness, but now only felt light and empty, a vessel impossibly fragile.

<<*Drink.*>>

Hannah floundered, struggled in the haze that surrounded her.

<<*Come to me,*>> the voice demanded. <<*Drink.*>>

Hannah rallied, focused on the sense of desperation in that voice, and then she was back in her body completely.

"<Drink, chaivin,>" she heard, and this time it was with her ears. Her mouth was warm, her lips wet, and she licked them tentatively. Blood filled her mouth, and she swallowed reflexively, feeling the blood rejuvenating her as only it could. She reached out blindly for the source, then opened her eyes, desperate for more. She was lying on her back, and Klauden was leaning over her with his wrist held out, the blood spiraling down to land on her face. She drank eagerly, then reached out to claim his arm, pulling deeply from the wound on his wrist.

<<*Yes. More.*>>

She could feel something building in her, something desperate and uncontrollable. She pulled even deeper, her instincts taking over. Klauden made a noise, but she ignored him, sitting up in a lurch and tossing his wrist aside for more fertile ground. She struck his neck quickly, whining desperately when she couldn't break the skin. When the vampire raised a hand and opened a vein with his nail, she moaned gratefully, drinking deeply as she wrapped her arms around his back. Even this, though, wasn't close enough, she decided. She needed more.

She pawed roughly against him, pushing him back onto the bed and crawling on top of him, mouth working frantically against his neck. She could hear the slow beat of his heart, the echo of his desire flowing into her mouth as she drank, and she began to fumble with her clothes, knowing that she was definitely wearing too many, that there was too much in between her and the vampire.

<<*More,*>> she thought again. <<*More.*>>

<<*Chaivin.*>>

Hannah slowed in her fumbling, but didn't stop. She had almost worked her skirt up enough. Then there was the matter of his robe. She started pulling that aside, tearing the fabric when it wouldn't come away easily enough.

<<*Chaivin.*>>

The voice was calm, collected. *Weak?* Hannah slowed in her drinking, trying to focus beyond the burning need. *Who is talking to me? It doesn't matter,* she decided, going back to work on the clothes at hand. More fabric ripped, and she felt skin beneath her.

<<*Chaivin.*>>

<*What?*> She snapped, angry to be so interrupted, falling back into the common tongue in her thoughts as she focused. <*What?*>

<*Think of what you are doing.*> Klauden's quiet voice in her mind replied in kind.

<*What am I doing?*> Her mouth came away from his neck with a little pop, blood trickling out to drip against her chin. She needed more. More of everything. <*I'm getting more,*> she replied, hoping that would be enough to silence that voice.

<*You want me?*>

The voice was carefully neutral, and it brought her somewhat back to herself. For a moment, she was Hannah again, a crazed Hannah who was somehow ripping Klauden's clothes off in her need to be closer to him. She knew there was a reason that she shouldn't be doing this, but it wouldn't come. She kissed the wound on his neck, licking the blood and feeling it stir her desire even more.

<*Yes,*> she answered decisively, <*of course, I want you. I want all of you.*> Her hips made a decided attempt to claim him, and then there were hands on her shoulders tipping her back. At the same moment, the voice said, <*Good. It is enough, then.*>

Then she was being pushed back and down, and when she would have lunged to latch back onto Klauden's neck, suddenly another body was between them, a body glowing with health and vitality.

A body with a bleeding wrist that it was holding out to her. Hannah seized the limb, glad that she didn't have to bother with her fangs, and pulled hard. The owner made a guttural sound, and suddenly Hannah's need for more blood sharpened again, refocused into a need for more, just more, and then she was climbing onto this body, not caring about anything except fulfilling that burning need for more.

This person was a lot more flexible, she realized as a strong arm came around her back and lifted her easily. She held onto the wrist with one hand, dragging the rest of the body on top of her, her other hand eagerly grabbing at even more clothes. *<Gods,>* she thought frantically, *<does everyone always have to wear so much?>* Half mad with her need, she tore these away as well, but instead of forcing her to pause, to stop and recollect herself, a different voice echoed in her mind.

<Mine, Hannah. Yes.>

She fought again with her skirt, this time tearing it instead of pushing it aside, and then, finally, their bodies were aligned, and he pushed into her. She moaned against his wrist and then was aware of nothing except blood and the pulsing beat of her body for several long building moments. When she thought she was about to explode into a thousand pieces, Hannah tossed the wrist aside and lunged for her lover's neck, desperate for fulfillment. Instead of soft skin, she encountered something that felt like a hand, and when she bit it instead, the warm flood of blood was just as satisfying as the neck would have been.

Finally sated, Hannah drifted off for a long moment, feeling the blood singing in her veins along with the low hum of a completely satisfied body.

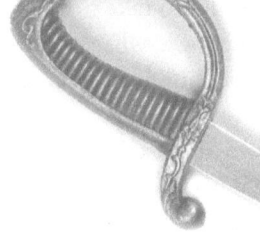

XXIX

When she came to herself again, Hannah took a slow inventory of her surroundings. She was on her back, and she had to keep taking deep breaths. Someone was lying on top of her, and even more interesting, someone was still somewhat inside her. She opened her eyes wide and was only somewhat relieved to see the side of Rory's face resting against her shoulder.

Gods, she thought frantically, *what happened?*

Her sharp intake of breath alerted Rory, and the elf turned to face her. He was very white, eyes wide with shock and blinking slowly. His shirt was still on, she saw, but spattered with blood. She was sticky with it, her face and neck warm with the liquid. She turned her head to the other side and saw a long-fingered hand resting on her shoulder. It, too, was leaking blood slowly from a bite mark between thumb and forefinger. As she followed the hand back to its owner, she caught a glimpse of Klauden, his face even more pale than Rory's, his chest heaving in the great gasps that signaled the onset of blood withdrawal.

"Oh no," she said, scrambling suddenly to sit up, to take stock. "Oh no." Rory pulled away from her, out of her, and sat back, what was left of his pants flapping around his hips. "Did I...?" she mumbled, then tried again. "Malfek, did I bite you?"

The elf was still quite disoriented, but he gave himself a slow once over, moving from the blood on his wrist to the rest of his body. He shook his head then, a short jerk that revealed just how out of it he was.

"I didn't know," she mumbled then, hands patting the bed around her to find the remains of her skirt to cover herself. "Gods, I didn't know it would be like that."

She felt a strange emotion then, an odd upwelling in her chest that seemed like ruefulness, but was really more like bone-deep weariness. She looked at Klauden, the vampire sitting listlessly on the edge of the bed, his robe in tatters. It was him, she realized.

Klauden was sad. She could feel it. She could feel everything now.

"Did you know?" she whispered, a hand reaching out to touch him, to complete the connection. "Did you know it would be like that?"

"I said it was intense," the vampire said, and that was when Rory dove on top of him. Before the vampire could even react, Rory had knocked him off the bed and onto the floor. The elf was straddling the vampire, completely unconcerned with his lack of clothes as both hands closed around Klauden's neck. The elf was cursing in a low slew of Elven that Hannah had only heard whispered in the back alleys of Kalford, hands crushing what life remained in the vampire. Hannah felt a curious closing of her own throat then, and she coughed, unable to breathe past the invisible hands on her own neck. It was more of her connection to Klauden.

"Rory!" she choked. She rolled onto her side, using her momentum to propel her onto the floor and knock the elf sideways. Rory slipped but did not let go, Klauden's body tumbling to the side as they all rolled. When Hannah came to a stop, she was lying behind Klauden, Rory on the other side of the vampire with his hands locked in a death grip. The elf's face was a mask of fury, mouth twisting in rage as he continued his litany of Elven curses, calling out Klauden for every sin known to the language.

"Rory," Hannah tried again, this time managing to lift her arm over Klauden's body in an attempt to pull the vampire out of Rory's grasp. "-top." She managed to get her other arm underneath Klauden, who was doing absolutely nothing to resist the elf's attack, and tugged him back, dragging Rory with them. When she hit the edge of the bed, she rolled again, pulling Klauden up and over her, and wedged her body between the two men. When the elf tried to readjust his grip across her body, she brought a hand up to slap him hard across the face.

Rory paused, his red face suddenly white again with the force of her slap, and he stared at her uncomprehendingly. She gasped again, the gurgling sound from her throat seeming to wake the elf up, and he pulled his hands back suddenly, sitting up and pushing himself away from them.

He landed hard on his butt, great shaking breaths racking his own body. Hannah took several grateful breaths.

"You..." he was saying angrily. "He..." He looked up at her then, angry tears in his eyes. "How..."

Hannah pushed Klauden to the side, noting the way the vampire's gasping breaths were more intense now. He would need blood, and soon, she knew, but right now, there were more important things. *But what? What can I say? Sorry I almost had sex with Klauden just now?*

She caught her own breath, resting Klauden gently on the floor as she slid out from beneath him. She didn't approach Rory but sat isolated from both of them, trying to calm the situation. When no one said anything for a time, Klauden shuffled awkwardly onto his side, then rolled himself up against the bed with a supreme effort, pale face staring at both of them in turn. When the moment drew out again, Klauden chuckled softly, the movement making the hitch in his breathing even more pronounced.

"What could possibly be funny?" Hannah asked, misery evident in her voice.

"We all know not to do that again," the vampire said, and Hannah knew just how funny the idea was to him and couldn't help smiling too.

The bond was strong.

And Rory was outside of it.

She looked at the elf then, seeing the haggard lines of grief and rage on his face, and wished there was an easy way out of this. "Rory," she began, hoping the words would come. "I didn't know," she settled for saying finally. "None of us knew."

"He knew," the elf said, but there was distance in his voice now. Hannah knew he was probably thinking of Firene, of the morning that he had discovered his wife in bed with his cousin and committed the murder that had banished him from his people. And she had nearly committed the same act and right in front of him. If Klauden hadn't stopped her, she would have...

<<*Stop.*>> The voice was clear, controlled, and Klauden's. She didn't look at him but knew he was looking at Rory as well.

<<*But...*>>

<<*No,*>> he ordered. <<*You will not tell him what you wanted.*>>

<<*But...*>>

<<*Look at him. He cannot take it.*>> Then a sigh, and he added, <<*Tell him later if you must, break him down slowly, but do not do it now. I don't have the strength to protect either of us.*>>

<<*He is not an enemy,*>> she snapped.

<<*Not yet,*>> the vampire thought to her. <<*Not yours.*>>

Hannah wanted to contradict him, but she recalled the ghost-like feeling of Rory's hands around her throat and said nothing. Klauden spoke instead. "I didn't know precisely what would happen," the vampire said. "Some get violent, some get angry, some burn with the need." He paused, "And I suppose some translate that need into desire. It's no matter."

"Easy for you to say," Rory snapped. "You didn't just watch your wife almost have sex with someone else."

"She couldn't help herself," Klauden explained patiently. "It's a reflex, a side effect of the bloodlust."

"You said she would be different, not herself," Rory said. "You never mentioned that."

"Be glad she turned her attentions on you and not on some innocent unfortunate," Klauden replied. "Many have died because a fledgling was made in their vicinity."

Hannah winced, wondering just how much of her apparently regained control was permanent. "Will it happen again? Will I lose myself?" she asked, voice shaking.

Klauden shrugged, the move making him wince. "I don't know," he said. "Maybe not."

"I thought you always had all the answers," Rory commented, anger faded out of him now as he cradled his wrist against his chest. "You don't seem to know anything at all lately."

"I know," Klauden said. "Funny, is it not?"

"Not really," Rory said, getting to his feet slowly. Hannah could see that drinking his blood had weakened him. In fact, of the three of them, she was the strongest, the most refreshed.

When the elf struggled to raise the lid of the chest that held their clothes, Hannah stood. "Let me," she said, flicking the lid open a bit too hard, the top squeaking as it hit the end of the hinges and bounced back.

"Wow," Rory said, staring at her.

"I don't know my own strength," she said, pushing gently on the lid to keep it open and pulling out a new pair of pants for the elf to wear. He took them awkwardly, one hand still holding the wound on his wrist closed.

"Come," she told him, leading him to the bed, and when he sat, she took the pants from him and examined the wrist. Sighing at the well of blood leaking from beneath the covering hand, she walked to the counter and reached underneath, removing the long roll of bandages that he often used to patch her wounds. She returned to him, gesturing to the wrist as she knelt before the bed. "Let me see."

He held out the arm to her, and she used the remains of her skirt to wipe up the surrounding blood. "Hmm," she frowned as the blood smeared and stuck to her. "I'll get some water." She laid his hand back over the wound, pressing hard to staunch the blood.

When it seemed that he would keep up the pressure, she stood and walked to the back door. It was only after she opened it that she remembered the sorry state of her clothes and made an effort to pull down her shirt to keep what remained of her modesty intact. She picked up the bucket from beside the door and filled it with water from the barrel, then sloshed back to the bed, removing the scraps of her skirt as she did so; it wasn't covering much anymore anyway. Besides, the shirt was mostly long enough. *After all,* she thought, *what does it really matter now?*

She used the scraps to clean Rory's wrist and bandaged the wound tightly. She checked him for other wounds but found none, and when he stood on shaky feet to get into the new pants, Hannah did most of the work. Giving her his blood had weakened him, but the fight with Klauden seemed to have taken the rest of the spirit from him.

"Rory," she whispered when he was mostly presentable again.

"Your face," he said, reaching for the bucket and the wet cloths inside.

Hannah reached up touch her face, feeling the stickiness as she did. She let the elf wipe her face then, wondering how she could repair this sudden distance between them. "I'm fine," she said after a moment. "I'm going to live now. Because of you."

"Because of him."

"Because of both of you," she settled for saying. "Rory, I'm so sorry."

He shook his head. "It's not your fault."

"It's the blood," she added.

"I know." He gave her a long look then. "Look Hannah, I loved you when you were a vampire steeped in blood. I loved you as a mortal in a different body. I don't see how I couldn't love you now as his fledgling." He paused, pondering. "But..." His voice trailed off. Hannah was overwhelmed by his sudden willingness to discuss his feelings. It wasn't that he had refused to be open with her, but this frank discussion of things was completely new.

"What?" Hannah prompted. *Can our relationship be saved?*

"What almost happened here tonight," he said, "with him."

Hannah nodded, willing him to go on.

"I don't think I could live with that," he admitted. "I would still love you, I think, but I couldn't live with it."

"I understand," she nodded. "I do. Believe me, it will never happen."

"But you said it yourself. The blood bond is..."

"Intense, yes," she agreed, "but so am I. I am yours, you see. No matter how bonded we are, I am still yours."

"<Welan?>"

Hannah cocked her head at him, curious at the Elven word he had used. She scanned her memory but couldn't place it. "What?"

"It means to take an oath. To promise."

"Of course," she replied. "I swear."

"You don't have to," he said then, shaking his head as if to clear it. "It's silly of me. I need to rest."

Hannah nodded at him, thinking that his request was not so silly after all. She hoped her word would be enough. She stood up again, taking a blanket from the chest and pushing the somewhat mangled bedclothes into a pile that she tucked in the corner. The laundry could certainly wait. She helped Rory lay down and tucked the clean blanket over him.

"What about him?" the elf asked, gesturing to the still form of Klauden leaning against the bed.

"He needs to feed," Hannah said. "I will take him." Rory seemed about to protest but didn't. Hannah found she was fascinated by the subtle throb of the vein in his neck and looked away. "It's my duty," she mumbled.

The elf nodded, eyes drooping in exhaustion.

She walked around the bed to where Klauden lay propped up against the side, pausing at the chest to pull out another pair of pants and shirt for the vampire to wear and another skirt that she stepped into quickly.

"You need blood," she said without preamble after dropping the clothes on his lap. He shuffled awkwardly into them, and she helped as much as possible without allowing his modesty to suffer as hers had. When he had pushed the tattered robe above his head and managed to get into Rory's shirt, she got an arm up underneath his and raised him carefully to his feet. "Come."

"Be careful," Rory said, but his voice was already losing its edge, fading into the silence of deep sleep.

"I will," she promised, then began shuffling Klauden toward the trap-door in the floor.

XXX

When she stepped outside of the tunnel, Hannah realized just how changed her body was. She knew it was cold, the night black and crisp around them, but she didn't feel the temperature as she had hours before. Her feet were bare, and she could feel the cold snow beneath them, but it didn't matter as it once had. Her body wouldn't freeze to death now. Her limbs might feel cold, but it couldn't slow her or hurt her at all. Though being a fledgling wasn't quite like being the vampire she remembered, there were some similarities. Her body wasn't indestructible, but it was sturdy and immune to disease or sickness—except the bloodlust of course. She could see in the dark with her nightvision now, though it would color her eyes a glowing red, and she could jump higher and run faster and longer than any mortal. Still, she had blood tears and hiding from the mortals might be more of a challenge than she expected.

She was stronger now, too, she realized, her arm around Klauden's back supporting much of his weight without effort. As they stepped slowly into the clearing beyond the tunnel, Hannah wondered just what she could find that might sate Klauden. She wasn't about to sacrifice any villagers, though at the moment she couldn't give a valid reason for the reluctance, and she thought that bringing him to close to Salva might be asking for more trouble than they could handle at present. Maybe they would stumble on some more of the men who had tried to sell her and Elsbeth to Salva, no doubt as food for the growing army of fledglings. Things would certainly go differently this time around.

"Klauden," she whispered as they entered the woods, "where did you go last time?" Glancing around at the trees outlined by the moonlight, she saw the distant bulk of the newly constructed wall that now separated her home from the surrounding forest. She checked the ground around her feet, careful to disguise their footprints as coming from a different path than the one that led back to the tunnel and Rory. It made her nervous to leave the elf alone, but she knew it was foolish. They had been fine in that house for a long time; nothing was going to happen in a few hours' time. Besides, the army must be recovering from the loss of the fledglings this afternoon.

Gods, she thought in awe. *Was it only this afternoon that I stood in my forge and argued with Klauden about how contented I was in this life? How has so much happened so quickly?* She shook her head, then turned to Klauden. The vampire was reeling beside her, face pale and eyes bloodshot as he blinked slowly.

"Malfek, Klauden. You didn't say how much this would hurt you."

"I'm not hurt," he said in a soft voice.

"You're aching for blood."

"I'm always aching for blood," he replied. "You know that."

Hannah shook her head. "No," she said. "I didn't know." She felt a wave of something then, a thirst so powerful it threatened to split her mind with the need, and she wavered next to him. "Klauden," she whispered, feeling the bloodthirst rush through both of them. "But I'm sated," she insisted, letting go of him and shaking her head to clear the feeling. "I've had enough."

"It's never enough," he said.

"No," she contradicted, stepping away. "It was enough. When I was a vampire, I only needed to feed every few days, and even then, the thirst was never like this. Why is it so different for you?"

He shrugged weakly, taking a few steps on his own into the woods. "Perhaps it is because of the mortal blood you inherited from your grandfather," he speculated. "I have to feed more often, and more desperately, I think, than you ever did."

"How?" she asked, beginning to follow his halting progress through the trees. The night air was crisp and cold; had it always been like this or was she only now really appreciating it due to her enhanced senses? "How did you manage it on the long road to this place?" She frowned. "How did you feed? Did you pass through many villages or towns?"

Klauden shook his head. "I made do," he said without looking at her.

"It's funny," Hannah commented, stepping quickly ahead of him to take his arm as he negotiated a pile of downed branches in a vat of snow and mud, "for one who spent three long months traveling among the mortals, you've learned surprisingly little of them." As Hannah thought about it, the odder it became. She had only spent a month with mortals before changing her entire view of them—it was impossible to be around so much life and vitality without certain rules of her existence creating dilemmas and forcing change.

And yet Klauden remained unchanged. He still saw mortals as inferior, weak, and mostly unnecessary. Hannah stared at him, at the careful way he was watching the ground and taking steps, completely unaware of his surroundings for one of the few times in his life. Was it possible that her old friend was just too entrenched in his old ways, or was there something else going on here? She sniffed, pushing her hair behind her ears as Klauden rested beside her.

"How could you make it all this way without any of your belongings?" Her voice was casual, but she watched him carefully, taking in the awkward fit of Rory's clothes, the way they hung on his shoulders, the pants loose around his waist. "Honestly, Klauden, you don't even have another robe."

"I managed."

"But how? And why? Why would you leave without your things?" She gave him a serious look then. "Did they make you leave? Were you discovered? Did Malbrek learn what you did in the ceremony?"

Klauden shook his head. "Of course not. I am not so careless as to be caught by the likes of him."

"So what, then? Gods, Klauden, did you even tell anyone that you were leaving?" she pressed.

He shook his head again, then smiled broadly at her. She could feel some secret inside him, some knowledge that he was proud to have kept to himself.

"Klauden," she said in a shocked voice, "your poor mother."

"My mother is fine, chaivin. She would be gratified by your concern. I shall have to tell her of it someday."

"What are you talking about?"

"Think, chaivin," he ordered. "What can you make of it?"

Hannah stared at him, the question reminding her of hours spent talking just like this when he tried to explain her magic to her. "Well," she began, "you've no belongings, which means you must have left in a hurry." She paused, taking in the smirk on his face. "You've managed to keep yourself well fed along the way, which means you either brought slaves with you or have been lucky in finding them since you left home. But that doesn't make sense." She stopped, considering. "You have some way of keeping in touch with the castle," she speculated, "a spy of some sort, but who?" The way he was looking at her gave her another idea, a crazy idea, but one that answered all of her questions. "Or," she said slowly, "you never really left at all." She paused again. "What is it, then? A spell? Some sort of dreamwalking in the flesh? What?"

"You can be quite smart when you apply yourself. Yes, you are right. It is a spell."

"What kind of spell?"

"Teleportation," he said with a grin, eyes blazing red. "I found it one of Karnik's accounts of his travels to the far north. You know," he prompted, "where he met the man wolves." Hannah couldn't help but notice the way that he could lecture, even starved as he was. He was dedicated, too, she realized, in his own way, as loyal as Rory to his own ideals as the elf was to his men. *They are not so very different, then.*

No, she contradicted what must have been Solyn again. *They are very different.*

Hannah shook her head, snorting a bit as she recalled her history lessons. "Karnik was insane," she reminded him. "The man came back from the north spinning tales to frighten children in an attempt to cover up his own failure to actually leave the Vanya at all."

Klauden shook his head at her. "But he did leave," he said, nodding. "He used the spell to open a door between dimensions. It works much the same as the Star of Elgiva," he commented, "opening a space between spaces that allows one to walk right through."

"So, what? You go back home every night? How?"

"I can only travel to places I have seen," he explained, licking his lips a bit, "so I had to actually walk all the way here." He gave her a sardonic look. "You could have settled a bit closer, you know. I had a hard time explaining what I was doing to ruin so many of my clothes so the slaves wouldn't get suspicious."

"You didn't really live among the people, then, did you?" She nodded, the thought confirming her suspicions. "I thought as much. There was no way you could spend three months south of the Vanya and remain unchanged."

"Am I unchanged?" he asked. "I think I've broken more promises in the last weeks than ever in my life." He blinked slowly, reaching out to her. "You have an odd effect on my self-control, Hannah."

She took his hand, wrapping an arm around him for support. "You must feed," she said again, stepping farther into the forest. "Let's go."

"Yes," he said, wrapping his other arm around her and tugging her into a hug. "Let's go."

The rush of magic was dizzying. As the power gathered around them and carried them through the portal, Hannah heard a great sound like rushing wind passed her ears, her hair whipped into her face, and then her feet were back on solid ground, except instead of ice and snow, she was standing on something soft and springy. Hannah opened her eyes, stepping carefully away and out of Klauden's embrace and noted that she was in Klauden's rooms. In fact, they were in his bedroom, standing on top of his bed. She reached out to grab one of the four posters to steady herself, pushing aside a swath of the sheer fabric that shrouded the bed as she did so, and peered out into the room. They appeared to be alone.

Shaking her head, she stepped off the bed onto the floor, noting the wet footprints she had left on the bedspread and reveling in the soft rug that covered the stone floor. It had been a long time since she had been exposed to such finery.

"I can't believe this," she breathed. "Are we really here?"

Klauden sank slowly to his knees, then slid cross-legged to a seat on his bed. He took a long, slow breath, smiling a bit. "Welcome home, Hannah," he said formally.

She stared at him, suddenly very wary. "Klauden," she said carefully. "Why are we here?"

He chuckled, getting slowly to his feet. "I need to feed. You wouldn't have me take one of your villager friends, would you?" When she didn't respond, he added, "You might want to stay in here for a moment. I'd rather not have to explain your presence to any slaves."

He pushed away from the bed with a sigh, then took a few halting steps past an ornate armoire and walked through the open doorway that led into the outer rooms. Hannah knew that his suite was the same size as her own had been, but what she had used as a dressing room and bathing area was actually Klauden's study. She could see the edge of the massive desk through the open door and knew that the walls around it were covered with shelves and shelves of books. His desk, too, would be piled with books, scrolls, and ancient dusty sheaves of paper. Somewhere in the mess he would have clean parchment and his quill and inkpot, since Klauden spent much of his time reading and the rest taking notes on what he discovered. Hannah wondered how much of that desk was filled with notes about her and her strange condition—two souls in one body.

She heard the small tinkle of a bell and knew that Klauden had summoned his slaves. She ducked quickly back onto the bed, pulling the curtain closed behind her. She could feel Klauden's contentment as he sank heavily into the heavy wooden armchair that sat before his desk, and she tried to distance herself from him. He deserved some privacy, at least.

She looked around inside the bed. It was dim inside the gauzy material, much darker than she would have been able to see in if she were still mortal. Her fledgling eyes could see quite well, however, even without actively concentrating on using her nightvision, and she noted the twirling pattern of gold thread that twined around the bedspread, interlocking with a blue thread that bobbed and weaved up and down the brown stripes that dominated the design.

That's not hard to do, Hannah thought, imagining the loom and the beats between lines of material that would create the winding arc of the pattern. She reached out to trace one line, saw how it was threaded both from the top and bottom, and calculated how much thread a bedspread of this size would need, how many hours of spinning with her distaff and spindle would be required. She saw that the design was both an inherent part of the blanket and also traced again on top of the bed to give the image depth.

Someone spent a long time making this, she thought. *Yes,* she answered herself, *the thread alone would take two weeks for one woman.*

It was an odd thought, Hannah realized after a moment. Before Solyn, she would never have sat and thought about how a blanket was made or how to get the delicate lines of tracing that ran up and down the sleeves and along the collar of Klauden's robe. Now she knew that such line-work wasn't difficult, but it could be time consuming if the material was thick or the needle dull. Now, she could probably make a blanket just like that. Her finger traced the blue thread up to the head of the bed, pushing the blanket down to reveal a stack of pillows properly lined up. Hannah pushed the bedspread down, slipping beneath it without much thought, climbing into bed much as she had every night for years and years. The blanket felt divine, the soft material smooth under her hands and wonderful against her bare feet. She sank down into the pillow, eyes closing, and allowed herself to revel in the softness of the mattress, the smooth silkiness of the blanket.

The bed itself was huge. Three of the bed she shared with Rory would easily fit inside the curtained area, and there were two of them. Klauden slept here all alone.

Hannah turned onto her side, her nose suddenly picking up a distinctive scent that she knew was Klauden's hair. She moved closer, breathing deep. The smell of clean water and firesmoke blended with the slightly sharp scent of ink that always hovered around the vampire, and the smell conjured a memory.

She and Klauden were on this bed, she bouncing up and down in her eagerness to get him outside again, and he had finally given into to her cajoling and abandoned the study. Though he hadn't bounced, he had stood up on the mattress near her, and when the motion of his feet made her nearly lose her balance, he had caught her easily. Her face had fallen into his chest, and she had gotten a lungful of that scent, a smell she always associated with the indoors, with books and study and everything she wanted to get away from. It had only been a moment, but when she regained her feet and looked up at him, there had been a different look on Klauden's face.

He was older than she was, but still barely in his fourth decade, hardly even a man yet, but he had looked at her with a new expression and his hands lingered on her back. Hannah remembered the rush that had gone through her at that look, a wisp of desire that she didn't understand, and she recalled the frown that crossed her face. The look made Klauden a stranger, made him one of the countless others who gave her odd looks like that, especially the Kargin, and sometimes Vailen, and she didn't like it. Even more, though, was that she didn't like the responding feeling his hungry look roused in her. She had backed away from him then, climbing off the bed and stepping quickly into the outer rooms. It was the last time she ever went into his bedroom, and in the decades since, she had begun to slowly understand why.

But here she was again. Not only playing on his bed, but laying in it. *What am I thinking?* He said to stay out of sight, not to make herself at home under his sheets. She sat up, pushing the blanket down. She noted the wet splotch made by her feet under the blanket, the smaller chunks of drying mud, and slid to the side, clearing the space with the side of her hand, swiping the dirt off the edge of the bed to slide to the floor along the curtains.

The sound of the door opening made her pause, and she froze for a second, her senses reaching out for the source of the disturbance. Mortals, she felt instantly, three of them. She marveled at the swiftness with which the ability had developed; perhaps fledglings did not have to study to make their senses work as she had. She touched the newcomers softly, visions from their minds and memories playing out before her eyes. The first was Klauden's regular slave, a man who bowed quickly and withdrew after walking the other two inside. Both victims had been charmed already, and so stood docile, but Hannah could feel the rush of the blood in their veins, and the pulse of their heartbeats echoed in her fingertips. She crawled to the foot of the bed, pushing the curtain aside slowly to reveal a tiny opening through which she could see partway through the door. She heard the rustle as Klauden climbed to his feet, and she could feel the eagerness in him, the need to feed overwhelming any conscious thought. Through her small window, Hannah could see his back as he crossed to the front doors, then he was out of sight again. She could still feel him though, and she knew the first mortal was a girl, a teenager pale with hunger and tinged with sleeplessness around the eyes. Even if she had lived, Hannah knew she would not live long. It was a common enough malady among the humans who lived north of the Vanya—they called it the wasting sickness—and though the victims had nothing that harmed the vampires or fledglings, they did not live for very long after the gray tinge touched them, and it was the afflicted who made up most of the food supply for the castle.

Hannah had a sense that the wasting sickness might not be just a fortunate accident, and she knew that Klauden was pondering some theory he had in development, and she was somehow getting an echo of that thought, but then she was overwhelmed by the sense of Klauden feeding. She felt the rush of blood past her lips, the slow beat of the girl's heart, and she too felt the blood working its way through her body, healing her and soothing the burning need within. She pulled away, aware that she was intruding on Klauden during a rather private moment, letting the curtain fall back and trying to sever the connection between them.

It was difficult, however, since a part of Hannah was fascinated by the rush of emotions, curious about the bond, and she wanted to see just how far it would go. She knew part of the interest was Solyn. The slave girl was paying close attention to anything her new fledgling body experienced, but she couldn't deny her own involvement. Though she knew it was wrong of her, she wanted to be this close to him, to feel what he felt. It felt somehow right, and that bothered her more than anything else.

When Klauden finished with the girl, he slowly lowered her body to the floor, then took the few steps to the second mortal, an older man who stood stiffly, eyes rheumy with age and knuckles knotted by hard work. The vampire struck quickly, this time more aware of his surroundings, and Hannah knew the moment he realized she was with him in essence, though her body was still hidden in the bed.

He made a show of feeding then, swallowing slowly so that Hannah could feel the warm blood in his mouth, swirling the liquid with his tongue and rubbing his fangs against the tough skin of victim's neck. As she felt him feed, Hannah became aware of her own hunger again.

It's not right, she told herself, insisting her body obey her, but she knew that feeling. It was a slow crawl across her skin, a throb in her fingers and a flutter in her chest. The need to feed again.

It's too soon, she told herself. *I just fed. And an elf, at that. I'm fine. I just need to calm down.*

But she could feel the blood in Klauden's mouth, could sense the slowing heart, could imagine how it would feel to drink blood of her own, and when she opened her eyes again, she could feel her teeth huge in her mouth. There was something she should be thinking about, she realized dully, but by the time she had another conscious thought, she had slithered off the bed and hurried into the outer room, insinuating herself between Klauden and the body. When the vampire didn't move aside quickly enough, Hannah elbowed him roughly, the resulting rise of fierce pride making her shove even more, and then she struck, huge teeth taking a moment to find the right spot on the other side of the man's neck, and a jet of blood sprayed her in the face before she managed to capture and control the flow with her mouth.

There were memories in the man, images and feelings that she could share if she wanted, and she knew somewhere deep down that that was something she had always enjoyed when she had been a vampire, taking the memories, but right now, all she could think about was the blood. The heat filled her mouth, washed her face and coated her hands, and she was just as thrilled by the sharp smell in the room as she was by the slowing beat of his heart. There was something more, a hint of some feeling building in her, but it was slow to start. As he faded away and the blood began to flag, the new feeling vanished, and Hannah stepped away, watching curiously as the body slumped fast and hit the stone floor awkwardly. The sound was loud in the silence. She looked up to see Klauden smiling at her.

<<*Yes,*>> she heard him say. <<*Fight for what you want.*>>

She smiled back at him, wiping the blood on her hands across her face, then taking a second to lick her fingers clean. *It is so good,* she thought, *to have fresh blood, to share that with my master.*

My what?

Hannah returned to herself with a jolt, taking a few steps back and wiping her face with the few clean spots that remained on her shirt. "Malfek," she whispered. "I'm sorry. I didn't mean to…"

"You were hungry," Klauden said. "Fledglings are always hungry."

Hannah cocked her head, listening to her body for a second. The blood rushed through her, sating, easing, healing. She was fine for now, but soon, very soon, she thought, the need might be on her again. She didn't even remember making the decision to come out here and feed. It had been like being possessed by something—a demon of sorts that made her move without will or thought.

<Don't look at me,> Solyn quipped. *<You can tell when I'm doing it. That wasn't me at all.>*

<I know,> Hannah told her. *<The bloodlust is strong, stronger than I am used to.>*

"How long will this last?" Hannah asked Klauden.

"What?"

"The hunger like that. I didn't mean to come feed. It just happened."

The vampire shrugged. "I don't exactly know. Some fledglings gain control in a month; some take years. It depends."

"If that happens back home," she said, "I will kill someone without realizing it." She paused, considering. "I'm dangerous. I should stay away."

"You are away."

Hannah glanced around the room, the books, the fireplace, the candles on brackets high above the book cases. They hadn't been here very long. She wondered if Rory was still sleeping.

"Rory."

"He'll be fine."

"We need to get back."

"You just said you were too dangerous to get back."

"I can't leave him all alone like that. He's too weak."

"I'm weak," the vampire said, and Hannah gave him a look. "Fine," Klauden admitted, biting his lip. "First we will get cleaned up, yes? Then we can head back to the village and the impending slaughter."

Hannah did not appreciate his sense of humor, nor his lack of hurry. "We should go now," she insisted.

Klauden looked down at his clothes, the foreign shirt and pants, then ran a hand through his tangled hair. "I need to get clean," he told her. "Not long," he answered her unspoken question. "I'm not nearly as finicky as you."

"I'm not finicky," she snapped.

He chuckled. "Not now," he admitted, "but you were the one who took hours getting dressed."

"That was a long time ago."

"I know, but certainly you can still appreciate a bath," he said. "You're covered in blood again." He held his hands out before his chest. "A brief respite, chaivin, no more. I can get you fresh clothes as well."

Hannah contemplated. She desperately wanted to get back to Rory, but the elf was probably still sleeping, and she was filthy, her hair matted with blood and her face streaked with dirt. It had been a long time since she had a bath. It would feel wonderful, especially with her new skin so sensitive.

"Not long?" she asked.

He nodded. "I promise."

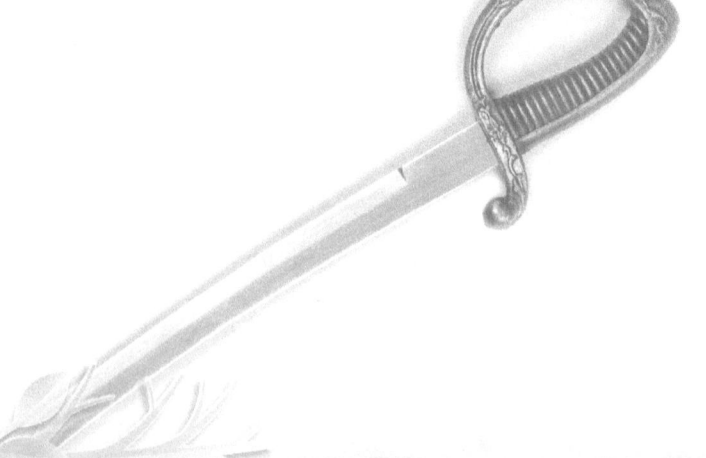

XXXI

Hannah lay back in the tub, freshly scrubbed skin singing with sensation as she submerged her head again. Her short hair felt odd underwater, like little snakes teasing her ears instead of the long veil she remembered from her last swim. She lay under the surface for a long time, reveling in the sense of freedom that not needing breath allowed. Truly, she was letting Solyn enjoy the feeling. Hannah remembered what this felt like. One year as a mortal could not erase eight decades as a vampire. Still, the girl was enjoying herself, her mind filling with lists of things she would never again have to endure.

<*Is it always like this?*> Solyn asked.

<*Not always,*> Hannah replied. <*When the bloodlust is unsated,*> she explained, <*that is the closest thing to breathlessness we feel. It's our body's way of letting us know we need more blood, though. It's nothing like getting kicked in the chest. It's slower, first of all, and more insinuating.*>

<*I don't understand.*>

Hannah considered. She knew that she could see Solyn's memories any time the slave offered, and even sometimes against her will, but she hadn't actively tried to share her own memories with the slave. <*Here,*> she said suddenly, allowing a memory of that night in Kalford to play in her mind. She was lying in bed, sweating and shaking and shivering, her breath coming in rattling gasps, her skin aching with need, her body burning with emptiness. <*It's like that,*> Hannah narrated, <*but it grows worse and worse as more time passes.*>

<*Can we die from it?*>

<*Yes, but not immediately. It can take a vampire up to a month to die from the sickness, though they go mad long before the end.*> She paused and

suddenly decided to forge onward. <*My own mother lasted two and a half weeks before she gave in and killed her best friend, a slave, and then she went mad and died two weeks after that.*>

Hannah swallowed reflexively underwater, recalling the locked door at the end of the hallway, her father and Malbrek whispering to one another as her mother's screams echoed through the entire level of the castle. Then Malbrek had cast a spell, a silencing circle, Hannah knew now, and the screams had cut off. She had been thirty-two that year, not yet a woman, and just beginning her magic lessons. Still, she had sworn that day to learn her spells, to become better than everyone else, even Kelvin Malbrek, so that he could never silence her like that.

Of course, she had forgotten that oath, much like the rest, after a time, lapsing in her studies as she always had. <*I made a lot of promises as a child,*> she told Solyn, <*but I rarely kept them.*>

<*Except to Klauden.*>

<*Even those,*> Hannah admitted, <*I only kept while I was here. It took me only six months to break my oaths to him as well. I am a terribly inconstant woman.*>

<*I know the feeling,*> Solyn said, and Hannah felt warmed then. *What was it? The start of a bond? A slow beginning to a relationship?*

<*Ease up,*> the slave snapped. <*No need to get all teary-eyed.*>

<*I know,*> Hannah snapped back at her. <*I was just thinking.*> She sat up in the tub suddenly, water rushing down her face, dripping from her hair. She pushed the short strands behind her ears and out of her face, glancing around the room for a towel.

She was in Klauden's bedroom still, the silver tub dragged in by the slaves filled while she lay motionless in Klauden's bed. He had bathed first, then called in more slaves to rinse and refill the tub, and Hannah had laid with her eyes closed and pretended that there was not a naked vampire a few feet away thinking about her. When he had risen to dry off and dress from the armoire, she had rolled onto her stomach, mashing her face into the pillow to restrain the almost overwhelming need to look, to see, to go out there and meet him as she knew he wanted her to do.

It was Solyn, Hannah told herself as she stood dripping. *I resisted what she wanted. It was not my own impulse.* When the vampire left the room, pulling shut a curtain that separated the bedroom from the study, she had been glad, her chest heavy with relief that she managed to stay in one spot.

<Please,> Solyn said. *<I thought you were a big believer in honesty, at least with yourself.>*

Hannah reached for the towel and began drying herself. *He could have made me,* she thought, squeezing her hair and shaking her head a bit. *With a word, a thought, a gesture, he could have made me come to him. Instead, he let me struggle.*

But did he let me win? Or did I win?

Hannah sighed, stepping out of the tub onto the soft carpeted floor, clean toes relishing the feeling. She wrapped the towel around herself, then crossed to the fireplace that took up most of the wall opposite the armoire. It was habit to warm herself, though she hardly needed to anymore. She wasn't even cold, though she knew the room was chilly. The water had steamed when she got in, and even now she could still see little wisps rising from the surface. She held out her hands, sighing as she realized just how little of her body the towel covered. Klauden had told her to call when she was ready, and he would see to fresh clothing. *That's not all he'll see,* she thought, glancing down at her long bare legs, the curve of her shoulders, and the cleft between her breasts. *This will not do.*

She stepped over to the armoire, enjoying the oiled hinges as she opened it—everything in her father's castle was made from high quality materials and craftsmanship—and considered the selection of Klauden's clothes. Though most of the space was taken up by hanging robes in various shades of the rainbow, some that went over the head and some that tied at the waist, there were drawers in here as well. She bent down to open the top drawer, holding the towel carefully as she dripped a bit, wet splotches landing on a pile of neatly folded shorts in varying shades of creams and beiges.

Well then, she thought, *now I know what he wears under that robe.* She picked up a pair from the top, shaking them free and holding them against her body to see if they might fit. She tossed the towel aside, remembering a lifetime of doing just that, and she had to smirk at the knowledge that she would not have to pick it up this time. It was a wonderful thing to have slaves.

<Sure it is,> Solyn quipped, *<when you're not one of them.>*

Hannah colored a bit but said nothing. She stepped into the shorts, tying the drawstring across her hips and taking a few tentative steps to see if they would stay up. Satisfied, she stepped back to the armoire, rifling through the robes.

"Hey," she heard Klauden say, "are you done yet?" The curtain rustled and she turned toward the door, arms crossing over her bare breasts to cover herself.

"No!" she shouted as he entered the room, his arms filled with a folded garment that looked like one of her old dresses.

Klauden didn't look ashamed at her appearance. In fact, he looked at the shorts she wore, shook his head, and blew out a long breath. "Those do not become you, chaivin." He stepped to the bed, tucked the curtain to one side behind a bracket, and draped the dress he carried on the surface, spreading out the folds of arms and neck.

"What are you doing?" she squealed. "Get out of here!"

"This is my room," he answered, his back to her now as he fussed with the dress. "Now, come here."

"No!"

He glanced at her over his shoulder and raised an eyebrow. "I have seen you in far more incriminating circumstances," he commented. He reached for the straightened dress, which Hannah noted was one that wrapped around the waist, then twisted up and around to highlight the curves of hip and breast before spreading out to cover the arms tightly. The bottom was loose fitting, the better to show the shape of her thighs as she walked, and the low bustline and low-cut back were designed to draw attention to key areas of neck and shoulder.

Did I ever wear such a thing? She wondered. *How?*

"Come here," he repeated, and this time there was an order in his voice, and Hannah began walking before she realized it. She stopped herself at the third step, muscles shaking, and glared at him as her body began to tremble with the effort of resistance.

He held the dress out, flipping it down so that he could slide it over her head. "Oh, come now, chaivin," he snapped. "You need help to get this one on." He paused, then added, "Unless you would rather stand there half naked?"

Hannah stepped jerkily toward him and turned her back. When he slid the dress over the upraised arms, she muttered, "I need an undershirt."

"You never needed one before," he said, sliding the material over her shoulders and patting it into place around her hips.

"I didn't have this body before," she snapped. She gestured to her chest, considerably larger than it had been when she wore clothes like this. But even as she spoke, Klauden fit the wrap of the dress around her chest, helping her slide her arms into the sleeves. The dress fit snugly but comfortably, almost as though it had been made for this body. "It fits," she said softly, remembering how dresses like this once felt, knowing that the blue would complement this body's blonde hair, the tightness of the waist and bustline outlining her attributes and the pale skin of her back and shoulders revealed to eager eyes.

"Of course, it fits," he said, turning her about to face him. He looked her up and down, then frowned. "Those shorts do not fit," he added. "I can see them."

Hannah gave him a frown of her own. "I'm not taking them off," she snapped. "Besides, you can't be serious. I am not wearing this thing back home."

"Why not?"

"It's ridiculous."

"You look wonderful."

"No, I don't." She stopped, realizing that she had been rubbing her hands along her sides, enjoying the feel of the material under her skin. "Fine," she admitted. "It fits well, but even so..." She let her voice trail off. "Klauden, where did you get this?"

"I had it."

"You are in the habit of having women's clothes in your room?"

"I don't know which to find more offensive," he snapped, "that you think I have many women in this room, or that you think I wear women's clothes."

"I'm serious."

He shrugged. "It was for her," he admitted finally, with a gesture to the body. Solyn's body.

"Why?"

"She liked nice things," he said. "I had it made for her." He was saying something else, but Hannah was already tugging off the sleeves, unwrapping the waist and pulling the dress overhead.

"No," she declared, struggling as the material caught around her head, snagging in her hair and wrapping around her elbows. "I am not wearing this." She felt him helping her then, strong hands freeing her, and then the dress was off, and she stood facing him, bare breasted and breathing heavy in her frustration.

Klauden's gaze did not stray, his eyes meeting hers with a question.

<Come on,> Solyn shrieked. *<Just get it over with!>*

<I will not,> Hannah told her. *<I cannot.>* But she could feel her body leaning toward him, and even more so, she could feel the call of her blood, her spirit, aching to reach out and touch him again, to complete the bond.

<Oh, you can,> the slave assured her. *<And you will.>*

Hannah closed her eyes, breaking contact with both Klauden and Solyn. Her hands were shaking with the effort of her restraint, and she turned quickly around. It was better not looking at him, though she could still sense him. She crossed her arms, tying up the limbs that might betray her over her breasts.

"What will you wear, then?" he asked her back quietly. "I cannot take a slave's clothes without creating yet another rumor I do not need." He paused. "Vailen is known for such behavior, but I am not." Hannah stiffened at Vailen's name, Solyn experiencing a violent shudder inside as she recalled the one who had raped and tortured her during her days as a slave in the castle. The memory cleared Hannah's mind, and that overwhelming need to touch Klauden faded away. *<Not anymore,>* Hannah heard Solyn vow, thoughts of Vailen clouding the slave's perception. *<Never again.>*

Hannah hoped the girl was better with vows than she herself had been.

"Give me one of your robes," Hannah whispered. There was the sound of movement again, and then Klauden held something against her crossed arms. "Take this," he said quietly. "I will leave you be."

By the time she opened her eyes, she was alone. The curtain between this room and the study was shaking a bit, as though someone had just stepped through it.

She took a deep steadying breath and sat down hard on the edge of the bed, clutching the robe to her chest.

Gods, she thought, *this is awful. How much longer can I resist?*

230

XXXII

Hannah woke suddenly, disoriented and confused, unaware of where she was, and for a startling moment, who she was. The bed beneath her was soft, much softer than where she normally slept, and there was a wonderfully smooth blanket over her, tucked beneath her head.

When did I fall asleep? She sat up, blanket folding in her lap. She tangled for a moment in the length of the robe she wore, and she adjusted the shoulders and tugged the waist back down. *Oh,* she realized. *I sat down for a minute.* She was alone in the bed and in the room, and she pushed the blanket away and got to her feet. The floor was soft as well. *Hell,* she thought, *the entire place screams luxury to me now*, but she crossed quickly to the doorway.

Klauden sat at his desk, head bent over yet another book, this one folded in the haphazard blocks that marked the change from ancient scrolls to modern books, but he looked up when he saw her.

"How long was I asleep?" she asked, wiping her eyes.

He shrugged. "Not long. It's not yet sevens, though the sun is up already. It's early this time of year."

"It's morning already? Klauden, we have to go back!"

He raised an eyebrow at her. "We will."

"Now," she urged, but he didn't move. "Well?"

"Well what?"

"Are we going?"

"Easy, chaivin. Rest yourself."

"I've rested enough," she snapped, approaching the side of the desk.

"Severin isn't going anywhere," Klauden said, leaning back in his chair and folding the parchment on his lap.

Hannah knocked the book out of his lap. "That's not my concern," she said, "and you know it." He gave her a dirty look before leaning over to collect his book. He made a show of folding it again, brushing the corners flat and pressing along the spine before resting it carefully in a spot in the center of the desk before him. His fingers were stained with ink again. Hannah wondered what he had been writing. A glance at the desk showed that the book was covering a fresh sheet of paper, but she could only make out the bottom half of the last sentence in Klauden's spiky writing: *Kevna has never been severed.*

Hannah raised her eyebrows and was about to ask him about it, but then she thought of Rory, and the need for action was on her again, and she was tugging Klauden out of the chair. He came reluctantly, limbs resisting her pull.

"You're acting like a child," he told her when they stood in the center of the room.

"Bring us back," she ordered, stepping close to him. When he didn't touch her, she grabbed each of his hands and placed them on her shoulders. "Now."

Klauden sighed, shook his head, and his hands trailed down her arms to take her hands. "Chaivin," he whispered. "I know you are ever a woman of action, but magic doesn't always work that way."

"What do you mean?" Hannah gave him a suspicious look. *What new plot is this? Another way to keep me here, to remind me of this new connection? To keep me away from Rory?*

He shook his head again. "Honestly, chaivin, you really don't listen to me when I talk, do you?"

"I listen," she said, but her voice was petulant and sulky, the whine of a child.

"But you don't hear," he admonished. "Karnik's spell takes a lot of power and concentration," he explained. "I cannot perform it at will."

"Don't play with me," she accused. "You are a more powerful magic user than even Malbrek. You can't expect me to believe a spell is beyond you."

"It's not beyond my ability," he replied. "It's just beyond my ability right now." He sighed heavily, dropping her hands and heading to a bookcase near the door that led to the hallway and the castle beyond. As he stepped, Hannah could see slow trails of light around his feet, the effects of walking through the spell he had around the door to discourage unwanted eaves-droppers. Since the slaves from a few hours before, no one had bothered them. Hannah assumed that Klauden's slaves only came when he rang for them. Hers were always wandering in and out of her rooms, straightening up her mess or her person, and it was somewhat surprising to realize that there had been a time when she hadn't even noticed their presence.

< You never were the observant one, > Solyn quipped.

Klauden had found the book he sought, wriggling the slim volume from beneath a tottering pile of leather bound portfolios. He handed it to her. It was Hansen's *Introduction to Magical Incantations*, a primer that she remembered from her earliest days in Essentials. She looked at Klauden curiously.

"Why are you giving me this? I outgrew it years, hell, decades ago."

"Open it," Klauden ordered.

"Why?"

"Just do it," he repeated, and Hannah complied, the waft of ancient ink recalling hours spent poring over his incantations, days of memo-rizing foreign syllables and hearing Klauden's admonishments to *focus, Hannah, focus.* The pages were even more worn than she recalled, but she could make out the introductory words easily enough. Since she had found a new way of casting her spells, Solyn had stopped interrupting her ability to read.

The study of the magical arts is not to be taken lightly, Hansen began, *and requires a mind keen on detail and sculpted for devotion.*

Hannah snorted. She had always hated Hansen and his pretentious approach to teaching spells, as if he were the only one worthy of knowing such magic, but he deigned to share such knowledge with the mere mortals.

"I read this already," she complained, closing the book over her finger and looking at Klauden.

"Clearly, chaivin, you didn't."

"Well, it's been a long time since I needed to remember the proper order of incantations," she snapped, though the litany went through her mind—*memorize, strategize, practice, and release.* She blew out a long breath. She really loathed Hansen and his cut and dry magical lessons. None of his descriptions had ever explained her own magic—the way it leaped out of her as if alive, the way the words of the spells sometimes wavered in her memory or abandoned her completely. Now, she had a new way of casting that worked reliably, but the thought of all those wasted days trying to learn Hansen's method made her angry. She glanced down at the book again. Maybe Klauden was right and she hadn't finished it.

"Wait," she said, an idea coming to her, "was he the one who talked about fatigue all the time?"

Klauden nodded.

"I remember now," she said. "I never could cast the way he said to, but I never got that tired either, so it worked out well enough." She smirked. "While the rest of you rested, I kept trying to get the spell to work, and by the time you guys could cast again, I had figured something out." Klauden was nodding. "You really get fatigued?" she asked.

"Yes, chaivin, I get fatigued."

"What's it like?"

He shrugged. "Empty."

Hannah considered. She could be tired out by the effort of casting the magic, but that was more an issue of willpower or strength of mind, not like she had a limited amount of magic she could use at one time. "I get tired," she told him, "but never the way he explained it. When you are fatigued, you cannot cast any more magic. I may be limited in what I can actually cast, but the power never runs out on me, not until the rest of my strength does, and I can hardly stand." If she ever memorized her spells as she ought to, she would be able to cast much longer than any of them. She looked at him. "So, right now, though you are rested and fed, you cannot cast any magic?"

Klauden shook his head. "I might be able to manage a small spark to light a candle if I waited for it, but anything larger than that isn't possible right now."

"How long does it take to return?"

He shrugged. "It depends. Sometimes a few hours, sometimes a day or so."

"We have to stay here all day? Rory will be worried sick!"

"Easy, chaivin. I've already regained some of my power. Another few hours and I will be able again. We will be back by late morning."

Hannah reminded herself that there was nothing she could do to speed up the process, tried to accept this news with dignity, and nodded as she flipped through the book, trying to find the passage on fatigue and failing. "I never was very good at books," she commented, closing the book and placing it back on the shelf.

"You were good at magic, though." He shook his head, running a hand through his hair. "You are not what you appear," he said. He moved past her, deft hands picking the book up from where she had set it, lifting three books up, and sliding Hansen in the new space before putting the other books back on top. "You are clearly better at magic than at organization," he muttered, then turned back to her. "No. To be honest, your magic is quite powerful."

"How can you say that? I was terrible at my magic. Half the time it didn't even work."

"But when it does work," he began, "you are..." He paused, head cocking. He looked at his desk, then back at her. "You remember Hathdern?"

Hannah frowned. The name was familiar, something about experiments with blood, trying to cure the bloodlust, perhaps? "Was he the one who tried to cure his daughter during the Masenin?" She remembered reading about the Masenin, the decade when plague ravaged the mountains and human blood became a very high commodity. Some of her people had starved then, but Hathdern had tried to save his family using some magical means of diluting the blood. "He tried to give her mortal traits, right? Much like a fledgling, only backward?"

Klauden was nodding. "But he didn't complete the process. The girl didn't grow stronger. She died."

"And your point?"

"Before she died, Hathdern claimed that he was very close to success. More than half of her constitution was human. She only needed a small dose of blood to survive. In fact, I've come to believe that he really did succeed, but then she died of the plague that killed the other mortals."

Hannah snorted. "There's irony for you. Why are you telling me this?"

"You have mortal blood in you, Hannah, or you did when you were a vampire. The question of the body, the physical, is crucial here. Do you realize how important it could be to discover whether the bloodlust is linked through the flesh or is anchored in the spirit?" His face was flushed, the eager scholar at work again.

"I would be a good experiment," she said carefully.

"That's not what I said."

"But it's what you meant," she accused. "What would you do, Klauden? Cut me open to see my veins? Pump out my blood to dilute in glass bottles? What?"

"You know I wouldn't. I've always been more interested in theory. Malbrek, on the other hand, is one who would do such things."

"You're right. He would."

"Which brings me to another point—he stole your body, Hannah. Maybe he let me help him inadvertently, but it was him all along. Who knows what he's been doing with it all this time?"

"Anna has it," she said, recalling the memory she had glimpsed. She tried not to think of what her body had been doing for the last year, tried not to think of Malbrek and any plans he may have. "It seems fine."

"But where has it been? What has he been doing to it? And, more importantly, what did he not find that he has created an army to sack the very village you decided to settle in?" Klauden seemed determined to say all of the things she so desperately was trying to avoid.

"He doesn't know where I am," Hannah argued, clinging to hope even though she knew it was foolish. "He thinks I'm dead."

"But what if he doesn't? What if the entire thing, everything, has been a setup?"

"I think you've been living in this castle too long," she said. "You see plots in everything."

"Maybe because there are plots everywhere."

"It just seems too convenient," she argued. "How would he know what you would do?"

"He knows me," Klauden said. "I may think I am cautious or that I can keep secrets, but perhaps I am wrong and I have been his puppet as well."

"What do you mean—puppet? Maybe he foresaw you helping me then, though I know you much better, and I didn't see it, but even so, how could he possibly orchestrate what has happened since?" Hannah thought about it. "That would mean that everything—Solyn, Rory calling you, the army, the fledglings, getting bitten—everything would be due to him. I'm sorry. I just can't believe he's that powerful."

"Maybe he wouldn't have to be so powerful," Klauden mused. "Maybe he's just gotten very lucky. Maybe he saw the way I look at you and gambled on it."

"Stop," she ordered. "You're paranoid. You're just tired," she added. "Rest up and we'll go back to Rory, and all of this will make sense again."

"Think of it. How else to test his theory further? To have your soul trapped in a fledgling's body, to test what might be done with your blood."

"He couldn't know I would become a fledgling!"

"Who sent that attack? What chance would a mortal have against a fledgling alone, not to mention a dozen of them? And to what purpose? They only killed fifty people and converted none. Why throw them away like that? The one we captured had been ordered not to say. It was a secret mission, a hidden agenda. Maybe the agenda was you."

"But if I'd gotten bitten by a fledgling, I would have died. They were too young."

"And that's why I bit you, like he knew I would if I were here."

"You're ridiculous. Besides, what does it matter how I changed if that was his goal?"

Hannah heard a phrase echo from his mind to hers, and she saw the bottom half of a line of spiky handwriting—*kevna has never been severed.* When she looked up, Klauden was nodding.

"Kevna," she repeated. "What is it?"

"It's ancient," he said, gesturing to the stack of books on his desk. "An old form of the blood bond. I've been researching it."

"And?"

"From what I can tell, it's a connection between mates that transcends everything else. The stories I read speak of touching from across vast distances or speaking without words."

"And you think that's what we have," Hannah guessed. "Kevna. The purest form of the blood bond."

He shook his head. "I don't know. Though strong, it is just a master fledgling connection." There was something in the way he said it that made Hannah think there was more he wasn't telling her, and she wanted to ask him how he knew what a normal master fledgling bond should feel like. After all, she had bitten the healer, and she knew what that felt like.

And this was a thousand times stronger.

Hannah leaned against the front of the desk, considering. "But why? Why do it at all?"

Klauden ran his fingers through his hair. "I don't know. The only thing I've found about the bond thus far is that it lasts even beyond death. One story claims a lover brought her mate back from the dead." He shrugged, shaking his head again. "I doubt I could raise you from the dead, chaivin. The old stories are filled with nonsense sometimes. It could have been anything—an exaggeration, a misunderstanding, a metaphorical rebirth. The possibilities are endless."

Hannah wanted to ask why she was the one who would be dead in this scenario but decided to focus on the bigger issues.

"For someone who claims there are a lot of alternatives," Hannah observed, "you seem pretty convinced it's Malbrek."

"I just want to examine all possibilities," he defended. "If I'm wrong, and I hope I am, then I am paranoid and this has all been chance. But if I'm right..."

"If you're right, then figuring out what to do with Solyn is going to be the least of my problems."

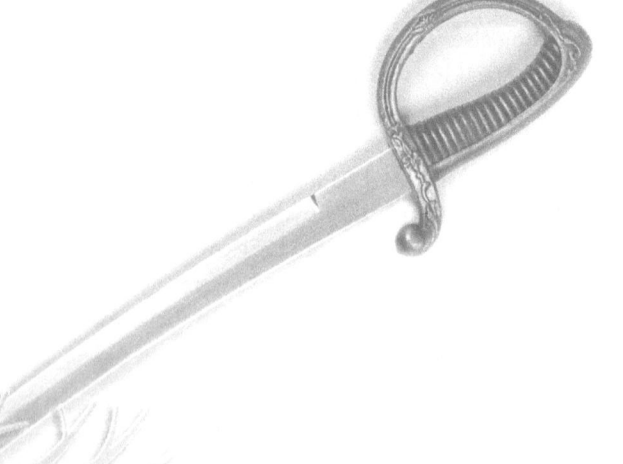

XXXIII

T he magic made her head spin, and Hannah stumbled a bit as they landed, her feet tangling in both the robes she wore and Klauden's own legs, and her weight knocked both of them to the snow-covered ground.

"Honestly, chaivin," Klauden griped, helping her off of him with a strong hand before standing himself, "turning fledgling has not improved your reflexes." Hannah caught his hand and tugged him quickly to his feet, the newfound strength in her arms amazing them both as he went nearly airborne before settling back onto steady feet. He gave her a look. "Point made."

She winked at him, then turned to brush snow off her hip. She checked the sun; it was late morning already. *Is Rory awake already? Did he discover we were missing? How much does he remember from last night?* Hannah glanced at the trees around them, orienting herself in the midst of snow covered landmarks and wet barked trees before heading to her right. She could get back into the tunnel, cross beneath the wall, and be back inside before she knew it.

Klauden followed wordlessly, his feet making no sound on the rock floor of the tunnel, and when she stepped up to the wooden chest that rested below their trapdoor, he didn't offer to help her. She pushed on the door, and when it resisted her initial test, she gave it a sharp push. She heard the wooden latch snap, then a *thunk* as the metal lock fell off, and then she could lift the trap.

Gods, she thought as she reached up to pull her body through the opening, *was it always so easy for anyone to break in?* She had felt so safe in the house. Then again, creatures with her strength weren't common in Severin, so there hadn't been any need to think that the lock wouldn't hold firm.

She reached down to grab Klauden's hand and help him up without thinking, and once again, her strength surprised her. She tugged too hard, and the vampire flew up into the room with her, her surprise at the ease with which she could lift him made her pause halfway, and this time it was Klauden who tripped on the hem of his robe and the edge of the trapdoor to stumble against her, knocking them both to the floor. As he collapsed on top of her, Hannah couldn't help a smirking giggle, "And you said I had no reflexes? Ha."

"Yes, well, chaivin, there are easier ways to get me on top of you," he retorted mischievously, and she gave him a warning look.

"Enough of that," she snapped, pushing him off and sitting up. She glanced around the room and stopped at Rory's smoldering gaze as he lay in the bed staring at her. "Rory!" she exclaimed, pushing herself to her feet and away from Klauden. The vampire stood with casual grace, straightening his robe and kicking the trapdoor shut.

"You're awake," she said, moving toward him with a smile. The elf didn't look very well this morning, his skin pale and waxy, his hair in sweaty waves behind his ears. As she approached, he sat up with a great effort to lean against the wall. Hannah saw that he wasn't wearing a shirt, his scar-crossed chest slick with a sheen of sweat.

"You're not well," she said, worry wiping the smile from her face as she sat down on the bed before him. "What is it?" she asked, hands reaching out to touch his cheek. His skin was cool to the touch. "What's wrong?" she asked, glancing at Klauden standing behind her. "Is it the blood loss?"

The vampire frowned, crossing swiftly to the other side of the bed. He, too, touched Rory's face, but he did not sit down on the bed. The elf pushed the vampire away weakly, his eyes very alive in his gray face.

"Where have you been all night, Hannah?" the elf asked, his voice a low croak in the dim room.

Hannah gave Klauden a sharp glance then back at her husband. "We had to f-feed," she explained, her voice tripping over the word. *How does he feel about me now? How will he react to my bloodthirst?* She rallied her attention again. "How long have you felt like this? Can you get up?"

"Why are you wearing his clothes?" the elf asked sharply, suspicious eyes taking in the clean lines of her face, her smoothly dried hair, his nose sniffing delicately at the perfume that clung to her from the scented bathwater. She stared at him for a second, not understanding, then remembered the robe she wore.

"Oh, mine were a wreck, so I took these. Are you lightheaded?"

"Took them from where?"

"My room," the vampire supplied helpfully.

"What?"

Hannah grimaced at Klauden's abruptness, then explained about the teleportation spell. Rory's eyes grew wide in his face, but his color did not improve. "So you spent the night in his room at your father's castle," the elf said slowly.

Hannah nodded, hands reaching to feel the elf's pulse at his wrist. The beat was there but very light and fluttery. "What's the matter with him, Klauden? Why is he sick like this?"

"I'm fine," Rory said, pushing her away. "I'm more concerned with you at the moment."

Hannah sat back, realizing that the elf would not relent until she had explained herself fully. "Yes, Rory, I spent the night at the castle. Yes, I'm wearing his robe." She leaned in to stare at him. "But that's it," she finished. "Satisfied?"

The elf looked away, swallowing clearly. Hannah was suddenly very aware of his throat and the small movement of his skin across his veins, could smell the life still in him, the blood strong and vital in his body. She bit her lip, the need in her roiling up. She took a steadying breath, then let it out, feeling the bloodthirst subside for the moment. *This is ridiculous,* she thought. *I just fed! I can't need it again so soon.*

She looked back up into Rory's eyes, but there was something there now, a burning distrust as he looked from her eyes to her mouth and back again. His pale hand came up to rest on his shoulder, and he slowly brushed his hair behind his neck. "Come, Hannah," he whispered, hand tilting his neck to one side. "Why not finish me off? You know you want to."

Hannah stared at him, stung. "You bastard," she whispered, "how dare you say that to me?"

The elf smirked, a coldness in him a barb in her heart as he turned his attention to Klauden. "Intense indeed."

"Stop it," Hannah whispered. "Just stop."

"He doesn't know what he's saying," Klauden observed.

"Yes, I do," Rory insisted.

"What's wrong with him?" Hannah asked the vampire again, ignoring her husband.

The vampire shrugged. "Could be blood loss, could be mortal sickness, could be a lot of things." He gave the elf a sidelong glance. "Could be jealousy."

Hannah took a deep breath. "Seriously, Klauden. Have you seen it before?"

Klauden paused, then nodded. "It's probably blood loss. He's still weak."

Hannah reached out to touch the elf's face again, and this time he let her, but his eyes were not forgiving. "What can we do?"

"Not much. Rest. Food. He'll recover."

Hannah gave the vampire a sharp look. "Can't you help him?"

Klauden did not pretend to misunderstand her. "I might, but I do not think my help is wanted."

Hannah looked at Rory. The elf seemed to be considering, then shook his head angrily. He glared at her. "If it's sleep I need, I can do that. Scotty has already been here twice. The men already know not to expect me." He smirked again, that look embedding itself in her memory. "You need not worry over me."

Hannah sat back, giving Rory some space on the bed. "I didn't know you would be so weakened," she told him. "I wouldn't have gone along with it if I'd known."

"Wouldn't you." It wasn't a question.

Now it was Hannah's turn to glare at him. "I do recall that it was you who insisted I let him bite me, that it was you who said I was being stubborn by hesitating."

"That was before I knew," he said stubbornly.

"So now we all know a lot more," Hannah stated. "And nothing to be done about any of it." She gave him a once over, ignoring the sudden stir in her skin as she noted the fine musculature of his shoulders and neck.

She stood up abruptly. "You need to eat," she said when he gave her a curious look.

"I'm fine," he insisted.

"You're not fine. You need to regain your strength. You need food." She headed over to the table and counter, scanning for something edible. When she saw nothing but an empty bowl and a spoon lying next to the metal candleholder, she moved to the fireplace. The pot that normally contained soup was sitting on the floor to the right of the glowing ashes, the inside scrubbed clean of any food. "Damn," she muttered, kneeling down to open the cabinet doors. There were some more metal containers within, but nothing with which to make a meal.

Hell, she thought, *how does Rory always manage to have something for us to eat?* She stood, giving Rory another look. He had not moved. Klauden stood perfectly still near the door, silent and passive.

"I will go to the inn and get some food," she told her husband. "I won't be long."

"I'll go with you," Klauden said immediately, ignoring Rory's annoyed scoff from the bed.

As Hannah headed for the door, Rory called out, "You might want to change before you go, or people will begin asking who your tailor is." She glanced down at the robe she still wore and sighed. Without saying anything, she stepped to the trunk at the foot of the bed, flinging it open with a little too much force, and began rummaging through squares of cloth to find decent clothing. When she had selected an outfit, she turned her back to them as she changed. She left on Klauden's shorts, the soft material comfortable beneath the skirt she pulled on, and once she tugged a clean shirt over her head, she didn't waste time to button the jacket she put on top. Though she seemed to ignore both men, she was intently aware of Klauden watching her without eyes. She couldn't hear his thoughts directly, but she was very aware of how much he wanted to touch her skin, how her blonde hair seemed to glow in the firelight, and how he seemed entranced by the delicate bones of her ankles. She didn't look at either of them as she tugged on her boots, and when she opened the door to head to the inn, she didn't check to see that Klauden followed her.

XXXIV

The walk to the inn wasn't long, but Hannah moved slowly, adjusting to the sights and smells of the village through her newly enhanced senses as she tried to calm her whirling thoughts. It made sense that Rory would be upset, she told herself. He probably felt used; she had taken his blood and then disappeared for hours. Of course, he would be unhappy with her.

Still, she couldn't help being a bit annoyed with him as well. It was hypocritical, she decided. After he had gone through all the trouble of convincing her to become a vampire, now he had the nerve to turn it around on her and make her feel guilty? *And for what? A few hours spent in Klauden's room?* Clearly, the elf was overreacting.

She heard the step of Klauden's shoes on the snow-packed street behind her and slowed to let the vampire reach her side. She didn't think about what he might want to say to her; she just knew he wanted to say something, the bond between them telling her that he was cautious, a bit apprehensive. She stopped, turning to face him.

"What is it?"

Klauden seemed surprised by her question, and she had a moment where she knew he was wondering just how much she knew about what he was thinking, exactly how close the bond had brought them together.

"Close enough," she answered his unspoken thought. "I can hear you buzzing with nerves. Out with it."

Klauden smirked at her, clearly thinking, *<I'm not the only one buzzing here.>* He paused, then added, *<How are you?>*

"You know," she said out loud, "words work just fine with me. This," she made a gesture between her head and in his general direction, "isn't something I want to practice."

"Very well," he said, stepping close to her on the deserted street.

Hannah took a step back, maintaining a comfortable distance between them. Every time he stepped closer to her, her hands started to want to do foolish things. She clenched her fists to make sure nothing untoward happened. "You have something to say," she told him. "What?"

"Being reborn hasn't helped your manners," he snapped at her.

"I haven't been reborn," she retorted, "and you're the one being rude."

"You are not the same, chaivin. You must realize that now."

"I am still myself," she insisted. She scoffed at him. "You honestly think that after dealing with Solyn for months now that a little bit of blood is going to make me change?"

He stepped toward her, face serious. "Listen to me," he began. "You don't yet understand."

"What don't I understand?"

He shook his head. "The bloodthirst will be different than you are expecting."

"I feel fine," she said quickly, hands opening and closing as she suddenly felt that little thrill again, her pulse beneath the skin of her hands, a subtle hint that the bloodthirst was not as sated as she hoped.

"You felt fine in my room," he reminded her, "and yet you still fed, mostly without realizing you had even moved, yes?"

Hannah looked away, taking in the wooden construction of the general store behind Klauden's back. Two buildings down stood the small hump of her forge, and even farther down the street was the inn. "I'm fine," she repeated. "Is that all?"

"You are newly turned," he insisted. "You will be unable to control your urges for a time."

"I know how to control myself."

"Under normal circumstances, you do," he agreed, "but this is not normal, even for you."

She scowled at him. "What is that supposed to mean?"

"Don't," he warned. "This is important."

"I'm fine," she repeated, turning to continue her walk toward the inn. "You didn't need to be all serious for that, Klauden. I know how it is."

He didn't reach for her with his arms, but instead overwhelmed her mind with an image—Jaston the farmer, standing in his shirtsleeves outside the inn, brow slick with sweat from working outside, breath huffing in the cold air, healthy young heart pumping warm blood through the veins of his shoulders, into the small bones of his wrist, pulsing in the lines of his neck…

Hannah paused, senses reeling with the overwhelming need that pulsed through her. She remembered the bloodthirst, the crawling desire for blood as it made her shiver, but this was something different. She didn't want to just smell Jaston or take a small nip from his sweaty skin; she wanted to throw herself on him, her body demanding satisfaction as she tore his throat out. She could see herself doing it, too, and nothing could make her stop, not the knowledge that other people stood nearby watching, that she was not the type of girl who threw her body at strangers, that she had never been the type of vampire to relish spraying blood, not to mention the fact that she knew Jaston, knew and liked him as a person. If she got close enough to him, none of that would matter. And when the others turned on her, as she knew they would once they saw what she had become, she would dispatch them just as easily.

As the image faded, Hannah became aware of her immediate surroundings again. Klauden was in front of her, hands holding her arms gently, face serious.

"How…?" she asked, and when she couldn't get the words out, she finished in his mind. *<How can I stop it?>*

<You can't.>

<But.> She could feel something in her growing wild, crazed at the thought of being unable to control herself. It was too much like the fear that Solyn would one day take over her body. *<I have to go.>*

"Go where?" He spoke out loud, trying to give her distance in an attempt to calm her down. It didn't work.

"Away," she rambled. "Away from here, away from people, just away until I get that under control."

"Chaivin," he said, grip tightening on her arms as she struggled to break free, "that isn't possible."

"It is," she insisted. "I can go into the woods, far into the woods, where I can't hurt anyone."

"And what would you feed on?"

She stared at him, that minor detail of her life as a vampire having slipped her mind. She would have to kill again, and more often than she ever had before, in order to keep this body alive.

"How often?" she whispered. "How long and how often?"

"For now, every few hours," he told her. "After, it depends. Sometimes once a day, sometimes a day and a half." He reached out to touch her face. Hannah had started to cry without realizing it.

"I can't stay here," she said in a calmer voice. "I'll kill everyone in the village." She paused, thoughts racing. "Maybe we should go back to the castle," she blurted. "There at least I'll only kill slaves." She felt Solyn in her rebelling at the thought, and she snapped, *<What else would you have me do?>*

<Knit a spine,> the slave suggested, and Hannah ignored her.

"What about Rory?" Klauden asked, and Hannah felt the tears fall even more freely as a great weight seized her chest.

"I can't," she whispered. "What if I hurt him? What if I don't realize it and I...?" She let the thought trail off, staring at Klauden with horrified eyes.

He shook his head, a sad smile crossing his lips. "Oh, Hannah," he whispered, a hand moving to wipe the tears from her cheek. He so rarely called her by her name now that it took her by surprise. In the sunshine, Hannah could see the red tint of her bloody fledgling tears on his fingertip.

"Oh no," she moaned, then began scrubbing at her cheeks with her sleeves, wiping the accusing redness away.

She felt the vampire sigh, then he spoke in a soft voice. "Much as it pains me to say it, you do not have to leave this village right now," he said.

"What do you mean?"

"I mean that there is a way to be certain you do not attack anyone you do not wish to."

"How?"

"Give your will to me."

Hannah stared at him. "What?"

"Give me your will," he repeated.

"What are you talking about?" She recalled him offering to help her shield her mind, before she left home so long ago. *Is this the same thing?*

"You feel this, yes?" he asked, and suddenly Hannah was aware of him in her mind, his soul in her blood, as if she were an instrument whose string he had plucked. She nodded numbly, overwhelmed by the completeness of the feeling as she wondered how much further this connection could go. *How much of this is because I'm not trying to get closer,* she wondered, *and how much of this is because he is shielding himself? What will happen if we stop fighting against it?*

"I do," she said quietly.

"Good. Give in to me, let me rule you, and I will not let you harm anyone."

"How is that possible?"

"I am a vampire," he said seriously. "I know how to control a fledgling of my making."

"I was a vampire," she replied, "and I didn't know how to control the fledgling I made."

"Unlike you," Klauden smiled, "I paid attention during our lessons. It is not a difficult thing to do once one learns the basic premise."

Hannah thought of her body, her real body, and the army of fledglings it had spawned. "Can you teach me?" she whispered. Klauden seemed to follow the direction of her thoughts.

"Oh yes," he whispered. "I will." Hannah caught a sense of some underground current then, a thought process that he tried to conceal from her. She only caught the end of it—*what great power to control such an army.* She gave him a sharp look.

"If we do this, if I give my will to you, how long does it last?" she asked. "And how much control will you have?" She didn't know why she asked, the flash of Klauden somehow stealing her away seeming ridiculous in light of their return trip this morning, but she couldn't help it. The idea of being controlled by Klauden while she controlled a mass of fledglings was ludicrous, but she was starting to realize that scenarios that seem impossible one day had an odd habit of becoming her reality the next.

"Long enough to keep everyone safe," he answered. "And I will not make you do anything you do not wish to. I will only keep you from acting on new impulses."

"Are you sure it will work?"

He nodded.

"And how will I get my will back?"

"I will return it to you when you have gained control."

She didn't like the sound of that. "What if you decide not to return my will to me? What then?"

"Why would I do that?" he asked, shaking his head.

"You hate that I don't do what you tell me to do," she explained. "If we do this, you'll be able to force me to do what you wish."

"Chaivin, I can force you to do my will right now. If that was my intention, it would have been done long ago."

"What do you mean?"

He gestured between them, mimicking her movement from before when she spoke of their bond. "The blood bond," he said. "You are my fledgling. You must do as I command."

"I do not," she insisted, but something in her gut was telling her that he was right. He could make her do anything he wanted, at any time. *Wasn't that one of the things I told Rory when I argued against this?*

He gave her a look but said nothing.

"Why?" she whispered, looking up at him suddenly, realizing just how carefully he had been treating her. "Why are you holding back?"

He sighed at her. "Sometimes, chaivin, I think you know me not at all," he complained. "I do not want another slave," he continued. "You would do my bidding, yes, but you would hate me for it, and I would not have that between us."

"So you hold back because you know I wouldn't like it," she repeated, feeling the thinness of that excuse. Klauden never did anything without a really good reason. A simple desire to keep her happy did not seem likely in this case. "Really."

"I would not do that to you," he said quietly, looking away. "I hope that someday you believe me when I tell you that I am not here to hurt you."

"So why can't you help me anyway?" she asked, changing the subject. "If you can already control me, why do I need to give you my will?"

"I can only make you do things, chaivin. I cannot stop you from doing them." He paused, considering. "That is not entirely true," he amended, and she stared at him. *Is he admitting a lie?* "I can stop you in a limited fashion," he explained, "but the bloodthirst. That I cannot compete with as we are now. You must allow me to help you gain control."

"And you will give it back once I learn control."

"Yes."

Hannah sighed, then decided. "Alright." She paused, waiting for some sort of sign that it had been done, but nothing happened. "How?"

"Look at me," he said softly. She did. Again, nothing happened for a long moment, and then she had a brief moment of complete immersion in Klauden's mind. There was a flood of feeling—worry for her, anger at Rory, frustration at the villagers, confusion about Solyn—and then something powerful gripped her.

< *You are mine,* > a stern voice said in her mind. It took her a moment to recognize Klauden in it.

< *Yes,* > she replied.

< *No,* > the voice insisted. < *You are Mine.* >

< *I know,* > she repeated.

< *You will obey me in all things,* > the voice continued.

Hannah rebelled for a moment, not liking the idea of being under anyone's orders, but then relented, recalling the need she had felt for Jaston. < *I will,* > she said.

< *You will heed the call of your master.* >

< *I will,* > she said again. As she said it, she felt something loosen in her chest, some small part of herself that she had never quite been aware of, and watched it float away into the overwhelming sense of Klauden that surrounded her.

She stood in the middle of the street, feeling the echo of spent magic thrum up her arms, and stared at the vampire to whom she had just surrendered.

Did I just manage to save the lives of these villagers at the price of my own?

XXXV

Rory did not recover as quickly as Hannah would have liked, but over the next two days, he improved enough to continue training the men on the third day. He did not speak to Hannah any more than was strictly necessary, and he did not acknowledge Klauden at all.

Though Hannah was able to restrain the bloodthirst with Klauden's aid, she spent much of her time away from the village, wandering the surrounding woods with Klauden. They stumbled onto another band of roving would-be thieves, and this time Hannah had no problems keeping herself safe. Afterward, she had sat in the snow and wept, though she couldn't get Klauden to understand why. It had been partly guilt for having to kill again, but mostly because she knew that without Klauden's help, she would not only have drunk their blood, but would have given in to new demands of her body as well, and that thought made her ill. It seemed that the bloodthirst and sex were linked in her mind now; she couldn't have one without the other, and only Klauden was holding her needs in check. Part of her was overwhelmed with gratitude, but another part of her was dying with embarrassment that she couldn't control herself.

How much longer can we go on like this?

Luckily, word reached them on the third day that men and goblins had been seen forming rank and file before the walls of Salva. It seemed that the interminable period of waiting was over, and the army would finally arrive. Hannah had given Klauden a long look, earning his silent approval, and had set off to find her husband.

He wasn't with the men, and when she asked, Fergus told her that he had been left in charge while Rory went to make some final preparations. The man did not know what those preparations entailed, but further inquiries of those she found busily moving through the streets told her that the elf had been seen heading back toward their house. She entered cautiously, wondering what he could be doing in the middle of the day on the afternoon before an invasion, but it wasn't necessary. The house was empty. The trapdoor on the floor was shut, but upon closer inspection, not locked. They hadn't had time to replace the latch she had broken when returning from the castle with Klauden, but from the way the latch rested on top of the bracket, Hannah knew that it had been lowered carefully so that it could be easily reopened.

Rory went this way, but why?

Frowning, she opened the door and slipped through, her fledgling eyes picking up shapes in the darkness of the tunnels. There were benefits to the blood. It was hard to remember that when she was still fighting the bloodthirst, but the strength in her limbs and the newfound agility and capability of her body was rewarding. Sometimes she forgot to be grateful for that, though Solyn was always there in the background to remind her.

The slave had gotten so close to her in the past few days that Hannah could hardly tell where she ended and the other began. Perhaps this was what Klauden had meant when he said she needed to blend with her. Still, she knew she could untangle herself if she wanted to; it would take some concentration, but she was certain that she could draw the boundaries between them again if it came to that. She wondered how much longer she would be able to do that and redoubled her efforts to find Rory. He wasn't in the tunnels. Unless he had decided to go scouting the enemy, which was unlikely if he hadn't given Fergus more specific directives, he had no real purpose beyond the walls. In fact, the only thing remotely nearby was the spring, and it had long since frozen over.

Still, she thought, *it's an idea.*

As she allowed her feet to trace the familiar path through the frozen trees, Hannah let herself feel Klauden again. It was different than the connection with Solyn, but she was always aware of the vampire on the edge of her mind. If she focused on it, he drew nearer, his thoughts sharpening in her mind, and his presence somehow melding with her own. She knew that the vampire was in the back room of the inn with Elsbeth, going over a relaxation technique that would help her control her power. Before he had turned Hannah, the vampire had spent much of his free time with the girl, and now that he sensed his fledgling's need to be alone, he had sought out the mortal's company. Elsbeth was a changed girl following the death of her father, filled with anger and grief. Hannah knew that Klauden would teach her to focus that rage, shaping raw power to a purpose that may help turn the tide of the approaching army. Hannah watched as Elsbeth closed her eyes, the girl mouthing the words to a simple spell designed to focus the mind, and then she felt the full force of Klauden inside her, as if he had turned to face her.

<*Yes?*>

She pushed away from him then, doing the mental equivalent of pushing him out of her embrace to arms' length and then taking a few cautious steps backward. She could not be rid of him completely, but she could distance herself from him.

Thoughts of distance made her realize that for the first time since she had been made, there was actual physical space between them. Klauden was in the inn, far from where she walked in the forest, and yet she could still reach out to him at a moment's notice. *Are all bonds this powerful?* Hannah didn't know. No doubt Klauden did, but she didn't want to bring the connection closer again.

There were things to be done that she preferred to do alone.

<*Tell me about it,*> Solyn whispered.

Well, as alone as she could be these days.

<*Soon,*> she told the slave girl, <*soon there will be a battle, and after that, I will find my body and reclaim it. You will be free.*>

<*I hope so,*> Solyn replied. <*I really do.*>

<*You will,*> Hannah assured her. <*But until then…*>

<*You need some time alone,*> the girl replied. <*I understand.*>

Hannah felt Solyn recede a little, a slight untwisting of words and thoughts and memories, and then she really was alone. She could still feel them at the very edge of her consciousness, but Solyn had gone wherever it was that she disappeared to sometimes, and Klauden was somehow shielded from her. It was like being in a very large room, and they had all retreated to different corners. Except the room was Solyn's body, and the corners were gaps in her mind.

Hannah shook her head, eyes focusing on the wet forest around her. Just because she was looking for Rory didn't mean that other creatures didn't lurk beyond the walls.

She found the elf at the edge of the ice-crusted spring, his tall form outlined with a cloak damp from the cold winter air and his hair slick with melted snow. She paused at the edge of the clearing, mind replaying the many days spent in this very place, laughing and loving with Rory. How very far they had come from that time.

"I hoped you would come," he said softly, and Hannah started a bit. She hadn't known he heard her approach.

She walked the few steps toward him but stopped a few feet away, staring out across the frozen pond. "Why?"

"You will have heard the news, then?"

"The army? Yes." She risked a glance at him and nearly looked away when she saw his complete attention was on her. Then she steeled herself. This was her husband, Rory, and she was not such a coward that she couldn't look him in the eye. "I heard."

He nodded. "They will get here early in the morning."

"Are the men ready?"

"As ready as they can be," he replied. "I think they will do me proud."

"Fergus was still running drills when I left him," she said.

Rory nodded again. "I should have told him to let them go for the evening. They could use the break."

She shuffled her feet a bit, boots making wedges against the snow-covered edge of the water. "What would they do instead?"

He shrugged. "What all men do before a big battle. Eat, drink, find women, and pray to their gods."

"Is that what you do?"

He cocked an eyebrow at her. "I wanted to find you."

"Why?"

He was very serious. "There are things to be said."

"Like?" She wasn't going to make this easy for him.

He scowled at her. "For starters, I wanted to apologize for my behavior that morning."

"You had the right to be angry," she admitted.

"Maybe," he said, "but that wasn't a reason to behave as I did. I am sorry for that."

"You were very ill," she said. "It's not your fault." As she said it, she knew it was true. It didn't change how angry she still was, or how frustrated she felt about their current awkward state, but she did understand why he had acted as he did.

What would I have done in his place, to have him use me, then disappear and return in the morning with a strange woman? Hannah felt her hands clench, and she wondered if it was her jealousy or Solyn's she was feeling.

He took a step toward her, and the angry heat in her chest faded a little. "But it is. And it's my own fault that we've hardly spoken over the last few days." He shook his head. "I've been an obstinate fool." He paused. "Again."

"It's alright," she assured him, unwilling to break the hesitant truce between them. "You've been very busy." Her chest was beginning to fill with something else now—was it hope?

"I could have made the time," he insisted. "I chose not to, and now..."

"Now what?"

"Now they're on the move, and we don't have time to waste anymore."

"The army? They've been coming for over a month now. We're as ready as we can be. Would you have them drag things out even longer?"

He took another step toward her, running a hand through his ragged hair. She saw that his eyelashes were glistening, though she thought it probably from the dampness of the air and the melted snow in his hair more so than any hint of tears.

"I would have had more time with you," he said.

Hannah stared at him. Of all things she had hoped for from this meeting, confessions of regret and love had not been a possibility.

"We've had our time," she said and then immediately regretted it. That sounded like things were over between them. "I mean to say..." She trailed off, not knowing what she meant to say.

"I know," he said, taking another step in her direction. He was very close to her now, intense brown eyes threatening to devour her. "But I've been unfair to you," he admitted, "and that is something I hope to remedy, if I may."

Hannah gave him a shy smile. "You have been a bit of a brute lately," she told him. "I know that things are different now, but—"

She never got to finish the thought because Rory grabbed her suddenly about the waist, pulling her tight against him and covering her mouth with his in a deep kiss. Hannah was too stunned to react at first, but her body knew this dance, and soon enough, she was kissing him back, hands tugging at his hair, slipping inside his cloak to caress the lines of his back. She remembered that afternoon on the floor of their house, Rory saying, *But being with me brings you back?*

"Hannah," he was speaking against her mouth, her neck, as he moved, "I am sorry. I didn't mean to be cruel. I didn't want this to come between us."

"I'm sorry, too," she gasped against his chin, his lips. "I didn't know, and I'm sorry."

She didn't know when he had picked her up, but suddenly, she was in the air, legs wrapping themselves about his hips. The movement put her face close to his neck, and she caught sight of the pale lines of blood beneath his skin. Another hunger rose in her, and it took all of her willpower to turn away, to move her mouth to the bunch of fabric at his shoulder and bite down on that instead.

Rory seemed not to notice, his own mouth working in a feverish pace along with his hands as he took a few steps to pin her back against a nearby tree. She let go of the corner of his cloak, clamping her mouth shut and biting down on her tongue as his hands worked their way under her skirt. She realized that she was moaning, both from the pleasure his touch evoked and the pain of restraining the bloodlust that was threatening to take over.

No, she pleaded, *please no. Let me have this,* she begged the hunger within. *Let me have this moment with him.*

Still, when he pressed himself against her, the warm length slipping into her, the desire for more didn't abate. Instead, she was overcome, the willpower needed to restrain herself from latching onto his neck nearly enough to split her mind, and when he began to move even faster, Hannah knew that she could not stop herself. She screamed then, and Rory, thinking her as caught up in passion as he was, redoubled his efforts.

His shirt had come askew in all the motion, and his neck was clearly exposed. She was moving toward it, teeth elongating in her mouth, and though she didn't want to hurt him, didn't want to break the moment or lose the pulsing building desire that flooded her body, Hannah knew that it was only a matter of time.

"N—," she managed to grunt.

Rory looked up at her, and it took him a second to recognize the danger. When he did, he brought his arm up between them, blocking her forward motion, and pinned her back against the tree with both arms and hips. Despite his restraints, Hannah was still trying to lunge forward. She knew she could do it; the strength in this body could easily outmaneuver the elf, but somehow she was managing to hold back.

"Hannah!" he was shouting, arms bulging with the effort to hold her at a distance. He was still pinned inside her, and when she made a more desperate lunge forward that nearly made her mark, he used the motion to fling them both from the tree and onto the snow-covered ground. He used his weight to pin her more firmly, and though most of her concentration was focused on trying to restrain her snapping mouth, she couldn't deny the thrill that coiled through her as he moved again.

This is madness, she thought. *Are we fighting or making love?*

Both, she decided as the thirst wracked through her again, the need building just as her passion grew. Rory clung to her, his body caught in its own trap of desire, but when Hannah was sure her next attempt would score a hit and damn him forever, it was he who lunged forward past the locked arms that held their upper bodies apart and kissed her. It was not a gentle movement, his tongue forcing its way into her mouth, passing her jagged teeth without any care of being bitten by accident.

Hannah almost gave in then. *After all, he wouldn't have kissed me if he didn't want to be bitten. Maybe that's what all of his apologizing was about. Maybe he wants to be a fledgling, to have the power to save this village, to share his wife's fate...*

<*Now there's a ridiculous theory,*> Solyn said calmly, and Hannah jerked away from his mouth. Rory could not be a fledgling. It was madness. But if he didn't get off of her, get off of her right now, she was going to bite him, damn the consequences.

In her desperation, Hannah did the only thing she could think of. "Klauden!" She screamed at him, and suddenly he was there inside her. The vampire tactfully said nothing, but she could feel him gathering her will. The bloodlust doused immediately, and Hannah could control herself again. Sex was just sex again. She was herself again. Klauden was gone as quickly as he had appeared.

She took a deep breath and opened her eyes to see Rory staring down at her, eyes wide and mouth slightly agape. He had gone completely still above her. Only then did she realize that she had shouted aloud.

"I..." she tried, but Rory was climbing off her, refusing to look at her as he put his clothing to rights. "Rory," she began, adjusting her skirt as she stumbled to her feet after him. "I didn't mean."

He whirled on her. "You never mean!" he shouted. His face was white with fury. "Even now," he sneered, "even now when we have barely hours left together, you are thinking of him." He shook his head. "Even when I am with you, you are thinking of him."

"No," she argued. "It's not like that!"

"Oh no? When you cry out his name when you lay beneath me, what else am I to think?"

"It's the thirst," she tried to explain. "It's all connected now. When I feed, I..." She couldn't speak, couldn't admit what this new bloodthirst had brought out in her.

"You what?" he demanded.

"I can't separate the two desires," she mumbled. "It's all tangled up in my mind. Klauden—" Though she had had the elf's attention, his face closed at the mention of the vampire's name. She grabbed his arm, forcing him to look at her again. "Let me finish! Klauden has been lending his will to me, to help me feed without ... without that."

"What do you mean, 'lending his will to you'?"

"He can control the desire," she explained. "He can restrain the bloodthirst for me."

"I see."

"No, you don't see! I could have killed you." She tried to make him see his danger. "Or worse, I could have bitten you."

Rory was shaking his head. "You're wrong. I do see. If it's not Solyn taking over your body, it's that damn vampire taking over your soul. I get it."

Hannah heard his words, knew that everything was happening too fast, that it was easy to get overwhelmed, but she couldn't help it. The words spilled out. "So that's it, then? I know things aren't right with me.

I've got the soul of a slave girl sharing my body, and a vampire so close to my mind that I can tell you every whim he entertains. I'm a mess."

She paused, then glared at him. "I would have thought that you might want to help me since you're supposed to be my husband and be there for me, but I see that I was wrong. Thanks for being so dependable, Rory," she spat. "I always know what you'll do when things get difficult."

"Difficult?" he repeated. "You call this difficult? This is intolerable. I don't even know who I'm talking to half the time, and with him inside your head, I don't even know what you want anymore!" He took a deep shuddering breath. "What is it going to be, Hannah? Him or me?"

"You!" she screamed at him. "It's always been you, if you'd stop being an ass long enough to listen to me! You... You..." She took a deep breath of her own then, steadying her pounding heart. She couldn't let herself get excited like this. Excitement brought on the bloodthirst. She had to be calm. To calm herself and walk away. "Never mind," she muttered softly. "I can't," she whispered, giving him a sad look. "I can't fight everyone else and you at the same time. I just don't have the strength for it."

She didn't give him the chance to respond. Instead, she took off running. He called after her, but she couldn't make out the words. Her vampiric limbs pumped, propelling her through the snow at an astonishing speed. It was good to do this, to engulf herself in movement, to stop thinking for a moment and just appreciate the newfound strength in her body. She ran until she had no breath, until her blood sang in her veins and her face ached with the cold.

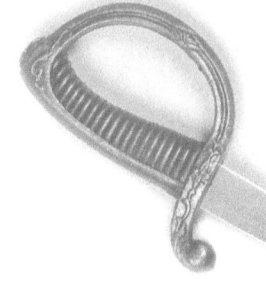

XXXVI

When she came back to herself, Hannah was standing amid a cluster of trees and rocks alongside the newly erected wall around Severin. Solyn kept trying to take deep breaths to steady herself, and Hannah kept trying to assure the slave that breathing wasn't necessary anymore.

<It's alright,> she told the girl. *<We could run like this all day and never run out of air.>*

<We never get tired?> Solyn asked.

Hannah considered. *<Not exactly,>* she answered. *<The body will tire eventually, but it will last a lot longer than it ever did before. We are strong now.>*

She felt Solyn twisting in her then, the girl stretching muscles and squeezing her hands, adjusting to the newfound abilities of her skin. Hannah let her take over for a moment, using the time to latch on to the calm she had found during her run. She knew that letting Solyn have even a small amount of control of the body should upset her, but she just couldn't bring herself to care at the moment.

There would be a fight in the morning. There were only a few more hours to endure. Then, nothing would matter anymore.

<Why would you ever give this up?> Solyn's question broke into Hannah's reverie, and she considered her answer.

Her instinctive response was to say for Rory, for love, for the chance at a life she had wanted, but suddenly she wasn't so sure that was the truth anymore.

Had it been guilt over the killing the body required? Not really. Killing had never really bothered her, and part of her knew that it only did now because she knew that it should. Rather, she knew that it would bother Rory, and so she thought it should also bother her. When it came down to it, though, she was still her father's daughter, and killing mortals came as naturally to her as it did to any of her kindred, despite her protests to the contrary. Klauden was right, after all.

So, why had she given it all up? Mere curiosity seemed ridiculous. Love seemed foolish.

<*I don't know,*> she told Solyn, feeling more at home in herself than she had in months. Maybe it was the freedom of finally admitting the truth to herself, maybe it was because she and Solyn had formed some kind of truce, or maybe it was because she was strong again, powerful again, and the bloodthirst, though lingering just out of sight, was under control. *This is me,* she told herself. *This is who and what I am.*

And if Rory couldn't deal with that, then she knew what had to be done. Her vampiric nature would probably have been a problem before, but everything had happened so quickly. Rory hadn't needed to come to terms with her nature. He had managed to ride to her rescue, but the woman he had rescued had been much easier to accept than the vampire he had met. He'd never been tried when it came to her, Hannah realized. Everything had been so simple between them. Even if Solyn wasn't in her and Klauden wasn't around her, Hannah knew that her very nature would have still come between them. It was a comfort in a small way, to know that not everything was because of her two constant companions.

Thoughts of her connections made her think of Klauden, and then she could see him. He was being herded toward the main room of the inn by a determined Elsbeth, the girl practically dragging him along with entreaties of "Come dance with us, Klauden" and "You have to!" Hannah got a sense of amusement from the vampire, and the random thought that Elsbeth would not be so eager to press up against him if she knew he was the same kind of creature as the one who had killed her father. Still, Klauden liked Elsbeth, liked the potential power she carried, and he allowed himself to be cajoled.

Once in the common room, Hannah got a sense of swarming bodies; it seemed that everyone in the village had decided to live it up on their last night. People were shouting, singing, drinking, and dancing. Klauden let himself be dragged into the fray, but he did not join in the raucous dancing, preferring to stand and watch Elsbeth sway and jump around from the side.

Hannah retreated from Klauden's mind, realizing that she was being terribly rude. She hadn't known that she could do that, could see from inside Klauden's eyes. His thoughts were a constant presence, though often running just below the surface, but to live through him was something else entirely.

<Forgive me,> she thought to him. *<I didn't mean to pry.>*

<No need, chaivin,> he replied, and she knew he was smirking, both at the foolish mortals desperate for life and at her hesitant apology. *<It is only natural to be curious.>*

<Is there anything else I should know?>

<Yes.>

<What?>

He laughed then, a quiet chuckle that was purely masculine. Hannah thought she might have blushed to hear that sound, but her blood was not so easily stirred now. *<Why should I lecture when it is so much more fun to watch you learn on your own?>*

<Fine,> she told him. *<Be that way.>*

She returned fully to herself, glancing around at the trees, the snow, the wet bark and muddy ground. The wall was only a few feet away. She prepared her muscles, took a few steps, and easily vaulted the eight foot height, her legs pushing off the ground with more force than Solyn had ever expected to feel from her body.

<It's like flying,> the slave observed.

Hardly, Hannah replied, a memory of a childhood episode flittering through her mind. She had been in her twenties then, still very young, and Klauden had discovered a new spell. He had grabbed her, held her close, and whispered the words that allowed his feet to leave the ground. It hadn't lasted very long, but Hannah still recalled the wind in her hair, the weightless feeling in her limbs, and how Klauden had held her hands as he fluttered back and forth and flew up and down. She had never been able to master the flight spell, but she knew Klauden was quite adept when he needed to be.

She landed silently on the other side of the fence, realizing as she did that if she could vault the fence, so could the fledglings that would be marching tomorrow. She ought to mention it to Rory, just in case he hadn't thought of it. He probably would have, but maybe he didn't know everything about fledglings. They had had long talks about the approaching army, she reminded herself. Rory knew everything he needed to know about the enemy. As for her, though, there were still things to be said.

That is, if he would listen to her speak, of course.

In the end, Hannah wandered to the inn, drawn by the noise and the lights, and when she entered, the villagers gave her a warm welcome, all half mad with drink and abandon. She found Klauden easily, the vampire standing out from the crowd as he always did, a few desperate girls hanging around him talking quickly. Hannah noticed the way their faces fell when she entered, when they saw how he looked at her, and for a moment, the ache in her chest eased some. Here was a man who would always care for her, even when she was at her most frustrating.

But that wasn't fair. Rory still cared for her. He was just angry, and rightfully so. *Damn,* Hannah thought, *why can nothing in my life be simple?*

<*You had simple,*> Solyn commented quietly, <*and you were bored.*>

<*Maybe,*> Hannah admitted, <*but it was better than this mess.*>

<*You say that now,*> Solyn added, <*because it is the easiest thing to say, not because it is true. Admit it. You love the excitement.*>

<*I do not!*>

<*So you say,*> the slave quipped, and rather than continue the conversation, Hannah made her way to Klauden's side. The vampire was smiling politely, his accented voice a familiarity as he answered Elsbeth's request for a dance.

"I cannot," he declared, and as Hannah reached his side, he added, "Ask her. She will tell you how inept I am at this sort of thing."

Hannah grinned at the girl, nodding. "It's true. Klauden never dances as he should. It's always proper lines and choreographed steps with him." She gave the vampire a sidelong glance. "He never quits being a teacher long enough to just let the music move him."

Elsbeth latched on to the one possibility Hannah had left her. "So, you know the same dances?"

Hannah laughed, remembering the hours spent at her father's formal gatherings, she and her betrothed marking out distinct diagrams on the floor of the great hall in her father's castle. Hannah had always left such events aching for some real dancing and some real music, but Klauden had always been content to follow the formal moves.

"We do," Hannah admitted, but giving a moment for the whirling music to infiltrate their conversation, added, "but this is hardly the right tempo for such seriousness."

"You did grow up together, then!" Elsbeth said, as if she had just unwound a major mystery. "Where?"

< *Thanks, chaivin,* > Klauden said in Hannah's mind. < *You have undone all that I have spent weeks developing.* >

"Far from here," Klauden replied in a tone that suggested more questions were not welcome.

Elsbeth was not to be deterred so easily, and Hannah warmed to the girl. Here was someone to give Klauden a real challenge. "So, could you dance to something slower?"

Hannah shrugged, grinning. "Sure." Before she could say anything else, Elsbeth was heading toward the musicians across the room.

"Are you determined to make a spectacle tonight?" Klauden asked her, a polite smile frozen on his face.

Hannah considered. "Not particularly, but if you think a little dancing is going to be the talk of the town, you're imagining things. Everyone is dancing. It could be fun."

"I don't understand it," Klauden mused. "I suppose I do grasp that everyone here is celebrating life on some level, but shouldn't they be preparing for the fight tomorrow?"

"They are," she told him. And she knew, as she said it, that the buzz of the room had somehow infiltrated her own spirit, and that instead of the bloodthirst, which she had feared might raise amid so many people, she could only think of living a few more hours. True, she might die in the fight, but it wasn't likely, but even so, she couldn't resist the human instinct to revel before the final battle. She wanted to dance. And she was thrilled to find that her desire to dance wasn't mingled with anything else.

It seemed that her exchange with Rory had dampened her appetite for other things.

As she stood near Klauden, trying to decide how to convey this to him, the current swinging song ended, and the musicians took up a slow, serious ballad. Hannah had recognized Frank Cirlus as the bard doing most of the singing earlier, but he did not sing along to this tune, and the slow drum beat built up with a few guitar notes into a song made for slow dancing. As she and Klauden watched, Fergus made his way into the center of the impromptu dance floor with Elsbeth, and the two began a slow and steady dance that had everyone entranced. After the couple had made a few revolutions, Elsbeth gestured to Hannah and Klauden.

"Come on," she mouthed in time to the music and her steps. "Join us."

At her words, a few other couples made their way through the onlookers to dance, and Hannah looked at her feet, suddenly shy. She ought to be dancing with her husband, but he didn't want her anymore. Not like this.

< Overly dramatic much?> Solyn's sarcasm made Hannah's cheeks burn, but she couldn't get rid of the feeling.

There was a movement to her right, and Hannah looked up to see Klauden standing before her, bowing in the formal pose that requested a dance.

"<Might I have the honor of a dance?>" he asked in the language of their homeland. The words were so out of place, his actions so formally removed from this time and place, that she heard herself respond without thought.

"<I would be pleased to do so,>" she said, and Klauden stood up, his full height revealed as he straightened his back and confidently grabbed her hands. Even in this new body, Hannah remembered the steps as Klauden moved her from one place to the next, the slow drum beat relaxing as they twirled. Klauden had always been good at this kind of dancing. Hannah found herself wondering if he had practiced in his room by himself. The thought called up a memory, and she was watching Klauden as he swayed back and forth with another woman in his rooms, a blonde woman, the slave that Solyn had been, and Hannah pulled away from the memory and from the vampire. It wasn't far enough away to interrupt the dance, but it made it harder for him to maneuver them.

<< You do not enjoy seeing me with her, >> Klauden said.

<< I do not want to know, >> Hannah admitted.

Klauden swung her around quickly then, using her own momentum to wind her closer into his embrace. "<Why not?>" he whispered in her ear.

Hannah pulled away, but he just tugged her gracefully back again. Hannah became aware of a widening circle around them as people paused to watch their movements. It looked like they were marking the steps of a choreographed routine to them, not like she was trying to get away from him. Klauden had tugged her close again, and the iron strength in his arm refused to let her go as they swayed together, the length of their bodies touching. "<Tell me why.>"

"<I will not,>" she replied, turning her head to his shoulder as he tried to force the answer out of her. The song was coming to an end, and Klauden let her go a little as he finished with a triumphant twist that ended with her looking up into his face.

"<You will not tell me now, chaivin,>" he said confidently, "<but someday soon, you will not be able to pretend there can be anything less between us.>"

Hannah glared at him, at the vampire who had made her jealous without even trying, bowed cordially as another song began, more perky and upbeat than the last, and stepped quickly backward, seeking the solace of the outside where she could pretend to be alone.

XXXVII

The moon was only half full, the dim light turning the lane into a shifting pane of blues and grays. Hannah moved away from the solace of the inn, down the empty street until the sounds of celebration coming from the rest of the villagers was a low humming. Hannah knew she could still hear every word, every song if she concentrated on it, but she focused her senses away from the people, looking at the night and enjoying the few moments of calm.

She had been standing in the street, watching her breath mist in the night air, long enough to start feeling the cold in her face when she saw the shadow moving down the street. As she watched, the shape coalesced into a man's form, a familiar outline in the dark, and she stood, waiting for Rory to reach her. He stopped a few feet away, his face cautious but calm.

"Hannah," he said, and she felt the thrill in her at her name in his voice. He always called her by her name, never deceived himself as to who she was or distanced her with a pet name.

"Rory," she replied, loving the feel of his name in her mouth, wishing she knew what else to say.

"I didn't know if you would be inside," he said after a moment.

"I was," she answered, "but I needed some space."

"Oh." He seemed to consider saying something, then sniffed in the cold air, and she could see him change his mind and say something else, "Would you like to be alone, then?"

Hannah shook her head, feeling her cold hair brushing against her cold cheeks. "I wanted to be away from them," she explained. "Not you."

He took a few steps toward her then, and Hannah was sure he was going to pull her into an embrace, when shouts cut across the night.

"They're coming!" A breathless voice was shouting, and then Hannah saw the staggering form of Jaston making his halting way down the street toward them. Rory turned abruptly to his scout.

"Fledglings or goblins?"

"Goblins now... but others..." Jaston paused, gasping to catch his breath before he could get the words out. "Not far behind," he finished.

"How many?"

Jaston shook his head. "Hard to see... even with moon." The young man reached them and hunkered down on one knee, chest heaving with effort. Hannah felt the pull of his blood then, galloping with his heart, and looked away, focusing on Rory instead. The elf was considering, planning even as he turned to Hannah.

"Get back to the inn," he ordered her. "Get them ready."

Hannah turned to move, but before she could, Rory grabbed her, tugged her close to his chest, and kissed her hard. He released her, looking to the struggling scout, and Hannah said, "I love you," before turning to run down the street.

She was yelling a warning as she approached, but the villagers were still caught in the confusion. Hannah shouted at them, barking orders as she had seen Rory doing, and soon the men were readying themselves, many kissing women frantically before they marched outside, forming ranks as they had been taught. Hannah left them to their orders as Fergus began shouting at them, making her way into the chaotic maelstrom that was the inside of the inn.

<Klauden, > she searched for him with her mind, knowing that any shouting in here would be a wasted effort. *< They're coming. >*

The vampire answered her immediately. *< The back door, chaivin. I've got Elsbeth. >*

Hannah pushed her way through the mob, elbowing aside two women who had decided that screaming was a good way to survive the coming battle, and made it to the back room. She was loosening both swords on her hips as she hurried out the back door, hands untying her cloak and handing it quickly to Elsbeth, the girl just starting to shiver in the cold. The cloak would only get in the way as she fought, and it wasn't as if the cold could really hurt her anymore.

CHAPTER XXXVII

Klauden was already scanning the darkness beyond the inn's yard, eyes glazed red with his nightvision. Elsbeth had gone quite still, the girl staring into the night with a mix of fear and exhilaration. Hannah could practically feel the low thrum of the girl's pulse, a fast beat of health and vitality, and she had to force herself to look away, to concentrate on something other than the smooth skin of Elsbeth's neck.

"Can you see them?" she asked Klauden, scanning the night herself but seeing nothing.

"Not yet," he answered. He took a deep breath of the air, and Hannah felt him reaching out with his senses. She followed suit, feeling for the presence of others. She felt them the same moment he did, a swarm of bloodthirst and excitement streaming toward them, and she opened her eyes.

"They're going to die," she said quietly, seeing Talperin's fate again in her memory. "We are going to die."

Elsbeth was staring at her now, the girl's face white with fear.

Klauden stepped toward her, hands resting on Hannah's shoulders. "We will not die," he assured her. "I will not allow it."

Hannah turned away from his comfort, walking to the corner of the inn and peering beyond to the street where she had left Rory. It was very dark there, but she could see the mass of men waiting, hear the desperate pounding of hundreds of hearts as they stood their ground, and her fear left her, replaced by a fierce pride in these people who stood against overwhelming odds.

Well then, she decided, *if this is to be the end, then I will die fighting.* She reached out again with her newly enhanced senses and found Rory, the elf standing at the head of line, eyes searching the darkness for the line he knew was coming.

Hannah didn't hesitate.

Ignoring Klauden's shouts both out loud and in her mind, she ran around the corner, darted through the lines of men, and stopped at Rory's side. The elf looked startled at her sudden appearance on his right, but then he recognized her, and his face broke into a grin.

"I knew you would come," he said, and there it was again, that lust for life and love for her that she knew was still in him.

"I wouldn't miss it for the world," she told him, grinning back at him, heart hammering in her chest as she drew her swords.

She heard them before she saw them, and her hearing must have been quite good because she knew they were coming long seconds before Rory did. She looked at him once more in the moonlight, almost laughing with keyed up tension. "This is crazy," she said. "You are crazy."

"I know," the elf answered, drawing his own blade, the ringing of metal echoing down the lines as men drew steel. As the line of moving shapes came into sight down the street, Rory turned to her once more. "You know I love you, right?"

And then the mass of bodies was on them.

XXXVIII

Hannah managed to stand her ground through the first assault more easily than she thought would be possible. Her new reflexes made the goblins seem slow, and her nightvision allowed her to see them in the dark. She had to wait until the fighting got underway to use it though, unwilling, even now, to let the villagers see her glowing red eyes. Even so, there would be questions after if any still stood to ask them. Hannah found herself hoping that there would be.

The goblins were disorganized, attacking without any patterns or overall design, but there were enough of them. Hannah watched as wave after wave of the short stocky creatures piled into the organized lines before the inn. Her body moved as it had been trained, swords swinging madly at each new target, but there were so many of them, and by the time she felt the new wave of fledglings coming, her face and arms were bleeding from stray cuts. Still, it was easy enough work. Every goblin she fought seemed focused on something else, and the hits they scored seemed almost accidental. Her mind wandered as she fought, wondering why the red demon and her elf would have waited to unleash the fledglings, why they were willing to sacrifice so many goblins uselessly, but then she understood.

It was the blood.

Even with her fighting skills and superior reflexes, she was bleeding from a dozen little wounds. The men who still stood in their ragged lines were bleeding even more. Some had fallen amid the piling bodies of the goblins, but those who were still fighting—and Hannah was glad to see there were still quite a lot of them—were all wounded at least a little bit. *All of that blood in the air...* Now that Hannah thought about it, she could sense it, and for a moment, she was afraid that she would lose herself to the bloodlust, but nothing happened. She could feel Klauden in her head, his will keeping her need in check. But there was no one holding the enemies back, and all of this blood would be just enough to push the crazed fledglings into complete madness.

It was a brilliant move, really. It was something her father would have done.

As she stabbed through the chest plate of another goblin and spun out of the way of two more thrusting blades that somehow managed to go completely around her before the two forms moved farther into the fray, Hannah realized that if everything she had been speculating was right, then everything she had feared was probably true as well.

Anna had her body, and she was using it to get her. Hannah had the terrible feeling that Malbrek was somehow behind all of it, though she couldn't imagine how.

She had the odd thought that if she just stepped back and stopped fighting, the goblins would move around her, ignoring her completely, as, she realized slowly, they already had been.

That's crazy, she told herself, but when she glanced in Rory's direction, she saw that his goblins were completely focused on him. Their attacks, though no match for the elf's superior swordsmanship, were direct and determined. The goblins who passed Hannah didn't seem to be running straight at her. In fact, they were all next to her or nearby when she attacked them, and then their pitiful defenses were useless.

It was almost as if they couldn't really see her, as if she was somehow invisible or cloaked from their view.

<Klauden!> She called out to him with her mind. *<Am I hidden somehow?>* The vampire took a moment to finish the two goblins in front of him with a flick of delicate fingers—Hannah felt the power of the spell crackle under her skin—and then turned to consider her.

Elsbeth hovered behind him, the girl's small frame hunched in the dark, but Hannah could feel her power now, too, a strange sensation that hovered around the girl in a dark halo that pulsed and echoed with the girl's fear. Fergus was at her side, the young man crouched in a semi-passable attack stance. He held on to his sword and took down a goblin that got too near.

Klauden narrowed his gaze, and Hannah felt him run his mind over her, the touch too familiar and invading, but she stood still and endured it, needing to know if she was being paranoid or if the worst could possibly be true.

As Klauden's inspection grew in intensity, Hannah felt something else growing in her—a certainty that the more closely Klauden examined her, the more obvious her position was becoming to those watching, as if he were stripping away layers of invisibility. The goblins still seemed disinterested, but as a new wave of fledglings slammed into the front lines, the bloodthirsty creatures quickly made their way to her position, forming a loose circle around the small plot of land she and Rory were defending. These may not be determined to end her life, but they were definitely trying to put her out of the fight.

She stepped back, putting her back to Rory's as her swords defended from three fledglings who kept reaching for her with their bare hands. She could feel the smooth moves of the elf's blades slowly growing more jagged as he tired, could hear the pounding of his heart, and the inevitable hitching of his chest as he began gasping. He could keep up this pace for a few more moments, but the effort expended here would cost him greatly.

Hannah reached deep within, conjuring all of her newfound fledgling strength, and focused her energy into a spell. As the words somehow formed in her mind, she felt the magic growing under her control. She didn't stop to think about how she had remembered the spell. The power was there, her mind could control it, and without further thought, she loosed the power into the fledglings surrounding them.

The first two began to burn even before she finished pushing the spell out, their skin crisping on their surprised faces even as they tried to understand what was happening. The third burst into full flames, body pausing for a moment before slumping to the side.

Hannah shifted to her right, feeling Rory move behind her as she did, leaving her room to take the place he had stood a second ago. The three fledglings he had been facing reached for her, faces snarling, and she stabbed out at them with her swords, feeling the last of the magic leap out of her. The outstretched hands nearest her face began to smoke and smolder, and the fledgling yanked them back in alarm, staring at his hands in confusion in the few seconds before the rest of his body caught fire. The other two spared a glance for their flaming comrade, and stepped back from her, faces considering.

Hannah could sense the war within each of them—the desire to reach her battling with their sudden fear of fire.

"Rory!" she yelled in the seconds of the break, "touch me!" The elf didn't respond, but suddenly his back was pressed tightly against hers, and Hannah let loose another spell, again the words suddenly in her mind, and she watched as several images of both her and Rory appeared, mirroring their movements. The remaining fledglings stepped back from them, but as Hannah watched, listening to Rory's heaving breaths behind her, they circled again, not attacking her or her images, but swinging wildly at the elf's appearances. As they connected with the magical images, the copies dissolved, and Hannah realized that her distraction would not give them enough time.

Rory was leaning heavily against her back. She could feel the pounding of his heart as he fought. He was good, her husband, but he was still only one elf, and he had his limits. She needed something bigger, something to give them some time to regroup.

Hannah took a moment to take stock of the situation, completely scanning her surroundings to make sure she saw everything. In front of her was a pile of bodies, mostly goblins, but some lanky fledglings sprawled on top. No one was actively attacking her at the moment, but she could see more fledglings running down the lane toward them.

She could feel Klauden behind her to the left, and a quick glance showed him casually blasting a fledgling with a fireball and deftly tugging Elsbeth out of the way of another's attack just in time. When the girl regained her footing, she concentrated, and the fledgling's face became a mask of blood as he began to bleed before crumpling silently to the snow-covered ground. Elsbeth quickly turned to find another target.

There were still a few villagers standing in the line, and Hannah felt a brief surge in pride for them, standing against such impossible odds. She saw Fergus take on an approaching fledgling, the farmer and Jaston attacking simultaneously from both sides. The fledgling was fast, but the two men were holding their own.

Hannah took a few steps, pushing Rory around behind her as she scanned the area behind him. None of the fledglings were still standing behind them, so that was a good thing, but the approaching group would reach them in seconds. *If I could only think of something to slow them down...*

She thought of the lane they were on, the dirt road as it was during the day, now turned to mud under so many charging feet. She thought of cold and ice and how sometimes mud can suck a person's shoes off, and then the power was pouring out of her, a force of ice and cold rushing toward the oncoming crowd, and she saw them slow, some stumbling, as their feet seemed mired in the ground.

Her vision went white at the edges for a second, and she thought it was part of the spell, but then she felt wet cold through on her knees and realized that she had collapsed. Too much magic—even for her. Apparently her seemingly endless supply of power faded when her physical body tired now. She needed to rest.

Trying to pull herself up, she shook her head to clear it. Rory had stepped around in front of her, steadying himself to defend her until she could stand, and she felt a fierce surge of love for him, this man who would defend her at the expense of his own life.

She had just gotten a wobbly foot underneath her, and she was nearly standing when she heard the voice. "Find the elf and the girl!" it shrieked.

She couldn't identify it, but it was somehow familiar, and the fledglings who had been struggling with her frozen mud were breaking free. They didn't come in a rush, some abandoning their boots and some fighting harder to get free, but it was a small comfort to Hannah as she stood to face the rush.

She had an unreal moment of clarity where she could see everything around her in slow motion. Rory as he took his stance, his outstretched sword meeting a charging fledgling, and the two of them spinning away from her. She saw Klauden with his hands pressed together before his chest, but his face was drawn, his look serious. Elsbeth squinted, let loose another of the blasts of her power, and then a fledgling knocked Fergus to the ground and caught Elsbeth a blow to the face, and the girl went down hard.

The fledgling didn't follow her to the ground for the kill though, turning instead to face Klauden. The vampire leapt out of the way, deft hands reaching out to grapple with the fledgling and twisting his body. Hannah heard the crack of bones breaking. She turned away, a sound drawing her attention to her right, and she saw Scotty Pailin, arms raised in defiance at the fledgling before him, his little dagger flashing in the moonlight as he swiped at the creature.

Hannah knew it was too late even as she started to move, knew she would never get there in time, but she still had to try. She heard Scotty's scream as the fledgling tore into him, the creature's head buried in the boy's shoulder. She drove both of her swords into the creature's back, but even as it loosened in the grip of death, falling mostly on top of Scotty, she could see that it didn't matter. The boy's throat had been torn out. His unseeing eyes stared up at the sky.

She didn't want to care, didn't know why she should, but suddenly she wanted to scream at the futility of it all. She looked over to where Rory was, the elf spinning and whirling around as two fledglings tried to find an opening.

The familiar voice screamed again, "Find the elf and the girl!" Suddenly, Hannah knew who it was. There was a distant echo in her blood, in her soul, and she could feel the Elven healer from Kalford nearby, could sense him as he looked for her, knowing he wouldn't recognize her body but realizing that she must have some kind of tracking spell on her. That was why the goblins had been mostly ignoring her, why even the fledglings only defended themselves from her. Her own fledgling didn't want to risk killing her—and maybe himself.

She grinned, knowing that his reluctance to kill her gave her an advantage. She readied her weapons and leaped forward into the fray, taking on fledglings as fast as she could maneuver. She stabbed one in the back, took another out from the side, and then she was in the middle of them, feet nearly stumbling over frozen hunks of mud and ice. A hand clawed her back, and she felt something terrible give way deep inside, but she ignored it, hearing Klauden's curse in her mind as he too felt the blow.

She spun, facing three fledglings. She caught one's leg, easily knocking him down, then twisted to avoid another's clawed strike, sword swiping across his chest. She was moving toward another cluster of fledglings when she felt the whistle of a blade coming too fast at her. One second she was fine, moving and swiping and fighting, and the next, there was a sword blade aimed at her neck, and she knew she wasn't going to be fast enough. She had time for one thought.

I'm not ready.

And then a body was slamming into hers, and pain screamed down her shoulder. She was knocked aside, hand immediately going to cover the wound that must be spraying blood, but then she realized that while she was covered in wounds, blood everywhere, she was not wounded in her shoulder, though it screamed in agony.

She looked to the person who had knocked her aside and saw Klauden standing before her, arm hanging listlessly as his side, the blow that should have taken off her head nearly severing his arm instead. His face was dead white, his eyes blazing red, and she knew that he wouldn't be able to defend himself as that sword swung again. She gathered her energy for one more blast, and then the sword-swinging creature was flung backward into the darkness.

Hannah decided that she would have to figure out what spell that had been later on; now, she was struggling to her feet as her vision started to darken at the edges. She took a step toward Klauden, a hand reaching out to touch him, and she turned, seeing Rory surrounded by a group of fledglings. They had him, but they didn't seem intent on killing him. He looked at her, and he grinned, one wild, crazy grin before he looked at Klauden standing just behind her.

"Take her!" Rory shouted. "Take her and get out of here!"

"Rory!" Hannah screamed, starting to head toward him, but a strong arm gripped her around the waist. Hannah struggled, but she was weakened from blood loss. She felt the spell gathering around her then, knew that Klauden was using the last of his energy to teleport them to safety, and she realized that there was nothing she could do to stop it. She had a moment where she could see Rory's face clearly, blood smearing his cheeks, hollowed eyes blazing as he struggled to stay conscious, and he stared back at her, his lips forming one word.

"Go!" he yelled, then disappeared under a mound of bodies. Hannah screamed his name again, but it was lost in the swirl of magic, then there was nothing but a soft darkness that beckoned her. The last of her strength gone, Hannah gave in to the silence.

XXXIX

Hannah opened her eyes, then closed them again as the world continued to whirl dizzily for a moment. She steeled herself, rallied, and opened them again. *What happened?*

She was lying on something soft, silky material cool against her skin. *A bed,* she realized slowly, *a really big bed.*

She tried to sit up, to take stock of things, but failed. There was something heavy draped across her chest. She glanced down and saw a blonde head streaked with blood resting on her breasts. She followed the shape to long arms that were wrapped around her back.

<Klauden!>

She wiggled a bit, trying to move him enough so that she could sit up, but he was so heavy. The movement made her head spin, and she paused, closing her eyes for a second.

When she opened her eyes again, the room was still dark. She lay still, waiting for her eyes to adjust, glad when they did. *How long was I out?*

Klauden was still lying on top of her. She couldn't move at all, and she was so thirsty.

"Klauden," she croaked, "wake up." He stirred but did not move. Hannah tried again, reaching deep within herself for something, anything that would get his attention. As she focused and located her hands, one lying useless against her side, though it seemed a foreign limb, something not a part of herself, but the other was locked in a death grip on Klauden's shoulder. *Focus,* she told herself. *You can do this.*

She sent the magic out in a sharp burst, the effort wracking her body with new pain, and felt Klauden jerk as she allowed the cold spear to encase his unwounded shoulder and her hand. The magic made the blankets even colder, and she could see her breath as Klauden moved quickly away from her touch.

He yanked himself back, then turned unfocused eyes on her again. There was no recognition in those pale orbs, just a hunger too profound to understand. But she did understand. Klauden had been seriously wounded, the attack that would have lopped off her head had nearly severed his arm instead, and she could still see the ragged edges of the wound. He must be starving for blood.

She tried to say his name, but he moved before she could force any sound through her parched lips. He struck, his teeth digging into her neck as his lips touched her skin, his mouth drawing her blood to the surface. There was a moment of pain, like when the fledgling had first bitten her, but it faded quickly, and soon, she was being moved, the wound in her back forgotten as her body cradled against his, his good arm coming around her in a comforting embrace.

She was comfortable at least, floating in a warm haze of relief and bubbling satisfaction. She was helping Klauden, was healing him, was giving him more of herself than she ever could before, and it was worth it. She could just lie here like this for all eternity now. It no longer mattered.

Klauden's pull on her neck was slowing now, and she struggled to open her eyes again. His lips left her as he moved away, and through a dim haze, she could see the series of emotions cross his face. First, dull satisfaction, the look she had seen on his face the last time she watched him feed; then confusion as he glanced down at her, trying to remember what had happened, how he had gotten here; then a breaking apart of his features as recognition finally appeared, followed immediately by horror.

"Hannah!" he shouted, his arms first pushing her away and then pulling her close again. "What? How? Hannah!"

He had laid her on the blanket, her hair stiff with blood against her cheek. *Gods, there is blood everywhere.* So much of the stuff, and she was dying of thirst. It was funny in a way, but she didn't have the strength to tell Klauden about it.

He was shaking her, and she felt the first drops on her face. Warmth, sweetness, life. She licked her lips, then realized what was happening. She opened her eyes again—*when did I close them?*

"No!" she objected.

"You will die, chaivin. I took too much. Drink." Hannah could see the set of his mouth, the determination in his eyes only marred by the tears she could see streaking his cheeks.

Oh, Klauden, she thought dreamily, *this life does not suit you. You always used to be so clean.*

More drops were collecting on her mouth again, and Klauden put his wrist to her mouth. "You must, chaivin. Please."

She didn't really want to. In fact, everything seemed so hard, even keeping her eyes open to watch Klauden's face was hard, and there was a dim edge of darkness trying to take over her sight completely. Hannah had always been curious; she wanted to see what lay behind that veil. Before that though, she wanted to tell him that she would be alright. She was a fledgling. Her body would heal. She would survive.

"Chaivin! Stay with me!" Something about the urgency in his voice brought her back, pulled her away from an abyss that was inching closer to her every moment. *Silly Klauden,* she thought, *I'm not going anywhere. Just let me rest a while. I'll be fine.*

<*If we're going to be fine,*> Solyn commented dryly, <*then why is he sobbing like that?*>

Sobbing? Klauden is sobbing?

Hannah used the last of her strength for a final rally, a moment of clarity. *Gods, am I dying? Just letting myself die while Klauden stands by offering help?*

She forced herself to lick her lips, the blood a shock and a welcome thrill to her parched throat, and then his wrist was against her lips, and more blood was flowing into her, and she swallowed again and again. She didn't realize when her hands had moved to grip his wrist and hold it to her mouth, but she came to when Klauden laughed weakly.

What's funny?

She took a deep breath, feeling the blood regenerating as she lay there beneath him, her eyes growing clearer by the second until she could see, could really see him again. She stopped sucking on his wrist, allowing the blood to take effect. Besides, between the two of them, there wasn't exactly enough blood to go around. She would live now. They would be alright.

"Klauden," she whispered, and her voice was loud in the silence.

He was smiling at her, the joy on his face overwhelming even the sight of him covered in blood and in complete disarray. She had never seen him like this before. He was a wreck. So was she.

"You—" she began, but then Klauden darted toward her, and he was kissing her, madly kissing her until she couldn't breathe, and then she remembered that breath didn't matter anymore, and she was kissing him back, her hands twisting in his hair and tugging him closer. He rolled onto his back, pulling her on top of him, one hand holding her face against his as his tongue ravaged her mouth, and the other wrapped like a band of iron around her back.

"<You are alive,>" he was saying, relapsing into their native tongue in his madness, "<I thought they killed you. I thought I killed you. You are alive, oh, my love...>"

Hannah wanted to stop, to ask how he was speaking when his tongue was wrapped around her own, and then she knew that she was hearing his thoughts, connecting to him as mates sometimes did when the blood bond was strongest, and wondered if he could hear hers. All of this was on a conscious level, but what she knew was running along like a swift undercurrent in her mind was a similar litany.

<<*Kiss me, yes, do not let me go, never let me go...*>>

They rolled again, and he rested his length on top of her, and she was aware of the male part of him, something she had always tried to avoid thinking about. The endless kiss finally broke, and he lay there motionless, staring down at her.

"Hannah," he whispered. "My Hannah."

She nodded, knowing that this was dangerous ground, knowing that she should push him away. She was a fledgling now, she could do it if he let her; besides there was Rory to think of, her husband...

But when Klauden lowered his mouth to hers again, she forgot all about that. Her entire being narrowed, shrinking to the point where Klauden's hands touched her, and when he dipped his head to her chest, the bloodied and torn dress no match for his vampiric strength, she let him tear the material away, baring her flesh to his gaze.

This was madness, she thought.

<*Yes, madness,*> Solyn agreed, but neither of them tried to stop Klauden's frenzied kisses because it was right, they knew, Hannah knew, this moment was right and meant and foretold.

Klauden's wandering hands were matched by her own, and then she was shoving his robe off one shoulder, enticed by the blood that coated his skin. She licked it, the stickiness on her tongue not quite as delightful as his fresh blood had been, but a treat nonetheless. He moaned, then started licking around the wound on her neck.

Yes, she thought, *that's right. This is the only right thing I've done in over a year.*

She made a feral sound, her hands simultaneously trying to pull his robe away from his chest and to push up the bottom so she could feel his skin. His hands were busily pushing her own skirt up round her waist, and Hannah knew where this was going and knew again that this was crazy, this was insanity, this made no sense, but her body seemed to have a mind of its own, and it wasn't Solyn's. The slave seemed to be watching the whole thing in amazement.

Hannah was on fire, her entire being yearning to be closer to him. When he pulled away to untie the belt that held his robe closed, she placed both hands flat against his chest, marveling at the smoothness, the paleness of skin that had never been touched like this by another. *My mate,* she thought drunkenly. *You. Yes, you.*

Then, without realizing she had intended to do it all along, she was sucking on his chest, her new teeth piercing the skin, her lips and tongue busily catching the small stream of blood. Klauden made a guttural noise, then she felt him against her neck again, his teeth easily breaking the same wounds from before, and then they were both feeding, and her hands were slipping along the blood on his back, and he was floundering alongside her thighs, and her hand moved to guide him within her depths, and then they were one. He made a noise she had never heard before, and then they were moving together, a frenzy of biting and sucking and meeting flesh, and when the moment came, she heard Klauden's shout in her mind, and she wondered how she could ever have thought that sex with anyone else was worthwhile, when this was what it was really about. This intoxicating freedom of biting him and loving him and not being afraid or struggling with herself was how it should always be. It didn't matter! She wanted to shout it. She could be herself with him, would never have to guard against her impulses, would never have to worry about doing something accidentally again.

Klauden collapsed on top of her, his lips nuzzling her neck as he lapped up the last dregs of blood. She wiped the last of the blood from his chest with a finger and licked it, eyes widening as she took in the enormity of what had just happened.

They lay still, Klauden's cool body pressed against hers, and Hannah tried to focus, to remember why this had happened, to understand why she had thought this was the right thing to be doing. Klauden was staring back at her, his eyes wide and vulnerable, his entire being focused on her reaction. He was bordering on embarrassment, but Hannah thought that might come later, when they picked up the pieces and had time to think things through. For now, he was speechless, his formality, his distance, his cordial treatment of her forgotten as he began to understand what had happened. She saw the need to speak building in him.

"Hannah, I..." he began, but it trailed off into silence. She could see the regret building on his face now, guilt she would share soon but not quite yet. For now, there was just the two of them, together in the dark and cold, two bright lights that had been meant to be together, once. She put a finger to his lips, to stop him from continuing.

"<You will always be my mate,>" she said, with a strange formality, "<and we will share this blood bond.>" She paused, trying to grasp her purpose in speaking. Everything was sharp and crisp, and yet, her thoughts were low and muddied. There was something...

A face swam into her mind, a daredevil grin with hair falling across the question in its eyes. Rory. A lead weight settled somewhere inside her chest.

She put both hands against his chest, feeling the low dull beat of his heart as it slowed down to a normal rhythm. "<But this cannot happen again,>" she added.

Klauden nodded. "<I know.>" He closed his eyes, feeling himself in her again, savoring a moment he had thought would never come. He kissed her once, gently, formally, and then pushed himself up and away. She shivered in the sudden coolness where his body had been, knees pulling up as she curled in on herself and rolled to the side.

She was a mess, sticky and filthy, clothes hanging off her in strips, waiting for her body to start singing with dozens of wounds that hadn't been healed by Klauden's blood, blood which would serve to keep her alive in extremity but would not truly heal her.

Wait.

Hannah lay still, feeling her body. Yes, she was definitely still wounded, she could feel the bloodlust lingering but as a dull ache, in the background, not as immediate as it should be.

Instead, she felt ... sated. Right. As if nothing in the world mattered because something that had long been wrong in her life was now right.

Oh, hell no, she thought angrily, whirling around to sit up. Klauden sat at the edge of the bed, his back to her, his legs dangling off the edge, head hanging down a little bit. At the sound of her motion, he straightened, then slowly turned to face her.

"What did you do?" she whispered, anger turning her voice low and dangerous as she lapsed back into her new language. Klauden didn't say anything, so she asked again. "What is this?" She gestured to herself, trying to convey the feeling she had, that sense of perfect rightness that seemed so very wrong.

"It's kevna," he said, and his voice was exhausted, devoid of emotion.

That flatness called to her, and she wanted nothing more than to ease him, to fill that emptiness in any way she could. She moved across the bed toward him, arms reaching around his shoulders as she leaned against his back, her chin resting on his shoulder. Her skin stuck to the blood there, but she didn't care. "I don't want to comfort you," she said, "but I cannot stop myself."

Klauden nodded, and the emptiness in him shifted to a profound sadness. He moved, shrugging his shoulders, and she let go of him. "Please don't touch me, chaivin," he said. "Please don't."

Hannah sat back, trying to understand what was happening. Clearly the magic had bound them together, bound them more securely than any fledgling bond could have done. She knew that magic was making her feel this way, knew it rationally, but she couldn't explain the emotions away. Knowing they weren't her own didn't make her feel them any less intensely. She loved Klauden. He was part of her, a missing part of herself that she had now found, a part that she would never lose again.

She knew some of that was true. Of course, she loved Klauden. She'd spent the first eighty years of her life expecting to marry him. He was her best friend. But that life had changed when she'd left, when she'd met Rory. Then she had chosen a different path for herself. A path that this magic remembered but was trying very hard to ignore.

She conjured Rory's face in her memory, not as she had last seen him, fighting for his life, or even as he had been the last few weeks, when stress of Solyn and Klauden had threatened to tear them apart, but as he had been those afternoons at the spring behind their house, those days when he had laughed and smiled and loved her.

She knew that these memories should be tinged with guilt, that she should be swimming in regret, and there was a heaviness in her chest, but it was muted, subsumed by that damned sense that things were now right, and any regret she had should only be that she hadn't had sex with Klauden sooner.

She stopped, the thought jarring. *I just had sex with Klauden. Malfek.*

She looked at her old friend, trying to imagine what this must be like for him. She knew that he had wanted her, but now that he finally had her, what had she said? Told him it could not happen again and that she was comforting him against her will.

I'm a terrible person, she thought suddenly. *I'm a terrible friend.* She pulled herself to the edge of the bed again, letting her legs dangle but careful not to touch Klauden. She looked at him, waiting for him to speak.

When he didn't, just kept sitting there with that broken look on his face, she sighed angrily. The sound caught his attention, and he looked at her, a flash of annoyance on his face.

"What?" she asked him. "What do you want me to say?"

"I imagine your elf was kinder to you after your first encounter," he said, looking away, and the words stung.

"He was," she admitted, and then she reached out to pull him back to look at her. "But he also wasn't delirious with blood loss and drunk with ancient magic. Would you please at least look at me?"

Klauden nodded, face set as he stared at her. "And you are saying that is the reason that this happened, yes?"

"Isn't it?"

Hannah didn't think it was possible for Klauden to look more exhausted, but he did. She could feel his sadness, a deep pool of longing that twisted her heart. But his face was hard. "No, chaivin. No." He stood up, slowly pushing the remains of his robes off his shoulders. Hannah tried not to stare at his naked back. "I did not lie with you because I was out of my head and didn't know what I was doing."

The material puddled at his feet, and he turned to stand before her, torso smeared with blood, then pushed the ragged pieces of his shorts down over slim hips. Hannah looked away. "You can tell yourself that, but I will not."

He stepped forward, pushing his naked body between her dangling legs. His body was lean with toned muscles. She could see the ragged line of new flesh across his shoulder, his arm firmly attached again, her blood doing its job. "And now, I ask you to please look at me, chaivin." His voice was calm, familiar, and she could feel him rebuilding the walls between them, the well of emotion disappearing behind his barriers.

Hannah wanted to look at him, wanted to face what had happened with some semblance of dignity, but she couldn't. *It was a mistake,* she told herself. *A magic-induced, blood-bond-fueled mistake.*

But she could feel him standing in front her, his chest still bearing the marks from her mouth; she could smell blood and sweat and even herself on him. And she still wanted him. Wanted him again. And again. And again. The closer he got to her, the more right it felt.

"You won't look at me, chaivin," Klauden said. He paused, then added, "Are you ashamed?"

Hannah looked up at that, cheeks burning. "What? No! How could I ever be ashamed of you?"

It had been a mistake to look at him. He was still Klauden, her oldest friend, but he was also her Maker, her mate, her everything, and she suddenly wanted nothing but to please him, to touch him and bring him closer. Her hands reached out to wrap around his hips before she could stop them, and she pulled him down on top of her, falling back onto the bed, her legs wrapping around his waist as her hands moved up to wrap themselves in his hair.

She wanted to kiss him, but he pulled away, pushing himself up with his hands, body hard against hers. "I did not suggest that you were ashamed of me," he continued, as if they hadn't just moved to a much more intimate position. "I think you are ashamed of how you feel, ashamed of wanting me."

"I do want you," she said, and her body pressed against him. "My body wants you."

And then Klauden smiled down at her, and the vampire she knew was back. "Of course, chaivin," he said. "Your body." He gave her a quick, teasing kiss and then pushed up, easily breaking free of her legs and pulling back to kneel on the edge of the bed. His hands traced lines of fire up her legs. "This body," he whispered.

Hannah shivered, wanting him to keep touching her, but he sat back, then stood again.

"Why?" she whispered, and though she didn't say it, she knew that he knew what she meant. *Why is he stopping? Why is this happening?*

He walked around the bed, loosening the sheer curtains from their hooks to enclose her in gauzy darkness. She could see his outline as he walked toward the door, his words floating back to her.

"I do not want merely your body. I want all of you, chaivin, and someday, you will come to me, all of you, and I will be here. Until then, I will not settle for just your body."

XL

Hannah leaned back against the cold stone wall of the secret corridor outside of Klauden's rooms. She was clean, at least, though she had shared the bath water that Klauden had also used, and she was sure she could still smell him on her skin, even if she couldn't see anything. Now the slaves were cleaning his rooms, removing the evidence while she hid out of sight. She wondered what he would say to them, if anything, to explain all of that blood.

She wouldn't have said anything to her slaves, but she never had thought about them.

<This is my shocked face,> Solyn commented sarcastically.

<Come on,> Hannah replied. *<You know what I mean; you remember how I was.>*

<Was? Do you think you are not the same?>

Hannah looked at her hands, the red glow of her nightvision highlighting the long fingers, the calloused palms. *<How can I be the same?>*

<I don't want to hear it,> Solyn snapped. *<I'm sharing my body with a stranger, and I'm a fledgling now, and I'm still the same.>*

<How can you be?> But Solyn had faded, stepping away from her and the conversation.

Hannah looked up and down the hall. They were carved into the same stone that the castle was made of, but the openings only went into certain rooms. Hannah knew these tunnels well, had used them often in her years in this castle, and in all that time, she had never seen anyone else in them. Surely others in the castle knew about them; perhaps she had just been lucky.

Chapter XL

She hoped her luck would continue, at least until she could get back into Klauden's rooms, and they could go back to Severin, or what remained of it. She was trying not to think of Rory or the lead weight that had settled in her chest, but she was fairly sure she would know if he was dead. He must have been captured.

And if he had been taken... he probably had been bitten. If not during the battle, then most certainly afterward. It had been hours since Klauden had brought them here. Any chance to avoid that fate had passed long ago.

Then again... Hannah couldn't help but think of what she would do in Anna's place. They had taken the town, had found the elf they sought, but they didn't have her. She was sure they only wanted Rory to use as a bargaining chip against her. So without her, what would they do?

I would keep him as a hostage, Hannah thought, *until I figured out what to do next.*

And what am I going to do next?

She thought of Klauden then, trying not to feel the wash of satisfaction that enveloped her at the image of his face, the remembered touch of his hands on her skin. Even now he was there, lingering in the shadows of her mind.

Shadows.

Hannah sat up sharply. They didn't know about Klauden. Anna and the elf didn't know. If they did, and Malbrek was behind it all, then someone would have burst into his rooms by now, likely Malbrek himself if her father's magician was in the castle.

They would know she had help, though, a companion and magic user, and how long would it take them to realize who it was? Klauden had done a wonderful job of balancing his life, she thought, staying with her in Severin to help with Solyn, and lingering for the battle because she was there, but also returning home just often enough to be seen.

That thought brought her back around to his slaves again. They would know he had been gone, but would they tell? Hannah didn't think so. She knew that her own slaves had gossiped, but Klauden was better to his people, fostering loyalty where she had simply expected it. It looked like that loyalty was being tested and, for the moment, was holding true.

Thoughts of Klauden made her want to get back into the room to be near him, and she could suddenly see Klauden look up from where he sat at his desk, lips curled in a slow smirk as he reached out to her with his mind. She turned violently away, standing up and taking a few slow steps down the hallway, then a few faster ones. She could come back to his rooms later. He wouldn't have enough power to teleport them back for at least another few hours, so she would just keep pacing until he was ready, torturing herself.

Maybe if she wandered these old halls, she could find some release.

XLI

Hannah had retraced her old steps down to the library and out to the surrounding cliffs, pausing for a time on the ledge to stare at the mountains all around, before she finally decided to let her feet take her near her old rooms. She wondered what her father had done with them but wasn't sure she really wanted to know. Maybe they were exactly as she had left them, a shrine to the daughter he missed despite himself. She had to chuckle at the thought. Her father would never be so melodramatic.

Hannah hoped he hadn't given her rooms to Livenna. It didn't seem likely, but the idea of her father's other daughter sleeping in her bed or wearing her clothes burned.

She was nearly there when she heard a sound that made her freeze in place. It was a wail, a cry somewhere between human and animal. And it was coming from her room. *Is that a child?* Hannah took three steps forward, then Klauden was in her mind, calling her back to the safety of his rooms.

<Hold on,> she told him.

<Why are you near your rooms? Are you determined to get us caught?>

<I heard something,> she insisted. *<It sounded like a child crying.>*

<I'm sure you heard many things,> Klauden snapped. She could feel the frustration in him, annoyance that she never would stop getting into trouble. There was something behind his frustration though, and she felt it for a fraction of a second.

Fear. Klauden was afraid of something, very afraid of them finding her... or was it her finding something out?

Another secret, she thought. *No surprise there. Klauden is full of secrets.*

<Look,> he added in a mental voice dripping with disdain, <it's fine with me if you stay here exploring these walls for the next few years. Just say the word, and you can remain as long as you wish. I don't want to return to the remains of your little village anyway.>

<No,> she yelled at him. <We need to go back!> She turned away from the sound, curiosity forgotten in the rush of her eagerness to return, to somehow figure out how to rescue Rory.

She meant to ask him what had become of her rooms when she reached the sanctuary of his, but the sight of him pushed everything else from her mind. When he held out a hand to take her back to what she still tried to think of as home, she accepted without a moment's hesitation.

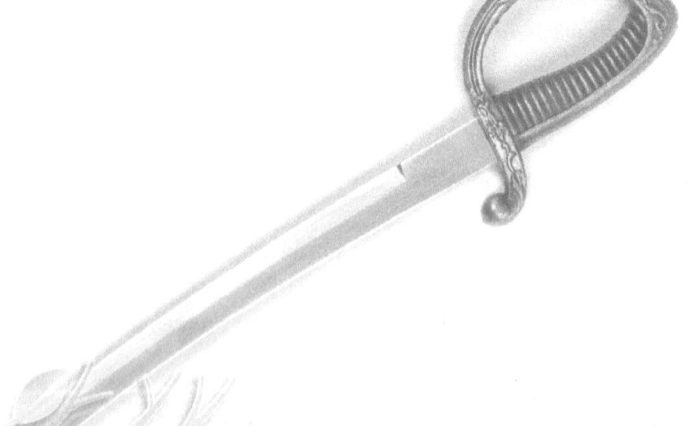

XLII

The magic was still overwhelming, even though she was prepared for it now. Hannah's foot caught on something as they appeared, and she stumbled forward, only Klauden's hand on her arm keeping her from sprawling outright on the ground.

"Sure," a voice drawled sarcastically. "Step on them. It's not enough that you abandoned us in the middle of the fight. You have to desecrate the corpses as well."

Hannah looked to the owner of the voice, staring wide eyed at Elsbeth, the girl standing tall and straight a few feet away, her face drawn and serious, her eyes and cheek still bruised and swollen from the battle. Hannah took a few delicate steps away from the neat line of bodies that Elsbeth must have been lining up for burial. The row of bodies ran up the street from the inn and down as far as Hannah wanted to look.

"Elsbeth," Klauden said, and it was as if his voice broke the spell. The girl looked at him, taking in his clean red robe, his healed arm, his healthy face, and then to Hannah, scanning her clean clothes, the borrowed robe from Klauden's closet.

Elsbeth nodded at them. "You are looking well."

Hannah tried to think of something to say. What was the right response? *I'm sorry that your entire village was destroyed, and it seems like it's my fault?* Rory would know what to say. Thoughts of her husband steadied her.

"We healed," she told the girl. For all of her angry words, Elsbeth didn't seem that upset with them. The girl seemed empty of all emotions, only her words containing echoes of judgement. "Elsbeth, where is Rory?"

The girl shrugged. "I thought maybe he was with you."

Hannah shook her head. "No." She looked down the long line of corpses, the faces familiar, but none of them the elf. "Is he...?" She let the question trail off. She was sure she would know if Rory was dead, sure of it, but her heart still pounded as she waited for Elsbeth to reply. The girl took pity on her, not dragging out her response.

"He's not dead." She nodded at the bodies. "Not here anyway."

"How did you survive?" Klauden asked, speaking for the first time. Hannah jerked her head to stare at him, at the rudeness of the question, but he didn't suddenly start bleeding from the eyes, so that was a good sign.

Elsbeth sighed, wiping her hands on her filthy dress. "Fergus," she said.

Hannah raised her eyebrows, confused. "What about Fergus?"

"I was hit a few times, down to my knees, and no doubt they would have finished me off, but then he was there, dragging me to safety." She gestured to the trees in the field across from the inn. The ground was a mess of mud, blood, and snow. It would have been impossible to follow any tracks after the battle. If Fergus had gotten her behind one of those trees, perhaps she could escape notice. Fledglings were eager fighters but not the best scavengers. Once the fighting was over, they would have wandered back to their camp, back to their mistress.

"He hid you?"

Elsbeth nodded. "I woke up a few hours ago. It was quiet. Everyone was gone." She looked at the long row of bodies. "The only ones here are dead."

Hannah didn't want to ask, but she had to. "Fergus?"

"Gone," Elsbeth said, and then the girl's shoulders started to shudder, and she was crying. "Everyone is dead or gone."

Hannah had never been very good with crying and certainly not with crying mortal teenagers. She was debating what to do when Klauden stepped past her, took Elsbeth into his arms, stroked her hair and back, and started murmuring soothing words. The girl shook as he held her, and he stayed that way for a long moment.

Hannah stared at them. *Why can't I do that? And when did Klauden start doing that?*

<*He's always done that,*> Solyn remarked, and Hannah turned away, not sure what she was feeling, but unwilling to watch anymore.

CHAPTER XLII

"I will find more of them," she said to no one in particular, stepping away to find more bodies. If she couldn't be useful to Elsbeth in comfort, at least she could finish the work of burying the dead.

XLIII

Hannah was glad for the cold weather. The bodies were in various stages, some a bloody mess, some missing pieces, some simply laying where they fell with no visible marks. Hannah knew that the smell would be overwhelming if the weather wasn't so cold, and she was grateful for it as she carried them to the line, placing them in long rows, crossing their arms across their chest if she could, closing eyes where possible. She wanted to cry when she found Scotty Pailin, carried his small form to the others, but instead, she just stood there for a long moment, staring down at his young corpse.

"They will die anyway," she had told Rory, trying to be rational. And it was true. All of these mortals would have died long before her even if the army hadn't come.

But Scotty Pailin would have lived before he died. He would have grown into those gangly arms, seen the promise of that face mature into a charming smile.

And now he never would.

And it made Hannah angry. *All of these people are dead, and for what?* The fledglings hadn't even bothered to feed from them. The goblins hadn't ransacked the bodies for useful trinkets. They were just dead and for no reason.

Except for the will of the red demon. *Anna. That bitch.* Hannah knew that she had always intended to go to the camp, to find and defeat Anna. She would rescue Rory if he was still alive. But she hadn't realized how very much she would enjoy it.

CHAPTER XLIII

She kicked the frozen ground hard, her boot cracking the top layer of ice and sending up a spray of red-tinged slush into the dying light of the late afternoon sun.

"We can't leave yet," a voice said behind her. She turned to see Klauden, face flushed in the cold wind, eyes clear and calculating. His hair was free around his face, blonde wisps blowing front and back.

"I know," she admitted. She was still tired. She needed to rest, to regroup, to prepare her magic, to change her clothes. And Klauden would need to rest as well, regaining his power before an assault on the enemy. "But we will go."

"I'm going with you," another voice said. They both turned to see Elsbeth. Her face was ravaged, but her eyes were determined. She held a lantern in one hand, the other holding her hair out of her face in the biting wind. She said a few words, then turned up the flame and brought the fire down to the edge of Scotty's sleeve. The light guttered for a second, but then the fabric caught, the fire slowly spreading across his clothes and then to the body next to him. Elsbeth stood up and walked over to where Hannah and Klauden stood.

"It's suicide," Hannah said, looking into the young face with the old eyes.

Elsbeth shrugged, glancing around. "I can't stay here. And I need to find Fergus. If they took him, I will find him. I owe him my life."

Hannah thought of the young man, his awkwardness, his fierce loyalty, and wondered idly how close he and Elsbeth were. There was a lot she didn't know about Elsbeth.

"Wait," she said, staring at Elsbeth with renewed interest. "That night when we were captured," she began, "you were outside. Why were you outside?"

Elsbeth rolled her eyes, paused, then apparently decided it wasn't worth the lie anymore. "Fergus and I have been sneaking away for a few months now," she admitted. "I just got unlucky that night and got caught before I could find him."

Klauden made a satisfied *See!* noise, and Hannah shook her head at him. <*I never said it was you,*> she thought at him.

<*You never said it wasn't me,*> he replied, but she could feel the lightness in the remark.

"I'm going with you," Elsbeth said again, and Hannah could hear the stubborn teenager in her voice.

"Of course, you are," she agreed. "But you need to rest. You'll need all of your power if we're going to make it there in one piece."

The girl nodded, eyes drifting to the line of fire now running down the lane. "I will meet you here at dawn," she told them, and then turned away, back to the inn for her last night.

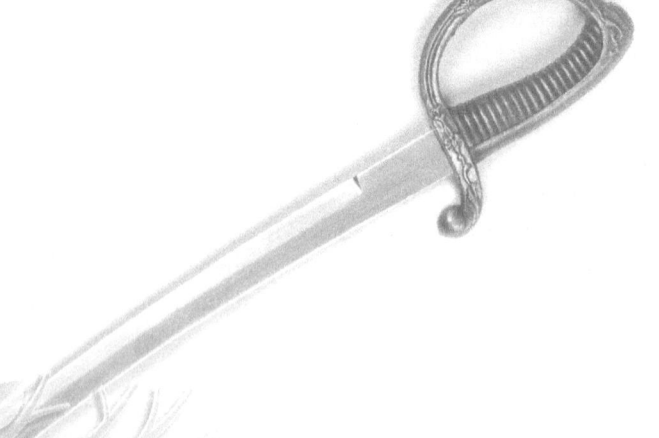

XLIV

Hannah stood in the home she had shared with Rory, staring at Klauden as he ran his hands down the shirt and pants he now wore.

"I feel ridiculous," he said again, tugging on the waistband of the pants while trying to simultaneously push down on the long shirt. The vest was a little loose across his shoulders; Rory was more muscular than he was.

"You look fine," Hannah assured him. "Come on, Klauden. You can't go in there looking like you. They'll recognize you right away."

"I know, but they will recognize me anyway. If I'm going to be caught, I'd rather I look like myself."

"If you ever want to return home," she reminded him, "you need them not to know it's you. Anything you can do to help disguise yourself, the better." She tossed him the hat, and he caught it gracefully but held it away from him, eyeing it with distaste. "It will hide your hair," Hannah insisted.

Klauden grumbled but yanked the hat onto his head, shoving chunks of his hair underneath the brim. "You should braid it," Hannah commented, moving toward him. She pulled the hat off his head, his hair coming down in a wave over his face, and she was suddenly awash in twin scents—Rory from his hat and clothing, and Klauden from all that hair. She remembered that hair brushing her face as he lay on top of her, moving in her.

She took a quick step back, head down, and focused on breathing for a moment. She knew it was silly to use breath to calm down—she didn't need to breathe at all anymore—but this body had a lifetime's memories of deep soothing breaths, and it worked to slow her racing heart.

Klauden moved away from her, giving her space as he moved to the table and the hairbrush there. He started working it through his hair, deft fingers twisting the strands into a short braid. Hannah tried to watch the fire instead, but her gaze kept pulling back to the vampire.

<Please,> Solyn said. *<You owe it to me.>*

<I don't owe you a damn thing,> Hannah snapped, knowing where the slave was going with this. She could feel the slave's desire, her fierce need to touch the vampire. Hannah told herself that she didn't owe the girl anything, but she knew it wasn't true and so did Solyn. Hannah had wreaked havoc on Solyn's life, whether or not the slave had longed for death before Hannah showed up. She had still stolen her body.

Hannah tried again. *<But I can't. It's not right. Rory...>*

<I know you love Rory,> Solyn agreed. *<And he adores you. It's been nice to bask in that affection for a time, even if I do despise the elf. But the way Klauden looks at you, at us, it reminds me of when I first came to the castle, when he would heal my wounds, when he would stare at me with that hungry look, though he never took advantage of me like the others. He was gentle and kind, and I respect him for that. I think I owe him something.>*

<You don't owe him anything,> Hannah insisted, hating that both of them had decided to focus on debt and obligation instead of the underlying reasons for their position. She could feel Solyn waiting for her to say more, so she added, *<And it's not right. I can't.>*

<Oh, please,> Solyn snapped. *<You can't even look at him without desire flooding through you. You think I can't sense that? The blood bond has made him practically irresistible to you now. It's only natural.>*

<Besides,> she added slyly, *<this isn't you. It's me.>*

<That's cheating, and you know it. I am in control of this body as much as you are. I am responsible for what we do.>

<Come on,> Solyn tried again. *<Give me this one thing, this one memory to take with me.>*

Hannah felt the tears that she couldn't cry for Scotty Pailin welling up at this. But she had to try again. *<But why? After I'm gone, you can do whatever you like with whomever you like. Can't you wait?>*

<It's just that...> Solyn broke off, and Hannah could sense the other girl steeling herself to say something.

<What?>

<He will never look at me again the way he does right now. It's you he loves. After you've gone, he will not want me.>

300

The tears broke free, spilling down her face, and Hannah sat down on the bed, eyes still slipping over to Klauden by the table. He was nearing the bottom of the braid now, fingers twisting the last few strands around his shoulders into place. *<Fine, then,>* she told Solyn. *<Do what you will.>*

<No,> Solyn insisted. *<If he sees me, he will know and resist. It has to be you.>*

Hannah glanced at Klauden, who had finished the braid and now plopped the hat back on his head. He stood awkwardly, the sword buckled around his waist an unaccustomed weight, his delicate hands resting uncomfortably on the hilt. "I feel like a fool," he said again, noticing Hannah's gaze.

"You look wonderful," she said, and they both meant it. Solyn had been right. Klauden was handsome, no doubt—he had always been so in Hannah's eyes—but something about their connection made him seem to glow. She felt a stirring in her blood, an undeniable impulse to touch him again, to stroke his smooth skin, to bite him and share his memories, bury herself in his body and lose herself in his mouth, his hands, those gorgeous deep eyes.

He must have felt it, too, for he paused in his nervous twitching. Hannah imagined running her hands underneath his shirt, her fingers pressing hard against his skin, pulling him close to her. "What—" he began but paused, eyes closing as he shivered. When his eyes opened again, he gave her a serious look.

"Don't," he whispered.

Hannah crossed the room to him, stopping when they were a mere foot apart. "Don't what?" she asked, picturing instead her hands tugging at the waistband of his pants, pulling them down and freeing the parts she was so newly interested in.

He closed his eyes again, hands curling into fists at his side. At the moment when she imagined his pants hitting the floor, Klauden's hands shot out to grasp her wrists. He pulled her close to him, pressing himself against her. Hannah could smell Rory on his clothes. He held her arms out, face carefully impassive. "Don't trifle, chaivin. It's cruel."

"Cruel?" she repeated, closing her eyes, imagining his face darting down to give her a kiss, his mouth warm on her lips and tongue hot in her mouth. His tremor was matched by one of her own as she suddenly felt his hands tight around her back, his tongue lightly flicking the sensitive skin of her neck. She opened her eyes, surprised to see him still standing in front of her, hands holding her wrists away from him in a death grip.

"But you..."

He nodded. "I don't even have to touch you, chaivin. All I need do is imagine," he said, and Hannah had a violent image of herself pinned on the floor beneath him, limbs a frenzy of anticipation as he yanked the clothes from her body, "and you will know."

Hannah caught her breath, hoping he couldn't tell how much that last image had affected her. "But why? Is it the bond?"

He shrugged, letting go of her wrists and stepping back from her. "I don't know. Probably not, since the bond has never been described in this way in anything I've read. Still, there were a few old texts that spoke of such things, though I never thought they were to be taken literally."

"How long will this last?"

"How long will you live?" he countered.

She thought of Rory, of Solyn, of everything she had shared with Klauden already. "It can't. It's not possible."

He sighed, shaking his head. "I am sorry to have done this to you. It was not my intention." Hannah could feel the truth in the words, but there was something underneath it, something she could poke at, but then Solyn was there, jabbering at her: <*Can you not just trust him for once? You're always thinking the worst of him. He's not the villain you make him out to be.*>

<*I know,*> she told Solyn, knowing that her need to paint Klauden as the enemy was part of her attempts to resist him. She knew he hadn't meant to do this to her. Not really.

"It's not your fault," she assured him, recalling the huge debt she owed to her old friend. "I would have died if not for you. I am not ready to die yet."

He nodded, but she could see the haggardness growing on his face, the desire that even he could not conceal, the agony of not touching her. He took another step away from her. "I ... must go," he said haltingly, then tried to step past her toward the door.

She caught his hand, allowing his momentum to pull her behind him and turn him around. "Please," he begged, and the word was foreign on his lips. "I cannot endure this."

"You don't have to," she replied, pulling him close and wrapping her arms around his back. "I know," she whispered against his chest as he enfolded her. "I know."

When he bent his head to her neck, she tilted her head, letting her hair fall to the side and allowing his mouth access to her skin. "Do it," she prompted when it seemed he would pull away. "Please."

The word was a moan, a desperate cry, a vocalization of the need that threatened to paralyze her. When he bit her and she felt the blood begin to flow, she pushed the vest aside, tugging the collar of his shirt down off one shoulder to reveal his skin, tracing light circles with her tongue before taking her own nip. He growled when she began to suck in earnest, lifting her from the floor as she wrapped her legs around his narrow hips. He pulled away to look down at her, and Hannah ran a finger across his blood-smeared lips, sucking her own blood from the fingertip and watching his eyes dilate into something alien and completely familiar. He carried her the few steps to the bed, setting her down gently as he knelt on the floor before her.

This time would be different, Hannah knew, this time would be slow and deliberate and damning all at once.

XLV

"This is where I go in," Hannah said, turning to Klauden and Elsbeth. She nodded at the girl, then waved Klauden away. When it seemed like he might speak, she raised a hand. "Follow the plan. You guys circle around until you spot Fergus. I surrender, and you wait until Anna..." Here she paused, then shrugged. "Until Anna does whatever she's going to do." She looked at Klauden. "You'll know, right?" At his nod, she continued, "Fine. You work the spell to put me back in my body, I push her out, and Solyn runs as fast as she can. Without Anna's will, the army should splinter." She nodded, the plan, rough as it was, solidifying in her mind.

"And Rory," Elsbeth supplied helpfully.

Hannah nodded. "Of course, Rory," she repeated, ignoring the jolt of emotion from Klauden, there and gone in an instant, but for that moment, it was like she had stabbed him, stabbed herself. She rallied, focusing. "He's probably with Anna. They will keep him close."

"And the fledglings?" Elsbeth asked, though they had gone over this already.

"They should fall. Some may die, some may not, but the shock of losing Anna, their Maker, should be enough to knock them out for a little bit." She looked at Elsbeth, who was clearly thinking of Fergus.

For a moment, she wished she could tell Elsbeth that Fergus would be fine, that even if he had been turned, he would survive—and more importantly for Elsbeth, that he would still be the Fergus she knew. But Hannah couldn't make any promises like that. And she had bigger problems to worry about.

CHAPTER XLV

"Will I still be me?" she had asked Klauden, their bodies touching as they lay on the floor of the small home she had shared with Rory. "After I leave this body and get back into my own... what will happen?"

Klauden had pulled her closer, his breath warm on her skin as he spoke, her head resting on his chest, "You will always be you, chaivin," he reassured her. "You just have to remember yourself. The body is yours. It shouldn't be too difficult to reclaim it."

"And Anna?"

He shrugged beneath her. "She will leave. You will make her leave. I don't think she will stay hidden in the body like Solyn did." He paused, and Hannah knew the grin he had, knew he was recalling the years spent with Anna back in her father's castle, that stubborn girl who always got her way in the end. "She's too proud to hide. If she can't have the body, she will leave."

"And Solyn?" Hannah could feel the slave girl inside her, close to the skin, reveling in the feel of Klauden's embrace, memorizing every sensation.

"This will be Solyn's body again. Solely hers. She should get away, as far as she can. I will find her afterward."

"How?"

"She is my fledgling, chaivin. I can find her anywhere."

Staring at him now, Hannah knew it was true. *<I'm sorry,>* she thought to Solyn. It wasn't enough, wasn't nearly enough, but it was something. She could feel Solyn's content, the girl finally accepting the apology that Hannah had been giving for several months.

<Why now?>

<Because you finally mean it.>

But Hannah could sense that a connection to Klauden was just fine with Solyn. It was what she wanted.

She took a deep breath, steeling herself for the inevitable. "Go," Klauden said, and suddenly Hannah saw herself standing at the end of a tunnel in her old body, then standing in another tunnel, this time as Solyn. *He is always saying goodbye to me,* she thought.

<But you always come back,> Klauden answered in her head. *<Come back to me, chaivin. Go get your body and come back to me.>*

<And Rory.>

<Yes. But come back to me.>

The compulsion was strong, the order undeniable, and Hannah thought it was more than the fledgling bond that made his desire echo in her bones. *Kevna,* she thought, and thought for a moment she could see the connection they shared. It wasn't a cord at all, she realized. There was no need for such distance. Wherever she was, whoever she was, Klauden was there. He was only a thought away.

She shrank away from the thought, horrified at the idea that she would never be alone again, never just be herself again. *One thing at a time,* she told herself. *Get your body back. Find Rory. Then figure out how to stop kevna.*

There was always the chance that the bond wouldn't follow her back into her body. It wasn't worth worrying about it now when the problem may take care of itself in the next few hours.

Right, she decided, nodding at Klauden and Elsbeth before stepping through the trees and into the sentry lines. *Get my body back. Find Rory. The rest will wait.*

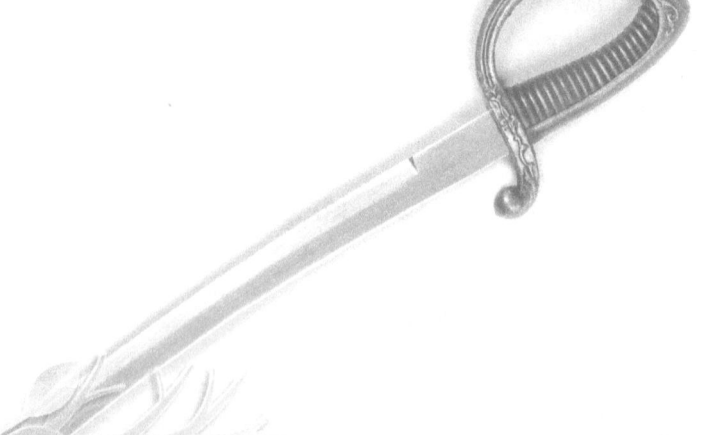

XLVI

Getting an audience with the red demon was surprisingly easy. The army had its orders, and even the goblins who found her was she strode into the camp recognized her right away. They marched her right through the encampment, muttering gruff comments to one another as she walked, spears at her back. Some of the goblins cheered as she passed—the enemy defeated. Hannah thought there were probably close to three hundred goblins here, give or take a few dozen. It was a considerable force, one she would not have an easy time getting free of, even in her fledgling body. She tried not to think of how utterly foolish her plan was, how simple and wrong, and how the Malbrek in her memory was screaming at her for walking into enemy territory without an exit strategy.

But that was the perhaps the brilliance of the plan—her complete lack of foresight. *The finer details never were my strong point, anyway,* she told the disappointed voice of her past. *And it always seems to work out somehow.*

<*Well...* > Solyn whispered, the girl a tight ball of tension inside Hannah.

<*I didn't say it worked out well,* > Hannah told her. <*But at least we're still alive.* >

<*For now,* > Solyn replied. <*This is madness.* >

<*Exactly. And madness is how you get your body back.* > Hannah didn't see any fledglings as they walked to the center of the tents. She also didn't see any horses. She wondered where the new vampires were camped, and if Klauden and Elsbeth would be able to find Fergus, and if the man would even recognize his former beloved. He might. And Elsbeth could take care of herself, clearly, or she wouldn't still be alive. Hannah tried to stop thinking of them, her only allies, and focus on her role in the next few moments.

The tent that held Anna and her body was in the center of the camp, an elaborate affair compared to the others that ringed it but still just a tent with dark colors. The goblin in front of her tossed the flap to the side, the material hooking and staying open. He stepped in before her, and she heard his low words to the occupants.

"I bring the prisoner," he said, bowing low to a dim shape in the center of the tent. Hannah tried to get her bearings as she stepped inside, eyes scanning the surroundings, reflexes primed to react to anything at all. There was little furniture inside the tent, a few chairs, a plain wooden table scattered with papers, a simple mattress against the far side with low hanging drapes tucked on either side. The bed was in disarray, the blankets pushed here and there, and the smell of fresh blood hit her just as the dim sound of a low heartbeat.

She didn't hesitate, pushing aside the goblin whose feeble attempt to restrain her was a joke, and moved to the bed, taking in the sight before her and waiting the few moments to gain control of the bloodlust. It wasn't hard, not with Klauden controlling her will, but so much blood was going to make anyone of the blood, born or turned, take a few deep calming moments. It was everywhere, coating the sheets, sprayed on the tent walls.

Anna had enjoyed her latest prisoner.

"Well, well, well," said an oddly familiar voice, "I never thought I'd see you again, sister mine." Hannah turned away from the bed to face the figure who stood in the center of the tent.

It was her body, dressed strangely in red leather that revealed far too much skin, but her face recognizable in the midst of curly red hair. Except the eyes. Hannah's eyes were green, bright green like her mother's. Anna had their father's eyes, the purple glow of the van Kreeosks since well before the castle had been built, but there was a hint of red to them as well. Anna had been gorging herself on blood. She was clean at least; the blood from the bed must have been washed off recently. Hannah was simultaneously disgusted at the idea that her body had done that, had been so messy while feeding, and was relieved that Anna had the decency to clean herself up afterward. At least she had been keeping Hannah's body clean, mostly.

Hannah tried not to lose herself in the moment, in the overwhelming wrongness of standing in front of her own body without staring in a mirror, seeing herself moving and speaking without her control, like a puppet taken on a life of its own. *Focus*, she ordered herself.

"I don't see *you* at all," Hannah replied, emotions settling into a cold fire that burned in her chest. She glanced casually around the dim space, trying to see who else was in the tent with them. The goblin who had brought her in was kneeling by the closed tent flap, head bent in supplication to his mistress. Another figure stood by the far wall, posture suggesting that he was guarding something. A quick glance showed something on the floor at his feet, something that may be a body. The heartbeat Hannah sensed was coming from there.

"Yes," Anna said, "of course. Always the literal one with you. You were never able to grasp the subtleties."

"No, I like to stick to the simple things like respect for other people's things, you know, like bodies."

"You are one to talk," Anna quipped, and Hannah flushed.

"You have something that belongs to me," she said bluntly, not wanting to play Anna's little games, tired suddenly of always talking.

Anna ran her hands down her sides, and Hannah could feel ... something faint against the edges of her skin. Hope filled her chest. "Oh, you mean this?" Anna asked, voice lilting in a way that Hannah never would have. It was so strange to hear her own voice used in such a way. Anna sounded ridiculous.

"No," she replied, "though that's mine too. I believe you have my husband."

Anna stared at her, surprised into silence. The figure standing near the wall kicked out viciously at the shape on the floor, and a low moan of pain leaked into the room.

Hannah didn't think. Suddenly, she was moving across the room, her fledgling reflexes allowing her to sidestep when the figure reached out to stop her, sinking to her knees beside the form on the floor. She rolled him over gently, wishing right up until the last moment that she was wrong, that it wouldn't be Rory's face she revealed.

But it was, though barely recognizable. He had been tortured, face bloodied, one eye swollen completely shut, the other a red-rimmed disaster. He whimpered as she moved him, and she felt gently down his limbs, pausing when she reached the mangled mess that was his right side.

He was curled around the wound, but when she rolled him over, she could see several lines gouged into his stomach, each as thick as her hand. The skin was ragged with blackened burn lines in some places. The blade must have been hot for some of the cuts. Blood was still leaking free of the wounds, but he wasn't bleeding dangerously at the moment. She glanced at the dirt beneath him, the ground a muddy mess of blood. She had seen wounds before, inflicted her fair share, but she hadn't seen anything this savage, this deliberate.

Despite the blood everywhere, she could see the skin of Rory's neck, the delicate lines of throat and shoulders unmarred by bite marks. If he was bitten, it was somewhere else on his body. It would be hard to tell with all of the other wounds, but that smooth neck made her think that Anna hadn't bitten the elf after all. They had tortured him for the simple sake of torturing him.

Hannah nearly choked at the red flood of rage that filled her. "What in the nine hells is wrong with you?" she snarled, letting Rory curl back into himself. "Why did you do this?"

At the sound of her voice, Rory stirred, his one good eye fluttering as he focused on her. "No," he mumbled, blood leaking from his mouth as he spoke, "run, Hannah. Run."

"I am done running," she said, lowering him gently on the floor and getting to her feet. Even the sight of all that blood was not enough to distract her. She could feel its call, the pull on her as old as her bloodline, but it was a distant echo. All she could feel was the pulsing in her ears, the pounding of her pulse as she tried to decide who she would kill first.

The figure who had been guarding Rory turned to face her, and Hannah was not surprised to see the face of the healer from Kalford, her would-be fledgling, smirking at her. The blood had been good to him. He was teeming with strength. She could feel it, almost the way she knew that her old body would feel everything he did.

"Why?" he asked, looking down at the elf at his feet with disdain. She recognized his voice from the village, the voice yelling for the fledglings to find her. "Why not?"

Hannah nearly lost control and hit him, but she knew it would be a waste. She was a fledgling but newly born. He had had over a year to master himself. He had let her reach Rory, even now was likely toying with her. She was the fighter, true, but he was stronger, for now. She was only going to get one chance, and she had to make it count.

Hannah glanced at Anna, the vampire wearing her skin standing carefully distant from them, face calculating as she stared at Hannah and the healer.

"You're playing a dangerous game here," Hannah said, deciding to go for the distraction. "He's bound to you, yes?" She reached out a hand to poke the elf in the hand, a quick gesture, harmless enough, and the healer didn't move out of the way. Perhaps she wasn't so outmatched after all. She saw how Anna moved her hand, too, a tiny gesture, but enough to suggest that she did feel everything that the healer did. "The bond between fledgling and Maker is strong."

Anna tilted her head at her. "It is. You wouldn't know, would you? You killed the one who bit you before you turned, didn't you?" When Hannah nodded, seeming to agree, Anna added, "Clever. It's the only way to be free of the bond. Had I owned this body the night you made him, I might have done the same thing."

Hannah looked to the healer then, wondering how he would react to this blatant discussion of his life. He didn't seem surprised or offended, so Anna must speak this way to him often.

"You would have, my lady," he said, nodding in deference to her, "but I am thankful that you did not."

"Of course," Anna sneered. "Dear Herrick here just wants to be a fledgling, to use his powers." She looked at Hannah, adding, "Did you know that Herrick here used to be a healer? Divine power, can you believe it?"

"Can you still cast like that?" Hannah asked him, curious despite herself.

Herrick smirked. "You assured me that I would not be able to, didn't you? You were so certain, so selfish."

"You're still alive, aren't you? Not so selfish after all," Hannah quipped, unable to stop herself. *It's fine,* she told herself. *Get them talking. Let them relax. Then make a move. Taking out one will take out both of them.*

"Not because of you," Herrick told her. "You left me to die. Malbrek was the one who brought me back."

"Malbrek," Hannah breathed. "And where is my old teacher?"

Anna answered, "He will be back soon. He has many things to concern himself with. But when he learns that we have you, he will come back right away."

"You have me, do you?"

Herrick stepped closer to her, a step away from Rory, who still lay curled up on the floor. He was quiet, but it was a tense silence. Hannah thought the elf may be conscious, listening and waiting. *Not yet,* she told him, wondering if he could hear her, knowing that Klauden would have.

"It's too easy," Anna said suddenly, red curls bouncing as she glanced quickly at the door. "Why are you really here?"

"You hardly left me any choice," Hannah said. "You have Rory."

"Oh yes, I had Rory," Anna agreed, and the tone made Hannah's skin crawl. "He was ... delicious."

"You didn't bite him," Hannah observed, hoping she was right.

Anna looked delighted. "No, sister mine, I wouldn't give you the pleasure."

Hannah stared at her, brows furrowing in genuine confusion. "What?"

"You wanted me to bite him for you, yes? So then you could have your fledgling but without all of that melodramatic guilt you managed to acquire from all of these dreadful mortals."

"Ummm..." Hannah couldn't even put it into words. Her relief must have been plain on her face, though, because Anna suddenly glowered.

"Wait," the woman in her body said. "Wait." She took a step closer to Hannah. "You didn't want him bitten?"

"Of course not," Hannah told her. "Thanks for that, by the way." She looked down at Rory, mangled as he was, and thought of Klauden's power, the healing magic that could repair her elf in a few hours. "He will be fine. You haven't done anything permanent."

"Haven't I," Anna said, and her eyes were cold, previous joy deflated as she realized her mistake. But her one-time sister wasn't finished yet. "Well, then, I will just have to satisfy myself with knowing that I have had him in every way possible." When Hannah went still, eyes drifting down to where Rory lay on the floor, wearing only his shorts, Anna added, "Oh, you know my favorite part, sister mine? That little sound he makes when he loses himself at the end." Anna giggled, then added, "He thought I was you, you know. He was really out of his head, poor creature."

Hannah lunged, unable to stop herself, but the healer grabbed her, intercepting her easily, strong arms wrapping around her from behind. Hannah didn't fight, knowing she couldn't defeat both of them at once. She took a moment to calm herself, adding this last detail to the mountain of rage she would unleash at the right moment.

Anna was looking at her quizzically, considering her as she stood shaking in the circle of Herrick's arms. "I still don't understand. You're headstrong, yes, and easily led, but you aren't foolish enough to just walk in here without a plan." She stared hard at Hannah, taking in the strength of her stance, the glow of her skin, the power of her magic that Anna could probably sense. "Who is helping you?"

Hannah forced herself to stay in control, to not lose herself to the black hole of fury within. "You think I need help to reclaim what is mine?" *Talking*, she told herself. *Talking is good. For now.*

"You survived a bite from a very young fledgling. How? Who is helping you?"

Hannah smirked. "I realize that you can't do anything yourself. That doesn't mean the rest of us have sunk to making pacts with goblins."

"The goblins are a distraction," Anna said dismissively. "Fodder. Food for the fledglings."

"And the fledglings?"

Anna beamed. "Mine. All of them, mine. Even him," she gestured to Herrick. "My Elven fledgling, Herculindarus Canadys." Hannah rolled her eyes at the long, formal Elven name. Anna gestured at her. "You bit him, but the bond is tied to the body." She pressed her hands to her body. "This body. They are all mine. Their strength is mine."

"Why would you do that?" Hannah paused, then added, "And how are you still alive? We killed so many fledglings."

"Funny things, bodies," Anna commented. "There are so many arbitrary guidelines, so many connections between the physical and the spiritual."

"I never thought you'd be one for metaphysical discussions," Hannah observed.

"I'm not surprised that you don't think of such things," Anna snapped at her. "You never think of anything beyond the moment."

"At the moment, I'm just confused. How are you alive if you are their Maker and they are dead?"

"This body is their Maker," Anna clarified, "but it's not quite my body. Not really. And that space between is just enough to distance me from them."

"This is Malbrek's idea, then, to use you as an experiment to make an army. What's his plan, then? What use is a fledgling army? Does he mean to take over the Houses?"

"Better to start with the elves, of course, but perhaps the Houses, yes," Anna agreed.

"How many have you made?" Hannah asked, suddenly sickened at the thought that her body had been violated in such a way. "What have you been doing with my body?"

"Your body? You are one to talk. Where is the host of the skin you wear?"

"I wouldn't have needed a body if you hadn't stolen mine!"

Anna peered at her, face deep in concentration. "Is she still in there? Is she the one helping you?" She glanced at Herrick, face darkening. "You told me it was just a slave body, someone she fell into during the ceremony." Her face grew grim. "By accident." Hannah could hear Malbrek's explanation in the words. Anna turned her scrutiny back to Hannah's body. "Who is she?"

Hannah smirked, feeling Solyn gather inside, the girl ready to jump into action the moment Hannah made her move. Hannah gave her one-time sister a patronizing glance, an expression worthy of their father, and spoke with a voice dripping with disdain. "Oh, Anna. You're still just outside, looking in, desperately wanting to belong but unable to grasp even the simplest concepts."

Hannah saw the look on her own face cross dangerously into madness as she gouged the old wound, recalled the hours Anna had lamented her third-wheel status, and she knew that Herrick would tighten his grip on her.

Anticipating the motion, she dropped to her knees hard, the elf losing his grip she fell. Herrick's blade snicked through the empty air where Hannah had been standing, and she ducked aside, kicking out to disable the former healer's knee. He fumbled, still not the fighter that Hannah had always been, and slid sideways, the short sword bobbling in his hand. Hannah snatched it from him with ease, using her other arm to shove his shoulder hard, pushing him over. He went down to the other knee, but when Hannah reached out to follow through, sword in one hand and the other hand hooked into a claw, he rolled out of her way in a display of agility she didn't expect, then he was behind her, one arm locking around her neck and the other reaching around to complete the hold.

Hannah leaned back, trying to knock them both down so he would lose his grip, then something hit them both from the side. Hannah recognized the dark hair of Rory as he wrapped himself around Herrick, and both elves went sprawling to the left.

Hannah looked at them, then back up in time to see Anna reaching out to her.

I'm ready, Hannah thought in the seconds before their fingers touched. The world exploded.

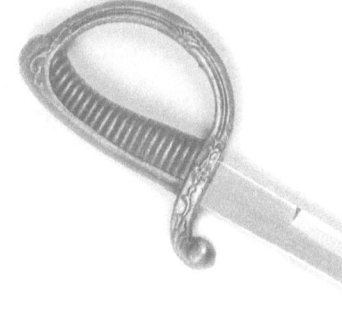

THE LOVERS

"This is a ridiculous idea," Klauden commented, trying to keep his mind from remembering Hannah's back as she walked away into the camp, her short golden hair shining in the cold sunlight as the goblins marched her deeper into the camp.

"You said this was a suicide mission," Elsbeth quipped, the girl turning her own head of glorious light hair to look at him from where they crouched behind the trees that edged this side of the camp. They could see the fledglings moving around in the camp, but there wasn't a lot of activity. Apparently, news of Hannah's surrender hadn't reached them, or they just didn't care. Klauden had counted at least a dozen young men after reaching out with his senses, but he was sure there could be more. These were newer blood, still learning to control themselves, still learning to conceal their presence. Anna was a strong Maker—he had no way to know how many more were hiding in the tents.

"I still don't see him," Elsbeth commented, neck straining as she scanned the few bodies moving about the camp.

"He's new," Klauden offered. "He may not be up and around yet."

"It takes a while, then?"

Klauden shrugged. "It depends on the strength. Your Fergus is a strong man, yes?"

Elsbeth nodded. "And this is the part where I don't ask you how you know so much about these creatures."

"Then this is the part where I don't tell you that we may not find him—and if we do, he will not be the same."

"Hannah is the same," Elsbeth breathed, face going white as she struggled with her emotions.

"Hannah is entirely different," Klauden said. "You cannot compare your Fergus to her."

Elsbeth gave him a pitying look then. It surprised Klauden, and he raised an eyebrow at the girl. "What?"

"You poor thing," she said, squatting back on her knees, abandoning her scan of the camp to really look at her companion. "You've got it so bad. And you really just don't see it at all."

"What are you talking about?" Klauden's words were simple, but his tone was growing colder.

Elsbeth rolled her eyes, and Klauden saw the girl she had been a week ago, the girl who would sneak out to meet her lover, the girl who would flirt with Rory and the new stranger in town. "Please. You are so completely in love with her."

Klauden looked away. "Am I."

"Yeah," she continued, eyes drifting back to the camp beyond the trees. "You sit here and judge me for hoping to find Fergus in this mess, and yet here you are, on a suicide mission for a girl who is so devoted to her husband, she came here ready to die to get him back."

"We came here to stop the red demon," Klauden corrected quietly.

Elsbeth snorted. "Right. Keep telling yourself that." There was a long moment when neither of them spoke, and then Elsbeth broke the silence. "Look. I've seen them together, Hannah and Rory. What they have..." She shook her head. "I don't care what magic hold you've got over Hannah or what kind of history you guys have, but you're not getting in between that."

"What do you know of magic or history?" Klauden snapped. "You are a child."

"Am I." The words were flat, and Klauden remembered the empty eyes they had encountered when they returned to find Elsbeth burying the dead in her village. Still, he could not let her words stay, could not allow them to have weight.

"You are certainly a child in matters of love," he amended.

"Then that makes two of us," she commented. "Me for foolishly hoping my Fergus isn't a monster, and you for ever thinking that she would choose you over that elf."

Klauden opened his mouth to reply, but then Hannah was screaming his name, and he was going to her, physical body teleporting in the process.

Elsbeth stared at the spot where he had been, feeling the magic echo in her skin and kindle a response in her own power, a feeling that seemed more inside her than the outside source she felt from Klauden. She pulled that feeling together, standing up and getting ready to find Fergus.

The fledglings should start dropping soon.

XLVII

Hannah remembered this feeling of being torn apart and flipped inside out, so she assumed it meant she had been pulled out of Solyn's body, but she was waiting for the heaviness that followed, the odd feeling of weight and substance that said she was back in a body. Her body.

For several long moments, nothing happened.

Hannah tried to open her eyes, then remembered that she didn't have eyes anymore, that she couldn't see anything.

Think, she told herself. *I have to get back in my body. It's mine. I should be able to feel it.*

She reached out with her senses, feeling tentatively through the nothingness, searching for something familiar in the emptiness.

Me. Myself. Mine.

There. A flicker. Something angry. Something red and angry. Something crazy and red and angry.

Yeah, that's definitely me, Hannah thought, and focused all of her energy on that space.

Mine.

She pushed out, feeling some slight resistance, and then Anna was screaming into the space.

<*No!*>

<*Yes!*> Hannah screamed back into that space. <*Mine!*>

<*No! This cannot be happening!*>

Hannah would have smirked if she still had a face. She pushed herself into that wall of denial but was repelled, Anna rallying and defending herself.

Hannah was about to push again, and harder this time, but paused, remembering Klauden's words. Anna had to flee the body. They would not be sharing, not like Solyn. It wasn't enough to push her way inside. She had to get Anna out of there.

So I need to get inside, she decided. *Really inside.*

She thought of Solyn, of the girl's hidden space inside her mind, the place she retreated to when all was lost.

I have that place, Hannah thought. *I didn't go there often when I was inside, but I know where it is. I've thought of it often enough.*

She would have closed her eyes to concentrate if she still needed them. She imagined the cliff at the end of the tunnel, then the open view of the mountains, the wind in her hair, and Klauden standing next to her, hand tight in hers. Of course he would be there with her. He was part of her.

She stood there, reveling in the feeling of a solid body again, the breeze pushing her dress against her skin, the sun in her eyes, the glare reflecting off the water of Nak Lake in the distance. *This place,* she thought. *It's always this place.*

I stood here the first time I found my way through the tunnels to the outside. I stood here and decided that I would explore all of the surrounding mountains. I stood here after dragging Klauden through the tunnels to my secret exit. I stood here with him and decided that I didn't want to explore those mountains, that I was fine, and I was home. I stood here when I wanted to get away from Malbrek, from my father. I stood here after reading my grandmother's journal.

And now I stand here in my mind. And if I'm in my mind, then I must be in my body.

Hannah reached out, pushed beyond the space, felt a slight resistance, but this time, when she pressed against it, it thinned out, stretching.

She was inside now.

Inside Anna.

Hannah grinned.

THE RED DEMON

The second her fingers touched the blonde slave girl, Anna realized her mistake. She knew physical contact with Hannah was a bad idea; Malbrek had told her so.

But her one-time sister had a way of infuriating her! No wonder Malbrek had spent so much time destroying the former First Daughter.

As their skin touched, the world exploded into fragments, and then Anna was hovering. She was still connected to the body, still tethered, but she wasn't in her skin the way she had been for the last few months. She looked down; the red-haired body lay slumped on the floor of the tent. The two elves were still tangled on the floor, limbs flailing. The blonde girl also lay on the floor motionless. The lone goblin guard had moved to kneel beside her prone form but was not doing anything else. Anna would have shaken her head if she had one. Goblins were so useless.

I wish I had known how to do this three months ago, she thought absently, staring at the thin tendril that linked her incorporeal form to the body. As she stared at it, she started to see other lines connected to them, some sprouting from the body, and some from her own form. As she stared, curious, the lines began to waver, some wandering closer to her, and some settling firmly into the body below her. She followed the lines as they left the tent, assuming they went to the fledglings quartered on the far side of the campground. She could feel them there, some of them anyway. As she concentrated, a few of the spots of heat and anger she associated with the fledglings grew stronger, and a few began to fade away. She was losing her connection to them, those fledgling lines cementing to the body below, Hannah's body.

No. My body!

Anna tried to return, to push herself back down, and for a second, she was sure that it would work. She was getting closer, the cord snapping taut as she moved back toward her physical form. But then another form was before her, practically between her and the body.

Hannah. Her half-sister pressed herself forward, trying to smash her way into the body. Anna resisted, tugging herself closer to the body, managing to shield herself. She wasn't quite back inside yet, but she was still closer to the body than Hannah. She pressed out again, easily pushing the ghostly shape that was Hannah away.

Malbrek was a fool, she decided. It didn't matter. Hannah could no more get back into her old body than he could. The body was Anna's now, even if she was still outside of it. Hannah would be repelled.

Anna concentrated, pulling herself down the line to the body, her spirit pressing against the skin. She felt the form that was Hannah press against her again, then the force faded away. Anna could feel the emptiness where she had been.

Hannah was gone.

Anna sank back into the body, fingers and toes tingling as she sat up.

"Stop!" she commanded, and the two elves stopped scuffling. Herrick scampered to a kneeling position before her, good little fledgling always bending before her will. Rory was slower to rise, but he did it, each movement a painful study as he staggered to his feet, unwilling to kneel. He was semi-alert, staring at her with something like hope, but he wouldn't last for long.

Anna smiled, trying to keep the glee from her face. This was too easy. "Rory," she said, hoping her voice had the right sound, the way Hannah would have sounded. She moved her legs so she was kneeling, infusing the motion with awkward unfamiliarity.

The elf fell for it. He took two steps toward her and then stumbled, weak with pain and blood loss, practically falling into her arms.

"Hannah," he breathed, eyes glazed as he slumped forward, the last of his consciousness ebbing.

"Yes," she said, gathering him into her arms. "Come to me."

THE VAMPIRE

When Klauden appeared in the tent, it took him a moment to orient himself. He had teleported before, many times, but always to a place of his choosing, a place he had been before. It had never happened like this, just being pulled through space and time to Hannah's side.

But he wasn't at her side. Because Hannah wasn't here.

Her old body was here, but he was fairly certain that Hannah wasn't in it because she wouldn't just be kneeling there on the floor, Rory's limp form sprawled on the dirt next to her. There was blood running down her chin, her eyes dazed, and she seemed lost in some kind of euphoria.

If he hadn't already known in his bones it wasn't Hannah, the purple eyes were a dead giveaway.

Where is she? He had heard her scream his name.

The other inhabitants of the room seemed as shocked as he was. Solyn lay on the ground, face covered by her hair, but he could feel her alertness, feel his fledgling's senses reaching out as she tried to decide what to do as the goblin leaned over her. Hannah wasn't there, not anymore. Solyn was just Solyn now.

The other elf, the damn healer fledgling, no doubt, was kneeling, face awash in worship as he stared at Anna, but when Klauden appeared, he got to his feet, face shocked, trying to figure out what had happened. The goblin also stood, and as it did, Solyn reached up with deadly speed and slid its sword from its belt, easily gutting the creature where it stood. She got to her feet, blade dripping as the body hit the floor with a heavy thump, and they both turned to look at the elf. He looked at both of them in turn, uncertain, then at Anna on the floor.

"Mistress," he breathed.

"Herrick," she said, seeming to return to herself. She looked at the elf laying on the ground next to her and then to Klauden, grinning madly as she swiped her hand across her chin, smearing the blood there. "He's mine now," she whispered. "She is gone."

Klauden stared at her, waiting. Hannah couldn't be gone, not for good. He would know. She wasn't here, that much was true, but she was still ... somewhere. He could feel her. In fact, the more he thought about her, the more it felt like she was holding his hand, even now. He glanced down at his hand, trying to distinguish between the touch that seemed so real, but his hand was empty.

Anna moved as if to stand up but then stopped, her own hand touching at her chest, fingers hooked into claws. "No," she murmured, both hands pressing against her body now. "No, no, no..." She looked up at Klauden, purple eyes fracturing as she screamed, "She's inside me!"

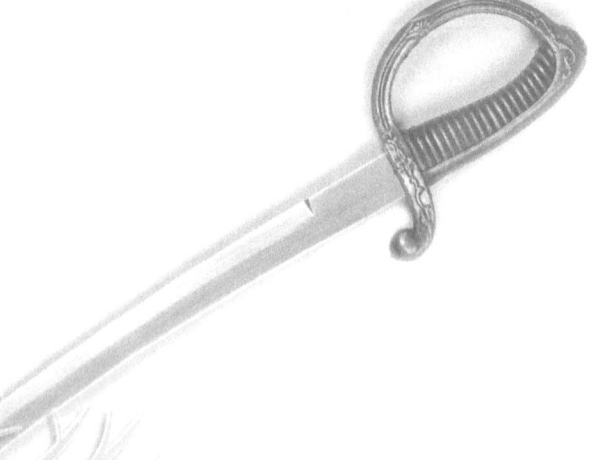

XLIX

Hannah was home. Her body. Her skin. She was so close she could almost feel it.

Almost.

She just needed a little push. Stretch out a little bit. Test the limits. Find herself again.

She had eyes again. She opened them. Klauden was standing in front of where she knelt on the floor. Herrick was standing off to the side, face uncertain.

Kneeling. She had knees again.

And then she was being smashed back, down and inside.

But all she had to do was stretch again, this time pushing herself to the limits she had found before and then a little bit further. And then she had hands again, fingers tight with tension and slick with something familiar.

Blood.

She was pushed back down again, but the struggle was fading, the stranger in her body losing hold, the form that was Anna thinning as Hannah pushed her from the inside, expanding her until she must eventually break from the strain or explode from the pressure.

<*No!*> She could hear Anna now, her half-sister screaming in defiance as she felt the body slipping away from her.

<*Yes.*> Hannah was calm, certain. This was her body. She belonged here. Anna could kick and scream all she wanted, but she wouldn't win.

She could feel the other girl's strength waning, but her will was not ready to break. She felt her sharpening, tensing up for one final assault before Hannah pushed her out far enough to where she could no longer hold herself together.

<I may not win,> Anna said in their mind, *<but neither will you.>* And she reached within ... and pulled.

Hannah didn't know what the girl had done, didn't understand why an empty space suddenly filled her chest, spiraling out from her center until she couldn't feel anything at all.

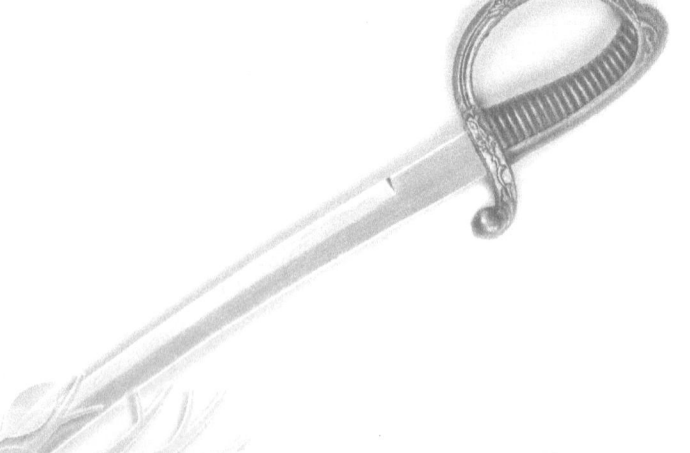

The Fledgling

Solyn waited, sword held ready, pausing to see what her Master would do. She was standing, watching Klauden as he watched the red demon kneeling on the floor. For a moment, she could feel nothing but the power of the magic in the room, some sense leftover from when Hannah had been inside of her, but she didn't understand it or know what it meant.

She stood still and quiet and waited. She was good at waiting.

So when the red demon started clawing at her chest, screaming about how someone was inside of her, Solyn was sure that Hannah had reclaimed her body and was just about to banish the imposter—something she had never quite been able to do—and then had decided she didn't really want to do.

Even Klauden seemed to think this was normal, standing there waiting for the magic to run its course.

Until the body shrieked and somehow managed to reach both hands through skin and bone and into its own chest, fingers disappearing in a mass of blood and gore.

Klauden reacted instantly, falling to his knees and grabbing at Hannah. The Elven fledgling, sensing his chance, turned and fled. Solyn considered giving chase, but then decided it wasn't her problem. She watched the tent flap swing shut behind him, waited a few seconds to see if any reinforcements would pile into the room, and then listened, hearing the confusion begin outside, gruff goblin words and mad shuffling. Some metal clanged, and there was motion outside, but no one came into the tent.

Solyn took a few tentative steps toward where Rory lay, the elf forgotten in the confusion, and tugged him over so she could see his face. He was barely breathing, but he was still alive. She ran a finger along the ragged flesh of his neck, wondering if any of them would make it out of the tent alive.

She didn't want to look at Hannah, at Klauden crouched over the crumpled form, at the desperate words and rising panic that threatened to swallow her whole as she was caught in her Master's emotions. Klauden's hands pressed hard against Hannah's chest, the glow of magic encasing them both. Solyn looked away.

When she looked back down at Rory, the elf was awake, brown eyes glazed red as he stared hungrily at her. Solyn sighed, then held her wrist out to him.

THE MOTHER

Keller van Sherinak was worried about her son. She sat on his untouched bed, his pillow in hand, wondering about the erratic behavior, trying to explain the long absences that he thought no one had noticed. He was right that no one else had noticed, but only because the silly boy had a loving and devoted mother who would not sit idly by and watch her only son fall victim to yet another one of Kelvin Malbrek's plots. The man had been trying to destroy her son for decades now; this newest attack was nothing new. Keller had been in the castle long enough to play the game well—she could keep Malbrek at bay for a little while yet.

Still, she hoped that Klauden would finish whatever it was he was off doing soon. There was only so much she could do to cover for him. The slaves were a big help, as they always were. She had known their devotion would be useful in many ways—though covering up her son's secrets was not what she had in mind when she'd convinced Jorus to see the mortals as something more than convenient snacks. She thought of her husband and shook her head. Though Jorus was a kind and considerate mate, there was no true passion there. The only thing she truly loved him for was for giving her a son that she treasured. A son that needed to get it together before he found himself facing the Master of the House and answering uncomfortable questions about the former First Daughter.

Keller had always liked Hannah, had been thrilled to have her son betrothed to her, not only because it meant he would not be leaving her to join some distant House across the mountains, but because she had seen how her son looked at Magnus's daughter. He loved the girl, and that made everything perfect.

And then Hannah had left. That had been damning enough for her family. But when she had returned in the jewel and Klauden had been unable to get her into the correct body... that failure had not been so easily overcome.

Keller had wondered about that "failure." Her boy was no fool. Not that she would ever say anything, of course, but she knew that Klauden wasn't telling the complete truth when he spoke of the ceremony. If he was hiding Hannah somewhere, so be it. It wasn't her place to press him about his secrets.

That is until he had started disappearing for days at a time. This last time, she had only just missed him, though she had seen the slaves cleaning up his rooms, and she had seen enough blood to make her worry. She wouldn't tell anyone, of course, but she had decided to stay in his rooms, waiting for him to return.

He had some serious explaining to do the next time he came home.

Keller had been sitting on his bed, pillow across her lap, wondering how she would bring it up, how to broach the sensitive subject with her secretive child, when she heard a noise from the study. She stood up quickly, pillow falling from her hands as she moved to the front room.

Klauden was sprawled on the floor, but as she entered the room, he stumbled to his feet with a lack of grace that shocked his mother even more than the blood that covered his arms and chest. At first she thought he was wounded, but then she knew that the blood wasn't his. He lurched to the desk and began frantically shoving things aside in his haste to find something.

"Klauden," she whispered, and it took him a few seconds of mad scrambling before he jerked his head up, eyes mad with desperation.

There was a long silence as he stared at her, and she could see the battle going on inside of him. Finally, something inside of him collapsed, and he was a child again, staring at his mother.

"Help me," he pleaded, face twisted with grief. "I can't do this alone. I can't find it. I can't save her. Please help me."

THE MASTER

Magnus van Kreeosk was not a fool, though it sometimes seemed as though everyone in his House thought otherwise. He stared at Kelvin Malbrek, his second-in-command so smug that the self-importance might soon lift the fledgling off his feet and send him floating skyward without need of any magic at all. Magnus kept his face blank, knowing that Malbrek assumed he knew nothing of the army the man was building down in the south.

"I believe my studies have led me to the idea of kevna," the wizard said, as if Magnus himself hadn't led the man down the path to the ancient magic. "I'm very close to something big."

"Of course, you are," Magnus agreed, keeping his face impassive as ever. Magnus knew all about his second's machinations. One did not rule a House for so many centuries without learning a few things about loyalty, and Magnus barely needed to glance at Malbrek to know all he needed about the wizard's true loyalties. A few ideally placed spies had done the rest.

His daughter had certainly made a mess of things. Just like her mother. Had she stayed here and married the Sherinak boy, the problem of kevna—and of Malbrek—would have solved itself in time. Now it looked like Magnus would have to do the work himself. He so hated having to lower himself to such petty things. But the time was coming soon where he could no longer afford to ignore his second's ambitions. The Elven city was one thing, but there was a real chance that Malbrek would use his army on the Houses, and that, Magnus could not allow.

"I just need a little more time," the wizard was saying. Magnus nodded in agreement, thoughts coalescing into a plan. He needed another distraction to toss in front of the wizard. Malbrek was ambitious and brilliant but also easily led astray.

Competition, Magnus decided. Something to get in his way for a time while the army situation works itself out. *Not something, then. Someone.*

Magnus reached out, waited for Malbrek to take his arm, and then led the man down the hallway to the Sherinak boy's rooms.

"I think I know what you may need, Malbrek," he told his second. "I believe young Klauden was studying a particular volume the last I saw him in the library. Perhaps it is in his rooms."

Malbrek continued to chatter as they walked down the corridors, but Magnus barely heard him. He was listening to his House, hearing the frantic pulse of Keller van Sherinak as she helped her beloved son find the books he sought. He slowed a few steps from the doorway, wanting the timing to be perfect.

"I'm sure the boy would be happy to share his work with you," Magnus said, stepping aside to allow Malbrek to open the door. "You could use his insight into the matter." The wards held for a second before releasing to the power of the House Master, and the door swung open.

Magnus van Kreeosk was a master of his emotions, but he was very glad that no one was looking at him during the next few moments. Klauden van Sherinak, the boy covered in blood that no doubt belonged to his troublesome daughter, had gathered a pile of books on his desk. His devoted mother walked into the room with a traveling bag stuffed to its limits and a leather cloak draped over one arm. Her expression was priceless as Malbrek stood in the doorway, but she didn't hesitate, and Magnus was pleased to see her react exactly as he had expected. She threw the bag and cloak at Klauden as he scooped up the pile of books, the cloak enfolding him in protective magic, and before Malbrek was able to do anything to stop him, the boy disappeared with a burst of power, the air echoing where he had been. His mother looked at Malbrek for a second, but then her gaze settled on Magnus, the Master of her House. She dropped to one knee before him.

"My Lord," she whispered but did not look up at him.

"I believe you may have to find young Sherinak if you want to read that book I spoke of," Magnus told his second. Malbrek left without a word, and Magnus stared at Keller van Sherinak. She didn't tremble, though she had reason to. He tapped her shoulder, and she stood, expression proud and defiant. He had always liked Keller.

"My dear," he began, "I believe we have much to discuss."

L

I t was dark and cold in the emptiness. Hannah would have shivered, but she had no limbs. She was a ghost, a spirit, a form without a body. It was like being inside the Star of Elgiva again—she felt weightless, yet she was still herself.

If I'm dead, she thought clearly, *then why am I still here?*

Because someone was yelling for her. *Klauden.*

Of course, it was Klauden.

And then they were standing on that cliff again, holding hands, the same never-ending breeze playing with her red curls. Her chest ached faintly. She reached up her other hand to touch it.

"Here we are again," she said, not needing the words but wanting to say something to fill the space. To make their presence here real and not just inside her head.

"Yes, chaivin," he agreed, and his face was tired, eyes hollow and cheeks drawn.

"You look like you need to rest," she told him.

"I will," he promised. "After."

"After what?" The pain in her chest intensified. She looked down but saw nothing. Her clothes were unmarred.

"After I bring you back."

"Bring me back where?"

"Look around, Hannah. Where are we?"

"Back home?" Hannah tilted her head, considering. She moved to release Klauden, to step away, but he held her hand tightly.

"No!" he barked, and she gave him a curious glance. "Don't..." He put his head down, and then looked back up at her, exhaustion written in every part of his body. "I do not think I can find you again if I lose you this time."

"Lose me? Where would I go?"

He gave her one of those impatient looks that was so shot through with love that she gasped. "I... Where did I go?"

He smiled weakly at her. "You tried to die on me, chaivin."

"I did?" She pressed her free hand hard against her chest, against distant waves of agony that were breaking through some impossible distance.

"Yes. But I won't let you."

"How?" Hannah asked, but one look at his face made her regret the question. "Never mind," she added hastily. "It doesn't matter." She looked around, then down at their linked hands. "How do we get back?"

"Just stay with me," he told her and tugged her close. "Don't let go."

"I won't," she said and buried her face in his shoulder.

"Oh, chaivin?" he asked as the world began to swirl around them.

"Hmm?" she mumbled against his shirt, world beginning to fade.

"This may hurt a bit."

LI

Coming back to her broken body was agony, but at least she had a body again. She couldn't quite open her eyes to see what was happening, couldn't do much of anything beyond curl around the agony that was the hole in her chest, but when the warm blood began to flow into her mouth, she was able to swallow, and her body knew how to do that without her help. She let it happen, feeling the blood soothe her as it once had, losing herself in the bloodstupid daze that followed, sinking into the relief that eventually came when the blood began to do its work.

She didn't know how much time had passed, but she knew that she had been drinking goblin blood, likely from a few of the stragglers who remained in the camp. She had heard snippets of conversations, Solyn's voice, so strange outside of her own body, Klauden's voice, which remained itself but tired, so very tired, and occasionally, another voice, Rory, muted and weary but very much alive.

Someone had picked her up, and there had been magic and darkness, but not the kind she would get lost in. Just dark warmth and slow healing as the pain in her chest faded little by little.

She opened her eyes, staring up at a familiar wooden ceiling, though she had never seen it in such detail before. Her eyes were so much better than Solyn's. So much better.

I'm using my eyes, she thought, a surge of delight welling up in her chest. *My eyes! I'm back in my house in my bed in my body!* She waited a moment, expecting to hear Solyn commenting on her situation, but when the silence stretched out, she remembered that she would not hear Solyn in her mind again. That connection was gone.

CHAPTER LI

She had a moment of sadness, of sharp loneliness, quickly replaced by the slow burn of hope. Her face was warm and wet, and she realized that she was crying.

A face hovered over hers, the bed dipping next to her as Rory moved to look down at her. "Hannah." His voice was a hoarse whisper, his eyes heavy with relief, face creased in old pain. He reached out to touch her face with a tentative finger. "You're crying."

Hannah reached up with her hands, marveling at the small fingers she remembered as she grabbed him, twining her fingers with his.

"Is it bad?" he whispered, his grip tight despite his clear intention to be gentle with her.

Hannah reached up with her other hand to touch his cheek, the fading bruises only just allowing his eye to open all the way. "It looks awful," she told him, and he laughed.

"Not me!" He chuckled, then winced, his other hand pressing against his side. He wasn't wearing a shirt, and his body was a kaleidoscope of colors, raw welts of barely healed cuts across his stomach. Hannah wondered why Klauden hadn't healed him, then immediately understood. Rory wouldn't let him. Thoughts of Klauden threatened to open an entire world of questions, but then Rory gently touched her chest, and Hannah looked down.

It was definitely her body. Her small frame. Her bare breasts. And a patchwork of scars winding this way and that right between them. She gasped, hand abandoning his to touch herself, to trace the ragged edges of flesh that had recently healed. It still hurt, but only faintly, the echoes of remembered agony more an effect of repressed memory than actual sensation. In fact, she could feel the skin with her fingers, but not with the skin of her chest. She had a sensation of movement, of pressure, but she couldn't actually feel anything on the surface of the skin.

"I have a scar," she murmured.

"I'm so sorry," Rory told her. "Even with all of the blood, this was the best we could do."

"No." Hannah looked at her husband, wanting to correct his misunderstanding as soon as possible. "I'm not upset about it." She looked back down at herself. "I've always been fascinated by scars. I could never get them." She looked at his body then, ragged but healing. "When we first met, I thought you had so many scars. I wanted to see them."

"I have a few more now," he commented, settling down beside her, one arm cradling her against him. She moved slowly but gratefully into his embrace, remembering how they fit together even though they had only spent one night together with her in this body. When they settled, Hannah sighed in contentment, at the rightness of it all. They lay in silence for a moment, and then Rory spoke. "What do you remember?"

Hannah thought. "I'm not sure." She craned her neck to look at him. "You?"

Rory shrugged beneath her, the movement labored, but still unconsciously done before he remembered that it would hurt. "I remember some things. Images. Moments. Pain."

Hannah nodded. "Yes, I remember pain." She glanced back down at her chest. "Anna, I presume?"

Rory nodded. "I didn't see it happen, but they told me. After."

"After?"

The question hung in the air, heavy. "After we got back here. After I healed enough to stay awake long enough to take care of you. After … everything."

"Where are they?" Hannah didn't want to say their names, didn't want to think of the two absent people.

"Not here," Rory replied, and Hannah let it go. She didn't want to know.

"Good," she said. "I just want to be here with you."

"You do?" The words were simple, but the naked longing in them made her move, scooting up on a shoulder to really look at her husband. There were things to be said, difficult words between them, but not now. Now, it was just the two of them and this bed.

"I do," she told him. "If you'll have me."

He grinned. "I'll have you, Hannah. I'll always have you."

She snuggled against him again, and he tugged the blanket up over both of them. As she teetered on the edge of sleep, she whispered against his skin, "I'm glad you're still here, Rory. I love you."

His arms came tight around her, almost painful for a moment, and then he relaxed, lips pressing gently against her forehead. "I love you."

Hannah let herself go then. It was enough to be alive and together. The rest would wait.

LII

The next morning found them slowly and painfully getting out of bed, Rory making a simple breakfast of oatmeal, the pot boiling over the fire before he turned to look at Hannah with a curious expression. "Wait," he said, voice still husky but light, as if he had just realized something funny.

"What?" Hannah asked, sitting up in bed, carefully propped up by the pillows, taking careful shallow breaths to see if she could, listening to her body, remembering.

Rory gestured at the bowl in the fire. "I'm making breakfast."

Hannah nodded. "I see."

Rory took the few steps toward her and sat down on the edge of the bed. "I'm making oatmeal," he said, "for breakfast." He paused, then added, "For you and me to eat."

"I know," Hannah told him, wondering where this was going. "And I appreciate it."

Now he did laugh, though he put a hand to his stomach as the sound escaped him. "Hannah," he said, grinning, "are you remotely hungry?"

Hannah thought about it. And realized what he already had. A silly grin spread over her face to match his. Laughter bubbled from her mouth. Food. She didn't need to eat food anymore. The only thing she needed now was blood. And looking within, she thought she could drink, of course, she could drink, but she didn't need to, not right now. Maybe tomorrow. Even as a fledgling, Solyn had still been able to eat and drink, though she could have chosen not to if she wanted.

Rory stood up to remove the pot from the fireplace, his usual grace only slightly stiff as he placed it on the counter, then spooned himself a bowl of breakfast. He looked at it for a moment, a hand reaching out to brush his neck, but then he shrugged, reached for a spoon, and took the bowl to the table. He sat slowly, then took a bite of the oatmeal. His eyes closed as he chewed, clearly enjoying the food. He opened his eyes, looked at Hannah, and gestured with the spoon in her direction. "You sure you don't want anything?"

Hannah considered, but the idea of oatmeal made her stomach quiver. "No," she told him. "Thanks, though." After a moment, she added, "Just think of all the food we will save now."

Rory nodded, taking another bite. "Sure. We just need to find some fresh blood for you."

Hannah marveled at the casual way he said it. "What have I been drinking?" she asked, recalling hazy images of goblins and then of more supple wrists. She looked around the room as if the memories would be written on the ceiling somewhere.

"Klauden," Rory said simply, pausing to chew. The elf was clearly hungry, eating as if he hadn't for days. Hannah hated the sound of the name in Rory's mouth, the word conjuring images that made Hannah flush with memory, with guilt, with unspoken words.

"What about him?" she asked, hearing the false note in her voice, hoping Rory would mistake it for something else. He didn't seem to notice.

"He saved you. I do remember that. Like I said, I was in and out for a while." He paused, scraping the side of the bowl, and looked like he would say something, but then he took another bite instead. "I don't remember much of what happened."

Something in the way he said it made Hannah think otherwise, but she let it go, recalling Anna's words, *He thought I was you.* The idea of this body but with Anna's purple eyes pressed against Rory was enough to make her skin crawl.

Hypocrite, a small voice whispered, and Hannah didn't stop to identify it. *Does he remember?* She watched her husband swipe a finger along the edge of the bowl, finishing his breakfast with a smile, and decided that there were some things she didn't need to know.

They had both done things that they would regret. If he didn't want to talk about it, neither did she. That little voice inside wanted to speak of the absolute hypocrisy and dishonesty of her plan, but she ignored it.

"Neither do I," she said and tried to bring some of the memories back. There was pain, a lot of pain, and then blood, blood from somewhere, and not from Klauden, not mostly. Her vampire could keep her alive with his blood, but the damage to her chest would have required a lot more than that. She looked at Rory sitting at the table, body lined with wounds, but nothing she though resembled bite marks. She had run her hands over his wrists that morning, fingers searching for the bites that Anna surely must have left somewhere, but found nothing. Even the mass of scars on his neck couldn't be bites—they were too ragged for that. Probably the result of that last lunge at Herrick; she thought she had seen the elf with his hands wrapped around Rory's throat at one point. That explained his rough voice.

"But I do know that he saved you," Rory repeated, standing up and taking his bowl to the back door, opening it quickly to access the water barrel outside. The cold air slid into the room, and Hannah pulled the blanket up to cover herself without thought before remembering that the cold wouldn't bother her anymore. How easily she had forgotten the benefits of her body.

"How?" she asked, watching as Rory cleaned the bowl and closed the door, returning the bowl to the counter and banking the fire now that he wasn't cooking.

"Goblins at first. I think he spelled them. They came, one by one, quietly, willingly, knelt beside you, and offered a wrist." He must have guessed her next question because he answered, "No, you didn't bite any of them. Klauden was very careful."

"And after that?"

Rory shrugged. "I was in and out for a while. I remember them kneeling over you in the tent. And then I remember walking. Solyn helped me a lot—she's so strong, stronger than I ever expected. She practically carried me back here. And I know there were some men left in the camp— they came too when Klauden did whatever he did—but then I think he carried you back here."

"Where is he now?" Hannah didn't want to ask, hoped that in her new body she couldn't reach out to her old companion, that he would be a distant vampire once more, but she didn't want to try, didn't want to say his name and find she knew exactly where he was.

"In the inn."

"With Elsbeth?"

"Elsbeth? No, with Solyn."

"What about Elsbeth?"

Rory shrugged. "What about her? Why? Was she with you?"

"She came to the camp with us. She was looking for Fergus."

Rory ran a hand through his hair, shaking his head. "I don't know. She didn't come back with us."

Hannah knew she could ask Klauden, that he would know, but she couldn't face the vampire, not yet. She wasn't sure their connection was still with her in her body now—and the uncertainty was a relief.

I'm such a coward, she thought, staring at Rory where he knelt on the floor, the fire taken care of. *I always knew it, somehow, but I could pretend. But not anymore.* The small fire flickered on Rory's bare skin, the silvery lines of new scars glinting, and Hannah felt a small wash of heat on her own skin. Rory looked up at her, and the feeling vanished as quickly as it had come. "Hannah," he said, and his voice was serious, "we need to talk."

"Do we?" she asked, her own voice a bit tremulous, wishing they could just skip this part.

He shook his head, looking back at the fire for a long moment, but then he got to his feet and walked to where she was propped in bed. "I think we do."

"Alright," she sighed, biting her lip as she waited for him to begin. When he didn't say anything, she prompted, "Well?"

He took a deep breath, shoulders heaving, and his hand went to his side without thought, fingers splayed out against his stomach as if it would help him heal faster. Hannah made a mental note to ask him about Klauden's healing before this day was through. Being stubborn was one thing, but there was no need for him to suffer through it when the vampire could restore his flesh with a few powerful words. Hannah thanked the gods that Anna had not bitten him—then Klauden's magic wouldn't be able to help him at all.

"I... I think we should talk about what happened in the camp." Rory's face was red, the blotchy color creeping across his cheeks and flushing his neck. Hannah stared at the redness, listening to the low thud of his heart, marveling at the restraint she now felt. Rory was attractive, no doubt, and if she wasn't aching with every little movement, she may have entertained other notions, but the fact that she didn't want to bite him was fascinating. True, she had been out of her body for a long year, but the memory of Solyn's bloodlust was so fresh that her own lack of interest seemed odd. She had only needed to feed every three or four days, though, likely a result of the human blood from her grandfather, but it was strange to be so close to the elf without wanting to taste him. Instead, she would be content to lean forward and touch him, just the comfort of skin on skin, of her lips pressing reassurance against his shoulder. Though, she realized, looking at his battered skin, she would be hard-pressed to find a spot to kiss that wouldn't cause him pain.

I don't want to hurt you, she thought, *and I don't want you to hurt me.* She recalled Anna's face: *that noise he makes at the end, when he has lost himself.* She shook the memory away, not willing to face it. "I think..." Rory said, but Hannah reached out a hand to stop him. Her fingers rested on his shoulder, damn the marks there, and he turned to face her. "I remember..."

"Don't," she said, and when he didn't stop her, she said it again, "Don't."

His face was so open, so desperate. He didn't want to tell her what little he remembered, and she didn't want to hear it. "We were both so badly hurt," she added. "Things were done. It doesn't matter." Rory looked away, eyes closing. She tugged on his shoulder, turning him toward her. "It doesn't matter," she repeated, and when he finally opened his eyes to look at her, "It's over," she told him. "She's gone. I'm back. It's over." She looked away, banishing Anna's smirking face from her mind. "What happened in that tent..." She stopped, reaching out to take Rory's hand instead. "What happened between the night they came and this morning, it doesn't matter."

"It doesn't?" Hannah's heart broke at the look on his face, at the way she was lying to him, manipulating his own horrible experience at Anna and Herrick's hands to hide her own magic-induced indiscretions, but then she thought of that night so long ago in that inn in Kalford when had spoken of his last wife and the circumstances that caused him to kill the prince of Firene. And then the morning after Klauden had turned her into a fledgling, the way he had told her, *I don't think I could forgive you for that. I would still love you, but I couldn't forgive you.*

Fine, she decided, swallowing her guilt. *If I can let go of the fact that Anna had him using my body, then I can let go of whatever madness happened with Klauden. It doesn't matter. We can start over from here.*

She felt the lie in her chest along with the massive scar, but there was hope on Rory's face, and relief. He rubbed his neck, the ragged skin there only just starting to mend. Hannah thought he might scar there for good if Klauden didn't heal him soon.

"It doesn't matter," she repeated. "We're here, and we're alive. We can just go from here."

Rory considered this, then gave her a long searching look. She met his gaze but was unable to read his thoughts. For a moment, she thought he was going to tell her anyway, tell her things she didn't want to know, but then he shook his head and smiled at her. "Alright," he said. "So you have your body back. No more Solyn taking you over a little bit at a time. But what do we do now?"

"Do?"

Rory gestured around them. "The house is fine, but the village is deserted. It's winter. We need to go somewhere with more supplies." He gave her a small grin. "You may not need food anymore, but I do, and I have a feeling that hunting in these woods may be scarce since the army has scavenged most of it already."

"What do you want to do?" she asked.

He shrugged. "Now? Curl up with you and take a nap." He helped her lay flat again, and then arranged himself on the bed next to her. "Later? We can figure it out after we sleep some more."

"Yes," Hannah agreed, snuggling into him, "later."

LIII

It was three more days before Hannah was hungry again. Rory had gotten up, looked at her intently, then bluntly asked if she needed to feed. Hannah squirmed a bit under this new honesty between them but nodded sheepishly. "I can go find ... something," she said, sliding stiffly to the edge of the bed. She was moving more easily now, and though Rory was still not completely healed, he was recovering faster than she had expected. She didn't think he'd gone to see Klauden for magical healing, but she didn't ask. He had been there each time she woke, but she had slept a great deal. He would tell her if he wanted to.

"I'll bring him," Rory said, and Hannah sighed heavily. She'd managed to avoid thinking about Klauden too often, almost pretending it was just she and Rory in the small house, alone in the world without any cares. That idyllic break was over. "Look," he said, turning back to face her as he grabbed his shirt from the chest at the foot of the bed. He pulled out another shirt and tossed it gently in her direction. "I know you don't want to see him."

When Hannah began to speak, he shook his head. "No, I don't need to know, but I see it. And I'm not a fool, Hannah." He pulled the shirt over his head while Hannah's heart began to pound. "You are worried about the fledgling bond," he said, and the bottom dropped out from Hannah's heart, guilt and relief washing over her. She looked from the shirt in her hands to the rug on the floor, the rug where she had lain with Klauden. She looked away. "You don't know if you will still feel it now that you are back in your body and away from him. But it's time to find out." He walked over to the back door and began putting on his boots. "What did he call it?" the elf asked as he bent down. "Kevna?"

Hannah's heart jerked at the word. "Where did you hear that?"

Rory raised his eyebrows at her. "Give me more credit than that," he told her, standing up and leaning against the door to watch her. "It was more than just vampire magic with you; it was ... powerful. Have you felt it since you've been back?"

Hannah shrugged, then tugged the shirt over her head, recalling the trial of her curly hair and glancing around for her hairbrush. "I don't know," she mumbled. "I haven't tried."

"Tried?" Rory walked back to the chest, rummaged some more, and came back with a black skirt. "Tried what?"

Hannah stood up, stepping into the skirt and tying it around her small waist. Solyn wasn't much bigger than Hannah, but the difference showed in her clothes. Rory handed her a belt to secure the slightly loose material, and she took it gratefully. "Tried to reach him. I haven't."

"Haven't been able to? Or haven't tried?"

"I don't want to know," she admitted, stepping around him to go to the chest for some socks.

Rory stopped her with a hand on her arm. "It's alright," he told her, tugging her gently back to him. "Whatever happens, it's alright now."

Hannah let him enfold her in a hug. "But what if we're still connected?" she whispered against his shirt, the warm reassuring smell of Rory as comforting as the arms around her back.

"Then you're still connected," Rory said, shrugging. "Nothing has changed."

"But—"

"But nothing," he said. "If it's magic, we can find out more about it." He paused, then released her so she stood within the circle of his arms but could see his face. "Hannah," he began, and he was serious, "do you want to be with me?"

She nodded, guilt filling her chest but nearly overwhelmed by hope. "I do."

"Then it doesn't matter. We'll get through it. Together."

She nodded again, embarrassed by the wash of heat that ran through her chest and up her neck. "Then let's go see him and find out," she said. "But first I need some socks."

LIV

Klauden was in the front room of the inn when they arrived, sitting at a table flipping through a large book. Hannah didn't recognize it offhand, but it was certainly something the vampire had brought from the castle. There was a stack of similar books on the table next to him, and he barely looked up when they came in. Hannah recognized the look of the scholar at work—a thoroughly familiar sight—but he was out of place in the inn's common room, a room that used to be bustling with life and was now empty. A small fire burned in the hearth, nothing like the blazes that Tarren had kept burning when this had been the town's busiest inn. Everything was so quiet in Severin now.

The quiet had been peaceful when it was just the two of them at home, but now it was eerie, a reminder of everything that had happened.

The silence stretched out, and Hannah wondered if anyone would ever speak again. "Where is Solyn?" she asked, if only to break the silence.

"It's good to see you, too, Hannah," Klauden quipped, hand leaving the book as he looked up at her. It was strange to hear her name in his voice. He so rarely used it. Hannah could feel the distance between them, and for a moment, she was heartbroken and overjoyed at the same time.

Hannah stared at Klauden. *<Can you hear me?>*

His face didn't change, and for another moment, she thought it had really worked, that the bond between them was broken, but then she felt it, a brick wall slamming into place, but not before she felt the wash of raw emotions—grief, relief, love, anger, resentment, sadness—from him. He was shielding himself, placing distance between them, but the bond was still there.

Still there. But it was a distant thing, and Hannah hoped that if she didn't focus on it, it might stay this way, divided with walls.

She sighed, shoulders heavy, the bloodlust burning, her head beginning to ache. She turned away from the vampire and would have walked outside, but Rory stopped her with a hand on her arm. "Hannah!" he exclaimed, surprised and not understanding what was going on.

Hannah looked at him, hoping her face showed her disappointment, but Rory refused to let her go. He shook his head. "No," he said. "No."

"No what?" she asked vaguely, trying to decide how she was going to feed when they were the only people left in the village.

"You don't remember," Rory said, looking from Klauden to Hannah and back again. He looked at the vampire. "Does she even know?"

"Know what?" Hannah forgot about feeding for a moment, trying to figure out what was going on. She looked at Klauden, the vampire sitting calmly at the table. He closed the book with a loud thump.

When it became clear that Klauden wasn't going to say anything, Rory used his other hand to pull Hannah gently over to the bench opposite Klauden. "Do you know what he did for you back..." His voice ran out, face clouding with memories, but then he forged on, "Back in that tent?"

Hannah looked down at her chest, recalling the scar there. "He fed me," she said tonelessly. "He kept me alive." She finally looked at Klauden. "And I'm thankful." The words were hollow, though she was truly glad to be alive.

"No, you aren't," Rory snapped, calling her out, "though you should be."

"I am!" Hannah insisted, nodding vigorously. "I was too wounded to feed myself," she added. "So, thanks for keeping me alive and saving my life." Though this body probably would have healed itself anyway, over time. Hannah was continuously surprised by the tenacity of this form.

But Rory was still shaking his head, hands holding hers. "No, Hannah. No." He looked at the vampire, who simply shrugged and nodded, as if granting permission. "He didn't keep you alive." He paused. "But he did save your life."

A shiver ran through Hannah, the small hairs on her arms rising. "What do you mean?"

"You died, Hannah."

Hannah looked down at herself. "What do you mean, I died? I know I was wounded badly, but I survived."

But Rory was still shaking his head. "No. You didn't." He looked down at their linked hands. "I don't remember a lot of what happened, not more than bits and pieces here and there, like dreams, but I do remember what happened when she realized you were inside of her." He looked away, eyes clouding over as he recalled the sight. "She reached inside. You are very strong, Hannah. So strong. And your hands..." He shuddered. "You weren't just badly wounded. You were dead. I saw your face. I've seen a lot of dead people, Hannah. You were dead."

"So then... how am I here?"

Rory gestured to Klauden. "He brought you back. I don't know how he did it, but he brought you back ... to life."

Hannah looked from Rory to Klauden. "Is that true?" She could feel that wall again, the barrier between them strong, and she let go of Rory's hands to reach across the table to touch the vampire. Klauden withdrew his hands. His face was thin, eyes exhausted, and Hannah remembered seeing him on the cliff in her mind, his face as he told her not to let go, that he wasn't going to lose her again. She glanced at the books on the table and back at him. "It is true, isn't it? And now you're researching it. Of course you're researching it. Have you found anything yet? How did you do it?"

Klauden shrugged, lips pursed as he considered. "Kevna," he said, the word simple and devastating.

Rory was nodding, though. "That's how you managed to do it," he agreed, looking at his wife. "That connection saved your life."

"I..." Hannah began but then fell silent. What was there to say? How should she respond to the person who had apparently brought her back from the dead? She looked to Rory instead. "How long was I ... gone?"

Now it was Rory's turn to look away. "I'm not sure," he admitted. "More than a few minutes." He glanced around. "Solyn might know. She was the one who..." He paused, hand reaching up to run through his hair, pausing at the barely healed scars on his neck and shoulder.

"She took care of me," he said. "She helped me get back here. He brought you back to the house a while later." He looked at Hannah, and his eyes were shiny with unshed tears, the bloodshot glaze nearly healed but suddenly very red as she heard his heartbeat speed up with emotion. "I was so thankful that you were alive."

"It's true," another voice said, and Hannah looked up to see Solyn standing in the doorway. It was strange to see her across the room and not in a mirror. Her voice sounded strange, not as low as Hannah had always felt it was when she was speaking.

"What's true?" Hannah asked, wanting to hear Solyn speak again.

"He was very happy to have you back," Solyn said, and there was a flatness in her voice, as if she were trying to tell Hannah something with her tone, but Hannah wasn't getting it.

"I'm happy to be back," she said, and suddenly, everything was fine. Even with kevna, even with the army still out there, even with the terrible secret she now shared with Klauden, she was going to get through this. She took Rory's hand, pulling him next to her.

"Well, that's good," Solyn observed. "But now I think we have some other things to talk about."

"Like?" Hannah asked, but Rory was already ahead of her. The elf looked at the three of them in turn.

"Like what are we going to do now?"

"Do?" Klauden asked, looking at his books with longing.

"Yes," Rory said sharply. "Do. There is now a large chunk of an army marching north to Firene."

"How is the army still together?" Hannah asked. "Didn't it fall apart when Anna left?"

Rory nodded. "Some of it did, yes. But some of the goblins stayed together under some of the fledglings."

"How are they still alive?" Hannah asked, but she had a dim recollection of strings, of connections to dozens of bodies beyond her own.

Klauden looked meaningfully at the stack of books on the table. "I'm not sure … yet." He looked at Hannah, then at Solyn. "But I will find out."

"And who's leading them if Anna is gone?"

"Herrick." Rory spit out the name.

Hannah swore. Of course her would-be fledgling would have escaped. "And he's heading to Firene?"

Rory nodded. "He has an old score to settle. What better time than when he has an army at his disposal?"

"So we need to warn them," Hannah said, following the lines of reasoning across Rory's face. "That's what you mean to do."

Rory nodded, his hand squeezing hers. "I have to go."

"Then I will go with you," Hannah decided.

"No, you won't," Klauden said, his voice quiet.

"What?" Hannah asked at the same time that Rory asked, "Why not?"

Klauden gestured to the books around them. "I need to find out what is going on. The answer lies in books. I can't have you wandering around the countryside chasing after an army you don't understand."

"But—"

"But nothing. What would you do if you get halfway across the country only to fall when the first of those fledglings gets cut down by the Elven guard? You are their Maker. We need to find out what that means."

"We killed fledglings when Anna was alive, and she was fine. I'm sure I will be—"

Klauden cut her off. "Sure, are you? You have no idea what any of this means. And not only to you but to me. Are you sure that nothing will happen to me, or to Solyn, if something happens to you?" He shook his head slowly. "I am not so sure. And I don't think these books have what I need. I need to get back into the library."

"So go," Hannah told him, trying not to think about the possibilities he raised. She hoped she imagined the quick wince on his face at her dismissive tone. Why was she constantly hurting him?

"I ... can't."

"Why not?"

"Hannah," he said, and his voice was so tired, "I did everything I could to get you back. Everything. Including going to the castle to retrieve some things." He shrugged. "I was certainly not as clever as I could have been."

Hannah stared at him for a long time, the realization of what he had said hitting her slowly. "They know you've been leaving? That you've been helping me?"

Klauden nodded. "No doubt they are currently ransacking my rooms for my research." He nodded at the pile of books. "Luckily, I was able to grab these the last time I was there."

Hannah paused, trying to let the magnitude of that sink in. Klauden couldn't go back to the castle without facing her father and Malbrek. He couldn't go back. They would kill him. "Klauden," she whispered, "your mother..." Why would he never stop sacrificing himself to save her?

"Never mind my mother!" he snapped, and there was something there, gone in a flash before Hannah could read it. "I can't go back alone," Klauden continued. "I need your help." He looked at Rory. "And I need her nearby while I learn more about kevna."

Rory nodded. "I understand." He looked at Hannah, then at Klauden. "But I have to go."

"And what about me?" They all turned to look at Solyn, the tall girl standing near the door.

"What about you?" Hannah asked, regretting the harshness of the words as soon as they were out. She was still staring at her husband, ignoring Solyn. Did Rory really mean for her to stay with Klauden while he headed north alone?

Solyn glared at her, and something flashed across her face, her blue eyes shining. She tossed her head, short mop of blonde hair moving around her lovely face. "Am I going with you?"

"By you, do you mean Klauden?" Hannah nodded. "Of course. You're his fledgling. You go where he goes."

"Well, I don't know if I ought to be going off wandering across the countryside or back to hostile castles in my condition."

Hannah felt the bottom drop out of her stomach at the words.

"What condition is that?" Rory asked absently, face furrowed as he tried to work out a solution with Klauden, not quite hearing her.

"I'm with child," Solyn said, and everyone turned to stare at her. Rory let go of Hannah's hand. Hannah could feel his heart pounding, and her bloodlust returned with a savage intensity. She closed her eyes, trying to slow her own blood at this news.

A child. Solyn is pregnant. A baby.

Rory was standing up, face red. He looked from Solyn to Hannah and back again, heart beating madly. "A child?" He ran his hands through his hair and then put both behind his neck, eyes wide. "But what will it be—fledgling or vampire? Half-elven?"

"That will depend a great deal on who the father is," Klauden said quietly. Rory turned slowly to look at them, the red dropping out of his face with alarming speed.

"Rory—" Hannah began, but then the elf was moving, lunging across the space between them, launching himself at the vampire. Klauden rolled aside, robe fluttering in the space where he had been, and then the elf was on top of him.

Hannah knew she should do something, knew she should intervene, but she couldn't move. She stood there, rooted to the spot, staring at Solyn. The girl looked at the men fighting on the floor, shrugged, put her hand to her belly, shook her head, and rolled her eyes as she looked at Hannah. Head still shaking slowly, she took a few delicate steps and hopped up to sit on one of the tables. She put her chin in one hand and watched the fight, face interested in a detached way.

Klauden had managed to roll out from underneath the elf and away, bouncing to his feet on the other side of a table from the enraged elf. Rory didn't waste any time trying to reach him; he grabbed the book from the table instead, yanking it toward him with such ferocity that Hannah was sure the cover would come off. She heard Klauden's outraged gasp at the treatment of his precious book, but then the elf threw it at the vampire, the heavy tome flying with startling accuracy to smack Klauden in the face. The vampire tried to catch it, hands awkwardly bobbling the weight, and Hannah was suddenly very aware of the blood dripping from his nose, a numb glow spreading out from her own nose in response to Klauden's injury.

There was a heavy pause in the room as everyone stared at Klauden, who managed to secure the book with one hand and use the other one to slowly wipe the blood away. Solyn wiggled her nose as if it hurt, but she didn't move.

"You bastard," the vampire said. "You've gotten blood on my book."

Rory looked away, face breaking apart, and his entire body slumped, shoulders falling, frame caving into itself.

"Rory..." Hannah whispered, and he looked up at her, eyes red with unshed tears.

"No," he said, and the word was cold. "You don't get to speak to me."

Hannah wanted to say something, anything, but what was there to say? Before any words could come, the elf looked around the room, eyes taking them all in one at a time. Klauden sniffed, then put the book down on the table, hands coming to rest in front of his chest in the universally known prep stance for magic users.

Rory cocked his head, considering, then without another word, turned and left the inn.

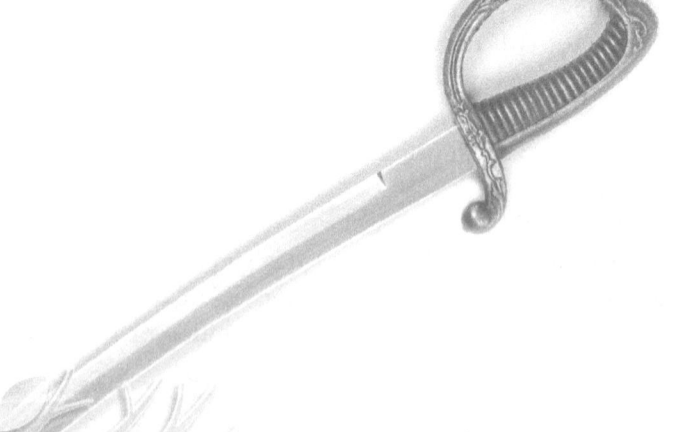

THE FLEDGLING MOTHER

Solyn was sitting at the table in the small house she had shared with Rory when the elf returned home. He seemed surprised to see her there, then confused, uncertain of how to act around her now. He shut the door and leaned against it, awkward in what had been his home.

"Have you..." he began, swallowed, then tried again. "Where have they gone?"

"I don't know. I came back to pack my clothes." Solyn looked down at the mug of tea she was drinking and shrugged. "She went to find you. I think he followed her."

Rory nodded, and Solyn appreciated how nice it was to look at the elf and just see another man instead of the lust-tinged adoration that colored Hannah's view. Though she expected their relationship to be strained now that Hannah had her old body back, it wasn't. In fact, she almost pitied the elf.

"I shouldn't have attacked him like that," Rory said in a low voice. "I don't know why I do it." When she gave him a pointed look, he nodded ruefully. "Alright, I know why I did it, but that doesn't make it right."

That's what she loves about him, Solyn thought, *this sense of honor or nobility that he drags around like a lead weight, shoving it in front of him whenever he wants to avoid really facing the truth.*

"You had your reasons," she acknowledged neutrally.

The elf began pacing across the width of the room. "I know that, but still. I should know better by now." He paused to look at her, questioningly. "You know what happened in Firene?"

Solyn nodded. "I do." He started pacing again.

"Well, then you know why I should know not to act like that. I can't explain it," he mused. "Sometimes I just can't stop myself, and now…" He seemed about to say something else but paused, a hand rubbing his neck. Solyn could still see the vivid welts of the healed bite marks. He would be scarred for the rest of his life. "Now it just seems too hopelessly confused."

Solyn got to her feet, plucked another mug from the counter and filled it with hot water from the pot on the hearth. She shook some tea leaves into it and then plunked it down across from where she was sitting. "Sit with me," she suggested. "There are words to be said."

He sat, and she could see the guilt crowding his face. Now that she was pregnant, he felt obligated to stay with her. Though there was nothing between them, he would not abandon her. He would stay by her side, would willingly trap himself. But she would not let him.

"About the baby," she began without preamble. "It's not yours." She had thought about this while the others were out running around. The only way the elf would leave, as she knew he longed to do, was if he was not bound to her. If she insisted that the child was Klauden's, he would be free to leave her to her own devices. It would be easier for everyone.

"How can you be sure?" His face was white, and Solyn realized that while this might be good for him in the long run, it was hard to hear right now. If the baby wasn't his, that meant Hannah and Klauden had been having sex, and perhaps lots of it, in the last few weeks.

"I know," she lied. *Well,* she thought, *if he's going to have it, make it quick.* "Look, you haven't been with me since before the fighting. I'm barely pregnant. It's not yours."

"You can't know that," he argued, but there was something in his face now. Solyn couldn't make it out. She knew if Hannah was still in her, she would have understood that look, but alone, it was a mystery.

"I'm a woman," she said. "Trust me. I know."

"But the timing," he tried. "You can't be so certain."

"Look," she said finally, deciding on a new tactic, "I've been this way before. I know what it feels like."

She saw how that surprised him, and he seemed about to ask but paused. She could see the debate spilling across his face. Finally, he asked, "Does she know?"

Solyn shook her head. "I never told her. It was a long time ago. Not even Klauden knew."

She could see the elf trying to process that with what he knew about her life at the castle. He gave her a curious look, and she spoke to dissuade him. "No, I was never with him before now. It was Vailen or one of the Kargin. I didn't know then, and I didn't care. The castle is not a place for mortal babies."

She had a brief flash of the old cook in the kitchen standing before the table as she held a cup of bitter tea to her lips. It had tasted awful, and the cramping agony that soon followed was not something she wanted to remember, but it was still preferable to other memories of that place. She remembered her swollen face, split lips, and aching insides, and compared to that, the pain of a few hours was nothing much. When her body had finally expelled what would have been a child, Solyn hadn't looked; she let the cook deal with everything, for once trusting another woman to help her as best she could.

She swallowed, the memory of that morning very vivid in her mind, tasting bitter herbs and fireplace smoke, and looked up at Rory. "Anyway, the point is that I know. I know when it happened."

He shook his head, then placed both elbows on the table and leaned into his hands. "Nothing makes sense anymore," he commented, and Solyn truly felt sorry for him then, for the elf whose life had been so disrupted by her presence. She reached across the table to cover one of his hands with her own. He welcomed the gesture at first, then seemed to remember that she was not Hannah and pulled away. He took a deep breath, nodded, and spoke. "It doesn't matter. I won't leave you."

She smiled at him. "Perhaps not, but I would certainly leave you," she snapped. "Don't play the honorable one with me. I have no need of your sympathy."

He seemed taken aback by her words, squinting at her in surprise. "You don't want me to stay with you?"

She scoffed. "Why would I?" He went to speak, paused, started again, stopped, then stared at her. "What?" she asked. "You didn't think you had to stay with me, did you?"

Clearly, he did, and she knew it, but it was easier this way. "Where would you go?" he asked.

She shrugged. "With him, I suppose, if he'd have me."

"You would be content there?"

"I would be with him," she said. "He would protect me, and the babe when it comes." She considered, then added, "Though if he chose to return home, I might not follow. I don't want my child to be one of the Kargin. I would rather live among the mortals than punish it like that."

Rory nodded. "You'll head north, then? What about the army?"

"I know how to avoid it, now. Besides, I am a fledgling. They pose no threat to me."

He nodded. "But what if—?"

"The child is yours?" she finished. "It's not." She saw he would not be contented with that and added, "Look, if it troubles you that much, I will send you a message when it comes to ease your mind. You may even come visit if you like, for old times' sake."

"I know it's different for you," he said, "but when I look at you, I see the woman I've lived with for almost a year. You are Hannah to me. It seems wrong to leave you thus."

"I know, but I'm not her. Not anymore. Besides," she added, "there's the army to think of. They are headed north now, right? You have a duty to your people. I know you want to head back to Firene."

He nodded. "They must be warned."

"So, there's no question, then. You will go to Firene. I will go with Klauden. It is settled." She took a deep gulp of the lukewarm tea and set the mug down. She tugged at the ring on her finger, pulling it up and over the knuckle, and slid it across the table toward him. "This is yours."

He picked the ring up slowly, clearly remembering what it had once meant to him. Finally, he slid it back to her. "Keep it. Even if it wasn't meant for you, I still want you to have it."

She picked it up, considered, then slid it back onto her finger. It was fair, in a way, after all; if Hannah was to keep Klauden's ring, she should at least get to keep Rory's offering. It wouldn't fit Hannah's dainty little fingers now anyway. "I thank you," she said formally, then stared at the table for a long time, waiting for him to say something.

"I should go now," he said finally, but he didn't get up.

"You should."

He waited another moment, then stood up. She didn't move as he rummaged through the chest at the foot of the bed, shoving shirts and pants into a worn traveling bag he tugged from beneath the bed. When he moved back to the kitchen, she watched him place a few apples, a loaf of bread, and a hunk of cheese, the last of the food in the house, inside a small pot and then stuff that inside the pack as well. He took the fire-making kit from the shelf above the fireplace and put it into a small pouch that he laid on top of the pot, and then he tied the bag shut. He was working daggers into various holsters on his waist and boot when she spoke again.

"You will leave now, before they return?" She hadn't meant it as a question, but she wondered what he meant to do about Hannah. *Is he just going to leave? Could he?* She watched him carefully.

"It will be ... easier," he said, hoisting the bag and glancing around the room.

"This was a good home," she whispered. "She was happy here."

"Not happy enough," the elf muttered and turned to her. "Be well, Solyn. Write to me in Firene when the babe comes."

She nodded. "I will."

He stood there a moment, ready to leave, but then he dropped the pack and stepped toward her. "Come here," he said softly, and she stood. It was oddly reassuring to find herself within the circle of his arms again, the corded muscles a reminder of his ability to keep her safe. "I am sorry for you," he whispered against her hair, then backed up to arm's length, pushing her hair behind her ears. "For all that has happened to you."

"Don't be," she assured him. "I am happy now. I am free and strong and about to be a mother. It is what I wanted."

He nodded. "Be well," he repeated and stepped away, shouldering his bag again and pulling up his hood.

He was halfway out the door when she called out. "Wait."

He paused but did not look at her.

"There is something you should know," she began, "before you go." At his expectant silence, she continued. "In her defense, it was only twice.

The first time was unavoidable, a result of the kevna which binds them together—it cannot be ignored."

"I see," he replied, "but the second?"

"That was for me."

He turned around to face her, breath clouding around his head in the doorway. "For you?"

Solyn looked down, then regained her strength and stared at him. "He would not want me when I wasn't her. I asked her for a gift, and she gave it to me." She looked down again, feeling the embarrassed heat climb up her chest. "I am sorry."

"Don't be," he said finally. She looked up at him. "I forgive you."

"Is there anything you want me to tell her?" Her hand strayed to her neck, fingers remembering the scars he now bore. "Anything at all?"

He considered, his own hand creeping to his neck. He shook his head. "No. There is nothing to say."

Solyn watched him leave, walking to the door when he went outside, and followed his form with her eyes until it vanished amid the trees, before turning away.

LV

By the time she returned home, Hannah was exhausted. She had searched everywhere she could think of, every last copse and grove, every building still standing in the village, every secret place and hidden tunnel she could recall, but Rory was nowhere to be found.

What should I do?

She couldn't find Rory, she couldn't make things right between them, she couldn't undo the things she had done with Klauden, she couldn't ignore that there would be a baby...

It's all hopeless now. A hopeless wreck.

< Come, come, now, chaivin, > she heard Klauden say, his voice echoing in her mind. *< You are not one for self-pity. >* He was on the move again, she knew, walking slowly through the surrounding trees, still seeking the elf even though he had no wish to meet him again.

< Leave me be, > she told him, wishing she had some way to block him out as he did her, wishing she could build walls to protect her thoughts. But there was nothing to be done about that. Even in her vampiric body again, Hannah's connection to him, kevna, was still very present, even more so than either Rory or Solyn expected.

She knew that even though he was at present in the woods beyond the house, heading back to the tunnels that led beneath the house, Klauden was thinking of her, of his desire to shake her, to somehow make her see reason, to force her to understand that this connection was permanent, that she would always be tied to him like this. Even with the baby, about which he was still confused—excited but hesitant, elated but nervous—he was sure that Hannah would always be there, his mate, his promised, the only one who really knew him at all.

<And what of Solyn? What about her?>

<She will stay with me,> the vampire assured her.

<And you know that for sure?>

<She is my fledgling still. We are connected too.>

<What, then? Are we to be a trio of vampires, Klauden and his two women followers, his mate and his fledgling? Where will we go?>

Hannah opened the door to the house, stepped inside, and shut it behind her, stamping her boots on the floor to get rid of the ice and snow. When she turned around, she had a moment where she thought Rory had returned, that he was the shape sitting at the table wrapped in a blanket, but a closer look revealed Solyn—a wet-haired Solyn who was twisting her short hair into little braids around her face—instead.

"Oh," she said, leaning against the wall as she untied her boots. "Hi."

Solyn nodded at her but continued with her twisting. When Hannah looked around the room again, she said, "He's not here."

"I know," Hannah snapped, but then took another look around the room. Something was wrong. No, something was missing. She took in the empty pegs by the door, pegs which that morning had held Rory's extra cloak, his shirt, and his extra belt. "Where is he?"

Solyn stopped her braiding and sighed. "He left."

"I see that. Where did he go?"

Solyn shrugged. "He doesn't want to see you."

"How do you know?"

"I saw him. He is very angry with you."

"What did he say?"

"That he had nothing left to say to you." Solyn paused, then added, "I am sorry."

"Did he say where he was going?" Hannah asked, leaning down to put her shoes back on. "Which way did he head?"

Solyn shook her head slowly, her expression pained. "He was going to Firene," she said.

"To Firene?" Hannah repeated, hands pausing in her efforts to get back into her boots. "Really?"

They were interrupted by a bang on the trapdoor. Solyn jumped, the blanket falling from her shoulders. "It's Klauden," Hannah said. "Can you let him in?" As Solyn got to her feet, Hannah added, "You know you don't need that, right? You aren't affected by the cold."

"I know," Solyn replied, "but it's habit." She leaned down to pull back the rug, flipped the latch, and tugged the door open. She leaned down to offer Klauden her hand and easily pulled him into the room.

"He's gone, then," Klauden said, watching Solyn lower the trapdoor back into place and lock it. She retrieved her blanket from the floor and wrapped it around her shoulders, then stepped before the fire, waiting.

Hannah nodded. "He's gone to Firene."

The vampire nodded, sat on the bed, and looked at Hannah. "What now?"

"What now? You're asking me?"

"This is your home, Hannah. It's up to you," he said.

Hannah considered. What was there to do? She couldn't stay here—the village was gone. There was nothing left here. She couldn't return home, not now, not ever. And what of Klauden? Where would he go with Solyn and a baby in tow? And whose baby was it anyway? Could she leave Solyn behind? Could she leave Rory's child?

She let out a sigh, sinking to the floor by the door. *I don't understand,* she thought. *After everything I went through, after all that trouble, I'm right back where I was.*

That's not true. The voice was her own, and it spoke enough truth to rouse her from what could have been a spectacular bout of self-pity. She was a vampire again, yes, but she wasn't the same. She was bound to Klauden now, but that didn't have to be a detriment. The vampire was strong and useful. And there was Solyn to think of. She owed the girl something at least, her protection, her company if it was wanted, a guarantee of safety for the child. She had obligations here.

But what about Rory? She thought of the elf, seeing him again as he had looked the first day they had walked into this house. It had been spring then, and everything was new and exciting and promising. After they'd agreed to take the house, he had picked her up, swung her around, and kissed her in the middle of the room. They had been so happy then.

Hannah wondered if they could ever be happy like that again. She wished she could talk to him.

But hadn't she tried that? Hadn't they tried to talk, to explain, to work it out? After she had gotten her body back, there had been such hope between them, such possibility.

That had all changed the moment Solyn made her announcement.

No, that wasn't true.

It had all changed when Klauden had made his. The one thing he couldn't forgive her, she had done. And how could she blame him for leaving her?

But where was he going now? Back to Firene, back to a city where he was wanted? He had gone there once for her sake and managed to escape, but could he do it again? But this time, he didn't want to sneak in and out. Now he wanted to warn them, to try to help them against the fledgling army headed their way.

He would need help.

Hannah stood up, decision made. "I don't know if it will do any good, but I won't let the army run around unchecked. I am somewhat to blame for its creation. And I can't let him go alone."

Klauden sighed, ran a hand through his hair, and stood up. "Very well. I shall find something to pack my books in."

"You don't have to come with me," Hannah said, knowing as she spoke that it was useless, that he would go where she went. "You have a choice."

"I know," Klauden replied, "and I made mine long ago."

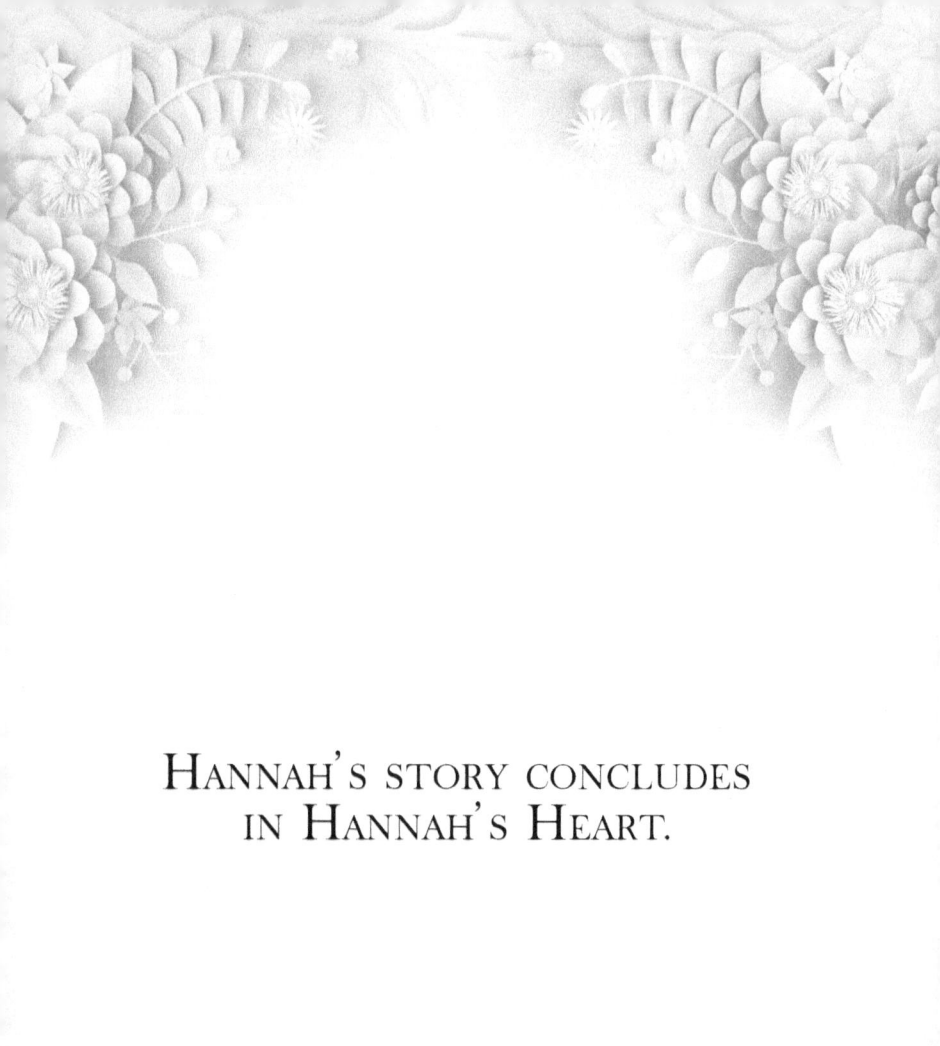

HANNAH'S STORY CONCLUDES
IN HANNAH'S HEART.

About the Author

Author of the Klauden's Ring Saga and the Conjuring Fascination series, JM Paquette writes fantasy and paranormal romance novels. When she isn't writing, she can be found teaching English to college students as Dr. Paquette or watching her favorite Russian shifter romance movie, *I Am Dragon*. Her areas of expertise include the history of the English language and the intricacies of grammatical rules, but her favorite class to teach is on *Lord of the Rings*. (If you've ever wondered why English is a crazy language, watch her video series on YouTube under Editor JMPaquette!) She enjoys editing manuscripts for academic and creative writers alike, and she adores tabletop roleplaying (THAC0, anyone?) where her halfling ranger/Twi'lek adept/vampire wizard/[insert race and class here] is often underestimated. You can also find her guest co-hosting the podcast Drinking with Authors—even though she doesn't drink, she loves getting to know fellow authors! Check out JM Paquette at authorjmpaquette.com and 4horsemenpublications.com and as Author JM Paquette on Facebook and Instagram.

Connect with JM:
www.authorJMPaquette.com
www.facebook.com/authorjmpaquette/
Email: authorjmpaquette@gmail.com

OTHER BOOKS BY JM PAQUETTE

Klauden's Ring (Klauden's Ring #1)
Solyn's Body (Klauden's Ring #2)
Hannah's Heart (Klauden's Ring #3)
The InBetween (Klauden's Ring #4)

Call Me Forth (Conjuring Fascination Prequel)
Invite Me In (Conjuring Fascination #1)
Keep Me Close (Conjuring Fascination #2)

Heart of Stone (Rock Star Fairy Tales #1)
One Mummy to Go, Please! (Shawarma Warrior King #1) with
Beau Lake

The General Guide to Worldbuilding

BOOK CLUB QUESTIONS

1. This story begins with Hannah in a human body, seemingly settled into life in a small village with Rory. If the events of this story hadn't happened, do you think she and Rory's relationship would have survived the years of Hannah's human lifespan? Why or why not?

2. Klauden comments at one point that he would not make a very good human because he needs more time. Do you think beings with long lifespans would feel that way about the passage of time? Would even eternity be long enough?

3. After Solyn's awakening, Klauden suggests that the only answer to Hannah's situation is to blend with the body's host. What do you think of this suggestion?

4. Hannah spends some time fighting with Solyn for control of the body. If you were in Hannah's position and the body host awakened, would you fight or would you return the body to the original owner?

5. Throughout this story, Hannah struggles with her humanity as well as her vampiric nature—both as a fledgling and back in her body. What do you think is the best life for her: a human Hannah, a fledgling Hannah, or the vampire Hannah? Why?

6. Klauden travels across the continent to help Hannah. What do you think of his motivations throughout? Do you trust him?

7. Hannah is quick to assure Rory that they can forget about what happened while they were apart, somewhat to spare him having to recount his trauma, but mostly to avoid telling him the truth

about Klauden. What do you think of her decision? Ultimately, it doesn't matter since the truth is revealed, but if there hadn't been a child, do you think Hannah would have ever told Rory what happened? Should she?

8. The story ends on a cliffhanger—Hannah, Klauden, and Solyn agreeing to follow Rory to Firene. What do you think of Hannah's choice to follow him when he clearly doesn't want to see her?

9. This book is about Solyn's body, but Solyn herself is often lost in the background. What do you think of her character, her history, and the new position she finds herself in at the end of this book?

10. You knew it was coming: Team Rory or Team Klauden? Why?

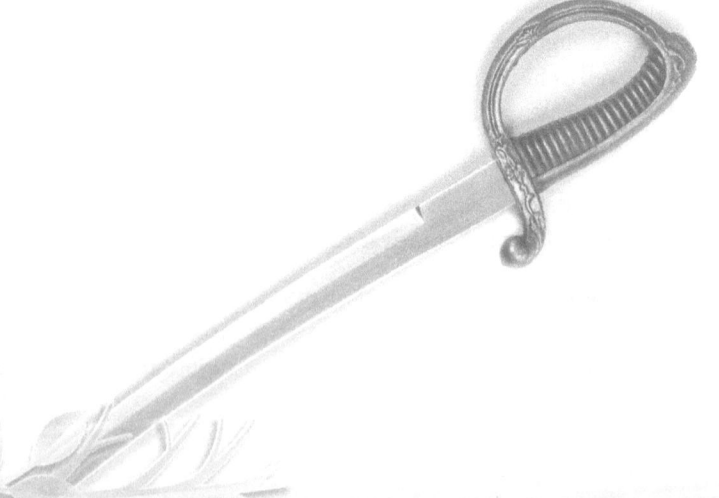

SNEAK PEEK AT HANNAH'S HEART

KLAUDEN'S RING SAGA #3

Hannah Tallerin, once Hannah van Kreeosk, stood at the end of an alley. She didn't recognize the place, but the buildings on either side were pale, probably white stone in the sunlight, though it was dark now, the only light from the half-moon drifting through the scuttling clouds. It was windy, Hannah's red hair blowing first back from her face, then swirling around before her eyes, the faint tinge of the ocean in the air. She quickly tucked her curls behind her ears, peering through the dim light, keen vampire eyes picking up the details of stone and dirt as she expected, but she couldn't see anything obviously out of place. Still, something wasn't right. She could feel it.

There were two people at the other end of the alley, the taller form embracing the other like a lover, a head bent into the other's neck. Hannah recognized the pose, having held her share of victims just like that, and she stayed where she was, allowing the vampire to finish. Time was strange, and Hannah waited for her mind to fill in the missing pieces.

When she saw the body of the victim slowly slump to the ground, gently drifting in a motion defying normal laws of gravity, Hannah understood.

This is a dream.

But that wasn't completely accurate. This didn't feel like her own dream. She had enough experience with other people's dreams to know the difference. This didn't feel like one of Solyn's memories, either. Since she had reclaimed her body, she hadn't had a dream like this.

That left another possibility.

The person at the end of the alley had abandoned the body and was now walking toward her. She knew it was Rory by the gait of his stride, recognizing her husband even before she could see the moonlight gleaming off his dark hair, the glint of silver hoops on the tips of his long elf ears. Those were something he hadn't had when she'd last seen him, when he had run from the inn in Severin, when he had learned Solyn was with child.

When he'd realized that she'd betrayed him.

"Rory…" she breathed, the sight of him stirring her heart despite the distance between them, but he didn't seem to notice her standing there, his form striding right through her. Her hand dropped to the necklace at her neck automatically, seeking the ring she'd worn there for so long, wondering if the artifact's magic allowed her to see the *real* Rory. She tugged Klauden's ring off her neck and held it out, staring as it spun on the end of the chain, the metal glinting in the moonlight. The ring allowed *Klauden* to see the wearer, though—it wouldn't connect her to Rory. She wondered if maybe she was seeing one of Klauden's dreams, though dreamwalking wasn't normally her ability. That didn't make sense either.

She tried to imagine why Rory would be dreaming about killing someone, but then she turned to follow him and abruptly, she was standing in a different place, a room this time, a much fancier space than Hannah had ever seen Rory in. She took in the fabric on the walls, the fine carpeting, the well-crafted furniture. It wasn't her father's castle, but the sense of luxury was familiar.

Hannah thought it might be the Elven city of Firene—but that didn't make any more sense than Rory killing someone vampire-style. He couldn't possibly be in Firene yet. She could have gotten there with her vampiric speed, but Rory was just an elf. An amazing elf, but an elf all the same, reliant on fresh horses at towns along the way. He would still be a few weeks away.

She took in the scene, seeking affirmation that this couldn't be an actual Rory dream.

Her husband sprawled on his back in a large four-poster bed, sleeping the way she'd seen him countless times, his hair in disarray, a hand flung above his head, and—Hannah noted with a start—a topless blonde elf wrapped in the sheet beside him. Her heart began to pound, an odd feeling of strong fingers clutching at her chest, and she realized she'd

stopped breathing for a moment. It didn't matter; she didn't need to breathe like a mortal, but it was still jarring. As she watched, Rory rolled onto his side, the moonlight glinting on the scars on his neck and shoulders, an arm reaching out to the strange woman and tugging her closer to him, tucking her into his embrace the way he had when he shared a small bed in Severin with Hannah.

I don't want to see this, Hannah thought as she backed away from the bed, necklace and ring falling from her hand, then bouncing on the plush carpet. *I don't belong here.*

She closed her eyes, willing herself out of the dream, away from the scene.

It's just a dream, she told herself. *This isn't real.*

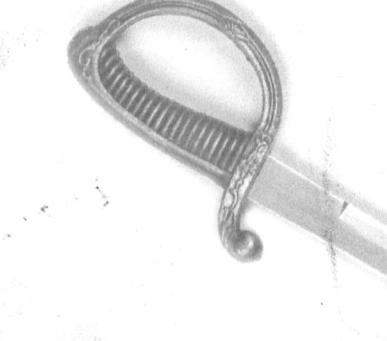

Discover more at
4HorsemenPublications.com

10% off using HORSEMEN10

www.ingramcontent.com/pod-product-compliance
Lightning Source LLC
Chambersburg PA
CBHW051529100726
47898CB00005B/1633